THE EQUIVOQUE PRINCIPLE

DARREN CRASKE

ISIS

LARGE PRINT

Oxford

First published in Great Britain 2008
by
The Friday Project
an imprint of HarperCollinsPublishers

Published in Large Print 2010 by ISIS Publishing Ltd.,
7 Centremead, Osney Mead, Oxford OX2 0ES
by arrangement with
HarperCollinsPublishers

British Library Cataloguing in Publication Data
Craske, Darren.
    The equivoque principle.
    1. Circus - - England - - London - - History - -
    19th century - - Fiction.
    2. Circus owners - - Fiction.
    3. Judicial error - - Fiction.
    4. Magicians - - Fiction.
    5. London (England) - - Social conditions - -
    19th century - - Fiction.
    6. Detective and mystery stories.
    7. Large type books.
    I. Title
    823.9'2–dc22

ISBN 978–0–7531–8722–7 (hb)
ISBN 978–0–7531–8723–4 (pb)

Printed and bound in Great Britain by
T. J. International Ltd., Padstow, Cornwall

Acknowledgements

I would like to pay homage to those who have helped me in no small way to shape my literary meanderings into what you hold within your hands.

They know who they are, but just so there is no confusion:

For enriching my days and nights with an abundance of love, laughter and fun, I would like to thank my wife Tracy, and my daughter Aimee.

For some priceless advice, support and input, I would like to thank Scott Pack, Heather Smith and all the crew at The Friday Project. A nicer bunch of truly passionate and professional publishers I challenge you to find.

For being an all-round good egg and great sounding board, I would like to thank my stalwart friend Karl Arlow.

For passing onto me his genetic talent for creativity, I want to send my thanks to my late grandfather, Herbert Edward Craske.

And lastly, but by no means leastly, the person without whom this book would never have happened, I would like to thank myself for having the determined doggedness to keep writing no matter what hurdles life threw in my path.

You have not seen the last of me.

Darren Craske, October 2008

CHAPTER
ONE

The Nod

London, 1853

The horse-drawn coach pulled up outside the row of dilapidated tenement buildings just after midnight. A lone driver sat high at the front of the carriage, holding his lantern tightly in his clammy hands, nervously scanning the streets around him for any sign of life. Wisps of warm breath trailed like spectres from his mouth into the bitter November wind.

"So this is Crawditch, eh? Can't say I'm thrilled about being here, Bishop," he said anxiously. "It's a bit of a hole, int' it?"

"Where else would you find a rat, Mr Melchin?" said the portly man inside the coach. He pulled a gold pocket-watch from within the folds of his dark-purple robes, and squinted in the half-light of the driver's lantern. "Don't worry, I've no wish to remain in this godforsaken place for long myself," he said, peering through the carriage's window into the ever-present smog.

Ever since the last days of the eighteenth century, steam and smoke had become the belt and braces of modern society. The masses of coal-burning furnaces and chimneys on the London skyline spewed their filth into the air relentlessly, birthing sulphur-dioxide smog that clung to the damp, cobbled streets like a milky shroud.

Across the street, a tall man dressed in a long mud-coloured coat and flat cap detached himself from the shadows of an alleyway and made his way over to the carriage. The fog spiralled and snapped at the edges of his coat as he strode resolutely through its formless blanket. Drawing a lungful of tobacco from a stub of a cigar perched on his bottom lip, this ghoul of a man rapped on the carriage door with bloodied knuckles.

"Rather off the beaten track aren't you, Bishop Courtney?" he asked, the vague light of the carriage's lantern illuminating the pale scar that tracked down the left side of his long, gaunt face.

"I am here on the Lord's business, Mr Reynolds, not by choice," said the Bishop dryly, a thin grin spread across his corpulent face. "I have need of a man of your talents. Surely you have heard of Queen Victoria's dictum? She wishes London to regain its rightful place as the jewel in her crown, and districts all over the capital are to be renovated."

The tall man matched the Bishop's sly grin with one of his own. "I'm well aware of Her Majesty's plans. She's been trying to evict the citizens of Crawditch for weeks now. Out with the old, and in with the new. So, what's that got to do with me?"

"She has tasked me personally to come here to Crawditch, and appeal to the residents' better nature,

2

and I do *not* wish to have to explain to her that the rebirth of the British Empire has fallen foul of one insubordinate little district," said the Bishop. "I want to employ your skills to help rid this cesspool of all its inhabitants."

Reynolds puffed his cheeks and pushed his flat cap back on his head. "You're not serious, surely? Getting someone like *me* to do your dirty work? That's not very Christian thinking, Bishop."

"The Lord works in mysterious ways," said the Bishop, his face entertaining rare warmth. "The Queen has set a very . . . *challenging* schedule, and even the Anglican Church must make questionable choices now and again. Tell me, Mr Reynolds, can this job be done?"

His pale face clouded in thick tobacco smoke, Reynolds shook his head emphatically. "Not easily. Crawditch is held together by stronger stuff than just bricks and mortar, you know. You'd need something pretty drastic to make this lot leave," he said, billowing twin plumes of smoke, dragon-like, from his nostrils. "But if they could be *scared* away . . . make them go *voluntarily*, that might do the trick."

"I admire the clarity of your vision, Mr Reynolds. If you were given free rein to do as you pleased, could you organise what needs to be done here?" the Bishop asked delicately, toying with the large ruby ring on his left index finger.

"I could," said Reynolds, his throaty, gargling voice sounding like a bubbling stew-pot. "But I'll need help. Blackstaff prison is a veritable market of men who would do your bidding for the right price. Have you got enough coinage and clout to get a man out of a place like that?"

"Mr Reynolds, you insult me," said the Bishop flatly. "Of course I do."

"And Scotland Yard will keep their noses out of it, will they?"

"Am I not God's messenger, Mr Reynolds?" said the Bishop with slight disdain. "If the Lord has no interest in what happens in Crawditch, why then should the Metropolitan Police? I will ensure they are kept restrained."

"Then I guarantee you, by this time next week, any resident of Crawditch still left alive will be bombarding Parliament, begging to be re-housed," said Reynolds. "Crawditch will be yours for the taking. When do you want me to start?"

"Immediately! With the hint of war in the Crimean peninsula at the moment, the Queen has one eye on London and the other on events in the Black Sea. She is distracted, and now is the perfect time. Until we next speak, Mr Reynolds, you have my permission to recreate hell within Crawditch's streets," Bishop Courtney said gruffly, and he pounded the silver-topped cane on the roof of the coach. "Drive on, Melchin."

The driver instantly cracked his whip, and the horse and carriage moved on, away from the grey, murky streets of Crawditch, and back into the enveloping darkness.

4

Reynolds watched the coach depart, a black-toothed smile crawling across his mouth. He had much to prepare. Murder was a complicated and serious business, but he was an expert. Removing another thin cheroot of a cigar from his jacket pocket, he forced it abruptly into his thin, lipless mouth. "My dear Bishop, if you only knew what kind of hell I'm capable of creating . . . you might think twice before making a deal with the Devil."

CHAPTER
TWO

The Strongman

Within forty-eight hours of that shadowy meeting, the renowned and respected Dr Marvello's Travelling Circus had rolled into London in preparation for a forthcoming event in Hyde Park. It would take the better part of two long, weary days to transport equipment from the nearby Grosvenor Park train station, where the circus's steam train was housed, and the crew were working hard into the night to ensure the show would be ready in time. A large oval area of the park, the same site that had entertained the gleaming spectacle of the Crystal Palace just two years before, was the perfect stage. The engineers were busy constructing the skeletal structure of the Big Top, along with various other smaller encampments. Climbing down from the construction, two technicians strode over to a gangly Asian man wearing a coiled white turban. He was crouched with his arms through the bars of a large metal cage, tenderly stroking the ruff of a muscular tiger as if it were his grandmother's tabby cat.

"Oi, Kipo? Is Prometheus about?" one of the men asked.

Kipo clutched his thick overcoat tightly about his body, and shuffled around to face the men, his face a picture of displeasure, "Mr Harry, Mr Bert, why must we come to this place? Spain was nice, I liked Spain. Spain was warm," he said with a shiver. "Even Rajah is grumpy in this place."

The two men looked at each other and grinned.

"He's a bloody tiger, man, he's supposed to be grumpy," said Bert, a scruffy man wearing blue overalls, and a large stripe of grease down his cheek.

"London in November gettin' to you then, Kipo?" said Bert's colleague Harry. "Listen, me and Bert could do with a bit of muscle to shift some scaffolds. Have you seen Prometheus about anywhere?"

"I understand the strongman is visiting the nearby borough of Crawditch, and I shall wager he is far warmer than I," said Kipo, and he shuffled away like a penguin, flapping his arms at his sides to keep warm. "I am off to my bed to dream of Spain."

Aiden Miller — "Prometheus" to his friends, after the titan of Greek mythology — was seated in an enclosed booth at the rear of The Black Sheep tavern, at a table built for a much smaller man. Cursed by nature with a body like an ox and an unwelcoming face, the gentle giant had fled from his native Ireland to join Dr Marvello's Travelling Circus many years before. Adopting the identity of the circus's strongman, Miller had found a new sense of purpose in his life. If the man had not been mute, he would have said that he was the happiest he had ever been in his whole life.

He wore a dog-eared and mottled grey frock-coat, and a thick, woollen cap covered most of his bald head. A low hem of dark-brown hair skirted the back of his head, like a fringe that had slipped somewhat. It flourished into a thick, bristling beard that enveloped the lower part of this face, with only his eyes and nose visible under the shade of the cap's peak. Four untouched tankards of ale were lined up like soldiers on the table in front of him, and his clay pipe streamed a flume of smoke towards the tavern's low ceiling. Purposely finding an area of the place built for secrecy, Miller wanted to be as inconspicuous as possible. Towering at over seven foot tall — this was no easy task.

A rickety old bar was positioned in the centre of the tavern, and several late-night drinkers were idly ghosting backwards and forwards inside the public house, either not caring, or not daring to look Miller in the eye.

"He's a queer one and no mistake, Arthur," said a lank-haired man hunched over the bar. "I mean, look at the size of the bleeder! He must be all of eight feet tall, if he's an inch."

The landlord glanced towards Miller's booth and nodded. "He's been there for over an hour, Alfie. Bought four ales, and not touched a single drop. Just been reading that letter in his hand, over and over," he said. "Must be bad news, whatever it is."

The customer grinned. "Probably a note from his bit o' fluff, tellin' him she's run away with someone who looks less like a bleedin' gorilla."

The barman and his customer erupted in hearty laughter.

"That's a bit rude, if you don't mind me saying," said a small, squeaky voice by the side of the customer.

The customer spun around to face the voice's owner, but no one was there. He felt a firm tug on the bottom of his long overcoat, and his eyes slowly panned down to face the wide, open face of a dwarf woman with a thatch of tousled blonde hair nestled under a stout straw hat. Large emerald-green eyes peeked up from under the brim, and her scarlet lips glowed like the petals of a summer rose.

"Who the bloody hell are you?" said the man incredulously, gawping at the immaculately dressed dwarf.

"The name's Twinkle," replied the tiny woman.

"What are you doing in here, lass? This ain't no place for a young'un," said the barman, leaning at full stretch over the bar.

"Yeah! Go on an' get home, little girl," chorused the customer.

"I'm no little *girl*, mister," Twinkle said, snatching the tail of the man's coat and yanking it as hard as she could. The customer slipped clumsily from his stool, and landed flat on his back on the sawdust floor. The dwarf swiftly cocked her leg over the man's body, and flopped all her weight down hard astride his chest. The air whistled from his lungs. "*I'm* the bleedin' gorilla's bit o' fluff!"

The customer's eyes bulged in disbelief as they flicked first from Twinkle's mischievous face, to the large shadow that suddenly blocked out the light. Aiden Miller's voluminous form towered over the man, his upside-down face grimaced into a cold, stone glare.

"Let's just calm down now, eh, big fella? Alfie didn't mean no harm; the man's got a loose tongue, is all," the barman said, hurriedly grabbing a bottle of whisky from a shelf behind the bar. "Here, why don't you go sit yourself down an' enjoy a dram or two on the house, eh?"

Miller glared at the quivering customer on the floor for what seemed like an age. Sweat formed in copious amounts on the barman's greasy forehead as he waited for Miller to make his mind up.

"Come on, duck, no harm done," squeaked Twinkle. "Let's go get drunk." And, with a playful grin, the diminutive woman climbed off the customer's chest, leapt up into Miller's vast arms, and the couple removed themselves quietly back into the booth. The landlord exhaled a heavy sigh of relief.

With her elbows perched upon the rickety table, the woman called Twinkle slid one of the tankards of ale towards her, battling to lift the tin cup to her lips. She was dressed in a long, flowing gown, with a high collar and puffed shoulders, thinning into tight-fitting long sleeves. She was decidedly overdressed for the grimy backstreet public house, but her pride showed on every inch of her face.

"So, come on then, spit it out, love. Why all the secrecy? Why couldn't we just meet back at the train?" she asked, eying Miller's dour expression.

The giant slid the crumpled note across the table towards her and, with his eyes, he bade her to read it. Twinkle obliged, offering the hulk of a man a supportive wink. Her eyes darted across every word, but her smile faded the more she read.

She glanced up at Miller. "This is rum stuff, love. When did you get this?" Twinkle demanded, with a fire in her voice that belied her stature.

Miller pointed a finger over his shoulder.

"Yesterday? Whilst we've been in London? And you're only just telling me now?"

Miller's eyes nodded for him. He lifted the bottle of whisky, and downed half the contents easily in one gulp. He was heavy with sorrow, and not even the sight of Twinkle's beaming smile cheered him. Chewing nervously at his lip, his bushy moustache twitching from side to side like a metronome, Miller anxiously waited for the reaction he knew was coming.

Twinkle gave his arm a painful pinch, and sucked air in between her teeth. "Prometheus, you daft lug! Did you tell Mr Quaint?" she reprimanded. Looking around her, she lowered her voice into a whisper. "Well, what are you waiting for? You *have* to tell the boss, you know that, don't you? We've all got our secrets, darling, you more than most, I admit, but he needs to be *told*. We're a family, remember? Tell you what, duck — we'll go and tell him together, right?" Twinkle said, as she slurped on the ale. "After we've had a few more pints, of course."

A little over ten minutes later, Twinkle slammed down the third of her four tankards and belched loudly, patting her chest with her hand. "Pardon me," she scolded herself. "By crikey, those ales are strong . . . let's have some more!"

Miller placed his hand on the top of the fourth tankard, rose from his seat and grinned broadly at Twinkle. He shook his head and tapped his breast pocket, where he kept his watch.

"Is it time to go already? What rot! You are such a killjoy, y'know that?" Twinkle chirruped, dejectedly sliding from the bench, and she tripped into Miller's arms as they headed for the tavern's door.

The late night air was immediately refreshing, and the winter wind nipped at any exposed flesh. It danced off the waves of the nearby Thames, bringing a moist chill along with the breeze. The docks were empty, but in just a few hours along the wharf at Blythesgate fish market, the trading barges and fishing trawlers would turn the area into a thriving hustle and bustle. Twinkle trotted happily at Miller's side through the towering claustrophobia of the crowded warehouses towards Grosvenor Park train station.

They unknowingly passed a skulking figure dressed in black, hiding amongst the shadows of a dark doorway, and he watched the giant and the dwarf with interest as they staggered a drunken zig-zag across the road. Not taking his piercing blue eyes from the odd-sized couple, the man observed their every move. He slowly removed himself from the darkness, and crept along the wharf after them.

Ignorant of the attention they had attracted, Miller and Twinkle shuffled along the street. Just then, a pained expression crossed over the giant's face, and he clutched at his stomach. He was giddy on his feet, unusually so for a man his size and he looked around for something to steady himself upon. His legs began quaking at the knees, threatening to give way at any second. Miller squinted into the misty half-light, staring down at Twinkle as her tiny form shifted in and out of focus. Colours blended into a wash of muddy mire, and suddenly everything around him seemed to lack definition and solidity. He doubled over as a sudden wave of nausea flowed over his body.

"Oh, my poor sweetie," Twinkle said, standing on tip-toes to pat Miller's back, as the large man-mountain vomited noisily into the gutter.

Miller the strongman lifted his heavy head, his eyes rolling madly, and suddenly collapsed onto his knees. This was unlike any inebriation he had experienced in his life. He felt like he was a marionette, and someone was snipping his strings, one by one. His large frame overpowered him, an unseen pressure forcing him down onto the cold dampness of the cobbled street. The dim of the night stole what little light he could visualise as he grabbed at Twinkle's dress, desperate to find something solid to hang onto. He mouthed empty, silent words, as he searched deeply into her green eyes, pleading for her help.

Miller was suddenly aware of a dark shadow falling over him from behind. Before blacking out, the last thing he saw was Twinkle's terrified face as she raised her arm to protect herself. In the midst of confusion, the man known in the circus as Prometheus heard her piercing screams, as unconsciousness draped itself over his body like a heavy, wet tarpaulin.

CHAPTER
THREE

The Eyes of the Law

"Bernie Yates says they've been there since first light, Sarge," said the young police constable. Twinkle's body was laid on her stomach across Miller's back, with her arms folded beneath her and fine splatters of blood polka-dotting her blonde hair. In the light of the early morning, the entwined couple resembled stone statues in a mausoleum, bathed in an azure glow. "I ain't ever seen the likes of it before. Look at the state of 'em."

"I'm looking, Jennings. The Commissioner's going to go spare now," said Sergeant Horace Berry, poking at the bodies with his truncheon. "This one's the third victim in as many nights. At least this time it looks like the killer didn't get away," he said, scowling at Miller's unconscious form lying in the gutter. "So how come I don't feel lucky, eh? Jennings, lad, get yourself back to the station. Bring back some men and a couple of body-carriers," he said, as he sized up Miller's vast body. "On second thoughts, you'd better make that three."

"Right you are, Sarge," said Constable Jennings, and he sprinted off amid the throng of onlookers and workers, surrounding the docks in the early morning light.

"Come on, folks, move on back. Go about your business now, g'wan," the sergeant said, as he glared at the assembling crowds. "Isn't it too early for you ghouls?"

The night sky was lazily making way for the day, and a cold November breeze rattled into Crawditch, lifting clouds of mist up into spiralling swirls in its wake. Sergeant Berry pulled out his pocket-watch and cursed. It was coming up to seven in the morning, and he'd only just come on shift half-an-hour ago. Berry had been hoping for a hot brew before he had to get his hands dirty. Sliding his helmet further back on his head, he mopped at his brow with a white handkerchief.

In his late forties, Berry had been with the Metropolitan Police since its inception over twenty years before, and had been a paid constable for ten years prior to that. In all that time, he thought he had witnessed the gamut of human criminality and depravity, but this was something different; he could feel it. One grisly murder was bad enough, two were a dreadful shame, but three? Three dead women in as many days meant that they were looking at something that would not easily dry up overnight. The paperwork alone could take a month. He stared down at the giant's face, inches from it, as if he were trying to read the man's thoughts as to what could possibly have occurred the previous night.

16

Suddenly, a tiny spark of consciousness lit within Miller's mind as he heard muffled voices around him. He tried to piece together his surroundings. His cheek was touching cold, damp, stone cobbles, and there was a weight upon his lower back. Miller cautiously flicked one eye open, then the next, and his bleary eyes came face to face with the eyes of a very shocked Sergeant Berry.

"What — What's all this?" Berry stammered, as his legs gave way beneath him, and he fell to the ground unceremoniously onto his backside. He kicked away from Miller as fast as he could against the damp cobbles. "Hold it!" he yelled, scrambling to his feet. "Don't you bloody move!"

Miller ignored Berry, desperately seeking sight of his beloved Twinkle. He half-turned his head, and noticed the shock of curly blonde hair, matted and caked in dark-red blood lying across his shoulder blades. He knew it was her instantly. If he were not already a mute, the pain in his heart would surely have stolen his words. Miller closed his eyes, trying to exclude the awful truth.

"Oi! I'm talkin' to you!" said Sergeant Berry, pacing up and down like a caged tiger. "I asked you a question, mate. What's gone on here?"

Miller was in no position to be questioned. The policeman's words barely even penetrated his ears. He buried his head in his large hands and wept heavily and loudly, his gargantuan frame quivering as he sobbed uncontrollably. No matter how much strength his massive body was capable of, it failed him now. Every bone, every muscle, and every fibre of his being was mourning. The giant was broken.

"What happened here, eh? Did you do this?" Berry demanded with a fiery rage in his voice. He prodded Miller in the guts with his truncheon, and the giant twitched, whimpering like a cowering child. Twinkle's lifeless corpse slipped from his body, and rolled onto its back, its arms flapping open. Sergeant Berry stared at it and gagged. "Of all the unholy . . ."

Twinkle's tiny, fragile body was horrifically disfigured, removing all semblance of the dwarf's personality, leaving behind a mere husk. Her dress had been sliced open down the middle, tearing through the material and gouging deeply through her undergarments, and into her chest beneath them. A bizarre death-mask adorned her face, transfixed into a grimacing, frozen scream. Blood was dried everywhere about her body, filling every crease of her clothes like a roadmap.

Sergeant Berry mopped at the corners of his mouth with a handkerchief. "Look, I don't know who you are, or who *she* is . . . but you're coming with me to the station to sort this out, mister." Berry turned as he heard a loud rattling noise coming closer to him, and was relieved to see three of his men approaching, pushing what looked like long wooden wheelbarrows. Each one stopped and gasped as they saw the scene before them.

"Bloody hell!" one of them said. "You weren't joking, Jennings. What a mess."

"You, men, get over here! Apprehend this . . . *man* immediately. A few hours locked in the cells should loosen his tongue," Berry said, as he bravely squatted down next to Miller's tear-stained face, catching a flicker of light in the giant's eyes. "You're going to pay for what you done, make no mistake about that! We don't take kindly to folk who murder little children here in Crawditch. You'll be hanging by your neck by suppertime!"

As Berry watched his men handcuff the giant and place Twinkle's corpse upon a body-carrier, something caught his eye down in the gutter. It was a small, crumpled piece of notepaper. Berry's natural detective instincts kicked in, and he picked it up. His grey eyes skirted from side to side across the paper, and he traced his fingers across the lines. "What's all this then?" he said quietly under his breath. "*'I will unleash a terror unlike any seen before, and the corpses of your loved ones will litter the streets.'*" Berry cursed, and folded the note into his pocket. "Oh, the Commissioner is just going to be cock-a-hoop about *this*!"

CHAPTER
FOUR

The Quaint Introduction

At Crawditch police station, circus proprietor Cornelius Quaint pushed hard on the double doors with intended force and they parted easily, crashing against the stout wooden frame. The man's flowing black cloak was cast behind him like a shadow, billowing open to reveal a dark, velvet three-quarter-length jacket over a white ruffled shirt. Well into his sixth decade, Quaint's face was hardened and well-lined, proudly displaying every year of his adventurous life, as well as a few more besides. Beneath the brim of an indigo felt top-hat, Quaint's obsidian-black eyes drove into focus under the woollen mass of grey-brown curly hair that surrounded them.

Following in the man's wake was a diminutive Inuit dressed in a long, oilskin anorak. His dark-skinned face peered cautiously from beneath a fur-lined hood, swathes of rich black hair poked out in tufts onto his forehead, and he walked cautiously a few paces behind Quaint, more because his tiny legs could not keep pace with the locomotive of a man than as a sign of servitude. The men's arrival demanded instant attention, and the policeman who manned the enquiries podium just inside the station had little choice but to stop what he was doing and simply gawp open-mouthed as they approached him.

"Good day, Constable . . . *Tucker*," Quaint proclaimed loudly, spying the small name plaque on the policeman's desk. "I am Cornelius Quaint, conjuror and proprietor of Dr Marvello's Travelling Circus, currently situated over the river in Hyde Park. My companion here is my deputy manager and squire, Butter."

The Inuit peered from behind Quaint's cloak and doffed an imaginary cap.

"Um . . . hullo to you," said the policeman, as he looked with interest at the two unorthodox men standing in front of him. One was a barrel-chested mule of a man, with broad shoulders and a steely temperament, and the other was an unobtrusive fellow who looked like he had just stepped off a ship from the Arctic regions. A strange couple, to be sure, and Constable Tucker found himself wondering what on earth these two could be doing mixing in the same circles. "That's an odd name, isn't it? Butter? What is he . . . some sort of farmer or something?"

"Hardly, Constable — the fellow comes from Greenland. He's an Eskimo. His body is gifted with a remarkable immunity to the cold, and he's a marvellous secretary. No one can juggle the books like Butter here. His real name is virtually unpronounceable, so I won't embarrass him by trying to say it. Folk just call him

'Butter' . . . as in, 'Butter wouldn't melt in his mouth.'"
Quaint grinned. "Which, of course . . . it wouldn't."

Constable Tucker was still agog, the explanation not serving to elucidate him. "Right, well, there you go then. So, what can the Metropolitan Police do for you two gents this morning?"

"I am searching for a couple of my employees, Constable; a mute, bearded, seven-foot-tall giant of a man and a dwarf female with a shock of blonde hair. This borough was their last known location. Neither arrived for work this morning, and . . . if I know Prometheus, in these circumstances he is nearly always incarcerated by the local constabulary — quite mistakenly, of course," Quaint sang, his voice shifting melodic gears from soft and caressing words, to severe commanding tones. "Are you aware of such a man currently under your charge?"

"We don't tend to get many mute, bearded, seven-foot-tall giants nor dwarf females in Crawditch, sir, so they do stick out in the memory," said Tucker. "I'm not sure of the female's whereabouts, but I'm afraid that your gargantuan friend is currently in our custody. Our men brought him in early this morning."

"Excellent! Then please contact your superior, if you would be so kind. I am here to secure his release," said Quaint with a disarming smile.

"Um, I don't think that's going to be possible, sir . . . you see, your mate's being held for murder, so he won't be going anywhere for a while. Nobody's to see him until the Commissioner gets here, and that's that."

"He's being held for — what did you say? *Murder?*" Quaint vented, stepping closer to Tucker's podium. "What utter nonsense, Prometheus is no killer!"

"Well, with all due respect, sir, you would say that, wouldn't you? You may not have heard, but we've had a few of these murders recently. One a night, as it goes, over the past three nights — last night being the third. There's a lot of concern amongst the locals, and obviously the Commissioner is keen to question your friend, what with him being found unconscious at the scene of the crime, and all that. So, sorry to tell you, until I get the say-so from my superior — you're out of luck."

Quaint shot a look to Butter, who merely shrugged, and so the tall, elegantly dressed man returned his cold stare to the policeman. "I can see that you're unlikely to budge, Constable, but I should categorically state that my man had nothing to do with any slayings. My circus and I only arrived two days past. We're entertainers, and it's hardly sensible to go around murdering the paying audience, is it? We shall take our leave for the time being, but return soon. What is your Commissioner's name, may I ask?"

"Mr Dray," the policeman answered obediently.

"Dray? Not . . . Sir George Dray by any chance?" asked Quaint.

"No, sir. His son. *Oliver* Dray."

Quaint threw back his head and rocked with laughter. "*Oliver?* Can it be true, after all these years? Don't tell me they made daffy old Ollie a commissioner? Now, this I just *have* to see. I've not set eyes upon the chap since our travels in Peru back in the thirties. It will be great to see the old Scottish terrier again, Constable. Tell me, when does the Commissioner arrive?"

"He's due in at ten o'clock," the policeman answered.

Quaint checked his pocket-watch. "Splendid!" It was nine forty-five.

"Tomorrow," said Tucker. "Ten o'clock *tomorrow*. If you want to see the Commissioner, or your friend, you'll have to come back then, I'm afraid."

Quaint exhaled slowly and purposely noisily in Tucker's direction. "But my man is being held for *murder*, Constable! You mean to tell me that he's to be locked up for a whole day without anyone being able to see him? Aren't you even slightly interested in his side of the story?"

"Listen, I'm just following the Commissioner's orders, right?" said Tucker. "Two days ago the mutilated body of a woman named Lily Clapcott was found off of Montague Street, near the disused bakery. A day later, a rose seller called May Deeley was found dead, also horrifically mutilated. Last night . . . it's another one. Now, we ain't got no other witnesses apart from your Prometheus fellow, so he stays put until Mr Dray gets here to find out what he knows about it all. So far, he has clammed up tighter than my wife's legs on a Friday night, so he ain't exactly doing himself any favours. If you've got a quarrel with that, Mr Quaint, then I suggest you take it up with the Commissioner himself."

"Constable, I am taking it up with *you*! Try and inject this with a modicum of common sense," said Quaint curtly. "Prometheus is a mute, for God's sake! He couldn't utter a single bloody word if he tried; did that ever occur to you? He's not being evasive purposefully." Quaint shook his head, grinding his teeth to quell his anger. "Tell me, how is he to vouch for himself? Smoke signals and blinking?"

"There's no need to be rude, sir. I'm just doing my job. I can't give you special privileges just because you're old mates with the boss, can I?" said Tucker, holding up his hands. "That's for the Commissioner to decide."

"Now see here, Constable Tucker, I am not a famous man, by any means, but I am well travelled, and command a fair degree of familiarity in many countries and provinces across the world. If you were to visit Peru, the Indigo Coast, Africa or even the Orient, you would meet folk who know and respect the name Cornelius Quaint."

The policeman blinked hard, uncertain what he was to do with this news.

"I'm very pleased for you, sir. And what's your point?"

"My point, Constable, is that in all of those countries — I guarantee that you won't find anyone who knows of me as a patient man." Quaint jabbed his finger repeatedly on Tucker's podium. "I have an employee of mine currently indisposed at Her Majesty's pleasure, I have no way of speaking with said employee, and I've got a circus to put on within the week! I simply do *not* have the time to sit on my hands and do nothing."

"I've already told you, sir," began Tucker. "The Commissioner —"

"Bah!" Quaint snorted, and waved Tucker away with his hand. "Did I happen to mention that my employee is the circus's resident strongman? You're lucky he hasn't ripped the bars from his cell and used them to grill your kidneys by now!"

Butter stepped out from behind Quaint and rested his hand on his employer's arm to dispel his temper. "Mr Quaint . . . please. The constable just do his job. Not his fault, and to shout will not help Prometheus's current situation . . . nor our own."

Quaint blazed his black eyes into the constable's, staring into him as if he was drilling directly into his skull, and the younger man lowered his gaze. "Look . . . I understand what you're saying, Mr Quaint, and I wish I could help you, but my hands are tied," Tucker said. "There is a proper procedure for this, and that's why I've said you'll have to wait until the Commissioner gets here."

One of Constable Tucker's colleagues had heard the raised voices, and came over to investigate their source. Tucker spun around to the policeman standing next to him.

"Marsh, do me a favour, will you? This chap here wants to go visit the giant in the cells, and he says it can't wait until tomorrow when the Commissioner gets in. He says the giant's a friend of his."

"Oh, does he now?" Constable Marsh eyed Quaint suspiciously. "The one we found at the docks with that girl?"

"Unless you are imprisoning more than one giant currently?" asked Quaint.

Constable Marsh sipped on a mug of steaming tea, and eyed Quaint up and down. "And what would a gentleman like yourself want with a murderer, mate?" he asked.

"How many more times?" asked Quaint. "Whatever happened to innocent until proven guilty?"

"It usually goes out the window once we find a bloke unconscious at the scene with the victim's blood all over him," answered Marsh.

Quaint ruffled his hair. "The man has been in my employ for many years and has exemplary conduct, I can assure you. This is all some unfortunate misunderstanding, one that I am attempting to resolve, if you two gents will allow me. Believe me; my friend doesn't have it in him to kill."

"Maybe he does now, sir. It seems he's graduated from middle-aged women to young girls now. Your friend is quite the monster," said Marsh.

"Young girls?" quizzed Quaint.

Marsh nodded. "I was there myself. This morning when we found him, he had the body of a young child lying dead at his side, her body all cut to ribbons. Sweet little thing an' all, she was. Lovely blonde hair."

"This is insanity," growled Quaint. "Child? What child?"

27

Butter tugged on Quaint's cloak. "Boss . . . remember Miss Twinkle did not arrive for work this morning . . . her hair is blonde . . ." he said in a quiet voice. "I am thinking something terrible has happened."

Cornelius Quaint's face turned ash-grey, his voice suddenly vague and hollow, and the spark of fire in his eyes gradually died. "Please God, no. Don't let it be her," he whispered. "Constable, the victim's body . . . I wish to see it immediately!"

CHAPTER FIVE

The Extinguished Spark

Twinkle's corpse was laid out on the simple mortuary table amidst the labyrinth of rooms in the basement beneath Crawditch police station. Cornelius Quaint and Butter stared at the small sheet-clad shape before them as if it were something of alien origin. Of all of Quaint's charges, she was the most angelic, the most innocent. Her death would surely send a shock wave throughout the whole circus. Quaint removed his top hat in respect, sensing a gnawing pain kicking at his insides like the mother of all indigestions. He didn't need to pull away the sheet to know the awful truth. He needed no confirmation other than that which his heart was telling him. As if he were being coerced at gunpoint, he carefully held the corner of the sheet, and steeled himself to reveal what was underneath.

Constable Marsh suddenly placed his hand upon Quaint's arm. "Mr Quaint . . . are you sure about this? You must understand . . . the lass was disfigured quite badly. Are you sure you want to *see* that? Perhaps . . .

perhaps it would be best to remember her as she once was. Do you understand what I'm saying?"

"Constable Marsh, I thank you for your sensitivity, but she was under my care, so I must see her . . . one last time. I owe her that much at least, man." Quaint slowly pulled the white sheet away from Twinkle's body. No amount of focus prepared him for what he saw.

Twinkle was virtually unrecognisable without the vibrant spark of life that was her trademark. She was stripped naked; her face and neck covered with tiny specks of blood, and a long, crucifix-shaped gorge was cut deeply into her chest. Her mouth was frozen in a silent scream of horror. Quaint prayed she had not suffered long.

"Your doctor made quite a mess of the body, didn't he?" Quaint asked, his eyes alight with anger. "The man's a butcher! Was he doing the bloody post-mortem blindfolded?"

"No, sir," said Marsh, shaking his head. "It wasn't Dr Finch. He hasn't arrived in yet. I'm sorry, but she . . . she was *found* like this. I did try and warn you."

The onrush of grief was akin to a father losing his child, indeed, in many ways that is exactly what it was. Cornelius Quaint regarded all his employees as his family. The big man's eyes glazed over as he stared down at Twinkle's body, and the gnawing hole in his stomach grew wider, as if this void were trying to consume him from the inside out. Upon seeing Twinkle so lifeless, he almost wanted to let it do so.

Butter removed his anorak's hood, and stepped closer. He looked to Quaint for some clue as to how he should feel, what he should do, but his employer and friend was as lost as he was. Grief has the ability to erase a man's soul, and empty his heart until only pain remains.

"My poor, dear, sweet girl . . . how ever will we carry on without you?" Quaint whispered, as he placed a gentle kiss upon Twinkle's brow. He glided his hand over her face, as if trying to feel the last vestiges of warmth from her body. "She was a good person, Constable. No good person should ever have to die this way."

"What was her name?" Marsh asked.

"Madeline," whispered Quaint, "Madeline Argyle. But we all called her Twinkle . . . because she was our little star." He paused, cupping his closed fist to his mouth to stifle his emotion. "Her life glowed just as brightly, and she would light up any room. Twinkle was no child, as you wrongly said earlier, Constable Marsh. She was a dwarf . . . a priceless, irreplaceable part of my circus, and she was Prometheus's lover. I know that he loved her with all his heart, and she him. So you see, it's impossible for me to believe that he'd ever harm a single hair on her head."

"She was . . . a *dwarf*? I don't know what to say, Mr Quaint, I didn't know, I'm so sorry. There was . . . so much blood, you see. But, you must understand . . . your friend Prometheus was found with her body by his side. Her blood was all over him, and with no other witnesses . . . we *had* to bring him in." Marsh rubbed at his jaw in contemplation. "But, you're right, we *do* need to get to the bottom of all this mess, and with your friend being a mute . . . maybe it *is* for the best if you see him . . . for a short while at least."

"Thank you, Constable," Quaint nodded. "I would like that very much."

"But you have to keep a lid on this. You're a civilian and if the Commissioner finds out, I'll be for it, whether you're an old pal of his or not."

"Understood. Lead the way, Constable."

Constable Marsh led the way out of the mortuary, directing Quaint and Butter back upstairs, where they faced a massive iron door barring their way. "The Commissioner will hit the roof if he finds out about this," he whispered, turning a large metal key in the lock. He swung open the massive metal door, sending a resounding scream of metal against stone around the corridor. "But as long as you aren't planning on staying for longer than five minutes, I don't see it'll do any harm."

Leading from the narrow hall were four other dark-grey doors with tiny, metal grated slats three-quarters of the way up them, identical apart from painted letters daubed on them. Marsh paced down the long corridor, brushing his hand against the doors as he went. He tugged on his bottom lip, trying to remember in which cell Prometheus was being held, and then he stopped in his tracks outside one of the grey doors. A small blackboard was affixed to the wall outside, and the single word, "MILLER" was written in chalk upon it. Marsh unlocked the cell door, and stepped to the side, allowing Quaint and Butter to enter the room.

As he entered the stillness of the cell, and spied the voluminous shadow sitting hunched in the corner, Cornelius Quaint was suddenly reminded of the many tombs and pyramids that he had explored in Egypt in his youth. Prometheus was hunched in the corner, unmoving and silent.

"Prometheus? It's me," Quaint said softly, approaching the giant as if he were a sleeping baby. His intense eyes searched the Irishman's shadowed face for a flicker of recognition, but there was not so much as a twitch of the man's beard. "My friend? Can you hear me? Are you all right? It's Cornelius."

At the mention of the name, the giant turned around slowly like a great prehistoric beast. His face was pale and withdrawn, his thick beard speckled with dust and grit, as well as the remains of his breakfast, and his eyes were red raw from incessant, merciless tears. In the space of only a few hours, Prometheus had seemed to age by ten years. He slowly lifted his arms and offered them towards Quaint, like a child to its parent. As if drawn by some powerful magnetic force, Quaint flung himself into the gaping abyss of his embrace. Prometheus sobbed heavily, and his body quaked as he let his pain flood out, as if his soul had been wiped clean by the sight of Quaint. The circus owner could almost feel the giant's heart breaking inside his chest, and he chewed at the inside of his cheek anxiously, uncertain what to say. For what words of comfort could he give, when he himself was in just as dire need of them?

33

"Prometheus . . . Aiden . . . I know about Twinkle. I'm so, so sorry. We all feel your loss, and share your pain," Quaint said, as delicately as he could. Even though Prometheus was only fifteen years younger than he, Quaint regarded the man-mountain as a surrogate son. "Are they treating you well?" he asked.

Prometheus nodded, resting his head against his chest, his neck without the strength to support it. He sniffed a lion's roar of a sniff, and wiped a huge paw across his nose like a disobedient schoolboy.

"What happened last night, Prometheus?" Quaint asked. "What did you see?"

Prometheus twitched his bushy beard at the question, and shook his head. He held his hands across his eyes like the See-No-Evil monkey.

"Nothing? You saw *nothing*?" Quaint translated. "Prometheus, you're in a great deal of trouble here. I want to help, but you've got to tell me what happened, man. I need to know specifics. Was there more than one of them? Was there a struggle? Are you hurt?"

Prometheus clawed at his bald scalp in frustration, and let his arms flap down to his sides like dead flesh. The giant motioned for something to write with, and Butter produced a small pencil and notebook from one of the pockets of his oilskin coat. His nostrils flaring, his muscles finding renewed strength, Prometheus began scribbling away in the notebook frantically. He tore off the page and handed it to Quaint:

I WAS DRUGGED.

34

"Drugged?" demanded Quaint. "Drugged by whom?"

Prometheus took back the notepaper and wrote some more words, just as the loud crack of Constable Marsh's key turned in the door's lock. He handed the note back to Quaint with haste, eyeing the cell door. Constable Marsh poked his head around the door, and stared numbly at the huge man sitting on the bench next to Quaint. It was the first time he had seen the giant moving about since he was brought into the station. The man was a lot bigger than he recalled.

"Are you nearly done, sir?" asked Marsh. "It's been five minutes."

"Of course, Constable," Quaint said, leaning closer to Prometheus, who thrust the notepaper into his hand. Quaint's eyes darted across the note:

LANDLORD BLACK SHEEP PUB GAVE ME WHISKY.

DIDN'T KNOW IT WAS POISONED . . . YOU DON'T BELIEVE THEM, DO YOU?

I DIDN'T KILL TWINKLE

"Don't be preposterous, Prometheus, of course I don't believe them," said Quaint, trying hard to keep out of the constable's earshot. "But they found you at the scene covered in Twinkle's blood. As far as they're concerned, they aren't looking for anyone else. Listen, I can't do anything right now to get you out of here. Just keep calm, and don't do anything stupid . . . leave this to me."

"Come on now, Mr Quaint," said Marsh standing in the open doorway, making a point of jangling the cell keys loudly. "I hate to rush you, but it's my job on the line here."

"Yes, yes, thank you, Constable, we're finished," said Quaint. "Come on, Butter, let's head back to the train."

A few minutes later, Quaint and Butter were standing outside on the grimy steps of the police station. Quaint pulled his cloak tight against his chest, trying to shield himself from the cold wind. He was unusually quiet, and this fact made the Inuit at his side very uncomfortable. Butter stared up at Quaint's weathered face.

"We now wait and let police handle, yes?" he asked.

"We now wait and let police handle, no," replied Quaint.

"But boss, we can do nothing until this Commissioner arrives."

"How long have you known me, Butter?"

"Perhaps nine or ten in years, boss."

"And in all that time have you ever known me to stand idly by and do *nothing* when people I care for are in trouble? Do you really think I'd let that lot in there deal with this? Prometheus wouldn't last an hour."

"But, boss . . . from here, where we go?"

"From here, Butter?" Quaint answered. "From here we go back to the train and try and form a plan of action. There's something rotten going on in this district, and if members of our family have been caught up in it, I want it brought to an end sharpish. If that means we have to take steps ourselves, then so be it."

"And wise for us to be involved?" the Inuit asked tentatively, eyeing the familiar steely determination in his employer's eyes. "Could bring more trouble."

"It's a little late for that, my friend," said Quaint. "Thanks to whoever drugged our strongman, I'm afraid we're *already* involved."

CHAPTER
SIX

The Inside Man

The skeletal Reynolds made his way down the thick-carpeted stairs and into a dingy, ornately decorated hallway. Dark-green curtains draped on either side of the front door, and faded oil paintings hung lifelessly on the walls, dusty and forgotten. The house didn't suit Reynolds at all. It was far too sumptuous, far too exotic, but at the same time, he seemed very much at home there. His face was no longer strewn with dirty smudges as it had been the other night, and his ripped and stained clothes were gone, replaced by garments of an altogether different class and finery. Reynolds wore a long velvet indoor coat, and frilled cauliflower cuffs flourished from each sleeve. His dark hair was slicked back tightly against his skull, like the shell of a bullet, and his face was neatly clean-shaven. All similarities to the man who previously met Bishop Courtney in the dimly-lit backstreets of Crawditch had vanished, replaced by a man very much in control of his own destiny, and with a devilish glint of mistrust in his eyes.

Reynolds's thin cigar, quivering on his lower lip, stopped dead as the house's doorbell rang throughout the ground floor hallway. His narrow eyes shot straight to the open drawing room door, to the lifeless body of the house's true owner. Lying with his feet protruding into the hall, the dead man's face was grey, and purple-brown bruises marked his neck where Reynolds had squeezed the life out of him.

"Sorry, old chap," Reynolds said as he picked up the old man under his armpits. The carpet ruffled under the dead body's heels as Reynolds dragged him into the room out of sight. "Highly undignified, I know, but needs must." The man had been dead for two days by this time and carrying his rigid corpse was like dragging a wardrobe.

Reynolds stepped out of the drawing room, straightening his neckerchief in the hallway mirror. As he strode to the front door, through the misted glass panes, he could make out the unmistakable silhouette of a policeman standing on the doorstep. He checked the carriage clock on the nearby reception table, and pulled open the door swiftly.

"Ah . . . Constable Jennings," Reynolds said. "You're early. I wasn't expecting you until lunchtime."

"Morning, sir, I 'ad a bit of business nearby, so I thought I'd kill two birds, like. Actually, I wasn't sure I 'ad the right address. I mean . . . didn't old Mr Lehman used to live 'ere? The old Polish chap?" asked Constable Jennings, examining the number painted on a plaque affixed to the outside of the house.

"He still does live here, Constable," said Reynolds hastily. "He's my uncle. In a bad state of health though, bless him. The poor fellow is simply dead on his feet."

Reynolds flattened down his hair. "So . . . you didn't come all this way for a social visit, I trust? You have some news for me, as per our agreement?"

"Yes, sir. Well, you see, we've 'ad some developments in town. There was another murder late last night. A young girl this time, down by the docks, it was. Real nasty stuff, I saw it myself. Folks at the station're pretty worried, let me tell you."

Reynolds's cold face forced a brief smile. "Really? Well, thank you for the information, Constable Jennings, here's a little token of my appreciation," he said, as he pulled his wallet from his inside breast pocket. "Same fee as usual, I trust?"

"Um, well, actually, sir . . . there's something else," Jennings gulped, his young face as white as a sheet. "That other thing you wanted to know about — that circus magician? A strange looking fellow in a cloak and top-hat you said, right? Mop of curls on his head?"

"Yes, yes! What of him, boy?"

"Well, he's been to the station, just like you figured he would. He left there with some weird little Eskimo geezer about ten minutes ago. Thought I'd come and tell you right away, sir."

"Did he indeed?" said Reynolds, rubbing his finger over his top lip. "Thank you, Constable, thank you very much indeed. Now, I shan't keep you any longer, I'm sure you're busy. Good day to you," Reynolds said, closing the front door.

Once he had seen the outline of Jennings step away from the front of his house, Reynolds rested himself against the thick, oak door and slumped down onto the floor. He slid his tongue across his teeth as a broad smile manifested itself on his face.

"Well, well, well. So . . . Cornelius Quaint has arrived in Crawditch, and is getting his hands dirty already, eh? That certainly makes things a little more interesting." He tapped his front teeth with his fingernails. "It will be such a great pleasure watching him die."

CHAPTER
SEVEN

The Gathering

As its name implied, Dr Marvello's Travelling Circus would be nothing without the means to travel. The steam train that carried all the circus equipment and crew was stationed a few miles away from the borough of Crawditch, at Grosvenor Park train station — a modestly sized, smoke-filled structure with a slatted glass roof and an atmosphere of grime and dust hanging persistently in the air.

The massive steam engine and its four carriages were gaudily painted bright green with red swirling trimmings, and a yellow lightning flash adorned its sides. Alongside all the rather more sombre engines and carriages housed at the station, it stood out like a jester at a wake. Quaint was a firm believer in tradition, and he was loathe to repaint the extravagantly decorated train. It wasn't proper for a circus train to be drab; it was a part of the show's character all to itself, there to offer the public a glimpse of the spectacle to come — and Dr Marvello's Circus thrived on spectacle. In fact it was renowned for it across many parts of Europe. The perfect synergy of traditional circus acrobatics, magical displays, feats of endurance, and the strange and the fanciful. The circus had performed to the likes of sultans and tsars, kings and queens, and always thrilled an audience. Of course, there was no such person as Dr Marvello. It was merely a theatrical pseudonym created to add an air of mystery to the circus. Cornelius Quaint had inherited the name when he inherited the circus, and he was quite unwilling to change it.

The man himself was sitting in his office in a loose white cotton shirt and black waistcoat. An array of twenty or so colourfully dressed folk sat around him in a semi-circle as he held audience. His office near the front of the train was usually a warm and inviting room — with theatrical posters on the walls, old magicians' equipment and costumes, keepsakes and heirlooms from his career. On this day, however, its atmosphere was dominated by an abundance of tears, sniffles and subdued silence as Quaint relayed the information about the loss of Twinkle, and of Prometheus's fate. As he had imagined, this double blow tore right at the heart of his family.

"I wish I had more to tell you, folks, but that's it," Quaint said, elbows on the table in front of him, bridging his fingers into a steeple.

He took a long, slow look around the room at the faces of those he had come to admire and respect. Every one of them had a vital part to play in his circus; every one was an essential cog in the machine. But Quaint was entertaining a thought that would see many of their abilities tested.

"However . . . I must tell you that tonight I intend to visit Crawditch myself and launch a search for the fiend who murdered Twinkle. This task will be fraught with danger, and I envisage conflict with the locals, the police . . . or both. I cannot ask any of you to come with me on this venture."

"Nor could you stop us, Mr Quaint," chirped a Chinese fellow from the back of the office. His identical twin sat next to him, and patted him on the back in firm agreement with his brother.

"Thank you, Yin . . . I hoped you would say as much," Quaint said.

"It's Yang, sir," said the Chinese man.

"My apologies, Yang. I do wish you two would wear name badges," Quaint said warmly, his black eyes twinkling in the half-light. "It would make identifying you somewhat easier!"

A beautiful woman with dark-brown tresses and large dark-brown eyes, wearing a peach-coloured sequinned dress, raised her hand in the middle of the room.

"Mr Q, I've got a question. It's about what happened to Twinkle," she said, her voice faltering as she spoke. "I don't understand . . . of all people, why do the police think that *Prometheus* did it?"

"Because they have no other suspects, Ruby," replied Quaint. "As far as they're concerned, they have their murderer — now all they have to do is find the evidence."

Ruby raised her hand again. "Just tell us what we can do to help, Mr Q. Anything you need us to do, and we'll do it. We're a family after all, right?"

"That is very sweet of you, Ruby, thank you. In fact, I aim to take you up on it." Quaint nodded sharply, his affection for his team reaffirmed. "Our first task this night is to be reconnaissance only. I don't have enough confidence of our footing to do anything more risky. We have a starting point, my friends, but we will need to act with haste if we wish to find anything that could help Prometheus." Quaint stood up from his chair and clapped his hands loudly. "Now, if you would please return to your duties." Quaint watched his troops depart his office until only a handful were left, and then he stepped in front of the door. "Not you, Ruby, Jeremiah, Yin and Yang — I need a word."

After Quaint's office was emptied of the various performers, crew members and technicians, the circus owner stood with his arms crossed, surveying the four remaining performers. The stunning woman in the sequinned dress, a middle-aged man with a balding pate and long sideburns, plus the Chinese twins, all waited behind in their seats, as did another woman who was seated at the rear of the room. Her face was concealed behind a dark lace veil, held in place by a golden headband adorned with a variety of tiny charms and trinkets. She sat bolt upright in her chair, silently observing the room. This woman watched Quaint intently, stroking the charms on her golden bracelet as if she were biding her time patiently to speak.

Quaint began: "Folks, here's my proposition: following a lead given to us by Prometheus himself, tonight we are going to start at The Black Sheep tavern in Crawditch, and search for clues. Prometheus claims he was drugged by whisky given to him by the establishment's landlord, so finding out what *he* knows is our objective. We'll do this quickly and quietly, as we can ill afford the spotlight of the police falling upon ourselves," said Quaint with a resolute clap of his hands. The room snapped to attention immediately, and all eyes and ears were transfixed by the man. "Ruby and I will enter the establishment at eleven o'clock and with a bit of luck the place won't be too busy. We don't want an audience. With Ruby's looks and the right attire, she'll hopefully grab the attention of the landlord." Quaint pointed to the two young Chinese men. "Meanwhile, our acrobatic twins, Yin and Yang, will enter the tavern via the rooftops and search the landlord's living quarters and office. Searching for what, I don't know, but somehow that man is linked to what happened to Prometheus — and so logic dictates, he knows something about Twinkle's killer also . . . gentlemen, lady . . . I want to find out just how much he *does* know — even if we have to squeeze the truth out of his bones."

The balding man raised his hand. "What about me, boss? I'm a clown, for crying out loud. What am I supposed to do, walk in there chucking buckets of water about?"

Quaint smiled. "That's a nice idea, Jeremiah, but no. Yours is a most important role . . . you're the distraction. This landlord will no doubt have a glut of scum in residence that would take umbrage with him being roughed up. It's your job to keep them occupied so that Ruby and I can play our parts."

"I find this unsettling, sir," said Yin, flicking his thick dark fringe away from his eyes. "It is inconceivable that this could happen to someone like Twinkle."

His brother Yang toyed with his neckerchief. "I agree with Yin, Mr Quaint. I cannot think what kind of person would wish to harm her."

"I share your sentiments, my friends, and your bewilderment. Twinkle was as close to an angel as I have ever known, and I am not going to stop until I find out who is responsible. What I *can* say with absolute certainty is that whoever this killer is, he's as dangerous a man as I can imagine."

The veiled woman at the back of the office gently coughed into her hand.

"Madame Destine?" Quaint asked. "You have something you wish to add?"

"Yes, Cornelius," she said, in a thick French accent. "But what I have to say must be for your ears alone."

CHAPTER
EIGHT

The Foreshadow of
the Past

"All right, Madame, you have my attention," said Quaint, once he and the veiled woman were alone. "What's on your mind?"

The circus fortune-teller known as "The Mystical Madame Destine" lifted her veil and stared at Quaint. Mid-way through her seventies, she was still in immaculate shape, and the curves of her face belied her age by a good twenty years. Her high cheekbones accentuated her catlike eyes as if they were created by a master sculptor, and she batted her eyelids as she waited for Quaint to pull up a chair before she spoke. Like a thick chocolate mousse, the Frenchwoman marinated every word with smooth, rich tones and flavours and, as always, Quaint was enthralled.

"Cornelius, have I not always tried to guide you away from perilous ventures in your life? Sometimes you choose to listen, most often not. But this time I beg you to take heed." Madame Destine breathed a heavy sigh, as if unburdening herself of a great secret. "There is more afoot here than simple murder. My gifts of clairvoyance are giving me conflicting thoughts at every turn. Emotion, contradiction, revenge, twisted pathways. The situation we find ourselves in is grave."

"Well, of course it is, Madame. One of our family has been murdered, and another is incarcerated at the police station," said Quaint, as he rose from his chair and squatted next to Destine's own, taking her hand in his. "Destine, you have been my guardian since I was seven years old. You have been more akin to a mother to me than my own was. You are one of the most gifted fortune-tellers in Europe, and my faith in you is unwavering. Both the circus, and myself, are glad to have you on board."

"Spare me, Cornelius," said Destine, with a hint of a smile. "When you compliment me this much it usually means you are about to tell me something that I do not wish to hear. I take it you are to continue with this folly anyway, despite my warning?"

Quaint snatched up the woman's hand, and kissed it gently. "This is too close to home for me to ignore," he said, his dark eyes searching for his guardian's blessing.

"No one is asking you to ignore it, Cornelius, but merely temper your response."

"Madame, you know me well enough by now. I am a creature of instinct, and I have seen far too many friends and loved ones suffer because I did not act sooner. That will not happen again, this crime *cannot* go unpunished."

"And how does involving this circus mean that it will *not*?"

"*I* did not involve this circus, Destine — the killer did. I would not ask my people to do anything that each and every one of them would not do themselves in an instant. Do you expect me to leave Prometheus to rot?"

"You aren't listening to me, Cornelius," the Frenchwoman implored, reaching out for Quaint's arm. "I am trying to *warn* you. There is something entwined within my visions of foresight . . . an undertone of secrecy. Something bubbling away that I cannot yet make sense of. Forget your pride . . . if you embark upon this quest I fear you may lose far more."

"Pride is an easy thing to lose, Madame."

"Cornelius, do not just simply listen to my words — *hear* them. Hear my counsel, else it be the last I give you," snapped Destine. "Ignorance of this underlying scent of deceit will be your undoing; I have no doubt of that."

"Madame, take a look around you," said Quaint, resting both hands upon Destine's shoulder. "There is deceit around every corner, behind every door of every house in every street — even in our Parliament. It's all around us. Deceit is practically what the present day world is founded upon."

"Cornelius, it is not the present that concerns me." Destine clasped at his hands, imploring him. "I fear that it is your past that is about to catch up with you."

CHAPTER NINE

The Black Sheep

Later, once the shroud of night had draped its cold, dark hand across Crawditch's streets, Cornelius Quaint stood opposite The Black Sheep tavern, and eyed the place with keen interest. He had shrugged off Destine's warning and continued with his plan, just as the Frenchwoman had guessed he would. Not the type to run from danger, he was more likely to sneak up behind it, tap it on the shoulder and announce himself. He looked around the late night streets of Crawditch. All his people were in position. The black-clad duo of Yin and Yang leapt like cats from one rooftop to the next in a synchronous fluid motion in the pitch darkness as easily as if they were walking down a familiar street. Ruby was standing by Quaint's side wearing a long, flowing dark-green cloak that covered her body completely, and Jeremiah waited pensively across the street, bathed in waning light from the gas lamp above him.

"It's show time," said Quaint.

The occupants of The Black Sheep stopped drinking in unison as soon as Ruby strode into the tavern. All eyes

51

were upon her, their necks craning to follow her every move as she approached the bar. The landlord followed suit as Ruby flicked coiled spirals of copper-brunette hair away from her eyes.

"Evenin', ma'am," he said with a nod of his head. "It's a bit risky for a lady to be out alone at this time of night, innit? Y'know, what with all these murders afoot? Most ladies are rightfully worried."

"My father was a merchant seaman, sir, I am not one easily *worried*," Ruby said, her eyelids fluttering a gentle tempo with the beat of her voice. "Might you be the proprietor of this establishment, sir?"

The barman nearly swallowed his own tongue. "I . . . I'm Arthur Peach, yes, the . . . ah . . . proprietor. Listen, you're not one of Hilda's girls, are you? I mean, I know I said I'd pay for what I owe . . . but business has been slow. Surely she'll allow me a few more days?"

Ruby unclipped the brooch fastening her dark cloak together, and it fell open at the front. Like a pair of drab theatre curtains, parting to reveal a magnificently decorated stage, her ample cleavage blossomed forth into the man's view. Her curvaceous breasts descended into tantalising shadow beneath the bodice of an emerald-coloured, low-cut dress, fitted tightly around the waist by a broad red silk sash. Ruby smiled a toothsome smile at the landlord.

"Mr Peach, I am not one of Hilda's *girls*, so you may relax," she said sweetly. "My name is Ruby Marstrand. A mutual friend of ours has requested that I visit you to . . . *repay* his thanks for the little job with the whisky last night."

"The Irishman?" asked the barman, scratching at his head. "But, Mr Hawkspear already paid me more than enough. Listen, why don't you —?"

Ruby pressed her finger against his lips. "Shhh. Is there somewhere a little more . . . *private* that we can go? Mr Hawkspear really is *very* grateful, you know . . . and he's asked me to *prove* it to you properly . . . if you get my meaning."

"What, you . . . you mean you want to . . . with me? What, right now? Here?" stuttered Peach, his lust silencing the logical, questioning side of his brain.

"Mr Hawkspear believes in bad rewards for bad behaviour, Mr Peach," teased Ruby with a wink. "And you have been very, very naughty."

"Christ, love, if you *ain't* one of Hilda's girls, then I must surely be the luckiest bleeder in the bar," snorted Peach.

"Not yet, silly, but you soon will be," whispered Ruby delicately into Peach's ear.

"Oh, right . . . well." The landlord looked around him at the small group of customers down the far end of the tavern, and smeared his cuff across his nostrils. "Well, I s'pose no one will miss me for a few minutes, eh?"

"A few minutes? My, you *do* know how to spoil a girl," giggled Ruby. "How about over there in the booth?"

At the far end of the tavern, the door opened and Jeremiah entered, cutting a swathe through the fog of tobacco. He was dressed in full clown make-up and

53

costume, and the alcohol-pickled occupants of the bar took second looks to make sure the rum and ale hadn't addled their senses. The clown demanded the attention in much the same way as Ruby had, but for entirely different reasons. Jeremiah approached a long table populated by some grisly-looking regulars and grinned broadly. Their eyes instantly caught sight of him, and a cacophony of laughter followed.

"Gawd!" one of the men laughed. "What's Arthur put in 'is ale tonight?"

One of the men nearly spat his drink across the table. "Crikey! Alf, look, it's your missus come to fetch you home."

"Good evening to you, lads. The name's Jerry the clown," Jeremiah beamed. The white greasepaint covered his entire face, except for bright red-painted lips and surprised eyebrows halfway up his forehead. He wore an orange wig, a jaunty bowler hat and a large, bulbous red nose perched on the end of Jeremiah's own large, bulbous nose. "Dr Marvello's Circus is in town, and I'm just drumming up a bit of trade, know what I mean? I can see you lads are of a discerning nature when it comes to your entertainment. Well, how'd you fancy some free tickets to the show, eh?" he said, throwing a handful of bright yellow tickets onto the table. "Hey, all of you lot over there, come on. Help yourself!"

Swarming from various parts of the bar, the other patrons ushered themselves over at the mention of the word "free". Crawditch's residents were not the sort to pass up anything that wouldn't cost them a penny, and the men huddled together, snatching at the tickets laid on the table. One of them cracked a joke about Jeremiah's baggy trousers, held up by braces over a yellow and red spotted shirt. Jeremiah flicked at his oversized bow tie, and stamped his feet onto the sawdust-littered floor.

"Oh, so you're after a free show right now, are you? Right then." He slapped his hands together, and grinned. "Did you hear the one about the whore with a wooden eye?"

At the opposite end of The Black Sheep, landlord Arthur Peach couldn't believe his luck. Ruby led him by his shirt collar to the secluded booths, and he practically stumbled the whole way there, where he suddenly came face to face with a grim-faced Cornelius Quaint. He had slipped in through the tavern's rear entrance unobserved when all eyes were transfixed by the wondrous image of Ruby. Quaint was reclining in a wooden chair with his dark-grey cloak cast behind him, and his arm rested casually on his knee as if he were expecting this visitor.

"Here, what's all this then?" Peach said nervously to Ruby as he spied Quaint's bleak face. "I wasn't expectin' an audience, love."

Quaint motioned to the bench to his right. "Be a good dog and sit."

The man was a bag of nerves at the sight of Quaint's ice-cold features, but he did as he was instructed. His forehead was speckled with droplets of anxious sweat, and his tongue darted about his dry lips like a serpent tasting the air.

"My name is Cornelius Quaint," said Quaint. "And you are?"

"Arthur Peach . . . the landlord of this place," the nervous landlord said, his parched lips making a clicking noise every time he spoke.

"Charmed, I'm sure," lied Quaint.

Peach shifted in his seat uncomfortably, his eyes darting left to right. "Look, what's this all about? I've got a bar to run 'ere, see, and I ain't in the mood for no fun and games."

"Well that *is* such a shame, Mr Peach, because *I* am. You and I are going to play a little game of life or death — *your* life, to be exact." Quaint stood up quickly, and slammed the heavy oak table into Peach's gut, its pointed corner gouging into the man's groin hard, pinning him against the wall. He gasped for air, his eyes watering and his forehead glistening like a star-filled night sky.

"Last night a young woman was murdered not far from here," shrilled Quaint. "What do you know of it?"

Peach scowled. "Nothing! I . . . I don't know *nothing*," he gasped, clawing at the table digging into his gut, trying to take in a lungful of air.

"That's a double negative, Mr Peach. But if there's one thing I hate more than bad grammar — it's a liar." Quaint shoved the table harder into the man's groin with all his strength, which was not inconsiderable. "The victim was a dwarf. She and a gentleman of great size were drinking in this tavern last night."

"So were a lot of people. What makes you think I had something to do with it?"

Quaint smiled ingenuously. "Because the giant happens to be a very good friend of mine, and due to your actions he happens to be in a lot of trouble. I don't like seeing my friends toyed with, Mr Peach, do you understand me? It . . . *aggravates* me, and I do so hate being aggravated. It plays havoc with the digestion." Quaint's dark eyes narrowed in on Peach, and fixed the man with a penetrating stare. "My friend was drugged . . . and drugged by whisky that *you* gave to him. What have you got to say for yourself?"

Ruby leaned towards Quaint and whispered in his ear. "He just told me that some Irishman named 'Hawkspear' paid him to give Prometheus the whisky."

"Hawkspear, eh?" said Quaint. He brought his weight down hard on the table, and an electric stab of pain resonated once again between Peach's legs. The landlord yelped like a dog whose tail had been stepped on. "My time is precious to me, Mr Peach, and if your scrotum is precious to *you*, then I suggest you hurry up and tell me what I want to know!"

Peach stared blankly at Quaint. "Why don't you go an' get buggered!" he spat, his lips quivering as he fought against the pain. "You'll get nothing from me."

With a flash, Quaint's fist darted from within the folds of his dark cloak and punched the landlord square in the face. Tears formed in the landlord's eyes instantly, and a dab of dark blood trickled from his nose. "Mind your language, Mr Peach, there's a lady present," he scolded.

57

"You're dead meat," Peach wheezed, trying to catch his breath. "Any second now, one of my lads down there is going to see what you're up to. They won't stand for it. They'll be on you like a shot. You'll be picking up your teeth, and she'll wish she'd never been born, know what I mean?"

From the far end of The Black Sheep, whoops and cheers echoed around the tavern, followed by a wave of gut-wrenching laughter, as Jeremiah entertained the locals.

"By '*your lads*', I assume that you're referring to the patrons at the far end of the tavern?" said Quaint, cupping a hand to his ear. "It sounds like your friends are otherwise engaged. I'm afraid that you, Mr Peach, are very much on your own."

"I ain't scared of an old man like you," Peach said defiantly, despite the quivering wreck of the rest of his body.

"My dear man, it is not *I* of whom you should be frightened," said Quaint with a smile, relaxing his weight from the table. "But my female companion here is another matter entirely."

Peach slumped into his chair, clutching at his groin.

"Ruby, my dear, I wonder if you would mind showing Mr Peach what I mean?" Quaint grabbed Peach's right hand and thrust it down hard onto the table, splaying his fingers. Peach winced, but his attention was wisely on Ruby, not Quaint.

"Love to, Mr Q," Ruby said, unbuttoning the fastenings on the front of her dress. Not removing her gaze from the landlord, she slid her nimble fingers

58

down into the shadows, and produced a slender silver dagger from a hidden scabbard in her cleavage. Holding it between her thumb and forefinger, Ruby flipped the knife up into the air, catching it perfectly by its point on her fingertip. Then, holding her palm flat with the knife upon it, she gently flexed her fingers, and the knife rocked in a see-saw motion before rotating in a complete circle. Peach's eyes were mesmerised by the display, as the knife almost took on a life of its own. With a deft flick upwards, Ruby tossed the knife high into the air once again. It fell in slow motion; landing with a dull thud in between Peach's outstretched fingers, a fraction of an inch from his skin. That was the second time that night that Ruby had nearly caused Peach to swallow his tongue. The landlord watched the knife like a man entranced as it swayed like a metronome half an inch into the wooden table.

Quaint's booming voice snapped him back into the room. "Miss Marstrand here was trained by a remarkably gifted German fellow named Viktor Dzierzanowski, arguably the best knife-smith in the modern world, and a favourite of Prince Albert himself, I understand," Quaint said, absentmindedly picking at his fingernails. "Ruby was Viktor's prize pupil, and she can skewer a bluebottle at twenty paces."

Ruby shrugged, coyly pretending to hide her embarrassment. "Well, that's awfully sweet of you to say, Mr Q, but I have to admit, I *am* a bit rusty. Perhaps Mr Peach would appreciate a more . . . *practical* demonstration. Tell me, what shall I aim for — his ears or his balls?" she asked innocently.

The nervous barman nearly fainted on the spot. His forehead was swamped with a sudden flurry of fresh, speckled perspiration and his lower lip quivered like a fish on an angler's line.

"W-W-What did she j-j-just say?" he stammered.

"Ears or balls, Mr Peach, ears or balls!" Quaint thundered. He pretended to mull over the question, closely inspecting the man's ears, before glancing briefly down at his already tenderised groin. "Well, he's got two of each, so from where I'm sitting they're much of a muchness, my dear. Perhaps Mr Peach has a preference."

"Hmm," Ruby said, as she plucked her knife from the table. She held it up and squinted, aiming at Peach's head. "The earlobes look a bit more of a challenge, don't you think, Mr Q? Look at them tiny little things. Like little rat ears, aren't they? But I might miss them altogether and catch him straight in the eye, and you know how much mess *that* makes."

Quaint enjoyed watching the colour drain from the landlord's face. "Don't remind me! You remember that poor fellow who accosted you backstage in Belgium?"

"Gosh, yes," giggled Ruby. "I threw the knife so hard it embedded itself in the poor man's skull and no one could pull it out! The funeral was a nightmare. They had a devil of a time finding a coffin to fit him."

"What?" squawked Peach, more of a bystander in this conversation.

"Perhaps the testicles would be a much safer bet then, my dear," said Quaint. "There'll be a lot less blood, and at least there's a one in three chance of hitting something painful." Quaint tapped the landlord on his shoulder, and the man leapt in fear. "I notice you aren't a married man, Mr Peach. Not planning on having children then? That's probably for the best."

Peach's skin was now so pale that it was practically transparent.

"All right, all right, man!" he said, slamming his hands on the table, petrified to the point of collapse. "I don't owe Hawkspear nothing. Just call her off, and I'll tell you anything you want to know, I swear!"

"Splendid," smiled Quaint. "You see how reasonable you can be with the correct level of motivation, Mr Peach?" He rocked back in his chair and linked his fingers together, delighted with his powers of persuasion. "Do tell me all — and leave out not one scrap of detail."

CHAPTER
TEN

The Messenger

It was close to midnight, and Westminster Abbey's annexe building was empty apart from a few priests and theology students scurrying about like minnows in a stream. Skirting from one place to the next, the students — known in the sanctum as "alumno" — were electric with something akin to gossip. There was a murmur on the wind — Bishop Courtney was in residence. Staying within the lush, ornate apartment situated in the west wing of the church away from prying eyes and spying ears, the Bishop was virtually a celebrity, and every one of the students wished to meet the man, him being one of Her Majesty's most trusted advisors.

Behind the varnished oak doors on the top floor of the annexe building, Bishop Courtney scoured through the reams of paperwork upon his cluttered desk. He scooped up a golden goblet with chubby fingers, and poured the contents down his gullet. There was a gentle knock on the door and the golden knob turned slowly, as the door inched open. The Bishop checked the ornamental carriage clock on the vast fireplace and clicked his tongue against the roof of his mouth. A young student priest was stood pensively in the doorway.

"Yes, what is it, alumno?" snapped Bishop Courtney, turning his portly mass around to face the door. "I thought I ordered not to be disturbed!"

"Sorry, your Grace, but a Reverend Fox is in the reception hall requesting an audience with you. Shall I permit him entrance?" the young priest asked, cowering as if he were pleading for his life.

"Reverend Fox?" asked the Bishop. He scowled into his goblet of wine curiously, and then his eyes suddenly sparked wide open, as if he had just been startled by gunfire. "Ah! Reverend Fox, you say? Well, by all means, show him in, boy."

"Very good, my Lord," said the alumno, bowing his head.

A few moments later, a tall, thin man dressed in black priestly robes and a white dog collar entered the residence, and closed the door firmly behind him.

"Evening, Bishop," snapped a heavily disguised Mr Reynolds. As well as bogus priestly garb, the man also wore a wicked grin across his gaunt face. "Burning the midnight oil, I see?"

Bishop Courtney didn't bat an eyelid. "I thought I told you that you were only to use the Fox identity if there was an emergency, Mr Reynolds. So what news is about to ruin my night?" he asked, nervously twisting his large ruby ring around his finger.

"You're more right than you know, Bishop." Mr Reynolds's face stiffened, as he approached the large fireplace. "Not long ago I received a message from my

63

eyes and ears in Crawditch. It seems that Arthur Peach, the landlord of The Black Sheep, has recently received a visit from Cornelius Quaint."

The Bishop raised an eyebrow. "Quaint? The conjuror you mentioned?" he said. "And so what? I don't expect to be disturbed for trivialities, man. You came all the way to Westminster just to tell me that?"

"Not just that, Bishop." He strode briskly over to the Bishop, his hands held loosely behind his back. "It seems Quaint put the frighteners on Peach, and he spilled his guts. Now he knows about Hawkspear, and he knows about the whisky! He knows it was drugged. Plus, he's been hanging around the police station, trying to see his employee . . . the one incarcerated for the murders."

"Once again, Mr Reynolds, I find myself asking how this affects me? Do you really think that I pay you to be involved in petty details? This man Quaint doesn't know of *your* involvement in this, does he? Or my own? Then I fail to see how this can be connected to my office and, as such — I don't care a whit about it. This is *your* plan, remember? Perhaps you should choose your men more carefully in future."

Reynolds gripped the back of Courtney's chair, his face tense. "Quaint is no fool. I told you, I have history with him. I know the way he thinks."

"Unless I am missing something, this man is a mere circus magician, is he not? An old has-been entertainer who now runs a circus? He's hardly a threat, Reynolds. I mean, it's not like he can read minds, is it?"

"Actually, some folk say he can," said Reynolds grimly. "He's a terrier, Bishop — once he gets a whiff of something, he'll not rest until he digs out the answers — and with his circus strongman involved to boot, it's practically lit a fuse right under him! We need to be on our guard, my Lord." The slender man paused, mulling over his next sentence carefully. "I think we should call off Hawkspear for a bit . . . let things simmer down."

"Absolutely not!" The Bishop's temper rose swiftly. "Mr Reynolds, may I remind you that Mr Hawkspear is on lease from Blackstaff prison to perform a service for me, and that service is to scare the wits out of everyone who lives in that flea-pit of a borough. You're just letting your nerves get the better of you, that's all. The plan will continue as we agreed — no deviation! So far we only have three corpses on the streets, not nearly enough to send a clear-cut message to those people, and certainly not enough to make them pack up and leave town. Do not forget, I need that district cleared of its inhabitants within the week, Mr Reynolds — or need I remind you of my schedule?"

"What? You think we should just carry on, and hope that Quaint doesn't get wind of our plan? You want me to be continually looking over my shoulder, do you, hoping Quaint's not stood there? That's taking a lot of unnecessary risks, Bishop."

The Bishop buried his head in his hands. "All right . . . let me think. This man you speak of . . . this Cornelius Quaint chap . . . if he really is as dangerous as you say, perhaps we can arrange for a little . . .

accident to befall him." The greasy skin of the Bishop's face caught a glint from the fireplace, as he leaned forward in his chair. "Get some men together, some good, reliable men lacking in morals and with questionable consciences. Pay them whatever it takes, and see to it that Mr Quaint finds himself in their company."

CHAPTER
ELEVEN

The Day After the Night Before

Sergeant Horace Berry was seated at his desk in Crawditch police station, idly tapping his knuckles with a pencil. He looked over at the clock on the wall and rolled his eyes in horror. Hearing the station's main doors burst open, Berry was about to stand and get a better look at who had entered, when a bellowing Scottish voice drifted over the tops of the desk partitions. Berry knew instantly that Commissioner Dray had arrived. Considering that it was gone midnight, and now encroaching on the early hours of the morning, he would surely be in a ridiculously foul mood — not that the time of day seemed to have any impact on Dray's demeanour. He was just as reliably grouchy in the morning as he was at midday or during nightfall. It was a permanent state for the man.

"Over here, Commissioner," Berry called, raising his hand in the air.

"I got your summons, Horace, and here I am. It's far too early in the day for all this nonsense, man. Mrs Dray was fast asleep — and you know how much I cherish the moments when that woman keeps her mouth shut! Night-time is the only respite I get from her incessant whining," Commissioner Dray barked, as he stormed through the empty station office towards a large oak door. "My office, Horace, and be quick about it, will you?"

Commissioner Dray was soon seated in his high-backed chair in his office. His desk was neat and tidy, with towers of paperwork placed into piles in order of importance. A misty sepia-toned photograph of his wife was placed next to an ornate glass statue of a prancing stag. It wasn't clear which was a symbol of a memorable hunt, and which was just a trophy to be proud of — but Sergeant Berry guessed Mrs Dray didn't fall into either category. The Commissioner was a heavy-set man with large, wide shoulders, a broad neck and podgy, chilblained cheeks. His grey-white hair was rapidly dissipating; a fact that he seemed entirely conscious of, as thin spidery strands were swept across his forehead in a vain attempt to disguise its thinning. Dray chewed at the inside of his cheek distractedly, as he rubbed his hands up and down his arms.

"Christ, it's cold tonight. Freeze the balls off a brass monkey out there, man!" The Commissioner opened his drawer and pulled out a bottle of whisky and two glasses. He placed one next to him and the other on the far side of the desk. "You want a wee dram, Horace? It'll get the blood flowing, so it will."

Berry shook his head. "Not whilst I'm on duty, sir."

Dray laughed. "Forget about that, Berry — *especially* whilst you're on bloody duty!" Dray poured two fingers of whisky into both glasses anyway, despite Berry's protestations. "Now, what the devil is so important that you send Constable Marsh round to knock me up at one in the morning, eh?" he said with his usual blistering tones.

Berry had known Dray for many years, but still, the man's bombast made his heart miss a beat. "Commissioner, if I had any choice, I wouldn't have bothered you."

"Well, I'm here now, Horace, so you may as well spit it out, eh?" Dray said, relaxing his grim face a little, and leaning back in his chair.

"As you might have guessed, sir — it's bad news," Berry said, removing a piece of paper from his uniform's breast pocket. It was the same crumpled note that he had found near Twinkle's body. "There was another murder last night. Jennings and myself were called to the outskirts of Crawditch at first light this morning. The victim looked as if she'd fallen foul of the same bloke responsible for the previous two murders in town. At first . . ." Berry paused to gain Dray's full attention. "The thing is, Commissioner . . . we found a man unconscious next to the latest girl at the scene, seemingly worse the wear for drink. You would naturally assume that all the evidence points to him being the perpetrator of not just that young lady's murder, but the other two, as well, wouldn't you?"

"I would hope so." Dray slurped his whisky noisily. "Horace, please don't tell me you dragged me out of bed for this. If you've caught the bloke responsible, well done! Slap the irons on him, and we'll measure his neck

69

for the gallows. Can I not just read your report once it's filed?"

"Well, sir, there are a few . . . variables we should consider."

Dray squinted. "Variables? What the bloody hell is that supposed to mean?"

"This latest victim was a dwarf, sir . . . and the man in custody is a hell of a size, and both are apparently part of a circus crew that's settled over in Hyde Park. Constable Marsh tells me the owner of the circus has already been here early this morning, trying to see his friend, convinced that he was innocent."

"Aye, and how many times have we heard that, eh?" Dray said.

"Indeed. The suspect is still down in the cells at the moment. I know you weren't due in until later . . . but I don't think we can afford to sit on this for long."

"Oh, and why's that?" asked Dray. "Don't mince your words, Horace; I've known you too long. If you're onto something, then let me in on it! What the hell's got you so bothered?"

Berry rubbed a hand over his forehead, and slid it over his hair. "These murders have been like a bolt from the blue to the folks round here, Commissioner, and if this gets out, God knows what could happen."

"Berry, calm down. What are you on about? If what gets out?"

Sergeant Berry toyed anxiously with his earlobe. "That's the reason why I called you in, sir. Just like the others, this poor girl wasn't just killed; she was mutilated horrifically in a most ungodly manner. Once

70

you see the state of her . . . you'll understand what's got me bothered."

"We've both seen murder before, Berry; nothing shocks me about that any more."

"You might change your mind once you've seen her, sir. I think we've got a real mess on our hands here, and I don't have the slightest clue how we're going to deal with it." Berry leaned forwards, pressing his hands flat onto Dray's desk. "Something tells me we're going to see a hell of a lot more bodies turning up."

CHAPTER
TWELVE

The Thicker Plot

Cornelius Quaint was sitting in near darkness in his office, the only glimmer of light provided by a single candle positioned on the cluttered table in front of him. Piles of paperwork were stacked up high on his desk awaiting his inspection, but he ignored them this night. His mind was simply not on the job. Admittedly, the circus finances were no fun at all, and there was never a good time to bury one's head amongst figures and sums, but he had at least hoped they would serve as some kind of distraction. Instead they were nothing more than one more thing to put off and do tomorrow. The very thoughts he was trying hard *not* to entertain remained stubbornly present at the forefront of his mind. The shutters over his carriage windows were down, and an eerie silence had taken hold within the room. It was rapidly approaching two in the morning, and Quaint's burst of energy from the night's adventure at The Black Sheep had subsided, giving way to beleaguered tiredness. As much as he hated to admit it to anyone — least of all himself — he was not a young man any more. He rubbed at the third finger on his left hand and stared into the flickering light of the candle, allowing the golden-amber flame to hypnotise him. He rubbed at his eyes, stifling a yawn. Quaint barely even noticed the gentle knock on his office door before Madame Destine stepped inside, carrying a silver tray with a hot pot of tea and two cups upon it.

"I thought you would still be awake, my sweet." Destine pushed a stack of papers to one side and placed the tray on the corner of Quaint's desk. "You do realise that pile won't get any smaller the longer it is left, you know. Unless you are trying to perfect a new magic trick to make all the bills disappear."

"I think that I would have better luck trying to turn water into wine, Madame," Quaint said with a wan smile.

Madame Destine seated herself in a wooden chair opposite him, raised her veil and looked at Quaint intently, her eyes taking in every minute detail of his worn face. She leaned forward to pour tea into his cup, never once removing her gaze from him. After a long pause, she spoke: "Is there something on your mind, *mon cheri?*"

"No, Madame. Why do you ask?"

She blew gently into her teacup as wisps of steam floated to the ceiling. "For three reasons; because I know you better than you know yourself, because you cannot hide anything from me, and because I know what the date is today."

Quaint froze, the teacup suspended in mid-air, inches from his mouth. A hollow silence was borne

73

between them. For a painfully long moment, he tried his best to avoid eye contact with the Frenchwoman, but he knew he couldn't resist a glance eventually. More than that, Destine knew it too, and when he finally looked up from the tea, her blue-grey eyes were already beseeching him for the truth.

"Has anyone ever told you that you would make a marvellous torturer?" Quaint asked.

"Frequently," replied Destine. "So there *is* something on your mind then?"

"Yes, yes! There is something on my mind. Are you happy now?" Quaint said, a little more harshly than he had intended. "You're right again, as always. I just suppose . . . the date sneaked up on me a little quicker than I had expected."

Destine nodded, choosing her delicate words carefully. "I thought as much. It is never an easy time of year for you, Cornelius, so why does this *particular* year cause you more anguish than the previous anniversaries of your wife's death?"

The directness of Destine's question made Quaint shudder, as if the words were forbidden, and by saying them aloud, some great taboo had been broken. The melodic control of her voice was like hearing each sentence as a symphony, deconstructed into its purest, most poetic form. Quaint had always said that Destine could read the cargo manifest of a spice merchant's schooner and it would still sound like angels singing. But that was not to say her words did not sting his heart.

Quaint locked eyes with her. "It's November the twenty-third and with all that has been going on recently, I've hardly even noticed."

"Perhaps that is a good thing, my sweet. A sign that the healing process has finally begun?" offered Destine. "It has been so many years now."

"Twenty-nine, to be exact," said Quaint. "But I have been distracted, Madame! This day almost passed by unnoticed, and I feel shame for that fact, as if I'm dishonouring her memory somehow."

"Poppycock! You remember Margarite in your own way at this time of year, Cornelius . . . within your heart. There has been much of late to occupy your attention elsewhere. That is not dishonour, my sweet. You have a life to lead, and one that is not frozen in time, locked in the past. As I said, perhaps you are now able to focus more clearly on other things. After all, does this day not normally put you in a most bedevilled mood?"

"Do I not look to be in a bedevilled mood now, Madame?"

Quaint leaned back in his chair, forcing the creaking wooden joints to complain. A broad sardonic grin forced itself onto his face. "I am always bedevilled — it is my lot in life. Even though I have subconsciously pushed these thoughts to the back of my mind, they are not forgotten. Maybe once I finally try and get some sleep tonight they will come back to haunt me once more. My bad dreams always seem to increase tenfold at this time of year."

75

"Is that why you are awake at this hour? Are you hoping to run from your nightmares, Cornelius, because I — of all people — can tell you that they have a nasty habit of recurring, usually when you least expect them," Destine said, as she moved her chair forwards, edging closer to the desk. "It does no one any good to dwell in the past. For what it is worth, I think all this talk of murder and death of late is the reason not why you *forget* Margarite's death, but why you allow the *symbolism* behind it to taint every thought you have. After all, is death not everywhere we look recently?" Destine made a point of a long pause, as she watched the cinders of recognition burn in Quaint's eyes. This was an important message that she was trying to impart, and she hated giving good wisdom to deaf ears. "Your rage is a great fuel for you, Cornelius . . . just be cautious that once that fuel is burnt out, your soul is not so spoiled that it cannot function without it." Destine stirred her teacup noisily, chinking the silver spoon against the saucer, signalling an end to the maudlin conversation.

"So . . . why do you not tell me of the night's adventures? I would so much like to hear of them. Make sure you begin at the beginning, dear, if you don't mind," said Destine calmly. "And do not leave out any tales of fisticuffs, for I am far from squeamish and you know how much I *love* to hear tales of you clobbering bad people."

Quaint nodded, reluctantly giving in to his companion's request. He regaled her with the night's visit to The Black Sheep tavern, and Destine hung on his every word.

"And whilst Jeremiah, Ruby and myself worked the floor downstairs, Yin and Yang searched the landlord's residence. I was actually hoping that they'd find something . . . *incriminating*, some titbit of explanation. But aside from a lot of unpaid bills, bad debts and a few bawdy love letters to a beau named Mary, the twins found nothing. However . . . downstairs in the bar, the landlord told Ruby and me that an Irishman had given him money to pass the drugged whisky to Prometheus," Quaint said. "The landlord had never seen him before, or since."

"We have been here for only two days and already we have made an enemy who is prepared to kill," Destine said, resting her top lip upon the ridge of her cup. "Things move fast in this town, Cornelius."

"Yes, well . . . Prometheus has always had a knack for attracting trouble, hasn't he?" Quaint said, recollecting more than one occasion when he'd either had to fight, bargain or plead for Miller's life in one country or another over the years.

"And how many times has he truly been at fault? He cannot help the way he looks, Cornelius. Prometheus is certainly no lover of conflict. Some people are magnets for trouble, whereas others seem to seek it willingly, like a wasp to jam," Destine said, catching Quaint's eyes. "Sound familiar?"

Quaint tried to look innocent, playing with the buttons on his shirt. "Not really. The only connection that I'm pinning my thoughts on is that this bloke was apparently Irish, as Prometheus himself is. Perhaps this is what triggered the conflict?"

Destine nodded. "*Probablement.*"

"Which beggars the question: how do you pick an argument with a mute? And if you wished to . . . would you do so with one who looked like Prometheus?" chimed Quaint.

"And why not use a knife or a pistol rather than poison?" agreed Destine. "You know that I am extremely sensitive to the emotions of others, Cornelius, and I know that it is usually emotion that is the trigger for murder. As you can testify, emotion and common sense are not mutually exclusive — or need I remind you of your tryst with the Hungarian Premier's wife a few years back?"

A smile (and one that balanced the delicate line between amusement and embarrassment) skirted briefly across Quaint's face, as his memory recalled the incident to which Destine referred. "That was years ago, but even now my lower back still aches on a cold day. Duchess Ariadne took a fancy only to my stage magic and illusion, Madame, not to me. She had such spirit, and such a voracious appetite!"

"You may paint that particular mental picture for someone else, Cornelius, I am a lady, and do not forget it," Destine said, sipping her tea. "We need to speak to Prometheus again. We need to try and find the connection, if there is indeed one to be found."

"The police said there have been two other murders the past few nights, oddly enough, all since our arrival. To me it's nothing but coincidence, but to the police . . . it's too *much* of coincidence to *be* one. Tell me, Madame Destine, oh great and wonderful reader of fortunes, what does your foresight tell you about this chaos? I mean, all this has just come from nowhere, as if we have stepped into a theatre performance half-way through an act. Something must be at its root, but what is it?"

"Ah, Cornelius . . . what a question, and therein lies the mystery," Destine said with a thin smile, crows' feet sparkling at the corners of her eyes. "The answers are well concealed, and my feelings tell me that these murders are more than just random street crimes."

"This killer is unconventional, would you agree?" said Quaint. "So to apply conventional reasoning to him is pointless. We went to an awful lot of bother to get information last night, and I know it means something, but I just don't know where it takes us."

"The truth shall be revealed in time," said Destine. "To get the right answers you have to ask the right questions, and of the right people. I have no facts to offer you, Cornelius, merely suppositions and propositions. As to why this man attacked Twinkle when his argument was with Prometheus . . . we may never know. Perhaps Twinkle was his target, and somehow Prometheus got involved. When he saw Prometheus lying in the gutter, perhaps he wanted to remove the only witness, and turned on Twinkle, or . . ."

"Or what?"

"Or perhaps he knew *exactly* what he was doing," said Destine. "Perhaps it was not his intention to kill Prometheus — merely to achieve that which in fact has transpired — to incapacitate him, and implicate him whilst he freely murdered and mutilated Twinkle. A decoy for the police to focus upon."

Quaint rubbed the back of his head in frustration. "What would make someone *do* such horrors to a complete stranger?"

Madame Destine sipped silently at her tea. "You are of course working on the assumption that this person *was* a stranger. We have no confirmation that this is so."

A chilling thought danced across Quaint's mind, and he clamped his eyes shut, trying to deny his imagination the chance to entertain it. Could this killer be someone from his circus? Quaint knew his people, and surely not a single one of them would harm — *could* harm — someone like Twinkle in such a maniacal fashion. It was abhorrent. Could a monster be hiding within his family undetected?

"As I said, my dear . . . *emotion* is a powerful master," continued Destine. "There are two emotions that men most commonly kill for. One is jealousy, the other, revenge. Both of these emotions inhabit the negative end of the wide spectrum of human emotion, and can blind a man to what is right and what is wrong. He can be tempted by them . . . tainted by them, blinded by their power." She leaned back in her chair, and stared deeply into Quaint's dark eyes. "I *warned* you about starting down this road, Cornelius, and yet again you choose to ignore me. I pray that more deaths do not come, and yet I know within my heart that they most certainly will."

80

Quaint pinched hard on the bridge of his nose. It was by now very early in the morning, and his body was on the verge of collapse. His wracked emotions were making short work of his strength. "Well, so far there's been a murder a night for the past three nights. I just hope there's another murder tonight," he said.

"Cornelius, what a thing to say!" Destine scolded.

"Think on it, Madame. If there's another killing whilst Prometheus is locked up, that exonerates him, does it not?"

"And if there is *not* another murder — tonight or any other night? What then do you think the local police shall do?" Destine asked, folding the corners of her lace veil between her fingers. "They will simply say that they have caught the perpetrator, which is why the deaths ceased. I suspect that they are ill-equipped to handle the complexities of a case such as this, Cornelius. I know I advocated restraint to you this afternoon, but I fear that if we place Prometheus's fate in their hands he may be hanging from his neck by the end of the week."

"Is that my governess or my fortune-teller speaking?" Quaint asked.

Destine smiled. "Perhaps a little bit of both. Did you not say that you knew the police commissioner? Can we not enlist his aid?"

Quaint swept a hand through his obstinate hair. "Oliver? Well . . . it's been a long time, Destine. I don't know how much pull I'll have with him these days."

"It is an avenue worth exploring, is it not? Our *only* avenue, in fact."

"I . . . I suppose it cannot hurt," Quaint said. "Dray's father, Sir George, used to own a shipping company working out of Singapore; cargo and trading ships mostly. I never really meshed with the old man's philosophies, but Oliver was all set to take over the reins, the last I heard. I guess something made him change his mind, eh?"

"Maybe your saintly influence rubbed off on him?" Destine jibed.

Quaint laughed. "I hardly think that likely. We first met whilst I was travelling through Peru . . . must have been all of twenty years ago now. I saved his life once, too, as I recall. But then, back in those days I was always saving somebody or other's life."

"Perhaps that is why you have never been concerned with saving your own, hmm?"

Quaint continued: "The word is that his father and Robert Peel were old friends from their schooldays at Harrow, and Sir George helped pave the way for Oliver's success in the police force."

"This case could get very nasty very quickly, Cornelius," said Destine. "Let us hope this Commissioner friend of yours has a strong stomach."

CHAPTER
THIRTEEN

The Letter

Commissioner Oliver Dray vomited all over the tiled floor of mortuary in the station's basement. He collapsed onto his knees, his body twitching in convulsions as a thick trail of sputum trailed from his mouth to the floor. Clutching the side of the mortuary table, he wrenched himself up onto his feet, watching through bleary eyes as Sergeant Berry replaced the sheet over Twinkle's body.

"Jesus, Horace . . . you could have warned me!" Dray said, trying to hide his embarrassment. He wiped spit from his lower lip with his sleeve. "She looks like a damn mackerel . . . sliced open to the gullet. And that . . . *thing* cut into her," he said, gesticulating with a shaky finger at the corpse. "What's the hell's that supposed to be?"

"It's a crucifix, sir."

"I can see it's a damn crucifix, man, but what on God's green earth is it doing carved into that woman's chest?" Dray yelled. "What is this, witchcraft or something? It's obscene!"

Berry shrugged. "Neither Lily Clapcott nor May Deeley looked as bad as this, especially with such . . .

83

religious significance. There was so much blood it was difficult to ascertain cause of death."

"Cause of death?" blurted Dray. "Are you insane, Horace? The woman's got a bloody big gaping hole in her guts — *that's* the cause of death!"

"You might think so at first glance, but the victim was actually killed by a single knife wound to the heart. The *crucifix* was cut into her body postmortem."

Dray palmed his eyes. "After? Are you sure?"

"Yes, sir," confirmed Berry. "You can tell when you look at the state of her arteries. The heart stopped pumping the blood, you see —"

"If I wanted a bloody pathology lecture, Horace, I'd go see Dr Finch!" Dray snapped. "And what about this devil you've got locked up? This . . . *abomination* of a man . . . what's he had to say for himself?"

Sergeant Berry looked back blankly. "Haven't you heard, sir? The man's a mute! It's pointless to try and communicate with him — he just sits there and stares at the wall with those big gaping eyes of his, like he's a hunk of beef, or something."

"Oh, and you think Whitehall will be satisfied with *that*, Horace? '*He can't actually speak, but take my word for it, Minister, he's as guilty as sin!*'" mimicked Dray. "They'll want a bloody confession, man, nothing less."

"Commissioner, we've as much chance of getting a confession out of him as we have of a full day's work from Jennings."

"Well, Horace . . . you'd better start getting creative, hadn't you. It's not the first time we've had to *assist* a prisoner with his confession, and it won't be the last!" Dray rubbed at his wrinkled forehead. "You mark my words . . . the bloke's probably escaped from some mental asylum somewhere, and then run off the join the bloody circus. Send a couple of men to Bethlem Hospital out Lambeth way; see what they can tell us about any escapees, especially ones with fixations for crosses. That should keep the brass off my back."

"There's more, Commissioner. You really need to have a read of this." Berry searched his pockets, and passed Dray a letter. "It's what I was hinting at earlier."

"What's this, Horace, your resignation?" Dray said with a smirk, removing a pair of thin wire spectacles from his breast pocket, perching them on the end of his nose. He cleared his throat, squinting at the spidery scrawls upon the letter, and read aloud:

Miller,

So, you have come to London at last, I see. That's right . . . I'm watching you.

You can't make a move in this city without me knowing about it. Travelling with a circus was a stupid idea . . . you may as well have taken out an advertisement for your whereabouts in the London Gazette.

You wronged me in the past, but that will not go unpunished for much longer. I have cultivated, nurtured and fed this desire for revenge for so very long. Once, you cut out my heart, and now I will cut out yours. I will destroy everyone you love . . . I will unleash a terror unlike any seen before, and the corpses of your loved ones will litter the streets.

This is inevitable, Miller. I will not give you the luxury of death; you will suffer a torment as I have done these past years. You will live with the pain that you have given me — and I will be stood right there enjoying every moment.

Dray looked up from the note. "What's all this is rubbish about, Horace? It sounds like the ramblings of a madman. Where did you get this letter from?"

"It was next to the last victim's body, sir. I thought it'd fallen from *her* pocket at first, but then, after I checked the prisoner's charge sheet with Marsh, I discovered something interesting."

"I thought the dead girl was called Argyle or something. Who's this 'Miller' character then, the one it's addressed to?" Dray mumbled, waving the letter at Sergeant Berry.

"That's my point, sir, *that's* why it's so interesting," said Berry, a grim look whitening his face. "We managed to get some details out of the giant not long ago, just the basics, name, age and that. Just stuff we got him to write down." Berry inhaled sharply. "It seems he's originally from Ireland . . . and his name is Aiden . . . Aiden J. Miller. The man the letter is addressed to! This whole case worries me, sir . . . it has since I first found him by the body. I knew there was something fishy about him, and this note adds a whole new way of thinking to this. It's too convenient, too simple."

Dray waved him away. "Simple is right, Berry. Simple mathematics. One dead girl, plus one unconscious murderer, equals we've got our man, case closed!"

"No, sir, I don't agree," appealed Berry. "Now we've got this note, everything's changed. The giant may well have been unconscious when we found him at the scene — but I don't think we can just *assume* that he's the killer. If he's managed to kill twice before and get away with it, why would he be stupid enough to stick around and get caught? And how come he was unconscious when we found him?"

Dray didn't budge. "It resolves nothing and complicates everything, is what that note does, Berry! We've got three dead women on our hands, and the only man who knows what happened to at least one of them is in our custody. Now what do you want me to do? Let him go? All because of some damned note? For all we know, the bloody giant wrote it himself."

"You'd be happy to imprison an innocent man, would you? Without proof? Surely you don't want *that* on your conscience?"

"One more thing won't kill me," muttered Dray. "There's already a lot of talk floating around town about these killings, Horace. Sooner or later, it's going to reach the Yard's ears and when it does, it'll be *your* head on the block if you're wrong about him."

"But if I'm *right*, there's a killer loose out there on our streets, and we've got an innocent man locked up!" Berry gritted his teeth to contain his anger. His superior was possibly the most stubborn man he had ever met, but this trait of his had never gotten to the point where it clouded his perception of justice before. Dray was being swayed by his anger, and his concern about being made a scapegoat, and it seemed to be up to Berry to be the voice of reason. "Commissioner . . . Oliver . . . we need to be a hundred per cent sure that the man in our custody is the killer. This won't just dry up and go away, you know, these things never do. I've got a really a nasty feeling in my water about this case. I just know that things are going to get a damn sight worse!"

Dray poured the remnants of his whisky down his neck. "Something will come up, Berry . . . something that ties all these loose ends up. We just need to be patient. An answer will present itself to us in time."

CHAPTER
FOURTEEN

The Meeting of Minds

By a quarter to ten the next morning it had become a bright, if slightly chilly day, and as Cornelius Quaint threw open the doors of Crawditch police station, the idle sunlight illuminated him with an aura of misplaced serenity. The man was anything but serene. Accompanied by Madame Destine, he was of a mind to see the captive Prometheus again — and he would not take no for an answer. Quaint walked determinedly towards the enquiries desk, and his hardened expression softened slightly as he recognised the familiar face of Constable Tucker at the podium.

"Constable!" he said cheerily. "Don't you ever go home, man?"

Tucker cracked a brief smile. "You've been speaking to my wife. Well, I can't fault your timekeeping, sir, the Commissioner is already here. He's in his office right now with Sergeant Berry, and he's been told to expect you." Tucker pointed to a large set of mahogany doors behind him. "Straight ahead, through them there doors. The Commissioner's office will be right in front of you."

Quaint and Destine nodded politely, and bustled through a small, knee-high wooden gate into the police station, past a variety of uniformed men busily writing reports and filing paperwork, flitting around like bees during springtime. Quaint raised his knuckles to knock on the Commissioner's door, when suddenly Destine's hand darted from nowhere and gripped his wrist.

"Wait, Cornelius," she said softly. "This friend of yours . . . can we trust him?"

"Need I remind you this was *your* idea? It's a little late for cold feet," Quaint said. "Stop worrying and come on. He's a police commissioner, for goodness sake. If anyone can ensure Prometheus gets a fair hearing — it's him."

"It's just that . . ." Destine paused, "after my vision yesterday, I am feeling a trifle nervous all of a sudden. It is probably nothing."

"Nervous? The vision from my past, you mean? Surely, you can't mean Oliver. A police commissioner? Come on, Madame, if we can't trust a policeman — whom *can* we trust? Oliver and I were friends a long time ago. Admittedly, we haven't set eyes on each other since, but he's certainly got no quarrel with *me*."

"Oh really?" questioned Destine. "What about that business you mentioned with his father? Did he not once threaten to kill you?"

"Ah . . . well, yes, but that was over twenty years ago. I'm sure that's all water under the bridge by now," Quaint said, knocking twice on the Commissioner's door. Not waiting for an answer from inside the room, he turned the knob, and strode inside.

★ ★ ★

As he entered the Commissioner's office, Quaint scanned the two men's faces in the room. One was unknown to him, and one looked familiar, but decidedly older than the one he recalled from his memory.

"Oliver!" Quaint said, grasping the somewhat bemused Commissioner's hand firmly. "How marvellous it is to see you again, old chap."

"And who the bloody hell might you be?" barked Dray. "Who let you in here? Hang on a mo . . . wait . . . is that . . . *Quaint?* Cornelius Quaint, is that you? What on earth are *you* doing here?"

"Just a bit of business, Oliver. What's it been? Eighteen? Nineteen years? I swear you haven't aged a single day, you old Scottish dog."

"I wish I could say the same for you, Cornelius! What a bedraggled mess you are," Dray said, flicking at Quaint's greying curls. "Look at that mop of hair!"

"And what of your own hair, hmm?" replied Quaint. "I trust you have your best men out searching for what's left of it?"

"Aye, and if they come across your fashion sense, I'll let you know. Look at yourself. Never have such fine clothes been so sorely wasted on a body," Dray said, looking Quaint up and down. "A cloak and velvet smoking jacket at this time of day? You look like you're off to the bloody opera!"

"A gentleman can never take too much pride in his appearance, Oliver, no matter what the time of day,"

Quaint parried. "But then, I suppose you wouldn't know anything about that."

"Cornelius, if I may?" interrupted Madame Destine. "Perhaps you two could postpone your verbal swordplay for another time, or do I need to remind you that we are here on most urgent business?"

"Ah!" Quaint chewed at his lip and nodded. "Quite right as ever, Madame. My apologies to you. I forget myself . . . and my manners."

"I suppose introductions are in order, eh?" Dray said, nudging Berry's shoulder. "This fellow here, Horace, is none other than Cornelius Quaint, an old . . . *friend* of mine from a misspent youth. Cornelius, this is Sergeant Horace Berry, the best beat copper on the force, bar none."

"Sergeant Berry, I'm pleased to make your acquaintance." Quaint turned on his heel and glanced at Destine. "And this is Madame Destine, my personal advisor. Madame, this fellow is Oliver Dray, commissioner of police, no less." Quaint cleared his face of all expression and focused his eyes upon Commissioner Dray. "And now that's out of the way, gentlemen, if you don't mind, I would like a word. Oliver, you currently have one of my employees locked up in your cells, charged with murder. It is imperative that I speak with him urgently."

"*Your* employee? You're the giant's *boss*? The one we found with that dead girl?" scoffed Commissioner Dray, slapping his forehead with his palms as if it were the most amusing thing he had ever heard. "Oh, *this* is ripe! Cornelius Quaint? Owning a circus, of all things?

Ha! Bloody typical, that is — I knew you could never go respectable, it's not in your nature."

"Yes, well, it's obviously in *yours*," Quaint said, poking at Dray's crooked tie. "I won the circus in a game of chance with two Prussian fellows. Fair and square, I might add, and it's a marvellous experience, trekking from one place to the next, entertaining folk. You really get to see the spark of the human spirit in full illumination. There is nothing like it on earth." Quaint's expression suddenly darkened, and the light faded from his eyes. "Of course . . . when something like this nasty business transpires . . . well, it does tend to stick in my craw somewhat. I do not like my circus getting involved in local matters, Oliver."

Dray snorted indignantly. "Local matters? You make it sound so clear cut," he said. "Murder is never clear cut, and thanks to your bloody circus lot, this one appears muddier than most. Actually, Horace and I were just discussing it. We've got three murders on our hands here in Crawditch, and murders that began just as *your* circus crew arrived. So what are you going to do about it, Cornelius?" asked Dray.

"Shouldn't I be asking *you* that question, Oliver?" enquired Quaint. "You do have a vicious murderer at large in this district, after all . . . I am not at all sure I wish to risk any more of my people. Perhaps we should postpone our show in Hyde Park."

"That would certainly deflect the blame from your circus, eh?"

"It sounds to me, Oliver, as if you have already closed this investigation, when in my eyes it is still very much open. My people aren't in the habit of going around slaughtering innocent people, and might I remind you that one of our *own* has also been killed. With my strongman wrongly incarcerated at the moment, my circus is feeling double the pain right now."

"Only you — a man who deals with the strange and fanciful on a daily basis — could be tied up in all this nonsense." Dray rubbed fiercely at his thinning scalp. "A great ox of a mute, a slain dwarf with a bizarre cross carved into her chest, and now a note from someone who says he's going to exact his revenge upon the giant!"

"Did you say a note?" Quaint's black eyes widened. "What note?"

CHAPTER
FIFTEEN

The Strange and
the Fanciful

Quaint looked from the note to Dray's face. "I assume that you've read this letter, Oliver. It is quite clearly a threat, and yet you *still* believe that Prometheus is guilty? The damn letter is *addressed* to him, for God's sake!"

"I've only got your word that this Miller fellow — '*Prometheus*' as you call him — is innocent and, believe it or not, your word won't stand up in court. Look at it from my perspective," Dray said. "Maybe your man had a dark side that you knew nothing about. Maybe he and this Argyle woman had some kind of argument and he did away with her, I don't know."

"What, and perhaps *she* wrote the letter? Look, Oliver . . . as I've said, Prometheus is no killer. Now, I don't have a clue as to what's going on in this little town of yours, but one of my best people is stuck right in the middle of it. This letter only perplexes me further."

"This is a triple murder investigation, Cornelius, not someone caught scrumping apples! We do take this stuff seriously, you know. So far I've managed to keep a lid on it and keep Scotland Yard out of the equation, but I can only hold them off so long. Otherwise we'd have Yard inspectors crawling all over my patch day and night! Do you know how that would make me look?"

"You'd rather wait for the *real* killer to strike again, whilst you tell everyone in Crawditch that you've got the man apprehended, and they're all safe? Come on, Oliver — surely it will make you look *far* worse when that's proved false! You've got a man locked up for a crime with *no* witnesses and *no* evidence beyond circumstantial. Is that just so it looks like you're in control when the Yard starts poking its nose in?" barked Quaint. "You're a chip off the old block, all right."

"Cornelius," growled Dray. "Mind your tongue now. That's territory you really don't want to tread."

"I remember." Quaint clapped his hands together loudly. "Look . . . all I'm trying to do is give my opinion about someone who's mixed up in all this, and need not be! You boys don't know him from Adam — but I have known him for years, and would vouch for his innocence until my dying day. He's not guilty — and if you just give me some time alone with him, I may just be able to prove it!"

"Cornelius . . . you know I can't do that," said Dray. "I just don't think —"

"And that's the point here, isn't it? You don't think! You never did have the capacity to think beyond the pack mentality, did you?" Quaint stared at Dray, their eyes meeting across the red haze of rage that filled the

96

room. Although neither man spoke, there seemed to be plenty communicated in the silence.

Dray took a deep lungful of breath, and threw himself down into his chair.

"I don't have the time for this right now, Cornelius," he said.

"Then *make* time, Oliver — this is important!" snapped Quaint, trying to get over his point and still keep the tinge of anger from his words. He was not doing a spectacular job so far. "I am not your enemy here, Oliver, and nor do I wish to be. Even as we speak, the real foe stalks Crawditch's streets, and I want the bastard hunted down and caught so I can put things back to normal, and concentrate on what my circus is in London for!"

"This isn't just about you and your bloody circus, man," Dray said. "When your lot pack up and move on, this will still be my district, and I want this mess straightened out just as much as you do, believe me. So . . . you want to speak to this Prometheus fellow of yours, right? Berry tells me he's deaf and dumb. What possible help can *he* be to this investigation?"

"He's *not* deaf and dumb, Oliver, he's a mute! He can *hear* perfectly well, and he can still write down what he knows, or what he's seen," Quaint said determinedly, ensuring that he kept his previous visit with Prometheus secret. He had no wish to get Constable Marsh into any hot water. "My crew have already gleaned quite a bit of information about what occurred on the night that Twinkle was murdered, but I need Prometheus to fill in the gaps."

Dray stroked at his temples. "Well, why don't you start by telling me what you *do* know? Stuff you can prove, I mean . . . not just your opinion."

Quaint nodded resolutely: "Very well. Last night my colleagues and I visited The Black Sheep public house not far from this very station. If you check with the landlord he will confirm that on the night of the murder, my circus strongman was drinking with his lover — the female dwarf who now lies in your mortuary."

"A concise recap for the latecomers," Dray grunted. "What else?"

"The landlord told me that on the night of Twinkle's murder, an Irish gentleman by the name of 'Hawkspear' paid him to give my circus strongman a bottle of whisky. The whisky contained a drug that would have probably killed a smaller man. As it goes, it merely rendered him unconscious." Quaint paused, watching Dray's expression closely. "Surely that is enough information to prove that Prometheus wouldn't have been in a fit state to do *anything* — especially murder the woman he loved. Arthur Peach's admission will surely absolve my employee, and I urge you to trigger a manhunt for this Hawkspear fellow, at least."

"Arthur Peach . . . yes, I know of the man. A sly one up to his neck in smuggled tobacco and cheap whores," said Dray with a nod. "All right . . . if what you say can be substantiated, and Peach will talk to us . . . maybe I'm prepared to delve a little bit into this — but on my terms, Cornelius. I won't have you influencing this investigation. You stay well away from now on. Just let

98

us do our jobs. I'll have someone go to the Sheep and look into what you say. But if Peach denies everything, what are you going to do then, eh?"

"He won't deny it, Oliver," said Quaint assuredly. "I believe I made a convincing argument for him to peddle his honesty to you."

"We'll see, won't we?" Dray said, shuffling distractedly with some files on his desk. "But until then, your mate stays locked up in our cells and no one sees him unless I'm satisfied."

"Well, you might not get very *satisfied* without *me*. Look, just let me speak to Prometheus for five minutes, Oliver, please . . . I can *help*."

"You can get *involved*, you mean," Dray snapped. "It's just like the old days, eh? I've not set eyes on you for twenty years, and you haven't changed a bit. You're still poking your nose into matters that don't concern you. I've told you — I don't want you anywhere near this investigation, and that's my final word. Now, Sergeant Berry will escort you out."

"Commissioner Dray, if you please," Madame Destine interrupted. "Surely you are more concerned with justice than arguing with a man you have not seen for twenty years," she said. Each word was energised with a devilish whiplash and Dray suddenly fell silent. "Now, admittedly . . . Cornelius may be as stubborn as a mule, but he speaks the truth. He *can* help you solve this case. More importantly, he can help our friend Prometheus. By allowing us audience with him, we may just learn something that can shed more light on this unfortunate affair. Would that not be a more preferable outcome than what you currently have?"

Dray was sizzling in his seat, his face beetroot red. Horace Berry looked over at the man, almost expecting to see steam rising from his collar, but somehow Destine's words seemed to penetrate his hard exterior, and the blustering Scot's temper waned.

"Commissioner," said Sergeant Berry, raising his hand. "Perhaps we should let Mr Quaint and Miss Destine see their friend, just in case a friendly face will make the man share a bit more information," he said cautiously, like a man disturbing a grizzly bear's hibernation with a sharp stick. "Lord knows our constables aren't having much joy. It can't do any harm, can it?"

Dray folded his arms tight against his chest. "I knew if I ever set eyes on you again things would go potty, Cornelius. I don't know how much information you can expect to glean from a man who can't utter a word, but I have to admit . . . I haven't the foggiest where else to begin. I think it's high time your employee told us the whole story, don't you?"

"Yes, Commissioner," agreed Quaint. "I rather think it is."

A few minutes later, Commissioner Dray grabbed the cell block keys, and strode down the long corridor that led from his office to the cells. Quaint and Madame Destine walked behind him in silent thought, and Sergeant Berry brought up the rear.

"You can have ten minutes with your mate and no more, Cornelius, and you can thank Horace here for that," Dray said quietly into Quaint's ear. "My job's going to be well and truly shot if this goes any further than this district, and if your monster has jeopardised my career — he'll hang for it, I swear."

"Always an open mind, eh, Oliver?" Quaint said, as he clamped his hand firmly on Dray's shoulder, making the Scotsman's heart miss a beat. "You're going to have to start entertaining the fact that maybe you're wrong on this one — and you're going to have to start thinking like that pretty damn soon. Your ignorance is your greatest weakness."

"And your stubbornness is yours," parried Dray.

Quaint grinned. "Well, you know what I'm like."

"I'd forgotten," said Dray, rolling his eyes.

"I admit, perhaps sometimes my mouth gallops ahead of my brain."

"I'll say! Every time you speak it's like a ten-gun salute. You've only got two settings, Cornelius — explosive and bombastic! You don't know subtlety. It's not in your blood is it?"

"Maybe so," said Quaint, as he drew a breath through clenched teeth. "But then, neither is giving up on a friend of mine when he's in trouble."

Dray unlocked the cell door, and it swung open with a grinding screech of metal against stone. The quartet stared into cell, their eyes adjusting to the darkness slowly and, one by one, they looked to each other for an explanation. An open-mouthed Sergeant Berry looked to Dray, who scowled at Quaint, who in turn then shot a perplexed squint towards Destine. A veil of silent confusion suddenly fell over them.

The cell was completely empty.

Prometheus's discarded woollen cap, lying on the floor next to the iron-grated window and piles of rubble, was the only sign that he had ever been there at all.

CHAPTER
SIXTEEN

The Strongman's Escape

The small, barred grate that had served as the only inlet for natural air and light in the cell had been forcibly ripped from its concrete moorings from the inside. The circus strongman known as Prometheus had escaped.

"Remind me again of your employee's innocence, Cornelius," seethed Oliver Dray.

"There has to be some mistake," gasped Quaint. "He wouldn't just —"

"Oh, but he has. He won't get far though, I promise you that," snapped Dray, as he turned on his heel, and barged past Destine and Quaint, dragging Berry with him in his wake.

Quaint squatted down onto his haunches and inspected the metal bars, discarded on the ground along with chunks of crumbled masonry from the wall. He looked to Destine for reassurance that what his eyes were recording was actually taking place, and he had not just set foot in a warped fantasy land. "So tell me, fortune-teller — did you see *this* coming?" he asked.

Destine stood at his rear, her veiled face hiding her expression of surprise, but her silence told Quaint all he needed to know.

"I see," grumbled Quaint. "What on earth is Prometheus doing? What does he think *this* will accomplish? Why would he be so *stupid*? If Dray didn't *already* have a noose measured up for him, he will have by now. How the hell do we repair this damage?" he said, peering at the window's grate. "Hang on . . . what's all this then?" He licked his finger, and gingerly touched the tip of one of the iron bars. He yelped, and withdrew his hand quickly. "Well, well," he said under his breath.

"What's all what, Cornelius?" Destine asked.

Quaint ignored her, and stood up sharply. "I knew there was more to this than met the eye!" he proclaimed, and approached Destine. She froze as he placed his arm on her shoulder, and plucked something from the tight bun at the back of her head. "Ah, perfect, Madame. Thank you!" he snapped excitedly, and squatted back down onto his knees, inspecting the grate.

"Cornelius . . . I know you take great delight in perplexing me," Destine said, teasing her bottom lip with her teeth. "But what exactly are you doing with my hairpin?"

Quaint ignored her again, and began poking tentatively with the metal pin at the window's grate in silence.

Destine tapped her foot on the floor. "The Commissioner will have mobilised his lynch mob by now, Cornelius," she said impatiently. "Whatever you are doing, it is costing us valuable time!"

"I don't think so, Madame, I think that — aha!" exclaimed Quaint, skipping easily to his feet for a man of his age and stature. With a broad grin, he held the metal hairpin towards Destine's face. "This mystery seems to have developed a new level of perplexity, Madame. Take a look!" A thin, barely visible wisp of smoke trailed from the tip of the hairpin, stolen quickly by the wind that blew freely into the cell through the hole in the wall. "Well, what do you see?" he beamed, like an eager child, proudly presenting a painting to his mother.

Destine lifted her veil and stared uncomprehendingly. "My eyes are not what they used to be. What exactly am I supposed to be looking at, may I ask?"

"Madame, do you not see? Those bars were not simply wrenched from the wall by Prometheus's strength alone. They have been eaten away! Look . . . eroded . . . by some sort of acid! It is burning the metal pin as we speak."

"Acid?" asked Destine, beseeching Quaint's impassioned eyes. "But how would Prometheus get hold of acid in a police station?"

"Anyone's guess. Perhaps there is a lot more to this than we had imagined." Quaint turned, and strode towards the open cell door. "Come, Madame, let us see what havoc Oliver's causing upstairs."

"Perhaps we should keep this mystery to ourselves for the time being, Cornelius . . . I am no longer sure whom we can trust."

★ ★ ★

With a crash, Quaint and Destine exploded through the thick set of double doors into the main station office and stared at the pandemonium before them. Commissioner Dray was holding court in the centre of the station as his men rushed about to and fro around him, obeying his every command.

"Hurry it up, men! We don't have all day. God knows when he decided to run for it. Didn't anyone *hear* anything? There's half a damn wall missing!" Proving that rage can be a most powerful fuel, Dray yelled with the vigour of a man half his age. "Sound the alarm, I want that man found!"

As Quaint approached Dray and Sergeant Berry, he looked around the madhouse that was the station. Policemen were rushing everywhere in panic, their eyes to the floor, desperately trying to comply with Dray's barrage of orders. Raised voices thronged the air, police whistles screamed and Commissioner Dray had Constable Tucker by his jacket lapels up against a wall.

"When was the prisoner last checked, Tucker?" Dray yelled.

"Sir? The giant, you mean?" said a flustered Tucker. "Well . . . he was given some breakfast I think, not too long ago."

"How long, lad?" Dray demanded.

"About an hour maybe," said the petrified Constable Tucker. "Could be a bit longer, I . . . I'm not sure. Why, what's wrong?"

"What's wrong, Tucker, is that he's bloody absconded! Ripped the bleeding bars out of the damn wall, he did. Have you got cotton in your ears, son? Did you not *hear* anything?" Dray demanded.

"Why, Oliver . . . did you?" asked Quaint, stepping up behind Dray.

The Scotsman shot a furious look over his shoulder. "You stay out of this, Cornelius, this is police business. Your friend just signed his own death warrant." He switched his stare back to his constable. "Tucker, get all the men we have available out on those streets right now. I want an immediate street by street search for the prisoner. Use whatever force necessary to restrain him and haul his arse back here, sharpish!"

"Seven feet tall, with a bushy beard and muscles like an ox. Shouldn't be too hard to find, Oliver, even for *your* men," Quaint said sarcastically, even though the situation clearly dictated against it. "Let me help. If Prometheus is anywhere nearby, or if he's returned to our transport, we'll find him. He *is* one of ours, after all."

"Oh, don't think I've forgotten *that*. Just you make damn sure you bring him back here, Cornelius," Dray muttered, flattening back the lapels on Constable Tucker's uniform. "Don't go getting any funny ideas either! Your lot are going nowhere unless I say so, got it?"

"Understood. But you needn't waste your men's time, Oliver. My train's not going *anywhere* until this mess is straightened out," Quaint said, feeling Madame Destine's fingers tighten around his arm like ivy around a drainpipe. She leaned towards his ear and tugged him firmly to one side.

107

"Cornelius, we may have further need of this man, if your temper hasn't burnt all our bridges," she reminded him. "So play nice. Exacerbating a grievance with the Commissioner will do us little good in exonerating Prometheus."

The pair exchanged glances as between a school mistress scolding her favourite pupil. Quaint lowered his eyes, and turned sheepishly towards the Commissioner.

"Look, Oliver . . . I am sure we'll get a speedy resolution to this unfortunate business," he said, holding out his hand towards Dray. "It is a shame we could not meet under less . . . *pressing* circumstances."

"Cornelius . . . we both know what I owe you," said Dray, grasping Quaint's open hand. "A long time ago, a world away from London — you saved my life. But this is just too big to sweep under the carpet. I've got no choice but to react with extreme measures. I have to do what's right by the letter of the law — whether your friend is in the firing line or not! Now, off you go. And if you really want to help your friend . . . stay out of my way."

CHAPTER
SEVENTEEN

The Twist of the Blade

"Right then, fellas, anyone got any questions?" Mr Reynolds asked a roomful of distasteful-looking ruffians, all of them dressed in brown or grey ragged, grime-stained clothes, practically the uniform of the common Victorian street criminal.

"Yeah, I got one," said a broad-shouldered Cockney. "This Quint bloke —"

"Quaint," corrected Reynolds. "Cornelius Quaint. What of him?"

"Quaint, right," continued the broad-shouldered man. "You said he's some sort of magician, so what's your beef wiv' 'im, then? What'd he do, saw yer wife in half, or summat?"

Reynolds grinned. "What a rum bunch you lot are. You mean you actually need to know what the bloke's *done* before you do him over? What's the world coming to when you can't even find a reliably dishonest bloke to do a little roughing up? You're getting paid, aren't you?" He clamped his hands over his eyes, and slid them down his face in frustration, distorting his voice. "You're not knights of the bloody realm, fellas, you're bad seeds. Rotten apples!

Shouldn't matter what he's done. Maybe he's killed my entire family, maybe he's done nothing — it don't matter! All you need to know is *where* he is and how *heavy* you need to get on him."

"We got it, boss," said another man, dressed in a scabby tan waistcoat with a fine mesh of grey stubble protruding from his jaw line. "No problem. How heavy do you want us to get on him?"

"Dead heavy . . . I want you to make sure that he —" Reynolds suddenly stopped mid-sentence as a doorbell clanged out around the house.

His eyes darted to the array of unscrupulous felons he had lined up in the house — the very same house that he had acquired since the unfortunate demise of its owner — and he pondered, his options falling through his fingers as if he were trying to grasp water. He wasn't expecting any callers, and he skipped over to the drawing room window, peering through the net curtains. Waiting outside, shifting his weight impatiently from one foot to the next, was Constable Jennings.

"Everyone stay in here, and don't make a damn sound! It's only the Peelers," said Reynolds to the shock of his audience. The men immediately shuffled around, looking like dumbstruck lemmings, anxiously searching for the nearest exit. "This one's my contact. Just keep it shut, the lot of you, and we ain't got a problem, right?"

Mr Reynolds opened the house's front door cautiously, his face softening as he saw Constable Jennings. "Ah!

Well, if it isn't my favourite constable! To what do I owe the pleasure?" he asked. "All is well, I trust?"

"Good day to you, Mr Reynolds, sir," Jennings said, nodding politely. "No problem, it's just . . . well, I can't stop long, in case someone sees me, like, but I just thought you should know . . . that giant fella from the circus who we had locked up on account of them murders? Well, you'll never guess what . . . he's only gone and busted hisself out, hasn't he? The boss is spittin' feathers!"

"I'll just bet he is." Reynolds's expression didn't falter. "And where is Cornelius Quaint at this moment? Pulling his hair out, I shouldn't wonder."

"Last I heard, him and some old French lady were heading back to Grosvenor Park station. I think that's where his circus steam train is held."

Reynolds's expression quickly changed. "Did you say a French lady?"

"Yes, sir. Quaint brought her along to the station. Apparently, she's the circus's fortune-teller or summink. Didn't get a good look at her meself . . . her face was covered with a veil."

Reynolds's face became a stone-cold glacier as he advanced towards the young constable. "Say that again!" he demanded.

Jennings stuttered, stepping backwards at Reynolds's intensity. "What? Oh, I . . . I just said . . . she was an old French lady, sir! She — she had a veil over her face! I couldn't make out much about her."

"Well, I never would have entertained the thought of it." Reynolds stopped dead in his tracks, and spun

111

around. He leaned his back against the hallway wall, and pinched his temples. "After all this time . . . she's still with him, is she? Why did I not see that coming?" He chewed his bottom lip between his teeth, and then his eyes suddenly snapped to attention, as if he'd just been startled from a trance. "And what of Quaint's plans now, boy?"

"I dunno, Mr Reynolds . . . all's I been told is that the giant's escaped . . . pulled the bloody bars out of the wall, he did. Thought you'd want to know *that*," said the constable. "As for Quaint, I ain't got a clue what he's doing, but he'd better pray he finds that mate of his before the Commissioner does."

"And are your colleagues close to catching this fleeing giant?"

"Not *so* far. You'd think a bloke 'is size would stick out like a sore thumb, but he's just vanished into thin air. Our lot are busy doing a sweep of the docks and checkin' all the boats and trawlers, but you know what that place is like at this time of day. Most of the fish trade of London is bringing in their catch to Blythesgate Market. The wharf's a bloody madhouse. Our lot 'ave been told by the boss not to come off shift tonight 'til we find that giant — never seen 'im so worked up," said Jennings, rolling his eyes. "Anyway, I'd best be off. The boss'll be wondering where I've got to. He only told me to report to you an' come straight on back," the policeman grinned. "He's got a lot on 'is plate right now!"

"Oh, I'll just bet he has," Reynolds said, running his tongue over his front teeth, barely containing his glee.

"Do pass on my regards to your boss . . . tell Commissioner Dray that he's sticking to his side of our bargain perfectly."

CHAPTER
EIGHTEEN

The Crumbling Wall

Madame Destine and Cornelius Quaint had not been returned from Crawditch long. Whilst Quaint busied himself with working up a plan to search for Prometheus, Destine was unusually gifted with some much appreciated free time. She sat alone on a wooden bench opposite the circus train in Grosvenor Park station, embroidering a shawl, replaying recent events in her head. She still found it inconceivable that Prometheus had escaped. His actions had made things far worse, and now the finger of blame would lie irrevocably at his feet. As much faith as she had in him, he was certainly not making things any easier — for himself, or for those who sought to clear his name. Clouds of smoke and steam squealed and hissed around her noisily from the train engine, as a man in filthy grey overalls fiddled around with a wrench underneath it. If the noise and dry stench offended Madame's senses, she did not show it.

"Hey, Madame," called Barracks the engineer. "Don't s'pose your premonitions've given you any hint as to when I'm going to finish Bessie's repairs, have they?"

Destine smiled over at the man. "Do you want the good news or the bad news, Raymond?"

"Ah," nodded Barracks. "Like that, is it? Righto! Whilst Miss Ruby is getting the rehearsals ready I'm a pair of hands down workin' on the ol' girl. I'd best not waste any more time chattin' to you then, eh?" the engineer grinned, returning to his chores underneath the engine. "Here, an' it looks like someone else wants an audience with you now anyway."

Madame Destine looked up quizzically, and spotted Butter scuttling along the platform towards her. The Inuit had a most uncharacteristically distant look upon his wizened face.

"Good day to you, Madame," he said, above the din of the squealing train. He approached the bench, and planted himself next to Destine upon it. "Do you mind if I may speak with you please? There is something concerning to me, and I . . . I wish for your advice upon its regard."

"Of course you may. Your English is improving nicely, Monsieur. Ruby is teaching you very well," Destine said, resting her embroidery on the bench next to her. She placed her hand on the little Inuit's shoulder. "How may I be of assistance?"

"Well, Madame . . . I suppose . . . I just want to be more of use to the boss."

"More use? Oh, Butter, where has this come from?" Destine turned to face him, sandwiching his hands within her own. "You are being silly! You are a wonderful organiser, a fantastic deputy manager, and most of the crew could not find their socks without you."

115

"That is kind of you to speak, Madame. I suppose . . . I just hope boss trusts me, that he knows he can rely upon me."

"Butter, *mon ami esquimau*, you have Cornelius's *implicit* trust, believe me! He already relies upon you far more than you could possibly know, *comprenez-moi*? Of late you are far more useful to him than I."

"I do not believe that is true, Madame," nodded Butter firmly. "The boss would be lost without your guidance."

"Once perhaps I would have agreed with you . . . but these days I am afraid my premonitions are not as reliable as they used to be. They seem to delight in perplexing me, rather than inform. I am almost afraid of opening up, afraid of what I may see. They do not provide much to offer Cornelius." Destine played with the hem on her veil, tightening her grip to ensure her features were obscured. "I do not always share all my visions with Cornelius, Butter . . . with anyone, come to think of it. Sometimes it is better to keep what I learn to myself . . . otherwise, will I not ever be the bearer of bad news, *mon ami*?"

As well as adding to the mystery of the fortune-teller, Destine's veil provided her with a welcome retreat from the telltale signs that could be seen within her eyes. She used the veil as a wall, behind which she could hide her true self. This was an escape much needed in her role as a fortune-teller, a retreat away from all she could see and sense. The veil gave her the power to detach her thoughts and fears from her words. She could quite happily lie in the face of someone, knowing that her eyes would not give away the truth. Not a lie as might be perceived a lie, but a mistruth, sometimes called a white lie, as if that somehow made it more palatable. A lie was a lie, Destine knew that, but just as there are sometimes valid reasons to tell a lie, there are often valid reasons to hide the truth. As she spoke to Butter of her concerns about her own reliability, Madame Destine found her thoughts and words merging as one. She was unable to lie to him, and in an instant the wall had crumbled, and she was suddenly unnerved by her nakedness.

Butter cocked his head to one side, and thrust his hands into the pockets of his anorak. "I am glad we could speak, Madame, I shall try not to let these bothers take residence in my heart," he said.

Destine lowered her head. "Good for you, Butter. Everyone has doubts it seems — everyone except Cornelius." She smiled warmly as her mind's eye entertained an image of the man. "He has a natural affinity with over-confidence, Butter, and that sometimes serves to inject us all with questions of our own importance. You will feel better in time, *mon ami*. You will find your place."

Butter nodded. "That is my hope, Madame. And you also?"

"*Oui*, that is my hope," confirmed Destine, as she gathered up her embroidery and clutched it close to her chest. "Now . . . I have other matters to attend to. Butter, if you will excuse me, I must return to my quarters. You are wrong to question *your* worth, *mon ami* . . . I only hope that my own fears prove just as unfounded."

CHAPTER
NINETEEN

The Rehearsal

Ruby Marstrand walked down the steps of the train's main engine onto the station platform, and swept her hair into a loose ponytail. Her fellow circus troupe were assembled into a long line, and their expressions reflected a myriad of emotions from excitement to boredom to anxiety.

"Inspection in five minutes, people," bellowed Ruby at the top of her voice through cupped hands. She was a gifted mechanic as well as a knife-smith, and was wearing a pair of tatty dungarees and a large, greasy smear of oil down her left cheek. Miraculously, she still managed to retain her natural beauty.

Tapping his feet idly, the lanky Indian animal trainer named Kipo toyed with a metal chain attached to the collar of his very large, very muscular tiger. Next to him — consciously standing as far from the beast as he could without breaking the formation of the line — was Jeremiah the clown, and next to him was his co-performer — a beaming, bearded dwarf clown by the name of Peregrine. Dressed in a crumpled, striped suit, and without his clownish makeup, Jeremiah looked positively dishevelled — the irony of his chosen profession obviously lost on him. His jowls hung low, his eyes carried a heavy grey undercarriage, and he was every inch the opposite of the persona that had graced The Black Sheep tavern the previous night — much the same as Ruby Marstrand was.

The young knife-smith pointed towards the large, circular clock that hung from the station's rafters, and yelled at the top of her voice. "Yin, Yang — hurry it up, will you? Mr Q wants to see what we've got, and we don't have all day," she called to the two Chinese acrobats, perched like pigeons atop the roof of the train above her. "You know what the boss always says —"

"You can never have enough rehearsal time!" chorused the twins in unison.

"And I am seldom wrong, gentlemen," said Cornelius Quaint as he strode onto the platform next to the line. He had changed his attire, and now wore a long-tailed, dark-grey woollen coat over a loose black suit, topped off with a half-height top-hat. He looked as if he were meeting a lady-friend for afternoon tea, rather than someone about to embark on a desperate search of the surrounding area for Prometheus.

Ruby looked to the floor in embarrassment. "Oh, Mr Q, you're early! I'm just trying to line everyone up like you asked. I'm just about getting there . . . slowly."

Quaint saluted her. "My thanks, Ruby, you've done an admirable job," the tall man said with an air of fatherly pride. "I'd hoped we'd get more rehearsal time in Hyde Park, but with all that's going on at the moment . . . I don't think we can afford the effort of skipping to and fro across London. Now . . . let's take a

119

look at our troops, shall we?" Quaint gave Ruby a wink, and began to stroll slowly along the line of performers. Not that he ever let on to the crew, but he rather enjoyed watching his performers — his family — stand tall and stand proud awaiting his word, knowing that he held their faith and respect completely.

Quaint stopped in the centre of the line, and held his hands up to his audience. "Now, folks, if we had more breathing space before Friday's show, we'd be doing a full dress rehearsal today, but as you know, there are a few distractions, so we'll go with what we have. You all know your roles far better than I, and you've all performed them so many times you could practically do the entire show in your sleep." Quaint gestured with his eyes towards Jeremiah's dwarf assistant. "And some of you frequently do from what I hear. Am I right, Peregrine?"

"Ah, just a bad case of the wind last night, guv. I think it was that mackerel Harry bought," Peregrine the dwarf said sheepishly.

Quaint afforded the man his blushes. "No need to apologise, Perry! Natural gas is a very healthy bodily product."

"It ain't that healthy when you're on the bottom bunk underneath it, boss," muttered Jeremiah. "I'm going to need a clothes peg if I want to get any sleep tonight!"

The line erupted into restrained sniggers, and Quaint clapped his hands to quell the rabble. "All right, folks. Part of why you lot are assembled is to make sure you're all still limber. And that goes double for you two chaps," said Quaint, looking at Yin and Yang atop the train carriage. "I'd prefer it if I didn't have to shout into the rafters; get on down here."

"Righto, Mr Quaint, on my way down!" Yin vaulted from the rear of the train, somersaulting in mid-air to land as deftly as a cat by Quaint's side on the platform.

"Impressive," Quaint said, half-approvingly. "And your brother, please."

"Look out below!" yelled Yin's twin. He and his brother were indeed two peas in a pod, either side of the same coin, but whereas Yin was calm, restrained and thoughtful, Yang had a daredevil streak that flowed through his veins. Whatever Yin did, Yang wanted to do it better, faster, higher. Leaping from the train like a dart into the air, Yang somersaulted, catching one of the station's iron roof supports, and swung himself around in a complete circle. He leapt from one girder to the next, more like an ape than a man, his fingers and feet seemingly finding stability everywhere they touched. He leapt into the air and performed a triple twist, to land with a cocky grin just as deftly as his brother on the platform next to Quaint.

"Save the theatrics, Yang. I can't have you breaking an ankle before show-time," Quaint said testily, glancing over his shoulder. And then more quietly, he said: "Nice final twist on the end beam though, son. You've been practising."

The hustle and bustle at Grosvenor Park station, commonplace at virtually any time of the day or night, slowed to a standstill as every other traveller or worker stopped and stared at the sight of the circus folk.

Quaint barely acknowledged the gathering audience, and seated himself down on a wooden bench opposite the train. He crossed one leg over the other, and linked his fingers together, his hands sitting loosely in his lap. He looked over towards Ruby, and gave a gentle nod.

"Begin," Cornelius Quaint said.

The word was like a starting pistol going off before a race, and in a second the group of circus folk pulled on the masks of performers, and the rehearsal commenced. Yin and Yang kicked off with a series of back-flips and cartwheels at blinding speeds along the platform. Like sporadic whirlwinds, the Chinese twins never stood in one place long before they were leaping somewhere else. They bounded, flipped, jumped and sprang from one end of the platform to the other with a succession of dizzying acrobatic displays. Quaint spun around in his seat to investigate, as a chorus of undulating cheers and applause echoed around the station. A group of onlookers had gathered around the station, and they were enjoying the free show.

"We have an audience now, people," said Quaint. "So make it count."

Even in the distilled afternoon light of the train station, with its many distractions of noise and smoke, the acrobatic display was still breathtaking — even to Quaint, who had witnessed it countless times. How the two little bumblebees managed to ricochet across the platform with such grace and speed was something of a mystery to the circus owner. As was how they managed never to collide mid-air, but perhaps this was due in part to the Chinese men being twins, as perhaps there was an unspoken, almost telepathic communication linking the two of them. That was the spiritual explanation, of course, and one that never sat too comfortably in Quaint's solid and physical world. Nevertheless, whether the display was the result of something beyond the boundaries of normality, or just the fact that the two had been performing together since the age of six, it was still spectacularly stunning to watch — and Quaint hoped that the forthcoming audience in Hyde Park would be sufficiently entertained.

As he watched the rest of his crew perform, he felt a nagging twinge within his heart. As good as his team were, there were still gaps in the programme, very obvious gaps that only served to reinforce what they were missing.

Twinkle's presence was irreplaceable. More than just a juggler, comedienne and all-round entertainer, she was the pulsing heartbeat within his circus, and now that heart had been torn out. Praying they were a strong enough community to weather the storm, Quaint knew that a lot of it relied on them finding Prometheus. Whilst not as effervescent as Twinkle, he was virtually an embodiment of the circus's recent troubles. If he could be found, and normality restored, perhaps they might all have a very real chance of repairing their wounds. But by the same token another question appeared in Cornelius Quaint's head. If Prometheus should die, would the hearts and minds of all in the circus be far behind?

CHAPTER
TWENTY

The Scent

A little over an hour later the rehearsals had concluded, and Grosvenor Park station gradually returned to a semblance of normality. Each of the performers was enjoying a well earned break from their duties and practising, and they congregated in small packs. They were sitting cross-legged on the station platform, some on the wooden benches, or atop stacks of luggage and canvas-covered circus equipment. Almost like a nomadic desert encampment, the small, scattered cliques were alive with pleasant chatter, idle gossip and good-natured warmth, not unlike most families. Seated within a throng of performers including Yin, Yang, Jeremiah, Peregrine and Kipo, young Ruby Marstrand sipped at a small metal cup of steaming tea, and tapped her feet against the ground incessantly. She was frustrated, and in no mood to hide her feelings.

"Something up, Rubes?" asked Jeremiah. "Or are you trying to burrow all the way to Australia?"

"Hmm?" she asked distractedly. "Oh, sorry, Jerry, it's just . . . all this waiting around. I want to be out there getting my hands dirty searching for Prometheus. How much longer do we have to wait? He could be anywhere by now, and it'll take us ages to get back to Crawditch."

"You're not going back to Crawditch," said a voice behind her.

Ruby swallowed hard as she saw Cornelius Quaint approaching her. His cold, steely expression immediately deflected any accusatory comments. His was the type of stare to silence even the greatest critic.

"We're not? How come?" Ruby asked.

"Because, Ruby, you and the rest of the crew are needed in Hyde Park getting things ready," Quaint answered. "We've still got a circus to put together, remember?"

"We are not going out to search for Prometheus?" asked Yang.

"Correct, Yang," confirmed Quaint. "We are not. Butter and I will suffice for now. As well as in the park setting up the tents, I need someone stationed here should Prometheus return to the train. It's a safe bet that we'll be having the company of some policemen soon."

"To stop us driving the train away, I'll bet," added Yin.

"Yes, well, if we wish to exonerate Prometheus, we must be careful not to add fuel to the fire. Commissioner Dray can be a conflagration all to himself," agreed Quaint. "Now, whilst Butter and I are absent, I am relying on the fact that everyone knows their roles and responsibilities. Madame Destine is on hand, should you require her assistance. We have promised London a circus this coming Friday, ladies and gentlemen — and I for one intend to deliver."

"But Mr Q, how are we supposed to do the show without Prometheus or Twinkle?" asked Ruby. "It just won't be the same."

"We will continue as normal, and hide the cracks as best we can — as Twinkle would have wanted. This circus was her life, and we must honour what she stood for. If I know Twinkle, she would want us to go out there and knock London's socks off! Prometheus will be found long before Friday's matinée show, of that I am sure."

"Will you still be requiring me, Mr Quaint?" asked Kipo.

"Oh, yes! You and Rajah are still very *much* required," said Quaint. "I have a most important job for you, as a matter of fact."

Yin patted Kipo on the back. "The boss is taking Rajah out on the town with him to search for Prometheus, isn't that right, Mr Quaint?"

Quaint stroked his jaw pensively, as Kipo looked on aghast. "As tempted as I am to see how Londoners would react to a tiger loose in their midst — Rajah's staying put, Kipo, so you may relax. He's a tiger, not a bloodhound, and he happens to be a very visible deterrent should the police decide to come and take a look inside my train." Quaint turned on his heels. "Now, where's Mr Barracks?"

"Down here, boss," called the train mechanic, crawling on his hands and knees down under the engine. "Up to me eyeballs in muck 'n' grime as usual."

"I should have guessed," Quaint chimed. "So, what's your prognosis on our faithful transport then?"

"Well, Bessie's been through a lot, boss. She needs a total overhaul, if I'm bein' honest," said the engineer, wiping a glistening trail of sweat from his forehead with his sleeve. "I'll need another day on the manifold, and the transmission's been shot since we left Edinburgh. She's held together by sheer stubbornness alone."

"I know the feeling," said Quaint. "Good work, man. Keep at it. I don't suppose you've seen Destine anywhere, have you?"

"The last I saw, she was on a bench at the far end of the platform," answered Barracks. "That lady could do with good night's sleep, if you ask me. She looks shattered."

Quaint cast his eyes through the smoke of the station platform. He saw Destine sitting detachedly alone in the distance. "You noticed that too, eh?" he asked.

"Hard not to," said Barracks. "When a lady glows as brightly as she does, it's obvious when she loses her shine, you know what I mean?"

"As a matter of fact, Barracks," said Quaint, "I do. You know how guarded she is . . . it is no easy feat getting her to admit it if she feels weary."

Barracks nodded. "You ain't wrong there, boss. She's like you; she'll just keep soldiering on until something breaks. She's no spring chicken any more, not that I'd have the balls to tell her that, of course," Barracks said with a throaty guffaw. "You know you're the only one who can get through to her."

"Hmm," agreed Quaint. "Perhaps it is time that I tried harder, eh?"

Quaint turned away from Barracks and made his way along the platform to where Destine was seated. She looked up in surprise as Quaint approached her.

"Hello, sunshine," he said. "How do you feel?"

Destine smiled. "How do I *feel*? Have you been talking to Ray Barracks again?"

"Always the fortune-teller, eh?"

"Barracks is a sweet man."

"He cares for you a great deal, Madame . . . but do I detect a little mutual fancy?"

"Nonsense, Cornelius! I am old enough to be his . . . well, let's just say I am more *senior* in years than he is. I am far too old for romance — let alone Ray Barracks!"

Quaint lifted Destine's hand and kissed it gently. "Love is blind to age, Madame."

"So what brings you here, Cupid?"

"Well . . . actually, I would appreciate your opinion on something, as it goes."

"My opinion seems to be in high demand today," Destine said. "I am honoured. What can I do for you?"

"Ah, would you care to take a walk with me?" asked Quaint. "Somewhere out of earshot, I mean."

He led Destine along the station platform, to a solitary wooden bench, away from the main congregation of circus folk. Quaint rummaged around inside his overcoat and produced a folded piece of paper.

"What do you make of this?" he said.

128

Destine knew instantly what it was, but still felt compelled to ask.

"Cornelius — is this the note we saw at the police station? The one found near Twinkle's body? Where on earth did you get it?"

Quaint smiled wanly. "No one has quicker fingers than I, Madame."

"But that's *stealing!* That's police evidence," shrieked Destine into her hands.

"Yes, I know that," said Quaint without batting an eyelid. "*Evidence* that I'm hoping you can make use of. From a sensitive's point of view. I'm curious as to your take on the sentiment, the emotion behind it all."

As well as clairvoyant, the Frenchwoman was highly sensitive to the emotions of others, and sometimes felt what they felt, saw what they saw. Usually this translated into faint, almost non-existent feelings, as identical twins such as Yin and Yang had experienced when one of them was in pain. There had been odd occasions when the flash of emotion was so strong that the Frenchwoman was almost rendered unconscious. It was a gift very different from the ability to read fortunes and was far more dangerous, far more uncertain, and Destine only attempted it when it was absolutely necessary.

She traced her fingers across the almost childlike writing of the letter. "I sense a high degree of hatred for Prometheus for one thing," she said. "A very personal hatred."

"That's plainly evident, Madame." Quaint nodded. "Anything else?"

Madame Destine closed her eyes, commanding her sensitive gift to work. "Very personal, very . . . angry, but that is also obvious," she said with certainty. "There is nothing more evident, nothing at all. It is cold."

"And yet the letter is the epitome of emotion, don't you think? Is that not your area of speciality? I had hoped you would be able to sense a lot more of the murderer's resonance from his words . . . allow me to paint a picture of him."

Madame Destine nodded thoughtfully. "Usually, perhaps I could. But this killer is different — the man we can presume is this Hawkspear — he certainly knows how to leave his scars, doesn't he? Physically and mentally, it seems."

Quaint's black eyes narrowed. "He could have been hunting Prometheus from the moment he set foot in Crawditch, and that's what worries me the most." Quaint motioned to the array of people gathered in scattered groups on the platform. "In that letter he said he was going to destroy everyone whom Prometheus loves, remember? Perhaps Twinkle was just the first target? When I look at those people over there . . . I can't help but think each and every one of them is also a potential victim — myself included."

"It would not be the first time you have had an enemy, *mon cher*."

"No, but I usually get to see the whites of their eyes before they try and kill me. This one's going to be hard to track down. He's elusive . . . faceless . . . like a mirage. I'll tell you this, Madame, wherever Prometheus is, I hope he's not in any danger . . . and that's why I need you to try and sense him again."

Quaint had no idea how Destine was able to do the things she could do, see the things she saw, feel the things she felt. As far as he was concerned, Destine had a gift, and that was that, and he was perfectly happy with his ignorance.

"As a matter of fact, Cornelius, I was hoping to find time to discuss something with you myself," Destine said softly. "My visions are behaving erratically. I am not sure how much we can rely on them. And I have been experiencing strange messages again . . . about a ghost from the past."

"Again? I do wish you would let that drop," laughed Quaint. "Look around you, Madame; these aren't the backstreets of Morocco, or the squalid shanties of India. We're in London — a city that I've hardly set foot in for years! I hardly think *anyone* would have a grudge against me here."

"I am starting to believe you," Destine said.

"Oh, yes?"

"Something has been bothering me . . . a nagging thought really, but it makes me think that perhaps I misinterpreted my previous messages. Taking into consideration how unreliable these visions have been, I am starting to think that this ghost has not risen from your past . . . but my own."

"Madame, that's ridiculous!" said Quaint. "Not only are you far less likely than I to have enemies, but here in England? Certainly not. If we were sitting outside a coffee house in La Rochelle, surrounded by a gaggle of women, angered at you for your beauty, then yes . . . I may be prepared to concede that thought. But it is simply not so, Madame."

"You seem very certain of my abilities, Cornelius," Destine said calmly. "Far more so than I, it seems. As you requested, I have been attempting to gain some connection with Prometheus's emotions since we returned from Crawditch. It has been difficult, with *some* success. Short bursts, nothing solid. I wanted to try and make a little more sense of them before I told you."

"And have you?"

"Barely," admitted Destine. "They are like a foreign language. The feelings are certainly confusing, unlike anything I have previously experienced. I feel so wrong-footed, no matter where I step. I just do not know what to believe."

Quaint nodded in understanding. "Well, that is understandable, Madame. None of us expected to be drawn into this web as we have been. We are all at the mercy of circumstance. I am surprised at Prometheus for one thing . . . why in God's name did he escape? What was he thinking? Or did someone provoke him — is that who melted the cell's bars? Another party?" Quaint rested his hand upon hers. "Who knows *what* happened — and that's why I'm so reliant on what you can receive from Prometheus. I know it is hard for you, Destine, I really do — but if only you could make contact with him . . . perhaps you could get some clue as to his state of mind."

"Cornelius, I told you that I have been trying to sense Prometheus constantly, but it is difficult," Destine said. "It is like looking at molten lava, and someone telling me to put my hand into it. They tell me that it will not burn, and yet I do not believe them. I am scared, my sweet . . . I feel as if my messages are willingly betraying me. I do not know if I can trust them."

"Madame . . . we have no other choice."

Destine's lips floundered silently. "I . . . I will try, Cornelius . . . but do not blame me if all I see is nonsense. I know you care for Prometheus a great deal."

"You don't need a crystal ball to tell you that."

"And you are not alone. We are all feeling as though we are at the mercy of something beyond our power to affect, and we have no choice but to give in."

"It is unlike you to be so pessimistic, Madame."

Destine fixed him with a stern glare. "Do not confuse pessimism for an advance warning, Cornelius. Now . . . I will try and connect to Prometheus." She took a deep breath, slowly exhaling through pursed lips. Destine's eyelids flickered like the beat of a hummingbird's wings, and she raised her fingertips to her temples. "He knows I am searching for him, Cornelius," she said. "He's opening up to me, allowing my mind to sense him this time. I sense a great turmoil within his mind, a feeling of isolation, but above all . . . hatred. He hates this Hawkspear most desperately. Give me a moment to make more sense of this, my sweet."

Quaint held his breath silently as he stared into Destine's eyes. It had been a long time since she had showed her true age to him. Her taut skin draped across her cheekbones like wet silk, and she looked pale and worn, but yet still held a timeless beauty like a porcelain sculpture. Ray Barracks was right. She needed a rest.

Destine was his spiritual centre of gravity, and for nearly fifty years he had never been without her. Since he was seven years old, she had been in his life — initially as his governess, and then later as an essential confidante and advisor. When Quaint inherited Dr Marvello's Circus she became his business partner, assisting him with the financial aspect of the circus, and she was his most valued and trusted friend. Now, looking as frail as she was, and in this climate of murder and subterfuge, Quaint just wanted to snatch her up and lock her away in a cage, to keep her safe from harm.

"Cornelius," the Frenchwoman whispered, snatching Quaint from his thoughts. "His fear is so raw; it is easy to pinpoint his position, or a rough approximation of it. He is very frightened . . . and very cold, but he is uninjured. He is being pursued . . . near the waterfront, and I smell . . . I smell *fish*?"

Quaint look baffled. "Madame, that tells me nothing. The wharf runs along the Thames for miles, and all of it stinks of fish — he could be anywhere."

"No . . . it is more than that. I am being shown the image of a large building situated on the wharf. A warehouse, perhaps? The smell of fish . . . and *ice*."

"Water, fish and ice?" repeated a thoroughly vexed Quaint.

"That is what I sense . . . I can almost taste the stench, it is so abundant."

"Wait on!" Quaint suddenly snapped his fingers. "Ice and fish . . . on the docks? Of course. It can only mean Blythesgate!" he said gleefully.

"Blythesgate? What is a 'Blythesgate'?" enquired Destine.

"It's a fish market," proclaimed Quaint. "A couple of miles along the docks from Crawditch — it makes perfect sense! He's got to be hiding in there. Madame, you're a genius." Quaint glanced at the station clock. "We shall have to make a move quickly; that place will be abuzz with fisher folk at this time of day." He strode back down the platform towards his assembled crew. "Butter?" he called, signalling the Inuit over to his side. "Hail us a hansom. We're off, my friend . . . to Blythesgate fish market."

"You're best getting a boat, Mr Q, if it's Blythesgate you're after," offered Barracks the engineer, overhearing Quaint's words. "Boat'll get you there ten times faster than any cab."

Butter looked up at Quaint. "We are to get boat, boss?"

"Yes, we are to get boat," Quaint snapped back enthusiastically.

The Inuit scratched at his dark mop. "Wherever we find ourselves boat, boss?"

"Oh, don't you worry about that, my little friend," said Quaint. "I know a chap not far from here who

135

works with a bloke whose sister married a fellow I used to play polo with who won't mind if we borrow one."

Butter's mouth fell open. "We are to steal one, aren't we?"

"Absolutely," replied Cornelius Quaint.

CHAPTER
TWENTY-ONE

The Trail

A few minutes later, Quaint and Butter exited the station, and headed towards the Thames embankment, where a number of small dockyards littered the river's edge. The late November wind was trailing a fine spray of cold, salty water in their direction, and Quaint shuddered, tucking his scarf inside his coat.

"My word, that's a chill wind. I'll bet this weather reminds you of home, doesn't it?" Quaint asked, turning up his collar.

Butter smiled. "Not much. There is too much rain here, boss. We have little rain in Greenland. It freeze to snow long before," he answered, his memory forcing him to reflect upon his homeland. "And of the chill, boss, I am long since capable of noticing such things."

Quaint stroked his chin. "Ah, yes. Your imperviousness to cold would be a very useful gift for me right about now, my friend. England is nothing if not damp. Damp enough to get right under your skin, as it always has been. Here we are. Look!" he said, pointing at a flaky painted sign above a rickety fence. "Barter's Boatyard. This will do very nicely."

Butter followed a few paces behind as Quaint strode into the boatyard. They weaved through the carcasses of several old and damaged boats propped up on stilts, and headed determinedly towards the wharf. A rundown shack, with a peeling turquoise-painted door hanging limply from rusty hinges, stood between the wharf and Quaint, and from inside the shack, the golden glow of a gas lamp shone weakly. It was mid-afternoon, but the clouds had congregated across the sky, shrouding much of the daylight. Quaint held his finger to his mouth, signalling quiet, as they crept underneath the shack's window, the gravel underfoot scratching at their soles as they went. Once they were past the outbuilding, Quaint relaxed and looked at a wide selection of rowing boats moored up alongside the wharf.

"Did I not say this would be easy, Butter?" he said.

The words had just fallen from his lips when an extremely large Alsatian dog bolted from behind the shack, a fire in his eyes, and a trail of saliva dripping from its jaws. Shards of gravel ricocheted around, smashing against the wall of the shack as the dog tried to get purchase on the ground, incensed to see two intruders in its yard. It didn't even bother barking, but just leapt with all its strength towards Quaint, the thick ruff of fur around its neck looking almost like a lion's mane. Quaint instinctively defended himself, and as the dog's vice-like jaws clamped themselves around his forearm, he let out an uncharacteristic yelp of pain.

"Christ, this bastard's strong!" Quaint yelled. He thought of his Indian friend Kipo's work in the circus with his tiger, Rajah, and remembered a flash of a conversation that they had shared once. Instead of trying to wrench his arm from the thrashing dog's mouth, Quaint relaxed, and forced his arm instead *towards* the gnashing jaws. He could see the ferocity in the animal's eyes as it tried to wrestle the tall man to the ground. With his other hand, Quaint delved deep into his pocket, desperately ferreting around for something he could use as a weapon, when suddenly — the animal stopped thrashing. It stopped snarling, and it stopped furiously trying to twist Quaint's arm from its socket. It just froze in mid-motion, its eyes rolled up into the back of its head, as if someone had flipped its OFF switch. Looking down at his bloodied and shredded sleeve, Quaint watched in transfixion as the dog released his forearm limply. As he stared down at the animal, something silver and glistening caught his eye, deep within the canine's open mouth. His eyes travelled up the length of the silver protrusion until they greeted the sight of Butter astride the now very dead dog. One hand gripped tight around the animal's neck, whilst the other grasped the handle of a long-bladed knife that was embedded into the dog's skull. The dog fell to the ground limply as Butter released his grip, sending a smattering of gravel into the air.

"My thanks, Butter," said Quaint exhaustedly, examining the state of his gouged arm through his ripped sleeve. Large patches of red blood seeped through the dark-grey material. "This coat is pure

139

Mongolian Kashmir. A second longer and that beast would have cost me an arm and a leg."

"Or perhaps just an arm," said Butter, his face a roadmap of craggy wrinkles as a smile breached his worn features.

"I shall have to have a word with Jeremiah about teaching you his sense of humour," Quaint said. He removed his scarf and tied it firmly around his wound. "Come on, let's move on. I've no wish to explain to that dog's owner the circumstances of its demise — especially as I'm about to thieve one of his rowing boats as recompense."

A minute later — passengers in a small pale-orange boat — Quaint and Butter pushed away from the wharf with the long oars, and the Inuit set about rowing them along the River Thames towards Blythesgate fish market. The afternoon fog was drawing in up the river, and visibility was getting steadily worse. Quaint produced a tinder-box from his coat pocket, striking a flint next to a small, oil-burning lantern. The wan flame flickered into life, albeit reluctantly, as Quaint hung the lantern on its pole at the fore of the boat. It gave them scant light, but hopefully enough for them to be seen through the fog should there be any other boats drifting nearby.

"Take it steady, Butter," Quaint said. "We don't want this pea-souper to be our undoing. Let's hope we can still see Blythesgate; we can barely be seen ourselves!"

But Quaint was mistaken.

They *had been* seen.

They were seen very clearly indeed by a set of piercing eyes that had been watching them with obsessed intensity from the entrance of Barter's Boatyard. The scruffy young lad wiped his mouth with a moth-eaten sleeve, and smiled.

"Off t'Blythesgate market are we, boss?" said the urchin of a boy, his thick matted black hair brushing against his eye line. "Mr Reynolds will pay 'andsomely fer that little titbit."

CHAPTER
TWENTY-TWO

The Snare

The winter sky was as dark as soot by late afternoon, with formless tufts of grey cloud obscuring the smattering of stars. Butter slowed the rowing boat to a crawl, as Quaint spied the docks through a pocket-sized pair of opera glasses. The fog had obviously put off other sailors and this stretch of the Thames was silent as a tomb, with visibility down to a minimum. Butter scanned around him, anxiously waiting for a sign that would indicate their destination.

"We should be coming up to Blythesgate pretty soon, Butter; I recognise the wharf's buildings. There's the Chinese textile emporium, and there's Arlow's mill," said Quaint. "There! Just ahead, that's it. That's Blythesgate!"

A short time later, Cornelius Quaint and Butter were standing in front of a vast warehouse. Its walls were a hotchpotch of colours and mismatched materials, from corrugated tin and iron, to large sheets of wood and salvaged planks. Trickles of rust seeped like gunshot wounds from the various bolts and nails holding the building together. Quaint stared up as far as the fog would permit him, and he raised the lantern to the door. A battered sign hung loosely from two hooks just above his eye level, creaking in the wind.

"Blythesgate fish market," Quaint said. "Shall we go inside and take a look?"

"But it is tight-up locked, Mr Quaint," said Butter, eyeing the massive chain wrapped around the warehouse door.

"Don't worry, old chap," said Quaint, with a devilish glint in his eyes. "We'll no doubt find a more suitable entrance around the rear of the premises."

As Quaint and Butter walked to the end of the warehouse, they pushed past a collection of large wooden delivery crates, not unlike tiny coffins. Each one of the crates was damp, stained white from the salty seawater, and reeking of fish from that day's catch. The trawlers would arrive early in the morning in Blythesgate, eager to sell their wares from the long, arduous day at sea and, to ensure their goods were kept fresh, they were packed in crates and covered in ice. The stench from the crates was fairly strong, and Quaint was pleased to move into the shadows of the alleyway that ran along the side of the market warehouse.

The buildings along the docks were positioned closely to each other to make the most of their highly sought-after dockland location. Huge, narrow tenements nestled next to storage warehouses, taverns to entice the seamen, as well as a variety of other more questionable pursuits. The entire stretch along the docks was virtually a different world from the rest of London, designed to cater to the needs of the passing traveller, or sailor, but as time had progressed, a more sinister element had taken up residence there, and more and more buildings had been built to accommodate the rash of interest in sea-faring commerce. Brothels were conveniently tucked away down every alleyway, and opium dens were even easier to find. Taverns were scattered about to pick up the flotsam and jetsam that wanted to empty neither their purses nor their minds on illicit sex or opiate distractions. The wharf was a disturbing, dark place once night fell, but Quaint moved confidently about with either ignorance or arrogance as his guide. The alleyway still presented potential for danger even at that time of day, and the wary traveller never dropped his guard. Not yet night — it was almost dark, and soon the local populace would be crawling from wherever they hid themselves during daylight hours.

Soon Butter and Quaint were in a much wider alleyway, bereft of light, save the slow-rising moon in the sky, barely visible through the crevices of the alleys. The fog was less evident now, the warmth between the buildings keeping it at bay, and Quaint was able to see the rear of the fish market more clearly. An array of large boxes were scattered about, containing the remnants of melted ice, and the same strong smell of fish as the crates at the front of the building. Quaint eyed the crates, his gaze drifting up the warehouse, to a small window above.

"These boxes have been intentionally placed here. They look as if they've been dragged from the front, according to these tracks in the dirt," said Quaint to Butter, as he bent down onto his haunches and placed his hand into a crate, pulling out a handful of crushed ice. "And not too long ago, by the looks of it."

"Are you sure, boss?" asked Butter. His eyes travelled up the marketplace wall, past the patchwork slates of iron and wood, to the open window. "It seem a lot of effort. Why he not just go to train, avoid police there?"

"I'm banking on Madame Destine's visions being correct, and that Prometheus was being pursued, so he went to ground," surmised Quaint, as he pulled at his bottom lip between thumb and forefinger. "Destine smelled fish, and this place is just about as good a place to start looking as anywhere. Come on, I'll hoist you up."

"Me, boss? Up there, boss?" asked Butter.

"Of course, man!" said Quaint indignantly. "Unless you think a little shrimp like you could lift a man my size?"

"Little shrimp? Boss, back home I slay a walrus of eight feet long, after tremendous battle lasted all of day and all of night. It was a spectacle!"

"My offence at the walrus reference notwithstanding, Butter, we don't have much choice, so let's just get going, shall we?" said Quaint, squatting down, and linking his hands together to form a stirrup. "*Allez-oop!*"

★ ★ ★

Around the front of the building, their shadows flitting like tomcats in the night, a collection of assorted ruffians arrived unannounced. Mr Reynolds's little urchin spy had earned himself a hot meal for informing the man of Quaint's intended destination, and with the Bishop's money paying for the hired muscle, the men had congregated outside Blythesgate fish market with the sole intention of causing Cornelius Quaint some grievous bodily harm . . .

CHAPTER
TWENTY-THREE

The Fish Net

Cornelius Quaint was totally oblivious to the gathering that had quietly and speedily accumulated outside the market's main doors. Each of the men was armed with an assortment of knives, chains, metal poles and wooden truncheons, and their faces entertained expressions of people who enjoyed inflicting harm on others. They were not a highly polished mob, these men, hired more for their ferocity than their adeptness with skilled weaponry. They were a means to a very sticky end for Quaint. Grunting like pigs hunting truffles, they held their cauliflower ears and scarred cheeks up against the corrugated metal doors, desperately trying to learn more about their mysterious target.

The man in question was busy climbing down from the open window, inside the market onto the slatted, wooden roof and through a skylight into a dank and dreary office. Many small tables were arranged throughout the room, littered with seafaring charts, bills of sale, maps, scraps of paper and discarded rubbish, and three large cabinets lined up against the far wall. This was the main hub of the marketplace, the manager's office. A small gas lamp had been left alight, giving Quaint and his associate Butter a faint sense of comfort.

"It's going to be murder getting the smell out of my clothes," said Quaint, giving the lapels of his long dark-grey coat a sniff. "I daresay Mae-Li at the Chinese laundry in Wapping will want extra for *this* stench!"

"Boss, look-see here," exclaimed Butter, who had exited the small office and walked out onto a metal staircase that ran along the side of the office, leading down to the far corner of the building.

From their vantage point, they had a bird's eye view of the whole place. The warehouse below was a vast, desolate area. Used primarily as a place for selling fish goods, it was basically just a skeleton of a building with weight-bearing metal struts placed at various intervals. Wooden beams formed the structure inside, looking just as randomly stitched together as the front of the market. Pools of water, a mixture of seawater and melted ice, covered most of the stone floor, but the warehouse was virtually empty, save for a huge, iron container positioned at the far end of the room, and a couple of metal storage sheds, nestled into the shadows of the corners. Great wooden pillar supports were holding a patchwork tin roof upon the building, and a vague semblance of stilted early evening dusk-light seeped between the cracks and gaps of the misplaced wall panels.

The market was frenetic with life the moment the sun came up, with hundreds of tradesmen vying for the best deal on the best catch of the day. Now, it was silent, damp and dark, and the perfect place to disappear. There was an endless amount of hiding places in the vast warehouse, and Prometheus could theoretically be in any one of them, if indeed he was there at all. An incessant hum made itself evident from the dark centre of the room.

"Boss, what is the noise I hear?" asked Butter.

"It's coming from that metal container down there. Seeing as we're in a fish market, it must be some kind of cold storage area; it's difficult to say from up here, but there do seem to be steam emissions spouting from the top."

"Hiding place?" offered Butter.

"Perhaps. Let me call out and see what happens." Quaint yelled through cupped hands, his booming voice echoing around the warehouse. "Prometheus, it's me! It's Cornelius! Are you in here?"

There was no sound, save a gentle drip falling from the roof onto the stone floor.

"Prometheus, if you're here, show yourself," Quaint tried again. "Damn it, Butter, I felt so sure he'd be here . . . Destine's premonition *said* so."

"Perhaps he goes elsewhere?" Butter asked Quaint, who was busy scouring the darkness seeking a sign that they were at least looking in the right place.

"I just want some kind of noise, a tap, a rap, something along those lines," he said.

Down within the dark, prevalent shadows of the warehouse, a metallic clang suddenly resounded. A clear beat of metal against stone.

Quaint and Butter exchanged surprised looks.

"Like *that*?" asked Butter.

"Uncannily so, my friend . . . just like *that*," answered Quaint.

They both raced as fast as they could to the rickety metal staircase that led from the small office on the second level down to the ground floor. The darkness closed around them instantly, and Quaint suddenly wished that he'd brought the lantern down with him. Now they were on ground level the warehouse seemed to open up in size tenfold, and it was impossible to isolate where the noise had originated from.

"Hello?" Quaint called. "Prometheus, are you here? Is that you?"

The metal clang sounded out again, this time fainter, located behind Quaint.

"Boss, you think we make better splitting up?" whispered Butter.

"Hmm. Maybe so. The darkness is blinding us. We need to distance ourselves from its grasp. Why don't you take a look down that way," offered Quaint. "Go and check that large metal ice box door, see if it's unlocked. It may just be the machinery making a noise, settling itself, for all we know. I'll investigate these sheds at the back here. That's where the noise just came from."

"No, boss, clang comes from this direction . . . ahead."

"You're mistaken, Butter. I think you'll find that it most definitely came from the area near those sheds over there."

A faint clink of metal came from the direction that Butter was pointing in.

150

"See, boss?" said Butter. "It *is* this way!"

But then another clang reverberated around the warehouse's ground floor, this time coming from the location of the metal sheds, directly behind Quaint.

"These sounds are all around us," said Quaint bemusedly, squinting into the dark as he walked slowly into the shadowed corner of the warehouse. "I don't know how that's possible, but I *do* know it can't be good news."

"Not for you, it ain't," said a grizzled voice from the shadows, as its owner brought a heavy wooden stake down onto Quaint's shoulder-blades. With a yell of pain, Quaint hit the ground like a ton of bricks. He rolled over onto his back, scowling into the shadows in the direction of his attacker.

"Who the devil just hit me?" he snarled, as Butter helped him to his feet.

"That'd be me, mate," said the gruff voice from the darkness, as a man with a grubby face stepped forth into the hazy light. "My first blow might not 've done the trick — but I guarantee you, my second one will," the man roared, as he slashed at the air with his wooden pole.

It came down in an arc, narrowly missing Quaint, striking the stone ground. Quaint quickly stepped towards the man, and stamped all his weight upon the tip of the wooden pole pulling it from the man's hand onto the ground. As the shadowed man tried in vain to wrest it from under Quaint's heel, the conjuror kicked up with his boot as hard as he could, and the metal cap on his heel made contact with the man's face. Quaint

151

watched with a certain sense of satisfaction as the bridge of the man's nose split in half, spraying a saturated curtain of bright red blood into the air. Quaint towered over the man, brandishing the wooden stave.

"Now listen to me, my good man, I'm sorry about all that, but *you* attacked *me* first . . . I was merely defending myself," he said, apologetically. "We don't wish for any trouble, we're only searching for a friend of ours — a big, tall gentleman with a beard — about so high." Quaint held his hand about a foot above his head. "I don't suppose you've seen him about anywhere have you?"

"Course I ain't!" spat the bloodied man.

"Worth a try, I suppose."

"I don't give a rat's arse *why* you're here, mate," said the bull of a man. "You ain't gonna be around for much longer — you're dead meat!"

"Be reasonable, there's a good fellow. If we've stumbled upon your sleeping place, we apologise," exclaimed Quaint, holding his hands up in appeal. "We'll just be on our way, and no harm done, eh?"

"You ain't goin' nowhere — I ain't finished with you yet," the bull yelled, as he pulled a small switchblade from his rear pocket. He cut the air, inches from Quaint's face. "By the time I'm done with you, Quaint, you'll be pickin' up your teeth with broken fingers!"

"I won't, if it's all the same to you," said Quaint.

"Boss," said Butter into Quaint's ear. "How does he know your name?"

Quaint froze. "That's a thoroughly good question."

"All *you* need to know, old man, is that my boss has paid me to make sure you don't walk out've this marketplace in one piece." The man brandished the knife menacingly. "And I'm going to make sure I earn every damn penny of it!"

"Good for you. Although, I feel it only fair to warn you; I used to box at county level, and was unbeaten for eight consecutive years! If it's a fight you're looking for, then congratulations — you just found one." Quaint clenched his jaw, and pulled off his overcoat, throwing it aside onto the sodden floor. He pushed his curly, grey-brown fringe away from his eyes, and raised his fists. "You'll last about three minutes by the looks of you."

"Yeah? Then you'll have plenty of time to take on the rest of that lot then," said the rough-voiced man, pointing at the far entrance as the main doors opened.

Quaint's eyes were naturally drawn to the sight at the end of the market. Early evening moonlight flooded in through the open doors, framing the silhouettes of a large group of grunting men approaching him at pace. They sneered, they jeered, and they cursed — each one with a fixed intention — to exact violence upon their target.

Quaint eyed the grizzled bunch. "Brace yourself, Butter."

Butter swallowed hard. "This is going to hurt, isn't it, boss?"

"Only if they hit you."

"What next we do then, boss? We run or we fight?"

"Considering the numbers, not to mention the obvious disposition of those chaps, if we had a choice, I would have to say that perhaps discretion was the order of the day."

"Then we run?"

"The problem is, Butter — we *don't* have a choice. This place seems to have only one entrance . . . and one exit, and we have to get through that lot to reach it."

"Fight it is then?"

"Afraid so, old chum." Quaint suddenly sprinted towards the oncoming rush of men, and launched himself upon the nearest one to him. His fists flailed wildly about. Within seconds, the pack of men was upon him, but Cornelius Quaint was not a man to go down without a fight. "Steel yourself, Butter!" yelled Quaint, like a battle cry, as he left his Inuit companion behind him.

Butter shot a nervous glance from Quaint to the looming storm of men, and then back to Quaint again. "Boss, what do these men want with us?"

"Who knows," replied Quaint, head-butting a man who'd just caught him a nasty blow on the jaw. "We'll ask questions once we're done."

"What shall I do, boss? I do not like to fight!"

"It's a simple theory, Butter — hit as many men as you can, as *hard* as you can — and don't stop until you're the only one left standing," shouted Quaint in reply as he jostled with a heavy-set foe. "If it makes it easier — imagine they're a pack of walruses!" He linked both his hands and smashed them down hard onto his foe's back, bringing his knee up at the same time. The man hit the floor.

Butter gritted his teeth, and threw himself into the raging pack.

"Good lad," said Quaint with a grin, but he couldn't keep his eyes on Butter long — he had more pressing matters of his own to consider.

As Quaint was the first to attack, his group of opponents was quite a bit larger than Butter's, and his furious fighting had to increase in ferocity also. No quarter could be spared, and he was damn sure none would be given. Drawing his fist back as far as he could, battling against grabbing hands from the rear, Quaint threw another punch at an assailant. The man tried to shrug it off, but the sheer force of will behind the showman's blow had sent him staggering off balance, wheezing like a prize-fighting boxer caught on the ropes. The man teetered, only his body's reflexes keeping him standing, and then he crashed unconscious onto the wet stone floor.

Given a little respite from the grappling pack, Quaint quickly joined Butter's side, just in time. "Keep your back to me!" he commanded. "Get in as close as you can like a rugger scrum. Don't let them land a solid shot. Got that?"

"I will try my best, boss," said Butter, surveying the swathes of clenched fists, raised weapons and gritted teeth before him. "But these odds do not favour us."

"What have I told you before, my friend?" said Quaint, snatching up his unconscious attacker's wooden stave from the ground. "Always play *against* the odds — it makes things *far* more satisfying."

"Only *if* you win," whispered Butter to himself.

Quaint threw himself into the mass of men, and was doing his best to disarm as many as possible with a few well-placed jabs with the stave. Considering the odds were indeed stacked against him, he was doing rather well. Using the stave as a brace, Quaint threaded the wooden post behind an assailant's arm, and wrenched it back as far as he could. The man screamed in agony as the bones in his forearm snapped. His metal staff fell to the ground with a heavy clang, and Quaint quickly snatched it up. Trading up on his weapons, he brought the metal pole into contact with as many heads as he could.

Quaint hated physical violence — but that wasn't to say he was no good at it. Many decades before in his wild, impetuous youth, he had befriended a bamboo-seller whilst travelling through the Yahn province of Northern China. The man had taught Quaint some basic attack and defence techniques — most of them involving a sturdy three-foot bamboo cane. The young Cornelius Quaint was a hungry learner, and this was advantageous considering the long metal pole that he now brandished between his hands. He jabbed frantically at the baying crowd, as sprays of blood smattered his hands and cuffs. Men were falling to the ground every second, clutching battered body parts, but still the combatants mindlessly continued their path, clambering over the bodies of the fallen to get at Quaint and his companion.

Smaller and far more nimble than his employer, Butter crawled on his hands and knees in the midst of the battle, amazingly untouched, letting the thrashing men around him consume each other. Every now and again he would leap to his feet and kick out when someone came near him. Even though Quaint's plan was working, the tide couldn't flow in his direction for ever. Butter was suddenly grabbed by his anorak's hood and dragged across the oily ground, as the pack of men split into two warring factions. This increased the overall area of the fighting space, and soon Butter was swallowed by the maelstrom of fists and feet.

Trying desperately to elbow his way over to his friend, Quaint clambered on men's shoulders as clamouring hands groped and scratched at him. A bald-headed man dressed in grease-stained overalls got lucky, and grabbed a handful of Quaint's grey-brown curls. The man yanked back with all his strength, and Quaint had no choice but to go with the flow, lest his hair be yanked from his scalp, and he kicked out with his heels against his aggressors as he was dragged onto the ground. As he felt an onset of feet kicking at him — striking his ribs, his legs, his chest — the metal pole was wrestled from Quaint's grasp, but he grabbed hold of one of his attackers, and managed to hoist himself back up onto his feet. Like a sledgehammer to the guts, Quaint landed a satisfying punch on a nearby attacker.

However, his sense of victory was short-lived as he noticed a flash of his Inuit companion's jet black hair, caught in a headlock by a huge grotesquery of a man. His immediate thought was to get to Butter as fast as he could — a thought suddenly marred by the appearance of a limp-haired youth barring his way.

"Come 'ere, you old bastard! You're dead!" he sneered, stabbing a dagger menacingly around him as he approached. "Let's be 'avin' you then!"

Quaint slapped the youth with the back of his hand, and brought his knee swiftly up into the lad's groin. The young man collapsed onto the ground clutching his privates.

"That'll teach you to disrespect your elders," quipped Quaint.

Suddenly, Quaint's blood ran cold as he heard an animalistic wail echo around the marketplace. With bizarre fascination, he watched as one by one, the men piled on top of Butter were thrown off as if grabbed by unseen hands, cast aside like toy soldiers. Men's screams littered the air. Pure, horrific, unfettered screams, and in the centre of the brawl, he saw Butter, his tusk-handled knife in his hand. An expression of malice was etched upon his wizened face, making him almost unrecognisable to Quaint. Again and again, the little man sliced around him with his blade like a warrior bred for battle. Blood spots decorated his cheeks and hands, and he was gaining the upper hand. But just as the tide seemed to turn in his direction, it was all over so quickly. Butter lost his grip on the mêlée as if he was suddenly fighting in quicksand. One of the men moved around behind him, and grabbed at his flailing arms, receiving a nasty gash to his arm for his efforts. With Butter promptly restrained, he was soon obscured by a mass of bodies. Unfortunately for him,

Quaint was so preoccupied with the sight that he quite forgot his own predicament.

He was suddenly grabbed around the neck by a large pair of mitten-like hands, and wrenched backwards off his feet. Quaint clawed at the thick arm around his neck as a heavy black shroud began to descend upon him. He was finding it hard to stay conscious. His attacker released him, and Quaint sank to his knees, all strength sapped from his body. He was surrounded instantly by at least four men, their blurred, elongated faces leering at him as if he were standing within his own circus's Hall of Mirrors.

"What . . . d-do you want from me?" he mumbled, wiping blood-spittle from his lips with his white cotton cuff. "You . . . c-can't interrogate me . . . if I'm dead."

"Who said we wanted to interrogate you?" asked one foe.

"You're goin' the same way as your mate over there," agreed another.

Two men brusquely pushed through the pack of men with an unconscious Butter in their arms. They cast the Inuit's apparently lifeless body onto the cold, wet ground.

"What have you . . . done to him?" asked Quaint, staring at the sight disbelievingly.

Whether his assailants answered him or not, Quaint didn't hear. Unconsciousness climbed up his body, coiling its icy clinch around him, and his battered frame hit the wet, cold concrete ground with a sickening thud.

159

CHAPTER
TWENTY-FOUR

The Chilling Tomb

With no idea how long he had been unconscious, Quaint was rudely awakened some time later by Butter slapping his cheeks, calling his name repeatedly. Immediately after the spark of life reignited Quaint's hazy mind, a multitude of questions jostled each other in an undulating swarm, all vying to be answered first. Where am I? Why is it so dark? Who were those men? Am I dead? No, I can't be . . . I'm in too much pain to be dead.

"Boss, please wake!" called Butter through the darkness.

"I'm here, Butter . . . I'm . . . awake," said Quaint hoarsely, his eyes slowly opening.

"I am so pleased you are alive!" said Butter elatedly.

"As am I, my friend."

Butter squeezed his hand tighter. "How are you?"

"I've been better."

"I am so sorry, boss; there were too many in number. They were victorious."

"Yes," said Quaint, rubbing at his ribs. "I noticed that part."

"I only woke myself a short while ago."

"Where the hell are we?"

"I . . . I am unsure, boss. It is so dark."

"And cold . . . it's blood-chillingly *cold!*" snapped Quaint, sitting up sharply. Immediately, he felt his body scream at him, and he clutched at his ribs. "Guess . . . I shouldn't have got up so quick . . . Head's swishing around like a fish in a bowl . . . and speaking of fish! From the stench of it, I'd presume we're still in the market . . . in that large metal container we saw earlier. From the sound of the machinery, my guess was spot on. It's an industrial ice box . . . to freeze the fish solid, ready for transportation," Quaint said weakly, rubbing at his bruised jaw, and trying to click his arm back into its socket. "And us too, if we don't find a way to get out of here pretty damn quick. If those bastards out there didn't finish me off, there's no way I'm going to let a bloody ice box do it!"

In the pitch darkness, Quaint struggled to his feet, with Butter helping to support his weight. He limped over to the wall and traced his hands across it tentatively, searching the cold, glassy wet walls for the door. His fingers brushed against a stack of wooden crates, and his nose told him they contained a consignment of fish.

"If this ice box is used to keep the fish frozen, we don't have long until it starts to chill us too. An hour at the most, I'd guess . . . but then again, who knows how much air is in here. We might have been out of it for hours; we might only get twenty minutes. After the pasting I just received . . . I'm not exactly at my peak." Quaint tousled his curls madly with both hands.

"Think, Cornelius! This is a machine. All machines work on the same principle — power in, function out. There must be an external cooling mechanism inlet somewhere, pumping in the vapours. If we can isolate *that* . . . maybe we can shut it down before we freeze to death. Then the hard part is getting out before we asphyxiate, because these industrial ice boxes are designed to be completely airtight — double-reinforced metal doors with rubber seals — which only serves to increase our peril."

"A machine, boss? To make ice?" questioned Butter. "How silly!"

"We British can't just step outside the front door and pick up a handful of snow to keep our food fresh, you know," explained Quaint, flapping his arms about him, trying to keep warm. "We have to improvise artificially . . . *mechanically*."

"Do you think we can make breakdown of this ice machine?"

"If we don't, my friend, we shall almost certainly freeze to death," said Quaint, trying to search in the pitch blackness for the gas inlet pipe. "Unless we get lucky and suffocate first, of course — but either way we're in big trouble."

"If only we had light," said Butter, scratching at his thick, black, matted fringe.

"Hang on, we do! My tinder-box is right here in my coat pocket," Quaint said, fumbling down his body. He slapped his forehead with his palm. "Blast! The coat that happens to be outside."

"I have no Plan B, boss."

"Join the club."

"Then . . . I am useless."

"Far from it, Butter, you're my sounding board — added to that, you prevent me talking to myself like a madman, and that's a *very* important job!" said Quaint, with a wince as he lifted his arm. The pain from where the dog had sunk its teeth into him earlier was now pulsating in sympathy with the rest of his battered body. "Come on, Cornelius, you're a bloody conjuror. You've gotten out of far worse scrapes than this. There must be something we can use to try and lever our way out."

Butter moved over to the heavy metal door and began slamming his weight against it, but it was pointless. The locking mechanism was designed to keep the door completely airtight, and true to its design, it didn't budge so much as an inch. His diminutive frame had all the effect of a rotten tomato against a brick wall. Quaint meanwhile, had gone decidedly quiet, unnoticed under the noise that the Inuit was making. He rubbed furiously at his arms and upper body, in an attempt to get his blood flowing, but it almost seemed an impossible task.

"Must . . . sit down for a little bit," said Quaint. Each word was a strain to speak, each breath a struggle to take as the coolant vapour burned his lungs. "Yes . . . that's it. I just need . . . five minutes' . . . rest." He curled his body into a tight foetal position on the ice box's freezing cold floor, desperate to keep warm, his teeth rattling in his gums.

Meanwhile, Butter continued his relentless assault upon the door's frame with his hammering fists — oblivious to the slumped figure of an unmoving and unspeaking Cornelius Quaint, drifting a hair's breadth from death's embrace.

CHAPTER
TWENTY-FIVE

The Buried Secret

Several miles away, the moon reflected the slumbering sun's glow like a golden teardrop suspended lazily in the starry sky. An off-kilter spire breached the diamond-speckled night, casting a long, crooked shadow across the muddy graveyard.

"So this is Crawditch abbey, eh?" said Mr Reynolds.

"What's left of it, yes," answered Bishop Courtney as he stood with his hands on his hips examining the church. "It's hardly a functioning place of worship any longer, Mr Reynolds, not since the larger building was built over in Lambeth."

Reynolds sucked on his cigar, and exhaled smoke rings into the sky. "I suppose the locals only use this place for weddings and funerals nowadays, Bishop, and there are precious few of both around here."

The Bishop clutched a small carpetbag under one arm, and a lantern in the other, and he called over his shoulder to his coach driver, sitting high at the front of the carriage like a pensive vulture. "Melchin, old chap, keep an eye out for Mr Hawkspear, will you? Tell him we have pressed on ahead." Melchin puffed on his pipe, and grunted a reply. "Come, Mr Reynolds, the crypt is this way," and he led Reynolds to an arched wooden door set into the side of the church wall. He shone his lantern down the haphazard stone steps into the darkness below. "There is something of interest down here that I wish to show you."

At the bottom of the steps the two men reached a wrought-iron gate. The Bishop pulled a small bronze key from a pouch affixed to his belt, and unlocked the gate with a jolting snap. Once through, the crypt opened up a little more, and Bishop Courtney used the lantern to light a wall-mounted torch. It sprang into life immediately, bathing the enclosed space in yellowish-brown light. Reynolds's eyes adjusted to the light, and he scoured every inch of the crypt like an automaton. It was difficult to see what could possibly be of interest to him in a chokingly dry cellar bereft of anything of value.

"I take it there's nothing left in this crypt worth stealing then?" Reynolds asked, with a sardonic grin. "Otherwise, maybe I would've been here before, eh?"

"Yes, well, that's the trick isn't it, Mr Reynolds, keeping the thieves out — or at the very least, dissuading them." Bishop Courtney swung his arm in an arc around the bare room. "Most common thieves presume this place was robbed of all its riches years ago. This is due largely to a rumour propagated by none other than the Anglican Church itself."

"They went to an awful lot of trouble for some poky old crypt, didn't they? That infers that there *is* something to find here."

"Astute as always, Mr Reynolds."

"Right . . . so what's here then? Treasure?" asked Reynolds.

"Of a sort," answered the Bishop, his eyes sparkling with something akin to gleeful pride. "But it isn't gold, silver or jewels, my lad . . . it is of far, far greater value than that. Allow me to explain; buried in that cemetery out there is —"

The Bishop suddenly broke off mid-sentence as he heard several scuffling footsteps approaching down the stone steps towards them. The lithe form of a man in his early thirties appeared at the foot of the steps, pushing a second man in front of him, and the torchlight flickered in the breeze as he entered the crypt.

"Ah, Mr Hawkspear," greeted the Bishop. "So glad you could join us . . . and you have brought company, I see."

Hawkspear was a bedraggled young man with pinched features and eyes like azure pools of water. Beneath tendrils of greasy black hair was a low brow and thick, bushy eyebrows that gave him a constant scowl. Hawkspear pushed the bound, gagged and bloodied landlord of The Black Sheep tavern in front of him, and the man stumbled awkwardly on the uneven ground. Hawkspear shoved Peach roughly to his knees in front of Bishop Courtney's portly frame.

"Aye, this is the landlord as you ordered, Bishop," said Hawkspear, with a thick, Irish drawl. "Arthur Peach, his name is."

A spidery grin crept across Courtney's fat face like a cracked window. "Splendid, Mr Hawkspear, simply

167

splendid!" The Bishop grasped Peach's head, twisting it from side to side. His eyes noticed the assortment of fresh bruises littering the landlord's face. "I see you had a little entertainment *en route*."

Hawkspear bowed. "Sorry, Bishop . . . he tried t'run. I had to *convince* him that it wasn't a good idea. In me own special way, like."

The Bishop smiled — a full, blossoming smile this time — with eyes alight like burning coals in a fireplace. "Well, you had better hope he isn't too badly damaged. I want him alive . . . before I kill him."

Peach moaned a mournful, sorrowful cry, and sniffed back petrified tears. His eyes bored into the Bishop, appealing for help.

He would find none.

The Bishop clenched his fist. "Stand him up! Now, you're probably wondering why I dragged your carcass all the way across town, Mr Peach." The Bishop didn't wait for an answer. "I have been given some disturbing news, you see. It seems that you had a visit from a man named Cornelius Quaint the other night, and like the gutless worm you are, you talked!"

Peach whimpered again through his gagged mouth.

"You informed him about Mr Hawkspear here," continued the Bishop. "A fact that led the man straight to the police. Luckily we have a man on the inside, and were able to contain that, but it has upset some carefully laid plans. Because of your slippage, I had to act quickly to secure the circus strongman's release from his cell before he could be questioned fully. My thanks to Mr Hawkspear for a wonderful job with the acid . . . I hear it had the perfect effect."

"Indeed it did, Bishop. Aiden Miller is still at large, last I heard," said Hawkspear. "Crawditch police are chasin' their tails as always."

"Splendid . . . the fool's doing a wonderful job of spreading the fear for me," said the Bishop. "I almost wish I could employ him myself!" Courtney suddenly bent closer to the landlord's face. "I happen to be in the middle of a very *sensitive* project here, Mr Peach, and cannot allow anyone to bring trouble to my door. Because of your loose tongue the police now know that an Irishman named Hawkspear paid you to supply one of Quaint's employees with a bottle of drugged whisky. You can understand why I'm a little *upset*, surely. And you —" he said, jabbing the Irishman in the chest. "Next time use a bloody alias! Did they teach you *nothing* in prison?"

Hawkspear lowered his clear blue eyes and stared down at his feet like an insolent child. "M'sorry, Bishop — I just wanted t'get it done, and get out. I didn't know that Quaint bloke would be sniffin' around."

Reynolds stepped forwards from the shadows. "Maybe we should remove the landlord's gag, Bishop? You did say you wanted him alive, right?" he offered, eyeing the landlord's pale, sweaty face. "Look at him. He's on the verge of collapse. It's not like he's going anywhere, is it?"

"If you must," said the Bishop. "You're right, Mr Reynolds, I don't want the bastard passing out yet."

169

Reynolds grabbed the ragged gag, and pulled it free from Peach's mouth. The landlord wheezed oxygen into his lungs, tasting the fresh air as if for the first time.

The Bishop cleared his throat. "Mr Reynolds, would you be kind enough to hand me my bag?"

Reynolds looked around, and spied the cloth carpetbag on the crypt's stone floor. The Bishop snatched it from him and rummaged inside, pulling from it a pair of long-handled brass tongs and some squat, stub-bladed shears.

"I found these items in Westminster Abbey's archive room, Mr Peach. They're from an age when peasants like you would be slaughtered for not obeying the word of the Lord. The Good Old Days, as I like to refer to them. Too bad it all had to end, eh?" said an almost nostalgic Bishop Courtney. "This instrument was designed to purge the Devil from a man's soul." He held the shears up for Peach to see them more clearly, taking pleasure from opening and closing the sharp, metal blades. "Shall we put them to the test?" He held the tongs closer to Peach's face, and a brief flicker of torchlight danced off the brassy metal of the tools.

The landlord's eyes glassed over with tears as he realised his fate. His hands bound behind his back, he begged for the Bishop's mercy.

"You don't have much breath left, Mr Peach. I wouldn't waste it if I were you."

"But . . . please! I had no choice!" protested Peach.

"You have a loose tongue, sir — and what do we do to people with loose tongues, Mr Hawkspear?" asked the Bishop.

170

Hawkspear cackled like an old crone. "We cut 'em off, my Lord."

"Indeed we do, Mr Hawkspear! Indeed we do," Bishop Courtney confirmed.

Reynolds placed his hand on Courtney's shoulder, and the Bishop spun around, as if disturbed from a hypnotic trance.

"Is this really necessary, Bishop? You have the man bound," he whispered.

Courtney's eyes flared. "*Mister* Reynolds, if you please!" he seethed, as droplets of spittle formed on his bottom lip. "I will thank you to remember your place."

This had the desired affect on Reynolds, and he removed his hand quickly as ordered. "I apologise, Bishop, I didn't mean to question you."

"This man must pay penance!" squawked the Bishop.

With Hawkspear holding his captive's face firmly between his dirty, blood-stained fingers, the Bishop pushed the tongs towards his mouth, snapping the handles together. Peach tried to twist his face from the Irishman's grasp, writhing like a fox caught in a trap, but Hawkspear was far too strong. The landlord was weeping freely now, begging for forgiveness, for release — but none came. Peach clamped his mouth shut, tears streaming down his sweaty face. The Bishop advanced with the snapping tongs.

Again the Bishop pushed the tongs further into the man's mouth, trying to force it open, scraping teeth and tearing gums as it went. A sickening crack suddenly echoed around the confines of the crypt. Several of

Arthur Peach's teeth snapped in half. The man himself was too stunned now to cry out, the pain too intense, as Courtney thrust the tools in further. The Bishop snapped with the tongs . . . and then slowly removed them from Arthur Peach's terrified mouth, revealing the landlord's tongue ensnared sharply between the brass pincers.

"Now, Mr Peach," breathed the Bishop hoarsely, "we shall hear how you plead for mercy without a tongue. Mr Hawkspear . . . take these, and show him what I mean," he said, and handed Hawkspear the small, stub-bladed shears. The Irishman gladly held them tightly against the wrestling Peach's cheek — and with one sharp snip — he severed the tip of the man's tongue clean off. It fell to the floor with a wet thud.

The sustained shock was too much for Peach, and he collapsed onto his knees, his eyes rolling into the back of his head. A spurt of dark red blood spilled from his mouth, coating his broken teeth and torn gums. The man coughed, tasting the blood that gushed down his throat. Suddenly, Peach began convulsing wildly on the crypt's floor, his blood-stained hands flailing as if trying to snatch something in the air. He collapsed, shaking spasmodically, and spat a flurry of blood from his mouth, daubing his face in a crimson mask.

Reynolds pushed past Hawkspear and bent down to investigate. "He's choking, damn it!" He searched Peach's eyes for some sign of life, but it was too late . . . the man was balancing one step closer to death than he was to life, and the scales were tipped in death's favour.

172

The Bishop and Hawkspear watched in fascination at the macabre scene playing out before them and, with a final twitch of his body, Peach arched his back, stiffened his fingers and then suddenly relaxed. The landlord's lungs exhaled like a bicycle with a slow, hissing puncture. The Bishop peered a little closer, rocking forward on the balls of his feet, risking a look into the dead man's eyes.

"The shock of it all was too much for him," said Reynolds, staring at the body.

"The Bishop did what had t'be done, so he did," snapped Hawkspear protectively.

"Mr Hawkspear, take the landlord's body up to the cemetery. Place it in the usual spot for the body-snatchers, as per our arrangement," said Courtney, wiping his bloodied hands on his robes.

Hawkspear did as he was instructed. He bundled Peach's body up over his shoulder, and carried it slowly up the stone steps to the outside night.

"Arrangement?" quizzed Reynolds. "You've got an *arrangement* with the body-snatchers now?"

"That is correct, Mr Reynolds," Courtney said. "As long as Mr Hawkspear provides them with a regular supply of fresh bodies, they have agreed to leave the cemetery untouched. I can't have those dreadful ghouls digging up the place looking for corpses now, can I?"

"And . . . why is that then? What do *you* care if they dig the graveyard up?"

"I was trying to tell you earlier, man, before we were rudely interrupted. It's far too late now. Don't worry, I'll reveal all in time. Now, I must retire to Westminster

173

. . . you should go back to Crawditch, keep an eye on things," the Bishop said, as he slapped Reynolds on the back like an old school chum. "The plan nears its fruition, my friend. Sooner than we thought, the residents will find the prospect of staying in that place extremely unappealing, and we can conclude our business. I told you all it would take would be a few dead bodies turning up."

"Yeah, but they're not turning up, are they? Not if you're selling them to the snatchers, at any rate. The folk of Crawditch are cowards, but all they're doing is *talking* right now," said Reynolds. "Talking about curfews, talking about businesses shutting up, and that's all. It's not enough. If you want this place ready in time for the Queen's orders, then we need to make a statement, Bishop! Something big."

The Bishop picked at his bottom teeth with his fingernail. "Now *that's* what I admired about you in the first place, Mr Reynolds — you've got vision, and that is *so* hard to come by these days."

Reynolds slicked back a stray tail of hair from his forehead, and his penetrating eyes seemed to grow slightly darker, accentuating the thin scar that bisected his left cheek. "We need a big name, my Lord . . . we need to kill someone in whom the locals hold a great deal of faith, someone they look up to."

"I have the perfect target in mind," said Bishop Courtney as he forced a wan smile. "His name is Police Commissioner Oliver Dray."

174

CHAPTER
TWENTY-SIX

The Prodigal

"It is of no use, boss, I cannot budge this from its frame," cried Butter, sliding his back against the door to the floor. He rubbed furiously at his eyes with the palms of his hands, frustrated at his lack of progress. "Would you like try?"

Cornelius Quaint did not answer.

"Perhaps you will fare better than I," called out Butter in the darkness of the ice box, crawling on his hands and knees. "Boss? Mr Quaint?"

The Inuit patted his hands through the air around him, searching for Quaint, and suddenly they found purchase on the man's shirt. Panting as if he'd just run a mile, Butter clamoured at Quaint's chest. He laid his head down onto it, listening for the beat of the man's heart.

Nothing.

Scratching along the cold, icy floor of the ice box in the complete blackness, Butter found Quaint's arm. He wrenched the sleeve open at the cuff, and rushed to check the man's pulse. It was incredibly slow, but just about there. The cold was slowing down Quaint's body functions to a crawl.

"Curse my stupidity," Butter yelled at the ceiling. "I should not have turned my back on you . . . now you suffer!"

Again he clamoured at Quaint's chest, and thumped his fists upon it. In truth this was more a way of him releasing his frustration than anything. To all intents and purposes, Butter was now alone in the ice box, and his curses fluttered in the air like confetti at a wedding. He had not realised just how much he relied on Quaint's company for all these many years, and now it was being painfully driven home to him.

Without Quaint, the tiny man would surely have died alongside his wife back in the icy wastes of Greenland ten long years before. Walrus poachers had encroached upon Butter's land, and when he had tried to defend his family, they beat Butter to within an inch of his life, before brutalising and then murdering his wife. The poachers' final act of evil was to kidnap his young daughter, and they stole her away from him aboard their icebreaker ship, mocking the injured Inuit as he clung onto his life in the snow. He very nearly died that day, and surely would have if Cornelius Quaint hadn't stumbled across him and dragged him to safety. What on earth the conjuror was doing out in the middle of nowhere that day, Butter didn't know and didn't care. He was salvation.

Quaint had promised to help Butter find his kidnapped daughter, and they became united in their dedication. But over the years, the world changed. Borders and countries expanded, empires were formed, and suddenly the globe seemed such a very large haystack within which to find his needle. Butter's precious daughter had simply vanished off the face of the earth, and despite the best efforts of both men over some years, they eventually had to admit defeat. It was not long after that when Quaint adopted Butter into the circus, but still the Inuit refused to mourn his daughter. The fire still burned inside him to find her, and he had never given up on his hope. As he sat by Quaint's side on the freezing floor of the wooden ice box, he realised that hope itself was fading fast.

Lifting Quaint's lifeless body up onto his lap, Butter wept openly, freely and loudly. The air was extremely thin now, and soon he would join Quaint in unconsciousness. He cursed at the door, finding the last, ethereal scrap of strength still left within him. He held onto it tightly within his clenched fists, nurturing its potency, cultivating it. Rocking his head back, Butter released his anger and bellowed with all his might. His tear-filled eyes were clamped tightly shut, and he prayed for a merciful release.

Suddenly, a flurry of scuffling footsteps outside the ice box door distracted him from his silent wanderings. Had the Lord sent him help already? That was quick work, even for a God. Butter inched himself closer to the metal door, but recoiled instinctively as a thought struck him. Perhaps it was his captors, come to finish the job? Maybe that merciful release would come soon. He listened intently for more sounds with his ear to the metal door, and sure enough, in the warehouse something stirred. It hammered a succession of heavy blows upon the door from the other side, and Butter felt a further chill rip through his nerves. He moved nearer, and pressed his worn hands flat against the freezing cold metal.

"Hello?" he called weakly, forcing back his tears. "Please, you must help. My friend . . . he is near death! Release us . . . please!"

"Stand away . . . from the . . . door, laddie," yelled a man's voice from outside.

The door shifted a little in its frame, accompanied by a rending scream of metal, as someone — or some *thing* — tore at the door's hinges. A thin seam of moonlight was slowly visible all around the door's edges. Butter felt his mouth quiver in anticipation. A sudden shock worked its way through his bloodstream as the door that he had spent nearly an hour hammering upon was forcibly ripped from its moorings and tossed aside as if it were made of balsa wood. Landing with a dull clang of metal against stone, it skidded across the warehouse floor. Heavy footsteps again pounded against the wet stone floor, drawing ever closer. Butter squinted through the onrush of sudden moonlight, trying to define what he saw.

A silhouette of a great, towering man stood in the ice box doorway, almost filling the entire space. Bathed in wistful light as if surrounded by a ghostly aura, the voluminous figure stooped down and gathered up Quaint.

His eyes still fighting to adjust to the light, Butter had no choice but to gawp at the large mountain of a man with Cornelius Quaint's inert body in his enormous arms. He rose to his feet, and cautiously

178

clambered from the ice box and followed the huge man, as he gently laid Quaint's body down onto a nearby table. In a daze, he watched anxiously as the shadowed form of the man rubbed busily at Quaint's chest.

"Got here . . . just in time, lad," said the juggernaut.

"Indeed," answered Butter automatically.

"He's . . . in a bad way. Need t'warm him . . . quick," said the bulky man in a thick, interrupted staccato drawl. Each word seemed to be a foreign language to him, and he fought to grasp each one clumsily between his huge fists. "Butter, are ye injured?"

"How do you know of me?" questioned Butter, squinting into the darkness. "Who are you?"

The giant of a man smiled, his thick, bushy beard hiding much of his broad mouth. He stepped into the shafts of moonlight streaming into the market through a crack in the wall, and Butter instantly recognised the face illuminated before him.

"Is it really you?" he gasped.

"Yes, lad . . . last time I checked," said Prometheus.

CHAPTER
TWENTY-SEVEN

The Reunion

"But . . . but . . . but —" stuttered a stupefied Butter, his mouth failing to respond to his brain's commands to speak. His eyes and ears tried to grasp the sight and sound before him.

"Butter?" said Prometheus. "Calm . . . yerself, lad. Take a . . . deep breath."

"But, no! Is not possible!"

"Look, if ye'll just let me —"

"But . . . but you are talking," Butter declared. "With a voice!"

"Barely, but it ain't easy," said Prometheus. "Words're like soap . . . can't hold onto 'em. Can see 'em in me head . . . but sayin' 'ems a . . . dif'rent matter."

"But this is not so," cried Butter, scratching tufts of thick black hair.

"Lad, that's four . . . sentences you've started . . . with the word 'But'." Prometheus wiped his hands down his face in frustration. "Now please . . . listen t'me! Cornelius is sick, we need —"

"Crazy! Yes, that is it," said Butter. He stared at the floor, as if that might provide him with some answers.

180

"I am crazy. Mad as Hatter! There is no talking Prometheus. The time in that metal prison has addled my senses!"

Prometheus tore off his thick woollen coat, untied his scarf, and placed them both over Quaint's body. "We don't have . . . time for this, man! Cornelius needs . . . help! And fast! Don't ye see? Where's the, ah . . . the Madame?"

"Madame Destine? Madame not here," mouthed Butter robotically.

"Yeah, I guessed that. Damn it," cursed Prometheus. "Gettin' nowhere. Like talkin' . . . to a bloody parrot. Butter . . . for . . . God's sake, man . . . snap out of it! I . . . need your . . . *help* here."

"Prometheus," whispered Butter, entranced. "Needs . . . *my* help?"

"Cornelius is . . . damn near frozen, Butter, y'get me? His whole body's . . . in shock — luckily for him, or else . . . he'd prob'ly be dead."

"Dead!" snapped Butter, stomping his foot upon the ground. "But not dead?"

Prometheus shook his head. "This is madness . . . We need t'warm him up . . . and we need t'do it *now!*" The giant clamped his bushy mouth onto Quaint's, holding his friend's nose with his hand. He breathed warm breath into the still lungs, and then quickly swapped the hand to his chest to pump the heart. It had now been at least five minutes since Quaint had drawn a full breath, and time was of the essence. Again, Prometheus breathed and pumped and breathed and pumped, and again there was no response from Quaint. Prometheus

181

massaged his heart in a rhythmic motion unrelentingly, as Butter's fragile mind slowly came around to the prospect that maybe it wasn't quite so addled after all.

With a sudden cough, followed by a gasp for air, Cornelius Quaint sat bolt upright on the table, with Prometheus supporting his back. He coughed again, a dry, hoarse cough, and he clawed madly at his throat. His forehead was speckled with perspiration.

"Wuh . . . Wuh . . . Where . . . ?" he wheezed.

Butter rushed to his side, snapped out of his confused state. "Boss, lie still. You are quite safe . . . and look," he exclaimed. "Prometheus is here!"

Quaint craned his neck to see the huge form by his side, rubbing away at his back.

"Prom? Is . . . is it really you?" he whispered.

"Aye, mate, but . . . lay still and rest."

Quaint responded to the giant's words with a furrowed brow. "But . . . you can talk?"

"That is what I said . . . he speaks!" said Butter. "But —"

"But —" began Quaint. "But you can't —"

"Oh, this . . . this is just grand. Now . . . it's infectious!" said Prometheus, shaking his head. "Will ye both . . . *please* stop saying 'But'? Just . . . ah . . . just take it easy, Cornelius. I'll tell ye all . . . once I c'n . . . grasp th'words meself!"

Quaint rubbed at his neck, casting aside Prometheus's thick coat. "Forget that! I can recuperate later, man. It's damn good to see you again, my friend, but we don't have time for a reunion right now. We need to get back to the . . . to the . . . to the train." Quaint tried to stand, his legs buckling like those of a newborn foal. He strained, and stared into Prometheus's large brown eyes. "Prometheus, my good man, do me a favour will you?"

"Anythin'," the Irishman replied.

"Catch me."

Quaint's eyes rolled to the top of his head, his legs totally gave out beneath him and he slumped limply into Prometheus's open arms. He was unconscious once more and, within moments, snoring loudly. Prometheus clutched Quaint's sleeping form to his warm chest.

"Some welcome home party this turned out t'be," said Prometheus.

Half-an-hour later, Cornelius Quaint re-entered the world of the living and came round again. His mouth was dry, and he stared intently at the huge figure in front of him. As if this was the first time they were seeing him, Quaint's eyes took in every detail of the strongman. His hands reached out, and clasped Prometheus's jacket tightly to prove to himself that he was no mirage.

"Christ, Prometheus, it really *is* you!" Quaint said, desperately trying to restore saliva to his mouth and dry lips.

"In the flesh, Cornelius."

"I thought we'd lost you for good, my friend."

"I *was* lost . . . an' bits of me still are I think," Prometheus said awkwardly. "From . . . th'look o'those bodies over there . . . we should move on. Someone's

183

sure ... t'come back and check on ye ... and they'll ... expect ye t'be dead. Where can we go? The train?"

"Not just yet, there'll be Peelers all over it," said Quaint. "Butter, how about the boat we came here in? Is it large enough for all three of us?"

"It is doubtful, boss," said Butter. "But I agree ... I have no wish to remain here long myself." The Inuit stared at the bodies littering the warehouse floor, and his mind wandered briefly back to the battle, and the lives he had been forced to take.

Quaint stared at his pocket-watch. "Let's try and make it to Hyde Park and to shelter as quick as we can; the circus is as good a place as any to hide out."

"Christ!" cursed Prometheus, as he scratched at his bald head. "Wish I could just ... get these damn ... words out, man. Surely ... th'circus will ... be the first place the police ... will think of looking."

"Or the *last* place, depending how smart they are. We'll have to take the side roads to avoid bumping into anyone. There's no better hiding place than in plain sight," said Quaint, sizing up Prometheus and Butter. "But look at the two of you ... an Eskimo and a giant. I doubt that I could be travelling with anyone *more* conspicuous!"

Prometheus mouthed silently, and smacked the side of his head as if trying to jar the right words into his mouth. "Mebbe we should ... split up, like? Three targets're harder t'find ... than one, right?"

"Well, you can forget that," snapped Quaint. "I've only just *found* you ... I'm not about to risk losing you

184

again. We need to get word to Destine at the railway station that you're safe, and let her know what's happening."

"Perhaps I go, boss?" offered Butter. "Boat not hold us all, but I alone? Yes! It shall be not a problem. I go back to station and tell the Madame we found Prometheus."

"Actually . . . 'twas *me* that found the two o' ye!" said Prometheus.

"And just in the nick of time, apparently," said Quaint. "Butter, if you're sure you want to go alone, then go by all means, but we don't want any unwanted attention. Just tell Destine to continue as normal. No need to drag her half-way across town tonight. Tell her to leave a skeleton crew on board the train, and bring her out to the park first thing in the morning."

Butter nodded dutifully. "It shall be done, boss."

"And Butter?" asked Quaint, watching the Inuit spin on his heels. "Those men mentioned me by name, remember? So it's a safe bet someone wants me dead. We don't know who our enemies are, but they surely know us. Be on your guard."

"Thank you, boss, I will," said Butter with a bow, and he skipped out of the warehouse towards the rowing boat.

Prometheus and Quaint watched as Butter pulled hard on the boat's oars, rowing away into the enveloping fog of the night. Within seconds, the misty shroud had swallowed him and he was no longer visible. Prometheus turned to Quaint, and slapped a huge hand on his friend's back.

185

"He's . . . a *plucky* little thing, isn't he?" said Prometheus with a tug on his bristles. "A proper . . . little lep . . . lep . . . lepre —"

"Leprechaun?" offered Quaint.

"Yeah . . . that's the word. Sorry, Cornelius . . . a bit rusty." Prometheus kicked at a wooden post on the wharf in frustration at the disjointedness between his brain and his mouth. Although he knew exactly what he wanted to say, and it was waiting there patiently on his lips, he was finding it immeasurably hard to communicate it. He had been mute for so long. The words teased him, floating from his grasp before he could vocalise them, like trying to catch a butterfly without a net. So much so that each sentence was constructed in such a way that it sounded like a completely random series of words strung together by accident. The haphazard inflections were all over the place, marred even more by his melodic Irish accent.

"No need to say sorry, Prom. I can imagine it is hard for you. And yes, Butter certainly is priceless. I only hope he makes it safely back. We need Destine up to speed when we see her. Come on; let's make tracks whilst we've still got an advantage."

"We've got . . . an advantage?" asked Prometheus dryly. "That makes a change."

"Of course we have, man!" said Quaint. "Whoever sent those men to kill me knew the name Cornelius Quaint. Now, I don't know who or why, but hopefully my enemy now thinks me dead. There's no greater advantage than that, trust me — and whilst we're on the move you can explain to me how a man who's been mute his whole life can suddenly speak, hmm? Not to mention how the hell you knew where to find us?"

"The tale o' how . . . me voice returned . . . is one for another time, Cornelius," Prometheus said, his heavy eyes lowered to the ground like a chastised dog. "I got . . . more . . . important things. Been . . . hidin' out . . . along docks for a while. Tell me . . . what've they found out? Police, I mean . . ."

"About what? About your escape?"

"Forget me . . . *escape*, man!" growled Prometheus. "M'talkin' about Tom Hawkspear! Are they any . . . closer t'findin' 'im?"

"Ah . . ." Quaint puffed his cheeks, trying to find the right words. "To tell you the truth, my old friend, I don't think they have even begun to look for him. They have a much larger target in mind. No, I think that if this Hawkspear demon is to be found . . . we shall have to get our own hands dirty!"

"I won't . . . let her death go unpunished, Cornelius," muttered Prometheus. "I just won't! Even if . . . I have t'dredge the depths o' hell meself!"

Quaint slapped his hand upon the giant's vast shoulder. "Then you will have my company in your task, my friend. She was a unique young woman," he said, his bottom lip floundering as he clenched the emotion behind his gritted teeth. "And I loved her like a daughter. She will not go unavenged, Prometheus . . . I swear to you."

187

CHAPTER
TWENTY-EIGHT

The Killer Connection

An hour later, after weaving their way through the labyrinthine backstreets of Lambeth, Quaint and Prometheus had made it to the near end of the Vauxhall Bridge, and they were close to their destination, crouched behind a large outbuilding.

"So, what's next?" asked Prometheus, trying his best to squat down into the shadows. "Or are *you* on the . . . run from the . . . law now, same as me?"

"We need Destine's advice as to which direction we need to take," Quaint said.

"A *plan*? That's not like ye, Cornelius," said Prometheus, with a knowing wink. "Surely, the plan is . . . I go t'Crawditch and speak t'the Police. I need t'hand meself in, Cornelius! Clear up this . . . mis . . . understandin', do ye not understand?"

Quaint bit at his bottom lip, and stared at his Irish friend. It was confusing hearing Prometheus talk, and how tentatively each word was delivered, in such a contrast to his physical bulk. On more than one occasion the Irishman had begun a sentence, only to clamp his mouth shut and keep silent. But he was slowly getting his confidence back, and renewing his acquaintance with his voice. Quaint was biding his time, waiting for Prometheus to explain how it had miraculously reappeared. He had never heard his friend utter so much as a single syllable in all the time he had known him, and yet somehow the deep Irish twang was how he'd imagined Prometheus to speak. He was transfixed, watching the strongman's big beard and moustache twitching from one side to the other like a ventriloquist's dummy as Prometheus spoke.

"I need t'hand meself in, clear up this mis . . . Er . . . misunder . . . misunderstandin'!"

"Commissioner Dray has the weight of Scotland Yard bearing down on him at the moment," Quaint said. "He may decide to make a scapegoat out of you, and he's certainly made it clear that *my* past friendship with him won't sway the balance in your favour. If anything, it'd work against you."

"But, Cornelius . . . I can speak up for meself now . . . just about."

"Yes, I'd noticed that . . . and I have been waiting . . ."

"Ye're probably . . . wonderin' how that . . . came about, right?"

"Amongst other vexing questions swimming around my head, yes," said Quaint. "Such as: how on earth did you get out of prison? I thought *I* was supposed to be the magician, and here you are performing not one, but *two* miracles in one day."

Prometheus had known this conversation was coming. There was little point in trying to sidestep it. Like a wart on the end of his nose, there was no avoiding the attention. A seven-foot-plus mute giant who could now miraculously speak was sure to be a conversation starter.

"Which . . . which one d'ye want t'hear first, eh?" he asked Quaint.

"The police station," replied his friend. "Forget just *why* you were stupid enough to escape when I had specifically told you to let *me* handle things . . . I want to know how you managed it. I inspected the bars on the window grate myself . . . they had been eaten away by acid. Now . . . how the hell did you get hold of acid in a bloody police station?"

Prometheus rubbed a thick hand over his bald head. "Well, the . . . um . . . the answer to *why* I was so stupid . . . and *how* I escaped . . . is the same." He tensed as he heard a rustle in the building behind them, and Quaint's hand darted out and grabbed his arm. The two hunched men relaxed as a ginger cat came scurrying out from the shadows, and they exchanged relieved glances. "Cornelius . . . I don't don't know . . . if this is the right place for this. It's not easy . . . hearin' me own voice, for a start!"

"I'm in no rush, and it's a long walk to Hyde Park," Quaint said, with a grin. "Did you suddenly get a visit from angels bestowing the gift of voice upon you, or something?"

"There was . . . nothing *angelic* . . . about it, man," Prometheus answered. "Cornelius . . . m'not sure . . . how much sense I'll make," he said, slumping his backside down onto the stony ground. "The truth is . . . it ain't some miracle how I got . . . got me voice back . . . 'cos it never really went away."

"What are you talking about, man?" asked Quaint. "No pun intended."

Prometheus's defences relaxed as he saw the glint of friendship in Quaint's black eyes. He exhaled noisily, his beard fluttering in the breeze, and he sighed a mournful sigh, as if he were unburdening a lifelong secret — which of course, was exactly what he was about to do.

"Well, the thing is . . . I . . . I *chose* not to speak."

"I think you're getting your words confused," said Quaint. "What do you mean, you '*chose*' not to speak?"

"I thought . . . it was . . . for the best . . . at th'time, anyways. Started out . . . like somethin' to protect meself . . . next thing I knew . . . it was a dec . . . decade later. Think . . . I almost . . . convinced meself I was a mute."

Quaint's brow furrowed. "You mean . . . all this time, all these years, you could have spoken . . . and yet you *didn't*? But . . . why?"

"It goes back t'years ago . . . back home in Ireland . . . someone very . . . close t'me . . . she was killed. Her name was Lily, an' me an' her got on just grand . . . the problem was, her family weren't as . . . keen on me, 'specially her two brothers."

Prometheus took a deep breath, as he laid out his past before Quaint. "They tried t'separate us time an' again, 'til one day . . . it all came to a head." He paused, catching the look of anguish on Quaint's face. "Don't you be lookin' like that, mate," Prometheus said, almost tenderly. "I ain't about . . . t'blub all over ye. I need to exorcise this demon . . . once and fer all. Y'see . . . Lily's two brothers . . . they *trapped* her when I was out workin'. They . . . they locked her up in a barn . . . threatened t'set it on fire. I got home . . . only t'see 'em waving bloody torches aroun' like some sort of witch-hunt. Lily's youngest brother . . . Tommy . . . said somethin' about me being a . . . a 'freak against God' or somesuch nonsense . . . I punched him so hard, damn near took his head off . . . he threw his torch into the barn . . . said he would rather . . . watch his sister *burn* than be wi' a monster like me. I'm too busy fightin' t'hear Lily's screams . . ."

"She died in the fire?" asked Quaint.

Prometheus nodded. "Aye, an' her brother Sean with her. O'course . . . Tommy blamed me for it all." He sniffed back a tear that clung to the tip of his nose like a bead of early morning dew. "He was . . . a bad seed, that one. He ended up doin' life . . . in Blackstaff prison . . . on account o' the Irish refusin' t'take 'im . . . somethin' about his religious fixations . . . that sent a chill up their bones . . . I think. Don't blame 'em . . . for what he'd done. Life wasn't enough . . . if ye ask me. Should've hanged th'bastard."

"And what happened to you then?" asked Quaint.

"Me? I dried up like a prune, shut meself away," Prometheus said, a rueful smile on his broad face, as he relayed the darkest chapter of his life. Talking to Quaint was a sobering experience for the man — for them both. Here he was chatting away, baring his soul, and it felt good. It felt right. He could have done so at any time in the past, but something held him back. Something held him cocooned within himself. But now, with Twinkle's death so raw to him, it was as if he didn't have the strength to keep up the barriers any more. He was crawling further from his cocoon with each new revelation. "I just . . . just shut it all off . . . in me brain," he continued. "Like . . . 'cos then maybe that way . . . no one'd get hurt again. From that day . . . 'til today . . . I ain't spoken a damn word to any soul." Prometheus pinched at his moustache, and scrambled to his feet. He clenched his fists, and then they hung limply at his sides. "When I found out about Twinkle . . . I realised it didn't matter whether I . . . was a mute or not . . . the people I loved still got hurt. But, it ain't easy to deal with, Cornelius . . . knowin' that . . . every woman I fall . . . in love with . . . is destined to die. Mebbe it ain't me . . . but, what if it is? What if . . . I'm . . . t'blame? What if I'm causin' it all somehow?"

"Don't be a fool," said Quaint, standing to join Prometheus. "You've been unlucky, but it happens to us all. You have suffered, more than anyone should ever have to, and you have my sympathy. But in life, everyone experiences their fair share of heartache and pain. It is unavoidable. It is not gravity that binds men's feet to the earth, Prometheus — it is Fate — and she will not be bargained with. She is like the wind, the sea, the rain. Fate is ever-present — and we are all at her mercy." Quaint ruffled his thick mop of hair, trying to find the right words of consolation. "Just look at me if you want proof of that. Here I am in my mid-fifties, and

I'm still crouching in shadows and hiding from the law. Fate has singled me out, and shaped my soul. What has changed in my life?"

"Perhaps you've become better at hiding, Cornelius."

"Better at running away, don't you mean? But I was *not* going to run out on *you*, Prometheus — and I still won't! So . . . with Lily's brother incarcerated in Blackstaff prison, at least that's an end to it all, then. You *can* move on."

"Maybe . . . except . . . I'm not sure it *has* ended, mate," said Prometheus. "Both the loves of me life've been . . . *taken* from me . . . by the same bloody man. Maybe it won't *ever* end. Maybe you're right, what you say about Fate. I'll bet she's 'aving a right good laugh at me . . . expense, so she is! I don't know *how* he got out but I'll find him — that's for sure. Drivin' me insane like this — it's all part of his game."

"Prometheus, what are you talking about?"

"He came to me cell . . . back at the police station . . . tauntin' me, rilin' me up through the bars from outside, he was."

"What? Who was? What do you mean?"

Prometheus ground his teeth, and started pacing in circles. "I got so mad . . . I went for him. Grabbed hold of the bars . . . and they just snapped right out . . . taking half the bleedin' wall with 'em! I know he's responsible. I just *know* it!"

"Prometheus, you aren't making any sense. Who? *Who's* responsible?" he asked, rounding on Prometheus, standing right in front of him.

He placed his hands upon the giant's chest to restrain him forcefully, and Prometheus stopped in his tracks. The unstoppable force had met the immovable object, and suddenly the rage that blazed in Prometheus's eyes faded.

"It's Lily's brother, o'course," answered the giant. "Th'same bastard who caused all this mess we're in . . . Tommy Hawkspear!"

CHAPTER
TWENTY-NINE

The Face in the Mist

Back across the Thames, at Grosvenor Park station aboard the circus train, Madame Destine was alone in Quaint's office, sifting through the running order for the forthcoming show. The absence of both Twinkle and Prometheus was proving to be difficult to accommodate into the schedule. Destine's veil was discarded on the back of her chair, and her head was buried in her fragile hands. The pallid light from the lantern on the desk served to exaggerate the woman's pale complexion. Despite the spark that shone brightly in her misty-blue eyes, she looked drained. The long days of late had certainly taken their toll on her. But there was something else behind it all, like a tenuous memory that, no matter how hard she tried to visualise it, she could never give it form.

Madame Destine had been a part of the circus long enough to know that it was pretty much a self-sustaining environment. All the crew and performers knew their roles, and everyone pulled together to make sure the show was a success. Even so, the days before the huge Big Top tent was fully erected, and the lesser exhibit tents were in place, were a strain on

196

everyone. Even though the first show was not until the coming Friday afternoon, there was still a great deal of preparation to be done.

Destine sifted through reams of paper, sipping from a bone china teacup, idly staring out of the window of the train. Down at the platform below, several circus members moved about carrying boxes, tarpaulin and timber. It was now rapidly approaching eleven o'clock, and there was little left of the day. She yawned, suddenly yearning for the comfort of her bed.

Without warning, like a spear of electricity striking her, she sat bolt upright in the chair, her eyes wide, her mouth trembling. For the second time in as many days, Madame Destine was petrified. Her visions were becoming less and less clear, and more and more infrequent, and when they arrived, they came with such ferocity that it was like a million hot needles pricking her skin. This vision in particular, a fleeting slide-show of images lacking in coherence or substance, invaded Destine's mind's eye, flooding it with pulsating pictures, scents, sights and sounds.

The train's office quickly melted away before her eyes, to be replaced with an out-of-focus image of a large, open-plan building. It was seemingly empty, and the French clairvoyant soaked up the vision in all its detail. Wisps of mist coated the floor up to ankle height, snapping and curling like coiled vipers. A silvery light flooded into the building from outside, casting an electric-blue glare across the barren floor.

In the doorway a fluctuating, undulating image of a man suddenly appeared, his face shrouded in darkness.

Destine watched breathlessly as the man walked into the building. He was clenching his fists and cursing madly. Destine couldn't make out the words, but she felt the emotion of the man all too clearly. It was hatred, pure and simple, coated with a frustrated lust for vengeance. The man approached closer, and with each footstep nearer to where Destine's spirit form was standing, she felt an unfamiliar sensation. She was suddenly taken by the idea that she needed to run.

Destine slammed her eyes shut tight and attempted to sever the connection — but something was wrong. Something was stopping her. The ghostly spectre of a man continued striding through the ghost-light, and then suddenly stopped stock still on the spot with his back to Destine — and then something happened. Something puzzling, frightening and something utterly impossible . . . something that had never happened before in all the seventy years of Destine's life.

The man noticed her.

He turned his head and looked directly at her.

Somehow, he knew she was there. He was definitely aware of her. A fact that was confirmed as a thin smile crawled onto his face. That wasn't supposed to happen. This was a vision from the future. Destine was supposed to be a disconnected viewer, observing events yet to pass — it was impossible for her to be drawn into some moment of the present. She brushed the feelings away, but as he began slowly walking towards her, the man's face drove into sharp focus amongst the wisps of the mist and moonlight. It burned its image into Destine's brain; so much so, that it was the only, overriding thought that existed there, and it was like being frozen to death from the inside out. An overwhelming wave of fear crawled across Destine's body. The man was now mere feet from Destine's position. Close enough for her to smell his breath. A twisted, malevolent sneer washed across his face as he walked into the shafts of blue moonlight. Destine slapped her hands to her face in sheer horror, as the image of the man flooded her senses.

"*C'est impossible!*" she gasped, "It cannot be . . . You're supposed to be dead!"

CHAPTER
THIRTY

The Walk in the Park

Quaint squinted at Prometheus, in a state of total awe. "*Hawkspear?*" he said. "Lily's brother . . . is Tommy Hawkspear? He's the fiend that I've been trying to tell the bloody police about! This is madness! I can't believe that Dray was so blind!"

"Tommy's escaped from Blackstaff prison, Cornelius. Somehow . . . he found out I was in London . . . sent me a note just before he killed Twinkle. A note swearing he would hurt her . . . and he made good on his threat, didn't he, eh?"

"I've seen the note," said Quaint. "And so have the police. They found it near Twinkle's . . . body." Quaint said the word "body" as if he were swearing in front of a priest. "I *knew* there had to be a connection between you and this killer, but not even Madame Destine foresaw *this!* We've been following this jigsaw one piece of the puzzle at a time and now finally I think I'm getting my first glimpse of the picture. My God, Prometheus, if only you hadn't bloody escaped we could have been way ahead of ourselves by now. Dray would've had no choice but to believe us!"

"Look . . . m'really sorry, Cornelius . . . Seein' that devil again clouded me mind, an' me anger just . . . took control over me, I suppose."

"So . . . Hawkspear drugged you at the tavern that night. He followed you . . . and then he killed Twinkle right in front of your eyes. Now, more than ever, we need to see Destine to make sense of this! Him just sporadically escaping Blackstaff and coming after you, just as we arrive in Crawditch to watch all hell break loose . . . the coincidence is staggering!"

Minutes later, fuelled by these revelations, the two men had resumed their course for Hyde Park. Quaint and Prometheus strolled down the centre of a moon-soaked street near Eaton Square, towards Kensington. Dark, foreboding clouds gathered in flocks above, as if spying down upon them. A metal fence cordoned off the centre of the square and sycamore trees decorated a small green area, like a tiny engraving of parkland, shrunk down in scale. Quaint and Prometheus crouched behind a bush next to the railings, and drew a long, restful breath after their long journey. Heavy hands of a thick sycamore branches hung over the railings like a giant eagle's wing, under which the men were cowering in the darkness. The road they needed to travel down was directly ahead, but it was intersected at crossroads, and they could be seen very clearly in the lamp-lit streets. Quaint could tell they were nearing Kensington. Only the idle rich were gifted with streetlamps.

"We're too much out in the open here," muttered Quaint. "And we've got another half-hour's trek through Kensington. We're going to have to keep on our toes if we want to get as far as the park unseen. You're not exactly pocket-sized. We'll need to use those terraced buildings up ahead as cover. With the docks far behind us we've run out of warehouses," said Quaint, eyeing the mass of a man next to him. "It's past midnight, so we should find the roads pretty empty, especially considering the weather."

"Aye, Cornelius," agreed Prometheus. "There's a storm coming."

"In more ways than one, my friend," nodded Cornelius.

"Shh," Prometheus held up his hand. "D'ye hear that? It's coming this way!"

A minute or two later, a horse and carriage steered swiftly past them in the darkness, the rattling cackle of the wooden wheels against the cobbled streets announcing its presence long before it was seen with the naked eye. Quaint stared at the sumptuous horse-drawn carriage, a spacious cart with a fine, muscular black horse pulling it. Two gas lanterns hung either side of the coach, and the driver was perched atop it, whipping the reins into frenzy, eager to be off the streets as quickly as the horse would take him.

"Fate, it seems, has seen fit to offer us a gift, my Irish friend," Quaint said.

"I hope you've got money to hire it, 'cos I sure don't," replied the giant.

"That's no cabbie, Prom," said Quaint. "Take a look at those markings. Hansoms are painted standard black, always have been. No, that's official Church transport, and I'm not thinking of hiring it . . . I'm thinking of stealing it."

With that, Prometheus and Quaint both leapt from the concealment of the shadows, and tore down the street at full pelt after the carriage. Despite his size, Prometheus streaked ahead of Quaint, reaching his arm out at full stretch to try and grab hold of the side of the carriage. His fingers found the groove of the coach door. But as his slapping footsteps resounded against the cobbles in the enclosed street, the mole of a driver glanced over his shoulder.

"What the bloody hell —?" squawked the man, as he whipped at the reins furiously, urging the horse to run faster. "Get out of it! Go on, gerrof!"

"Prometheus!" called Quaint from behind. "Get on top of it!"

Prometheus gave a lunge, and threw himself towards the carriage roof. He gripped onto the luggage rack and used his momentum to swing himself up towards the driver. The hunched man tried desperately to bat the giant away with his horsewhip.

"We ain't about t'hurt ye, man!" said Prometheus, hanging onto the carriage's roof for dear life as his thunderous feet tried to keep pace with the vehicle. "We only need a lift — it's an emergency."

"You're a bloody loon, you are — but you're a huge loon, and I want no quarrel wiv' you," said the man, slowing his carriage to a crawl. "Strictly speakin', I'm not supposed to do this, y'know — 'specially at this time o' night. Me boss'll 'ave me guts fer garters."

"I'm sorry," said Prometheus, climbing inside the transport. "We didn't mean to scare ye, honest. Y'see, me an' me friend need t'reach Hyde Park quick-smart! It's a matter of life and death, so it is."

Quaint eventually caught up with the carriage. He was bent over double, clasping his kneecaps, and panting like he'd just been forced to run a long-distance race at knifepoint.

"Thank you . . . for . . . stopping," he gasped to the driver.

"Di'nt 'ave much choice, did I? Yer bleedin' mate saw to that."

"Where are you off to?"

"Westminster Abbey . . . an' as it goes, I'm goin' right past the park on me way," the driver motioned the exhausted Quaint inside. "So get in now, or get left behind, mate."

"You are doing a great service," said Quaint, clambering into the carriage. "You have our thanks, Mister . . . ?"

"Melchin," said the driver, "Stanley Melchin." And with a crack of his whip, the coach driver rattled off along the street like a rocket.

"Bloody hellfire," said the giant, fingering a silk curtain, admiring the interior. His voice had now returned to full effect, and his heavy Irish accent coated every word with a comical, undulating twang. "Whose carriage is this then — Prince Albert's himself? Christ!"

"Exactly," said Quaint, pointing to a lavish picture of angelic cherubs painted upon the coach's ceiling. "It's not regal, Prometheus — it's religious. Look around at the art in here. Albert prefers the pomp and circumstance type of décor, not flying angels and cherubic scenes. Anyway, we have been most fortuitous, my Irish friend. Not only are we well concealed inside, we shall reach the park in no time, and we might as well travel in style, eh?" Quaint said, pulling closed the carriage's curtains.

Twenty minutes later, Prometheus and Quaint were standing admiring the stark beauty of Hyde Park. The cold winter wind was shaking the naked branches of the trees, sending grit and dust up into the night air. An unwelcome chill skirted around Prometheus as he spied the expansive, rolling fields, and the lines of trees that bordered the vast green space in front of him. The darkness stole most of the park from his vision, but compared to the stifling closeness of most other districts of London, this wide open space felt like another world to the man-mountain.

"Y'know, Cornelius . . . I've spent the past few days either locked in a police cell, or hidin' out in the docks . . . I gotta say, this place is just about as beautiful as I c'n imagine."

"You should have been here a couple of years ago, my friend," said a reflective Quaint. "The Great Exhibition of 1851 — an amazing spectacle, full of the exotic and the fantastic. The Crystal Palace was simply sublime. Joseph Paxton outshone himself with that building, to be sure," he said, picturing the gleaming glass-domed roof, and the expansive halls of wonderment within the grand exhibition hall. "The culmination of the greatest triumphs that Science had to offer, and we sure knocked the socks off those Frenchies — just don't tell Madame Destine I said that."

Prometheus laughed. "Cross me heart. So, where's the circus tent stationed, then?"

"Just up past The Meadow," steered Quaint, strolling along the hilly plains. "We know the police are watching the train, but this place is out of Crawditch's jurisdiction. Even so, we had best make sure we keep our eyes and ears open!"

CHAPTER
THIRTY-ONE

The Unfurled Agenda

A loud rap on the door echoed around Bishop Courtney's palatial residence in Westminster Abbey's annexe, and the heavy-set man clasped the glass door knob and briskly yanked the door open.

"What time of night do you call this?" Courtney demanded. "I said no later than eleven, and it's past midnight, Melchin! What on earth kept you?"

Melchin ambled inside the room with hunched shoulders. "Sorry, Bishop . . . I was on me way 'ere, and these two blokes just ran straight out of the bushes, right in the middle of the road."

"Just make sure it doesn't happen again, Melchin," interrupted the Bishop curtly. "So . . . what news do you have from Crawditch?"

"That, Bishop, is sure t'put a smile on yer face," Melchin began. "There's a committee on their way to Crawditch police station tomorrow. A lot of them locals are really jumpy now. So far they reckon they've 'ad about five people or so go missing, although the Peelers're only sayin' there've been them three women you said you wanted 'em to find, like."

The Bishop nodded. "Yes, the ones that Mr Hawkspear got a little too . . . *indulgent* with during the kill — they were of no use to the body-snatchers. We intentionally let the police find them to light the fuse of fear. I'd be very keen to hear the outcome of that meeting. Anything else of note, Melchin?"

"Yeah, apparently there was some to-do down at the docks tonight, and the coppers found a load of dead blokes, looked like there'd been some kind of scrap. Caused a right bleedin' storm, that did! Word is that the locals want Commissioner Dray to call in Scotland Yard, 'cos of all what's going on. They reckon the place 'as gone to hell . . . if you'll pardon me reference, your Grace."

Bishop Courtney gently rocked on the balls of his feet. "Blasphemy is all relative to your God, Melchin. I am more concerned with what occurs in Crawditch! That committee is exactly what I need . . . the problem is . . . Commissioner Dray is no fool. He'll deny their request, of course, if he wishes to retain a semblance of control."

"He should do," said Reynolds, stepping into the room from the hallway. "After all, that *is* what we're paying him for, isn't it? To turn a blind eye? A man in his position is the linchpin in a place like Crawditch. This needs to be kept contained within Crawditch's jurisdiction."

"Indeed it does, Mr Reynolds, and a high coup it was indeed for you to ensnare him in the first place. Who knows what you used to convince him, but it worked. We do however need to be mindful that the locals don't lose confidence in Dray. Thank you, Melchin, off you go," said the Bishop, ushering the driver outside the room. "I wonder then, Mr Reynolds, if the townsfolk are demanding the Yard's involvement — how will that balance be affected in Dray's absence should we do away with him? We don't want to make things even harder for us than they already are."

"Certainly not," agreed Reynolds, snatching up a glass decanter of dark-red wine and pouring himself a glass. "If Dray goes down, he'll most likely be replaced by his second, one Sergeant Horace Berry. He has been with the Force practically since its inception, no wife, no children."

"No leverage then? Nothing you can squeeze?"

"And nothing to blackmail him with either, he's as clean as his regulation whistle. Aside from the threat of physical violence, we're out of luck if he gets in charge. I've been thinking, Bishop . . . perhaps Oliver Dray works best for us right where he is."

"Although, I must admit that I was somewhat nervous about having a police commissioner of all people on our side, he has so far kept these crimes localised to Crawditch, as you so rightly surmised. That is vital to my plan . . . this must remain contained." Bishop Courtney wiped a thin slug-trail of perspiration from his forehead with his handkerchief. "I don't want to stir up a hornets' nest that's going to come right back and sting me in the posterior — my eyes are fixed upon the grander agenda."

Reynolds focused his gaze upon the Bishop. "What *is* the grander agenda? I'm not sure I'm following it any more. I thought this was all about Queen Victoria's grand plans of renovation . . . that's how you sold it to me. What's all this stuff about Crawditch and its cemetery got to do with what the Queen wants?"

"Victoria's decree is but a smokescreen, Mr Reynolds. A cloak behind which my own personal ambitions are hidden. It is not Crawditch itself that I wish to claim . . . but a right that should be afforded me as Bishop."

Reynolds strode to the long windows and rested his hands against the glass. "Look, Bishop — it really doesn't matter squat to me what your grand plan is. You could be raising an army of the undead to storm Buckingham Palace, for all I care — but I'd just like to know what side I'm fighting on, know what I mean?" Reynolds's face looked almost bone-white in the moonlight, giving him a ghoulish appearance.

"Very well," bowed the Bishop. "After all, you're not like Mr Hawkspear. He is a blunt instrument, whereas you, sir, are a keen edge. You have been a great help to me this past week, and I suppose you deserve to know just *what* is so important to me.

"What I seek is power. A power greater than words from dusty old Bibles . . . I mean *true* power. It is high time the Church of England reclaimed its place as a position of strength . . . to become again what it once was . . . an impregnable fortress of authority across this Empire — an authority far beyond that of mere kings and queens . . . an authority that is Godlike."

Reynolds clapped his hands noisily. "An impressive sermon, Bishop," he said casually, as he walked over to the table by the Bishop's side. "When we were in the crypt at the cemetery you started to tell me something, but you never finished. Is there something in that crypt that you need, Bishop? You have access to the crypt any time you want, so why not simply walk in there and take what you need? Why do you need the whole of Crawditch emptied first?"

Courtney stroked the corners of his grin. "Like I have said before, Mr Reynolds . . . you possess a keen intellect. All good questions, and to answer: what I desire is not hidden in that crypt, Mr Reynolds."

"It's not?"

"Not any longer, at any rate."

"I don't understand . . ."

"It is in my possession, Mr Reynolds — but it was only half of what I need."

"You're speaking in riddles, Bishop."

"You asked why the Church was so interested in a dingy dockland borough like Crawditch, Mr Reynolds, and why I am so interested in its cemetery. Well, I shall tell you all, if you really wish to know."

"Oh, I *do* wish, your Grace . . . I really, really *do*," pleaded Reynolds sarcastically, like an eager child begging for a toffee.

The Bishop played along, clearing his throat dramatically. "Many, many years ago Crawditch cemetery was selected as a location to store a very special prize, devised by the Church to secure its future and cement itself as the one, true religion to which all must heed. Part of this treasure was buried in the crypt; the other in the cemetery grounds itself."

"So, the crypt did have *some* treasure worth finding then, after all?" asked Reynolds, his beady eyes aflame with interest.

"As I said before, treasure is not always gold or jewels, Mr Reynolds. In this case, the treasure in the crypt happened to be a glass vial containing . . . an *antidote*, of a sort."

"An antidote? That's *treasure* to you, is it? A bleedin' antidote?"

The Bishop swatted Reynolds's caustic remark away with a wave. "The antidote itself is not the treasure . . . it is what it is an antidote *to*, that certainly is. The true prizes that I sought were both purposefully hidden in separate locations. One location contains the primary chemical, and the other a neutralising agent."

" 'Neutralising agent'? This is all getting a bit above me, Bishop . . . I'm a mercenary, not a chemist. If this 'solution' is such a treasure — why'd you need an antidote?"

"In case someone using the treasure should have second thoughts, Mr Reynolds," answered the Bishop, "for it reverses the effects of that vial's solution — although why one would wish to do such a thing is beyond me. I suppose the word 'antidote' is a bit misleading, for what the primary vial actually contains is a very special and unique elixir!"

"An elixir? What does it do, cure the pox, or something? Turn lead into gold?"

"Nothing as churlish as that, Mr Reynolds."

"But this . . . this *elixir* thing is hidden in the cemetery?"

"Within the cemetery grounds, yes," confirmed the Bishop. "In an unmarked grave."

"An unmarked grave? So, how come you don't just pay the body-snatchers to dig it up then? Why go to this great plan of yours for something so simple?"

"*Simple*, Mr Reynolds? I can assure you, if it were *simple* don't you think I would have the elixir in my hands by now? There are over five hundred unmarked burial sites in that cemetery — and what I seek could be hidden in any one of them."

Reynolds smiled as the penny dropped. "And I'd guess the locals would have something to say about you digging up their loved ones, eh?" he asked, purposefully showing the Bishop a furtive smile.

"Which is precisely why I am trying to clear the district," snapped Courtney. "It has taken me the best part of twenty-three years to finally track down the location of what I seek, but it's impossible to go any further with the district fully populated ... I'd be locked up within five minutes."

"And then along comes Queen Victoria ... with all her talk about reclaiming London as her Empire's capital, and that just falls like a gift-wrapped present in your lap, eh?" said Reynolds. "Pretty convenient."

"Have you not heard that the Lord works in mysterious ways, Mr Reynolds?" Bishop Courtney said. "Victoria gave me the perfect excuse to continue with my plans, and now ... now we are close to its fruition, Mr Reynolds, so very close."

"And all that stands in your way are a thousand locals, eh?"

"Thanks to Mr Hawkspear, that number is decreasing by the day, but it's not enough . . . I need the place empty of all witnesses."

"Now I get it," grinned Reynolds. "Why didn't you just say so at the beginning? We could have surely come up with something that wasn't quite so . . . *messy*, something a bit more *direct*. All this *subterfuge* for something that's buried in a bloody grave? How do you know some grave robber — or someone from your lot — hasn't already beaten you to it?"

"I would know . . . the Church would know, the whole world would know! The Church has closed its mind to the fact that it even exists. They feel it is just a myth, something lost to the legends of the past. They would not seek something of which they know nothing."

"I don't want to go digging around for some chemical that could burn my skin off! What on earth is this elixir for?"

"On earth?" said the Bishop with a throaty chuckle. "On earth it is nothing less than the touch of God's hand." The Bishop leaned closer to Reynolds, close enough that the gaunt man could feel the warmth of Courtney's breath against his cheek. "Mr Reynolds, that grave holds a prize that has been elusive since the beginning of time . . . a dream that many have endlessly searched for, only to watch it slip through their fingers . . . a prize that man has ever sought." Courtney rose to his feet, and cleared his throat, like an actor about to deliver the finest performance of his career.

"Answer me this, Mr Reynolds; what are your feelings on the secret of eternal life?"

"Beyond it being complete horseshit, you mean?"

"But you are at least aware of the notion?" said Courtney, clapping his clammy hands together. "It is far from fancy, Mr Reynolds — it is irrefutable fact. Throughout history, every religion across the world has spoken of such a thing . . . eternity! Not just of the living soul, but of the physical body itself. Perpetual, interminable life! A chance for mortal man to become . . . immortal! It's a tantalising thought for anyone, is it not?"

"I've met a lot of people over the years seeking eternal life, Bishop, and not a single one of them ever found it. Misguided fools, the lot of them — and they wasted what lives they had left searching for it."

"Mystical amulets, Holy Grails and alchemists' stones, Mr Reynolds? Indeed, they *are* all works of desperate fiction, and the beliefs of overactive imaginations. This quest we are currently embarked upon at this moment is one based upon reality."

"And I suppose you can prove that?" asked Reynolds.

"Proof? You ask a man of the Church for proof of his word?" the Bishop said with a sarcastic smile. "My, you *are* a breath of fresh air, Mr Reynolds. As a bishop I'm used to spouting all kinds of rubbish for the avid consumption of unquestioning minds, Mr. Reynolds. But if proof you seek, then how about this; if one were to produce one of these twinned vials, would that surely not prove the existence of the other?"

As Reynolds watched in awed silence, from under the folds of his deep dark purple robes, the Bishop pulled a six-inch-long, jewel-encrusted silver crucifix attached to a broad leather strap. Holding the cross aloft, he twisted it in half, unscrewing it to reveal a hidden compartment in its base. He tipped the cross upside down, and a small, filigree-decorated, cork-topped glass vial fell into his open hand. Bishop Courtney plucked at it with his thumb and forefinger and tilted it towards the staggered moonlight through the window.

Reynolds stepped closer, carefully inching himself towards the Bishop, his jaw gaping open. "You're serious, aren't you? Is . . . is that it? The elixir of life?"

"Unfortunately, no. This is but the reversal solution, Mr Reynolds, practical only if consumed within one hour of the primary solution, but like I said, why on earth would someone wish to reverse immortality?"

Reynolds sighed noisily. "If your alchemists went to the trouble of making an antidote, perhaps they realised that eternal life could be just as much a curse as a blessing."

CHAPTER
THIRTY-TWO

The Consuming Mire

Like a whisper on the wind, Madame Destine heard a voice calling her name in the darkness. She blinked hard, and when she reopened her eyes, she was blinded. She waved her fingers in front of her face, feeling the breeze against her smooth, porcelain cheeks — but she still couldn't see. It was as if she were in a windowless, wall-less void, surrounded by reams of black curtains, frozen to the core of her being, too scared even to move. Suddenly, she felt herself grabbed by her shoulders. Someone was there in the blackness with her.

"Madame Destine! Madame, please wake," said a very anxious voice. "It is me . . . Butter. Please wake up."

Something stirred inside Destine, and it was as if she was drowning, but the voice was giving her buoyancy, something in the distance on which to focus her attention. She gritted her teeth and pushed with all her might through the folds of black silk that encapsulated her, breaching through the material, into the real world, gasping for air. She rolled her pale blue eyes, searching the room for a recognizable face. Finding Butter, she fell limply into his arms, and he guided her gently to a seat, laying a crocheted shawl across her shoulders.

"Madame, are you all right?" Butter asked.

Destine eyed Butter's bruised face and split lip. "I could ask you the same thing."

"I arrive not five minutes past and found you lying on floor, face twisted in terrible pain. You weep. Only a few moments ago you awoke," said Butter, caressing the Frenchwoman's hair. "You fainted perhaps, Madame?"

"It's nothing to be concerned about," Destine lied. "It was just a bad headache. But what on earth has happened to you?"

"I am well now, Madame, it looks worse than it is."

"I doubt that. Got into some trouble, did you? And how is Cornelius? Don't tell me he's gone and got himself killed?" Destine asked, half-jokingly.

"Not yet, but tomorrow is another day," said Butter.

"So? Tell me what happened."

"We were in search of Prometheus. Fish market. Heard noises, and were beaten by many unknown assailants, Madame. We became locked in large . . . er . . . the boss call it 'ice box'. But we survive. Prometheus arrive in the nick of the time!"

"*Prometheus?* You *found* him? Oh, thank God! Is he all right? Where is he now? I must see him," said Destine excitedly, as she tried to rise from her seat.

"Rest, Madame, is to be your first action, I think," said Butter, gently easing her back down again. "You do not look so well. Get back your strength."

"I am fine, *mon ami*. I have survived much worse than this."

"The boss has asked me to take you to him; they hiding at circus in Hyde Park until we get there. The boss desperately seeks you for what options to take. Seems lots of bad men in that Crawditch . . . one even know name of the boss. It is very late now, but in the morning time we shall leave."

"Of course, let me just get up." Again Destine tried to stand, and this time her legs gave out beneath her and she fell clumsily into the high-backed chair. "I think that headache took more out of me than I imagined."

"But that is uncommon, is it not?" asked Butter.

"Very. Although recently, getting more frequent, perhaps the older I get."

Butter cocked his head to one side. "Madame . . . it was a vision, yes? We spoke earlier of your worry over their clarity."

"I cannot hide anything from you, my friend," admitted Destine. "Sometimes, if I experience a particularly intense vision, my senses simply cannot cope with the overload — and my mind shuts my body down. I collapse."

"And this is what occurred today? May I ask . . . what was it about?"

"It was . . . something that I wish to keep private for the moment," Destine answered, teasing her bottom lip with her teeth. "I am sure it was nothing."

Butter did not remove his stare from her form. The concerned expression that engraved itself upon his face was obvious to Destine. She turned her head away to hide her own apprehension.

"Do you think this vision is to come true?" the Inuit asked. His innocent, almost childlike grasp of the English language made it difficult for Destine to ignore.

"Let me answer your question with another question, Butter," she said, a mask of dread swamping her features. "Would you betray the trust of someone you loved if you knew it was the only way to keep them alive?"

CHAPTER
THIRTY-THREE

The Lingering Dread

Bright and early the next morning, the lethargic daylight filtered through every window of Dr Marvello's Travelling Circus train, gilding the occupants in a golden hue. Madame Destine rose silently from her bed, her head still heavy from the previous night's premonition. She had never experienced one so real, so penetrating that it felt like she would be swallowed by the darkness, consumed by the void. She could still see the image of the grey-blue face when she closed her eyes, and it horrified her, just as the realisation that she recognized him — of that she had no doubt. She was sure that he was aware of her presence in the vision also, and that was possibly more terrifying to the Frenchwoman.

Usually, when Destine experienced a glimpse of the future, it was as if she was the only audience member in an empty theatre, watching a show designed purely for her viewing. The vision she had experienced the previous night was entirely different. Aside from being more real than she had ever previously felt, it was as if she was an unwilling participant in the unfolding performance. It was as if she was sitting in the front row of the theatre, inches from the stage. It was an unsettling feeling, as if she had somehow taken a step into a much darker, much more uncertain domain, and her confidence was in tatters — not least due to the face of the man. It was a face she knew only too well, but had buried deep inside her memory.

A loud knock rapped upon her cabin door, and Butter darted his head around the frame. "Bonjour, Madame! Are you soon ready for leaving?" he asked.

"What time is it?"

"Nearly six o'clock, Madame," Butter chirruped, with a smile.

"It is unforgivable of you to be so happy at this hour, *mon ami*," Destine teased, stifling a yawn. "So, how are we to get to Hyde Park?"

"I have spoken to station manager. There will be horse-cab waiting after one hour's time at front entrance. I will come for you in minute forty-five, Madame, and knock upon your door."

"Excellent," said Destine. "I shall need at least that long to look presentable."

"Nonsense, Madame," Butter said, slowly making his exit from the room. "I shall engage breakfast straight away and deliver just here outside your door. Eggs, toast and hot tea will be ready soon."

As Butter had promised, everything had proceeded according to his precise timetable. The man's organisational skills made him indispensable to the more lackadaisical Cornelius Quaint. The horse-drawn hansom carriage took nearly forty minutes to reach

Hyde Park from Grosvenor Park station, and Madame Destine felt every bump in the road, and every stone underneath its wheels. It was a welcome, if slightly uncomfortable distraction from the myriad thoughts racing through her mind. Once she was away from the station, the fog began to clear from her eyes.

With Butter to aid her, Madame Destine stepped down from the cab gracefully onto solid ground, decorated with a blanket of brown and green leaves upon the grass. She took a long sniff of the fresh winter air, and was instantly reminded of her home in France. There was a familiar scent on the wind. A crisp breeze skipped playfully around the hem of her long, billowing dress, but it was not something to darken her mood. Destine was safe now, amongst friends, and soon she would be by Cornelius's side — to her, the most safe and secure place in the whole world.

After a brisk five-minute walk through Hyde Park, Destine was able to see the site where the circus was in the final stages of construction. The huge yellow-and-red-striped Big Top tent, positioned proudly as soon as they reached the top of The Meadow's hill, immediately stole her attention. Five smaller tents were scattered like tiny islands around the main tent, all decorated with the same bright colours, and Destine took in the full magnificence of what the circus folk had achieved so far. She could just imagine the circus in the midst of its prime time come the following day, with hundreds of people milling about from stall to stall and tent to tent laughing, cheering and cooing with delight. Butter pointed out Cornelius Quaint, standing in the distance next to a small canvas tent, his hands on his hips, beaming widely.

He was wearing a short-cut, dark-purple velvet coat, reaching down just past his buttocks, over a thick, wide-collared shirt and a neat black waistcoat. A short, black silk scarf was wrapped around his broad, muscular neck, tucked into the velvet coat. Immaculate he may be, thought Destine, but this week had taken its toll upon him as much as her. In truth, this fact gave her little comfort.

Above Quaint, a lavishly painted sign reading "*The Mystical Madame Destine: Fortunes Foretold, Futures Revealed*" was hung above the opening entrance to the canvas tent, and Destine knew she was home.

"Good day, Madame, come on inside," said Quaint, motioning Destine inside the tent with a peck on her cheek. "I trust you are well rested?"

"I am feeling much better, Cornelius, thank you." As Destine got closer she inspected the man and his wounds more closely. She saw the same dappled bruises about Quaint's face that Butter shared, with a gash to his cheek and a nasty purple-black hue under the rim of his right eye. She silently reprimanded him with a stern glare, and his eyes looked to the floor.

"Don't look like that, Madame," protested Quaint. "It was hardly my fault."

"Some people are a magnet for trouble, like a wasp to jam, remember?" said Madame Destine, as she pushed past a dark curtain decorated with silver stars and glittering sequins. She stopped suddenly as she noticed the voluminous form of Prometheus, standing waiting for her with his arms wide open. Her eyes sparkled as she lifted her lace veil; and she skipped across the tent to embrace him affectionately, literally throwing herself into him.

"Oh, do come closer, my great big bear, I am so, so pleased to see you," she beamed. "I thought we would never set eyes upon you again. You have my condolences for Twinkle's loss. Our little star will forever shine in the heavens above, Prometheus, you can be certain of that. She will be missed greatly by us all."

"I miss her so much already, Madame," Prometheus replied.

Madame Destine's jaw dropped and she spun around to Cornelius.

"*Sacre bleu!* You can speak? What is this trickery?" she demanded. "Cornelius — did you know he can speak?"

"Yes, Madame," confirmed Quaint. "It's getting him to shut up that's difficult."

"Madame, c'mere yerself! Aye, an' it's good t'see *ye* again!" Prometheus said warmly, as he bent down and nuzzled his bristly beard into Destine's neck.

The Frenchwoman batted him off playfully. "*Mon dieu*, Prometheus, you smell like a dustbin! You need a bath."

"I can't argue with that, Madame," agreed Prometheus.

Destine stepped up onto her tip-toes and ran her hand along his cheek. "Since when have you been able

225

to speak, *monsieur*?" she asked. "You simply *must* tell me."

Prometheus laughed. "I thought you knew everything, Madame Fortune-Teller?"

"No, you are confusing me with Cornelius," Destine said with a wink towards Quaint. "Oh, it is so good to have you home and safe, Prometheus." Destine closed her eyes, and buried her head into the Irishman's expansive chest.

As emotional as she was at seeing him, his words served to bite at her even more. Her faith in her ability to see into the future had been a nagging worry that had plagued her mind non-stop since she had seen the face in the mist. With Prometheus back amongst those who loved him, surely things would start to get back to normal soon, she thought.

Soon, Madame Destine was up to speed with all current events, and Quaint had requested that she try her hardest to foresee which direction was the best one for them to take, one that would yield the best results in discovering just what was afoot in Crawditch. Quaint had often put his life into suspended animation until Destine had assisted him in finding the right road to follow. As his "compass", he knew that if she pointed him in a direction, it would always ring true. But now, sitting in her tent, with Cornelius Quaint and Prometheus's faces appealing for her counsel, Destine was fighting an inner turmoil of her own.

She recalled her question to Butter from the previous night: "Would you betray the trust of someone you loved if you knew it was the only way to keep them alive?" and those words stung at her conscience. She thanked the stars above that it was she and not Quaint who was able to perceive the emotions of others, for her fear was hidden just beneath the surface, almost on parade for all to see.

"Well, Destine?" asked Quaint. "What should we do? We have a number of possibilities presented to us, but one thing I *don't* want to do is deliver Prometheus back into Oliver Dray's hands! I think it better that I visit Crawditch, if only to find out who wanted me dead — well . . . frozen first, but *then* dead — and we also need to poke around at Blackstaff prison to find out more about how this Hawkspear chap escaped. We know he's involved in this business up to his neck, but we don't know who's pulling his strings."

"Hawkspear's as close t'the Devil as ye can get, Cornelius, bar the pitchfork and pointy tail, but he don't have the brains for subterfuge. I'm surprised he's hidin' an' not out in th'middle of the street dancin', braggin' about his crimes. He wanted me t'know it was him that killed Twinkle . . . he knows it's tearin' me up . . . an' I'll bet he's just lovin' the fact that everyone in Crawditch thinks of me as a killer," said Prometheus grimly, teasing his beard with his fingers. "Don't forget I'm still a wanted man right now, Cornelius, so I am. I need t'clear me name, man."

"Prometheus, I understand how important it is for you, of course I do. We need to listen to the Madame here, and await her advice," said Quaint. "Destine, if you wouldn't mind . . . what are our options?"

Destine's voice was tempered, and each syllable floated from her lips like the gentle caress of a butterfly's wings. "Cornelius . . . I will try my best to aid you, but you must agree to take heed of what I say."

"Don't I always?" Quaint asked, looking the picture of innocence.

Destine shot him a look that said "Are you joking?" and smiled. "You have an uncanny knack of prospecting my advice, Cornelius. You sift out the words that you do not like, and turn a deaf ear to them. What I am to reveal — if anything at all — will only give you the bare bones of what your options are. It will not spell out what to do, step by step, word for word. The future is not like that. If I get the feeling that a particular avenue is your best road to travel, I'll need your assurance that you'll listen to me."

"I'll *listen*, of course," Quaint said.

Madame Destine nodded. "But can you promise that you will *hear* me?" she asked with a knowing flicker of her eyelids.

Prometheus nudged at Quaint's elbow.

"What? Oh, yes, yes, Destine . . . I promise," said Quaint begrudgingly. "I will take heed if you say anything bad. Now come on . . . don't keep us all in suspense."

"Very well, I shall begin." Destine rested her fingertips on her temples and closed her eyes. She was thankful that no one in the tent realised just how nervous she was at that moment, or she would have been even more so. The vision of the man in the mist was a heartbeat away, and this was her first attempt at a connection to the future since then. Carefully opening her mind's eye just a fraction, like the aperture of a camera, Destine allowed the sensations to flow in, a maelstrom of emotions to anyone without her lifetime of training. She allowed herself to float above the cacophony, filtering the white noise to make sense of it all. Sometimes she was flooded with images, sometimes a spoken word, or a snatch of a conversation, and sometimes it was only a vague feeling, like a barely forgotten memory. It was not her ability to see the future that made Madame Destine so special — it was her ability to make sense of and translate what she saw.

Not without an appreciation of irony, predicting the future takes time and after a gruelling fifteen-minute wait, Quaint was getting restless.

"Madame, I don't wish to rush you," he said, "but time is of the essence here."

Destine's eyelids flickered as she removed herself from her entranced state, and looked up at Quaint's appealing face.

"Oh . . . sorry, Cornelius . . . I . . . have been given many powerful images and it is taking some time to determine their meaning," she said quietly.

"I understand, Madame . . . my apologies," said Quaint. "Well?"

"You wish to return to Crawditch, Cornelius, but I sense that that place contains nothing of interest for you. You will not learn anything more there. I am sensing many angered and fearful people. Fearful for their very lives, it seems. They aim their hatred at the police, and they are concerned that the killer in their midst remains unfound." Destine licked her lips gently. "I foresee a great deal of pain centred on the police station, Cornelius. You must avoid that place at all costs."

Prometheus stepped forward. "But *I* don't! Cornelius, I told ye, man — I need t'go back there and clear me name. The police're looking for the wrong person, remember? Which means they'll never catch Hawkspear!"

"Prometheus, how many *more* times must I explain? Especially now, you must not set as much as a single *footstep* in Crawditch. If Dray is under pressure from the locals, then the first thing he'll do is set up a public hanging for you. Handing yourself in at this stage won't help anyone," said Quaint abruptly, baring his teeth, such was his passion. "Madame, if not Crawditch, then where must I go? Where is the key to all this strangeness?"

"I sense a dark tower full of the screams of men," Destine said in nothing more than a whisper. "Within this tower lies the answer to a great many secrets. I cannot tell you more than this." Destine pinched the bridge of her nose, and raised her fingers to her forehead. "I feel rather weary all of a sudden. Cornelius, if you have no objections, I would like to rest."

"Certainly, Madame, please do," agreed Quaint. "You have been of great assistance as usual, and I am sorry to cause you distress. At least now, we have a direction to focus upon."

★　★　★

Quaint and Prometheus stepped outside the tent into Hyde Park. Upon seeing them exit, Butter trotted up to them, an expectant glint in his eyes.

"We have plan, boss?" he asked, tugging on Quaint's long coat tails. "Madame Destine was able to help?"

"Indeed she was, Butter. Things are going downhill fast in Crawditch, my friend, but there is a place that Destine referred to that could hold the key to this mystery. She can only mean Blackstaff prison. I shall go there right away." He turned to face a glum-looking Prometheus. "I don't want you going anywhere near Crawditch until I return, understand? And Butter?" said Quaint, spinning to face the Inuit. "Keep an eye on the Madame, will you? Until I return, be on your guard. We could get a visit from the law at any time, so Prometheus — keep out of plain sight if you can."

With that, Quaint turned on his heels, walked across the park towards Cromwell Road, and the exit from Hyde Park that would lead him to the nearside of the Thames. From there he could charter a tug to Blackstaff prison. Discovery of his foe — or foes — was starting to feel as if it were nearly in his grasp, but Quaint did not know whether that made him feel better, or worse.

Laid upon a temporary bed at the rear of her tent, the uncomfortable mattress was the least concerning thought upon Madame Destine's mind. She had just deliberately misled Cornelius, and dissuaded him from a course of action that would have supplied a great many answers. That betrayal was hanging heavily upon her thoughts. But what could she do? Her voices had spoken, and she had no choice but to listen to them. What use was the gift to perceive the future if you couldn't avert the tragedies that you foresaw? Destine knew for certain that if Quaint were to proceed to Crawditch as he intended, it would set him upon a road that led in only one direction — his death.

But she also knew that secrets never stay buried for ever. As the fog cleared from this mystery, the truth would certainly soon be revealed, and Destine knew that she could not hide her greatest lie for ever. As she had once told Cornelius, nightmares have a nasty habit of recurring, and usually when you least expect them.

CHAPTER
THIRTY-FOUR

The Equivoque Principle

Blackstaff prison was inescapable. Many had tried and all had failed. Constructed in 1841, it was England's first barge prison, unique in the respect that it was able to relocate to positions along the Thames, or out into the English Channel or the North Sea. Containing just over a hundred and fifty prisoners, the structure was akin to a lighthouse, a tall, circular iron and wood tower affixed to a huge, specially designed barge platform. Very few cells had adequate toilet facilities and none had windows. The fear of incarceration in Blackstaff was the thought that had kept many a wrongdoer on the straight and narrow, and those who were lucky enough to be released from the prison rarely committed a further offence. Its reputation alone was enough of a deterrent.

Cornelius Quaint had called in a few favours to organise this unscheduled visit to Blackstaff. Luckily, Warden Melbury had once seen Quaint perform his act and was a big fan of sleight of hand magic. Quaint was treated like visiting royalty.

The prison was currently moored near Colchester, and the North Sea winds were scratching against the iron and wood hide of the tower. Quaint sat opposite the tobacco-stained, bearded Warden in his dank, grey-painted office, sharing a tin cup of some foul-smelling liquid that the Warden had sworn blind was Jamaican rum. It was certainly unlike any rum that Quaint had tasted before, but he needed the Warden's help, and he politely forced down each sip through clenched teeth.

"Christ, you should 'ave seen it," said the Warden, rocking back in his chair. "We pulled in, right into the Thames, trying to find shelter, but when you're as exposed as we are, there ain't nowhere safe. This place is great as a prison, but in a fierce storm like that, it's a death-trap!"

"And how long were you marooned for?" asked Quaint, appeasing the gruff Warden's zest for conversation.

"Four days," Warden Melbury barked. "My men were pullin' their bleedin' hair out."

Quaint looked around the cramped quarters. "I'll bet. So tell me, Warden, how many men have you got here on your staff?" he asked, gingerly sipping the rum.

"Twenty including me, and another twelve more can be called at the east end of the Thames if we need them, but we rarely do. Now and again we might 'ave an emergency . . . maybe one of the idiots somehow sets their bed sheets alight, or summat like that. Aside from bein' at the mercy o' bad weather, Mr Quaint, we don't really get a lot of entertainment round 'ere."

"And Blackstaff's escape record? What's that up to nowadays?" asked Quaint.

"Same as always, mate — spotless! And if we catch anyone trying to escape — we kill the bastard," guffawed the heavy-set Warden, his rosy cheeks glowing with delight at being able to discuss his work with a civilised stranger. Working in the prison was such a monotonous job, with the same old faces day in and day out, the warden welcomed the interruption to his daily repetition. "We run a tight ship 'ere, let me tell you! Prisoners are kept in line . . . they 'ave to be. We've got some of the most vile, depraved monsters alive imprisoned here, so it doesn't bother *me* none if the lads need to get a bit . . . *physical* now and again, know what I mean?"

Quaint grinned. "Actually, it's one of your most vile, depraved monsters that brings me here, Warden. I'm hoping you can shed a little light on something for me. An Irishman by the name of Hawkspear, I understand that he recently escaped, and I am very interested in how he managed it."

The Warden scratched at his head, flakes of dandruff falling like snow onto his shoulders. "You don't mean ol' Tommy Hawkspear, do you?" he questioned.

"Yes, that's the one. I believe he must have escaped about five or six days ago."

A broad smile appeared on the Warden's round and pink face, his chilblained cheeks littered with fine red veins like centipedes. He pushed his black cap further back on his head and poked at his temples. "You trying to test me marbles, fella? Or you 'aving yourself a little

235

prank at me expense, eh?" he asked merrily. "Mate, Tommy Hawkspear didn't *escape*! He was bloody released!" chortled the Warden. "Just the other day, in fact, an' a right to do that was, an' all."

"Released?" said Quaint sharply. "But I thought he was supposed to be imprisoned for life? Two murders apparently — his brother and sister."

"Well, yeah — supposedly! But he got a Stay of Absolution, didn't he! Lucky sod too, 'cos he weren't makin' many friends 'ere, let me tell you."

"A Stay of Absolution? What's that?"

"Ah, it's what we call it when we get a priest in 'ere to request a prisoner's release," said Melbury. "They come in, tryin' to get the crims to join their bloody flock. Only so they can score extra points with 'im upstairs, I reckon. Repent and all your sins will be washed away, and all that guff! A police constable brought the release order with him by hand and, like I said, Hawkspear was one lucky bastard." Melbury leaned back in his creaking seat, taking a sip of rum. "Like he was gettin' the right royal treatment, it was!"

Quaint's eyes flared like black flames. "Warden, it's vital that I track down exactly *who* sanctioned that prisoner's release. Do you think you can help me with that?"

Melbury nodded slowly. "Oh, aye, for a small fee, maybe I can, mate."

"A small fee?" asked Quaint cautiously. "How much?"

236

"Not money! I'm talking about your magic tricks! I've always had a fascination with you blokes who can perform such feats. I wonder . . . would you mind teaching me a few things — just for fun, like — I ain't about to try and compete with you or 'owt!"

Quaint laughed. "In return for a look over your release files? Well . . . I suppose that is a fair trade, although we illusionists do have a strict code of ethics, you understand. I could tell you — but then you would be sworn to secrecy, you cannot divulge secrets of the magic order to a non-magician . . . Deal?"

Melbury spat into his palm and thrust out his hand. "Deal!"

"Excellent, Warden," cheered Quaint. "Do you have any playing cards at hand?"

A few minutes later, Cornelius Quaint was sitting opposite Warden Melbury across a round wooden table. Melbury was practically salivating, wiping his bristly face with his sleeve, eager to gain an insight into the spellbinding world of the illusionist. His eyes flicked from Quaint to the table, to the pack of playing cards in his hand, back to Quaint's face. Like an expectant puppy waiting patiently for a bone, he sat bolt upright in the chair, panting heavily.

"Warden . . . this trick is called 'The Equivoque Principle', and its secret is only known to a few souls upon this earth!" Quaint said, drumming up an air of mystery for the susceptible Warden's benefit.

"Oh, aye?" asked Melbury. "And this . . . EK . . . WE . . . VOKE . . ."

"Equivoque, yes."

"Yep, that's it! A good 'un, is it?"

"A good 'un?" asked Quaint, placing his hand upon his chest, displaying his pride for the illusion. "Sir, it is simply the best!"

"So what does it do then?" the hungry Warden asked.

"It is a lesson in the gift of misdirection, Warden . . . and you will have no protection over its power. The Equivoque Principle, as it is known, was first performed at the turn of the century by Chinese sailors, and then later adopted by my fellow illusionists for the purposes of astonishing entertainment," explained Quaint, and he placed the full deck of cards flat on the table. "You will be bound to obey my unspoken commands, and present to me everything that I desire to know. Interested?" Quaint took the anxious look of stupendous excitement on Melbury's face as confirmation.

"Am I ever!" cheered Melbury. "When do we begin?"

Cornelius Quaint offered him a playful wink. "My dear Warden Melbury . . . we have *already* begun."

The Warden clasped his clammy hands together excitedly, eating up Quaint's stage persona. "The lads are going to love this!" he cheered.

Quaint circled his hand in the air a foot above the deck of cards. "As you can testify, Warden, I have not interfered with the pack in any way. Indeed, this is your very own deck of cards, do you agree?"

"I do indeed, sir," agreed Melbury.

Quaint flicked a quick, last-minute glance at his audience. Appreciation of the spectator's gullibility was as much a part of The Equivoque Principle's power as anything, and Warden Melbury might just as well have had a target painted on his forehead. When selecting an audience member to come up on stage, the conjuror chose very wisely indeed. Melbury had already made his love of sleight of hand known to Quaint. That was his first mistake. A willing participant whose mind was already convinced of the wonders of magic did half of Quaint's work for him — in other words, the perfect stooge. Quaint picked up the cards and shuffled merrily, rolling his eyes to the Warden as if it were the most mundane part of the act, whereas, in truth — the shuffling of the cards was key to its success. The Equivoque Principle was as much about timing and preparation as misdirection.

After the cards had been well and truly shuffled, Quaint offered them to Warden Melbury. "I have split the deck thoroughly, would you concur?" he asked.

"Con . . . *cur?*" asked the Warden numbly.

"*Agree* . . . Would you agree?"

"Yes, yes, I would, Mr Quaint! 'Course I would."

"Splendid. Now, I want you to choose a card, any one, from that deck. Do *not* let me see it, whatever you do. Once you have selected any one of these cards from the pack — even a picture card such as the King of Diamonds, not only will I be able to name it for you — I will also do so blindfolded," confirmed Quaint. "And are you sure you do not wish to shuffle the cards

239

yourself to be sure? You are perfectly welcome, you know."

Warden Melbury shook his head adamantly. "Nope. S'all right. Carry on, mate."

Quaint smiled.

That was Melbury's next mistake.

Quaint fanned the cards out in front of him and looked over at the Warden.

"Pick a card."

Melbury sucked on his stout thumb, and conjugated as to his choice — as if it really mattered what card he chose anyway. He coyly stabbed his stout finger onto a card, and looked up excitedly at Quaint.

"This one!" he declared.

"Oh . . . really?" Quaint asked flatly. "Are you sure you want to choose *that* one? Not this one over here?" He pointed to another card.

An element of doubt suddenly crept into Melbury's mind. He changed his mind, and placed his finger on top of another card, but not the one Quaint was pointing at.

That was Melbury's third mistake.

"You are absolutely sure now?" Quaint asked. Melbury nodded firmly. "Excellent. Now, please take a good look at it. Just to make sure I cannot possibly cheat, I will go and stand over in the corner, and blindfold myself." Quaint did as he related, and stood in the dank corner of the room. He removed a handkerchief from his coat pocket, and proceeded to tie it around his head, covering his eyes completely.

240

Melbury thrust his card up close to his face, peering round the corner of it just to make sure Quaint couldn't see it. It was the King of Diamonds.

Quaint cleared his throat and continued: "Now if you would be so kind as to place your card back in the deck. Anywhere you like . . . the top, the bottom . . . anywhere. Remember, I cannot see where you place it, I am totally blindfolded. Once you have done that, Warden Melbury, please shuffle the cards again . . . as much or as little as you desire. Let me know when you are done."

His palms sweating, a permanent fixed grin on his face, the Warden did as he was instructed, and grunted, which Quaint understood to be his way of saying "I'm finished."

"Are you happy the cards are well and truly mixed, or do you wish to shuffle further?" asked Quaint, his nose pressed into the corner of the room. He knew Melbury would say no.

"No," said Melbury.

For the psychological aspect of the illusion to be successful, Quaint knew that the more control an audience member thinks he has, the less he has in reality. A good conjuror only gives what he can afford to lose, and Cornelius Quaint was a very good conjuror indeed. Quaint could almost hear the little cogs churning inside Melbury's head.

"Are you absolutely sure? I don't want you to make this *too* easy for me," chimed Quaint.

With that, Melbury looked shocked, and tried as silently as he could to shuffle the cards again without

Quaint hearing him. "No, it's fine. I'm ready!" he proclaimed.

Quaint spun around and removed his blindfold. "Wonderful. Thank you, Warden. Now if you wouldn't mind . . ." Quaint rejoined the table, and held out his hand to Melbury. The Warden handed him back the deck of cards.

With a glint in his eye, and a gleaming smile upon his face, Quaint took great pleasure in splaying out all the playing cards face down onto the table in a long line. This was the fun part, the part when he shocked and amazed his audience. To the conjuror of course, he was merely replaying a script, as he had done hundreds of times. In Quaint's particular case, The Equivoque Principle was the very first trick that he had learned and, truth to tell, it had always been one of his favourites. In the world of the illusionist it was fairly straightforward, and such a staple, tried and tested trick that it was rarely performed. The more colourful magicians and conjurors of Victoria's age tended to prefer a grand spectacle over skill. Tanks filled with water, women sawn in half, levitation — there was far too much escapology to be found in halls and theatres throughout Europe, and Quaint was reticent to be caught up in that trend. Relying upon trapdoors, rigged machinery and visual fakery was less about skill and more about craftsmanship. The art of sleight of hand prestidigitation would not die out if Quaint had anything to say about it.

"Now, Warden Melbury . . . the trick is for me to name your card," said Quaint. "I was blindfolded, with my back to you, six feet away — so do you agree that there is no way I could have influenced the cards in any way?" he asked, licking his lips.

"No way at all, far as I know."

"Jolly good. Well . . . let me see now," Quaint said, holding his finger in the air. He made a big effort, for the Warden's benefit, of pretending to commune with mystical forces, acting as if he were navigating his consciousness through a spiritual mire. After milking Melbury's lust for magic for a good minute . . . Quaint suddenly flicked open his eyes, and stabbed his finger down firmly onto a playing card on the table.

"This is your card, Warden Melbury!" he announced, grinning broadly.

Melbury glanced down at the card. Surely the conjuror was incorrect?

Quaint slid the card towards Melbury, tidied the remainder of his pack up into his hands, and stacked it to one side on the table. "Would you like to confirm?" Quaint asked. Of course he had known the card from the moment Melbury's podgy fingers had touched the deck. "The King of Diamonds, I believe."

Melbury's heart sank as he flipped over the playing card, and saw the image of the King of Diamonds. He slapped his hands to his face in amazement. "But how did you —? You were blindfolded!" squawked the flustered Warden, clapping his hands gaily. "Out of all them cards! How did you do it?"

Quaint smiled, and tapped the side of his nose. "I'll show you."

★ ★ ★

An hour later, and after another tot of rum to steady his nerves, Warden Melbury directed Cornelius Quaint to a large, circular door. He rattled around with a large iron key in its lock; the Warden swung open the door, and led Quaint down a spiralling staircase, deep into the bowels of the prison, to a dusty room, piled high with filing cabinets.

Melbury picked up a large stack of card files, and a mountain of loose papers. "You should find what you're looking for in 'ere, Mr Quaint. Sorry about the state of this place," he said, thumping the pile onto a rickety old table.

"Thank you, Warden," said Quaint, and after a good twenty minutes of trying to decipher what indexing system the prison used to store its files — only to discover that it seemed to be totally random — he found a file marked "*Releases: Oct/Nov '53*" and traced his finger along the paper, searching for a name. "Aha!" he exclaimed suddenly. "Warden, it says here that Hawkspear's release was authorised on Sunday evening by the office of Bishop Courtney of Westminster Abbey, countersigned by Constable Percy Jennings of Crawditch District Police Force." Quaint tapped his cheek with his finger, deep in thought. "If I were a believer in coincidences, Warden, I would be most intrigued."

Melbury scratched his head. "Crawditch he came from? Just the other side o' the river that place, innit?" he said, drumming his teeth with his fingernails. "Well,

I s'pose then that means that Hawkspear's release would've have to have been authorised by —"

The Warden was interrupted by Quaint's chair scraping across the floor as he stood swiftly. "Oh, you needn't bother telling me, Warden Melbury," he said through clenched teeth. "I know *exactly* who authorised it."

CHAPTER
THIRTY-FIVE

The Seeds of Hate

Back in his office in Crawditch, Commissioner Oliver Dray poured himself a generous amount of whisky and slumped into his chair. The stilted afternoon light stuttered through his window, suffusing its light with a misty sheen. Fog was already beginning to rise, streaming about the streets. The station house was close to the docks, and highly susceptible to the chilled mists carried in from the Thames.

A knock on his office door suddenly alerted the Commissioner, and he quickly stashed his glass inside a drawer. He beckoned the caller to enter, and hastily picked up a handful of forms and papers, trying to look busy. He relaxed considerably as Constable Jennings poked his head around the door.

"How do, guv'nor," Jennings said with a nod. He stepped inside the room, and pulled up one of the Commissioner's chairs. "Just thought I'd pop in for a bit. You know, to see what's what, an' all that."

"What's what, Jennings, is that I'm looking incompetent!" Dray snapped, a ruby flash flourishing in his cheeks. "Not only have we got this Irish lunatic leaving more bodies in his wake than the pox, but I've been informed that your mate Mr Reynolds's band of so-called 'professionals' couldn't even do away with Quaint and his bloody Eskimo."

Jennings nodded in agreement. "I'm findin' it all a bit hard to fathom meself. I mean . . . all these murders — we know exactly who's doin' it, but we're powerless to stop 'em! I know I'm prob'ly out of line here . . . but how come you're lettin' Mr Reynolds get away wiv it, sir?"

"I wouldn't go so far as say I'm 'letting' him," seethed Dray, "but what I will say is this: that man is party to some information that I'd rather wasn't made public, know what I mean?"

"Yes, sir . . . but p'raps it's all gettin' a bit out of hand."

"Out of bloody hand is right, laddie! Reynolds promised me Quaint would be dead by the week's end, and so far the bastard is still walking!"

Jennings picked at his fingertips. "I'm sorry, Commissioner, but what's Quaint done to you that makes you hate him so much? The Sarge said you an' him knew each other from ages back."

Commissioner Dray rested back into his chair. "Back when I was no policeman, and he was certainly no bloody circus magician. Yeah, our paths crossed for a short time," Dray began, removing his whisky glass from his drawer again. "I used to travel all over the world with my father, y'see, with his shipping business. We went to all sorts of places. The Orient, South America, Bolivia, Ecuador — all over. Quaint had spent most of his life — and a large part of his inherited

247

fortune, I gather — traipsing from one country to the next, searching for what, I don't know. We met in Peru, back in the late twenties, early thirties I think, when he hooked up with our band. We were both a lot younger men, back in those days ... I was in my middle twenties, but God knows about Quaint. He's probably always looked like a grizzly old bastard his whole life."

"So, this Quaint was some kind of ..."

"Opportunist," snapped Dray. "Or so he used to call himself, whatever *that* means. We found all these secret caves once, up in the Peruvian mountains, so we thought we'd stick around, searching for anything we could trade on back home. The locals were besotted with gold, you see, and the stuff was everywhere. They had these great big temples just full of the stuff, sitting around gathering dust! The tribe located there were simple folk, content to just sit in the sun and pray. So ... seeing as it was all going to waste, my father decided that we'd make good use of all that gold ourselves." Dray paused, watching the flicker of glee upon the youngster's face ignite.

"Now, my old man, he was a rogue in his youth, an' no mistake, but he was one shrewd operator. He'd been tipped off by a ruthless young French thug — a man who seemed to care even less for the locals than we did. A right nasty piece of work, he was ... up until Quaint shot him, but that's another story. So, Father cooked up a deal to take over the tribe, and ship out all the gold back to England, where we'd all be rich men. So, we pitched up our camp, and made ourselves at home.

We'd only been there a short time, when Quaint turned up and started shouting the odds at my father."

"What's up with the bloke? Didn't he want to be rich?" asked Jennings.

"Quaint's the kind of person who loves to get involved, laddie. He'd set himself up as some kind of high authority or something, like he was better'n the rest of us. He stood up on the moral high ground and preached about this and that. How we were 'messing with other cultures' and should learn to leave well alone!"

Jennings laughed like a guilty schoolboy.

Dray continued. "When the final move came to overthrow the village by force, Quaint stood against us — against my father. Everything went haywire, and if it weren't for me, my father would've put a couple of bullets in him for sure. There was a big set-to with the villagers, and Quaint managed to turn the bloody lot of 'em against us. We had to grab what we could and get out of that place."

"And that was the last you saw of Quaint, eh?"

"Well, you know what they say about bad pennies, Jennings," said Dray. "I made a deal with your mate Reynolds. He's supposed to be making sure that the bastard gets what he deserves . . . in exchange for me keeping our boys off Hawkspear's scent, and out of his business."

"Right, I've got it now," said Jennings. "That Reynolds bloke has been blackmailin' you. Can't you just buy 'im off, like? Can't we just lock 'im up

249

somewhere? Or, better'n that, 'ave someone sort 'im out, good an' proper?"

"It's not that easy, Jennings," said Dray sharply. "I've never even met the man — he uses you as his bloody messenger boy. I can't risk that information getting out. It'd be a bloody disaster."

"So, what's he got on you then? Somethin' from the old days?"

"Not on me, Jennings — on my father. Back in Peru, he was involved in a couple of . . . I guess you could say 'questionable' cargo deliveries . . . the type that you don't make receipts for."

"What . . . like smugglin', you mean?"

Dray scratched at his chin. "Big strong folk, those Peruvians. They fetch a pretty penny, and the women . . . very *exotic*, laddie, y'know what I mean?"

"What, your father was smugglin' . . . *people*?" asked Jennings. "Slaves, you mean?"

"And somehow, this Reynolds fellow has found himself in the possession of evidence against my father. If it ever got out — not only would it kill my father, but it'd probably drag me down with him."

"Crikey! And ain't your old man some kind of lord?" asked Jennings.

"Sir George Dray, successful businessman, and personal friend to a lot of people in high places, so he is. Royalty, aristocracy, clergy . . . just about anyone who's got any clout in this damn country these days," said Dray, forcing a mouthful of whisky down his throat. "He'd be crucified if this knowledge ever came out."

"Maybe Reynolds is in league with Quaint? Maybe Quaint told 'im all he knows?"

"Blackmail's not exactly Quaint's style, Jennings," smiled Dray.

"So what can we do, guv?" asked Jennings eagerly.

"Against Reynolds . . . not one damn thing," said Dray dourly, running his finger over his teeth. "Against Quaint though . . . now that's another thing entirely."

CHAPTER
THIRTY-SIX

The Restless Doubt

Madame Destine watched meekly from behind the folds of her tent's entrance, as Prometheus argued furiously with Butter nearby. The discharge of the Irish giant's voice almost blew the tiny fellow off his feet, but to his credit, the Inuit stood his ground.

"That's easy for ye to say, lad, it's not *ye's* head on the block, is it!" Prometheus yelled. "How'd ye feel if ye couldn't even close your eyes at night in case the law decides to sneak up on ye?"

"Ye might find this hard t'believe, Butter, but Cornelius ain't right all the time! We don't all see him with rose-tinted specs like ye do." Prometheus spun on his heels and set off down the slope of the lawns. "Stay here with the Madame . . . that's where ye can do all the helpin', lad."

"I heard 'im well enough, laddie," snarled Prometheus. "But the locals in Crawditch are knockin' down the police's door, bayin' for me blood. If I don't do this now, what d'you think's goin' to happen? They'll find me, man . . . they will! I'll be tucked up asleep one night and get a wee knock on me door. They'll chain me up and they'll drag me away . . . I won't know when and I won't know where."

"Wait until Mr Quaint returns."

"No, Butter — I'm goin' back t'Crawditch t'face what's comin' — before it comes after me first. Geddit? At least this way I get t'have a say in me own fate!"

Butter buried his head in his hands. "Then . . . take me with you. I might be helping."

Prometheus stared at the man as if he had just discovered an entirely new species of human being. "Take ye with me, are y'insane, man? A second ago ye were tellin' me how I wasn't s'posed t'be going *anywhere* — and now you want to come n'all?"

"If I am to come, then when the boss ask why I did not stop you, he will know that I force myself to accompany you for own good."

Butter watched silently as Prometheus's voluminous silhouette walked off into the distance. "That man is almost as stubborn as the boss," he muttered under his breath. The Inuit chewed on his lip, considering his options, but within a few minutes, the Irish giant had disappeared completely from view. "Now Prometheus is able to talk again properly, no doubt he gets himself in even *more* trouble."

"Indeed he will, Butter," whispered Destine, spying unseen and unheard from her tent. "Prometheus should have heeded Cornelius's warning . . . for the only thing waiting in Crawditch is death."

253

CHAPTER
THIRTY-SEVEN

The Enemy Unmasked

As far as the Crawditch police were concerned, Prometheus was still number one suspect for the series of murders that had recently taken place, and as the man himself rounded a corner on the outskirts of the district, not far from The Black Sheep tavern, he smiled at a roughly sketched picture of himself — all beard and bald head — tacked to a wooden support beam of a grocery store. The word "WANTED" was written in bold letters underneath. Various people ghosted past him, and around him, a few looking over their shoulders at the vastness of the man, but no one stuck around long enough to pay him much mind.

It was mid-afternoon, and the Irishman was idly strolling down the centre of Merchant Street, with his concentration focused upon reaching the police station as quickly as he could. For his plan to work, and his name to be cleared, he needed to enter the station willingly, for no one would believe his story if he were captured and brought in. He saw the unmistakable blue-painted double doors of the station up ahead, closed tight against the November wind, and a large pang of uncertainty suddenly formed inside his

254

stomach. He knew he was feet away from freedom, but a part of him also knew that despite what he had said to Butter earlier, one of the most annoying qualities of Cornelius Quaint was that he was seldom wrong.

Prometheus grabbed the door handle, and was just about to open it when he heard the heavy pounding of footsteps coming in his direction. Looking around, he spied a low-lying fence, and leapt over, landing on his backside in the dirt. Pushing through the fence into a wall of large conifer trees, he tried his best to hide himself, aware that if there was one thing a seven-foot-tall man is no good at — it was hiding. His heart pumped like a jackhammer at the sudden flurry of activity, and he pressed his head tight to the wall, praying the enclosing trees would shield him. After a time, Prometheus heard the station door closing, and all was quiet in the main street once again.

Once Prometheus was confident that the officers had gone, he was just about to dart out into the street again when he heard raised voices behind him. He dove back into the branches of the trees as stealthily as he could considering his size, and moved cautiously towards the sounds of the conversation.

He soon reached another fence, and the voices were mere feet away. Something like the inevitable pull of a magnet dragged him towards the chatter. There were two voices, clearly heard. One was a broad Scottish accent, and the other, a far younger, local voice that Prometheus recognised instantly as belonging to one of the constables who had briefly visited him in his cell at the station. He couldn't remember the name, but he knew that the Scot was the young constable's superior officer. Prometheus held his breath, and his nerve, and concentrated on the two policemen's conversation.

"I thought you said this Reynolds beggar would be here at two o'clock, Jennings?" questioned Commissioner Dray, standing at the rear entrance to Crawditch police station. "It's now getting on for three, and if he doesn't show up in five minutes, the deal's off and I walk, you get me?"

Constable Jennings shifted on his feet nervously. "He'll *be* here, sir. He came to me, remember? He *has* to turn up!"

As if on cue, Jennings and Dray heard the scuffing of feet, and soon, dressed in a long overcoat and sporting a flat cap pulled down low to hide his scarred face, Mr Reynolds clambered over the station's yard gate, landing gracefully like a cat on the other side. As if he were another person entirely from the man who had graced the Bishop's lush apartment in Westminster Abbey, Reynolds seemed to carry himself differently now. The same cocksure attitude was still there, but his back was less hunched, he seemed wirier, and the fire that danced within his pale eyes made him look far more dangerous than Constable Jennings had previously seen. Reynolds approached Dray and held out his hand.

"*Bonjour*, Oliver, it's been a long time," he said. The Cockney drawl was suddenly gone, and there was a new, melodic accent to his voice.

"You!" Commissioner Dray was stunned at the image of the man before him, and he strode over to

Reynolds, pacing around him silently, as if he were a phantom. He took Reynolds's hand and shook it limply. "My God . . . it . . . it really *is* you!" Dray said, as if all his strength had been sapped by the image of the man, like Samson after Delilah had sheared his hair. He blinked hard; clamping his eyes shut tight, and then opened them quickly — expecting the mirage to disappear. But, to his dread, it remained. "But . . . but I thought . . . you were *dead*!"

"I got better," said Reynolds.

Jennings scowled at the man. "Boss? What d'you mean dead? This 'ere chap's my Mr Reynolds . . . d'you know 'im or somethin'? I thought you said you'd never met him?" the young constable asked.

"Oh, I know him all right, lad," the Scotsman replied. "Does Quaint know that you are still alive, that is the question?"

"Not yet, Oliver," grinned Reynolds, "but he soon will."

CHAPTER
THIRTY-EIGHT

The Conjuror Returns

At that exact moment, Cornelius Quaint returned to Hyde Park. The white sky was beginning to turn pale grey, as the invisible sun prepared for the long, chilly night to come. Quaint turned up the collar on his coat, and strode briskly across the park, catching sight of the circus in the distance, now taking on even more shape, practically completed. Quaint made a mental note to congratulate his team.

As he approached Madame Destine's tent he whistled the national anthem, the tent having no door upon which to knock and announce himself.

"It's me, Madame. I have returned, and I'm exhausted. Tell Butter to boil some water, will you . . . I need a brew. On second thoughts, crack open that cognac I know you've got stashed in your tent."

Destine pulled the tent entrance to once side, and swiftly dragged Quaint inside. Ruby Marstrand was seated at a round table set for two, a crystal ball in the centre of the table. There was an uncomfortable silence tangible in the tent, and Quaint's curiosity was immediately piqued.

"Madame?" he gasped. "Oh, sorry Ruby, I didn't realise you were busy. Shall I come back later?"

"Oh, Cornelius — it is you!" Destine said, her veiled face unable to hide her anguish. Her voice faltered as she saw him.

"Well, of course it's me, Madame," he said, gripping hold of the Frenchwoman's shoulders firmly, as she fell into his embrace. "You look scared to death, woman. Who were you expecting it to be?"

Ruby stood from the table and joined Destine's side. "Ah, well, we thought that maybe it was . . . Prometheus coming back, you see."

"Coming back? Coming back from where?" asked Quaint.

Ruby looked towards Destine for assistance.

"Back from where?" repeated Quaint. "Where is he? One of you must know."

"Um, have you asked Butter?" Ruby said, resting her hand on Destine's shoulder. "Maybe he'll know. We saw him talking to Prometheus earlier, didn't we, Destine."

Quaint stared at Ruby's expression. Her toffee-coloured eyes were wide, and her swathe of thick hair was entwined around her fingers, the very image of someone trying their hardest to look innocent. Madame Destine was no different, deliberately avoiding eye contact with him.

"Very well, ladies," Quaint said sternly, placing his hands flat on the table in front of him. His bold black eyes zeroed in on Destine and Ruby with an uncompromising glare. "Tell me everything . . ."

CHAPTER
THIRTY-NINE

The Warning

"How in God's name did you survive?" yelled Commissioner Dray.

"God had nothing to do with it," replied the man called Reynolds, a native French accent suddenly rising to the fore.

"Yeah, but . . . but Quaint shot you right through the heart!"

"Serves me right for not having one, then doesn't it?" smiled Reynolds.

"First Cornelius Quaint turns up out of the blue, and now *this*? What is it — the week for skeletons in my wardrobe? I knew someone was pulling my strings, man, but I had no idea it was *you*," Dray said, and was forced to steady himself against the wall. "My God . . . all this time . . . you've been *alive*? Why didn't you tell anyone? Why did you let people *believe* it?"

"Oh, come, Oliver, what would you have done if you had known the truth?" Reynolds challenged, his thick, European accent showing itself more freely now that the façade he had used as a mask was no longer needed. "Would you really have been pleased to see me? Would you have said: 'It has been fifteen years since you murdered for my father, Antoine, how's tricks?' Don't make me laugh!"

Jennings removed his helmet, and mopped at his brow with a handkerchief. "Hang on a mo, boss," he said. "I'm gettin' a bit out've me depth here. How do you know Mr Reynolds?"

"Reynolds is merely a *nom de plume*, Constable," said Reynolds, "as dear Oliver knows very well. But I did not come here for formal introductions; I came to pass on a friendly warning."

Dray responded with a guttural growl. "So, you've been masquerading as this 'Reynolds' character all along? Right under my nose? Using my own constables to do your dirty work? Blackmailing me with my father?" He clawed at his thin strands of hair. "I just can't understand it . . . but why go to all that bother? Not just for Cornelius Quaint's benefit, is it? Wouldn't you prefer to see the look on his face when you turn up alive and well after all this time?"

"Revenge against Quaint is just a bonus for me, Oliver. It is personal," said the Frenchman, stepping closer to Dray. "This is *business*. I'm revealing my identity to you *now*, should our paths cross again in the near future." Reynolds swept a thick strand of hair from his forehead. "*Quid pro quo*, remember? You're no fool, Oliver; you know how the Hades Consortium operates."

Dray inhaled sharply at the words. "The Hades Consortium has interests here? In . . . in Crawditch? I . . . I didn't know. Why did I *not* know?"

"The Consortium is not likely to broadcast its involvements. Our projects have strict time schedules to adhere to. It was not necessary for you to know what did not concern you, Oliver. Although you are unaware, I have been trying hard to save your neck all week, *monsieur*."

"But . . . but why are you here?" asked Dray. "Why now?"

The Frenchman's nostrils flared. "Let's just say that the Consortium requires something of value in this pitiful little borough, and they sent me to negotiate its collection. Of course, when I heard my old friend Cornelius Quaint was en route to London as well . . . I just had to stick around for a few more days and have a little fun with him."

Listening intently from within the seclusion of the nearby conifer trees, Prometheus felt a cold chill run up his spine as he heard the words. He knew very well from the intent in the Frenchman's voice that he was anything but a friend to Cornelius. What he was hearing now was a conversation that he needed to pass onto his employer urgently, and his secret position, hidden from sight, was essential. The more he heard and the longer he pushed his luck concealed within the nearby bushes, the more information he would have to pass on. Such was his concentration on his own stealth that he was completely oblivious to the person sneaking up slowly from behind.

* * *

"So, all this *Hawkspear* nonsense . . . that's you as well, is it?" Dray questioned.

"Certainly not." The Frenchman laughed under his breath. "Well, he's partly my fault, I suppose, but we're both working for someone else . . . someone other than the Consortium, someone with *heavenly* connections."

Constable Jennings glanced across from Dray's to Reynolds's faces. "I'm totally bloody lost, I am. This is all gettin' a bit too confusin' for me."

Reynolds grinned at Jennings's naïvety. "Oliver, I wanted to let you know that no matter what my business is here in London — Cornelius Quaint will get his just reward. I have been waiting so very long, patiently biding my time, just for the right moment. I know just how to test him to his limits — and I know what his weaknesses are." The man flicked his tongue about his lips, savouring the images he took from his words. "Oedipus had nothing on me!"

Prometheus's temper had reached critical mass, and he was starting to get white spots before his eyes, he had restrained himself for so long. He clenched his jaw and prepared to leap into the yard, tearing this newcomer limb from limb. Just before he leapt, his muscles like a coiled spring, he felt a firm tug on his sleeve. He spun around sharply. At his side, Butter grinned up at him mischievously, and held his finger to his lips.

★   ★   ★

"Right," said Dray, quaffing a swig of whisky from a silver hipflask. "So, in exchange for keeping your mouth shut about my family's dealings . . . what more do you want from me, hmm?"

"Nothing," said the gaunt man with a shrug. "Not a thing. I didn't come here for more demands, Oliver. Like I said, I am only here to offer you a warning."

"For free?" scoffed Dray.

"The Hades Consortium has invested a lot of time and money in your career, Oliver — remember that. They are not about to throw away one of their best assets." The man walked over towards the tall gate, unlocking the bolts at the top and bottom of the frame. "Your life is in danger, and soon someone will arrive and try and take it. I have gone to extreme measures to ensure that that someone was not *me*. You have enemies, Oliver . . . and they do not bow down to the law. If I were you, I would keep my eyes open, and never walk alone, no matter what time of day or night. I'll be seeing you. *Au revoir, monsieur, et bon chance.*" He stepped out into the lane that ran parallel behind the station, departing from the yard. The gate swung shut on the yard, leaving a dumbstruck Dray and Jennings to themselves, as if Reynolds had never been there at all.

Jennings skipped over to the swinging gate and went out into the lane. "He's gone, sir. Nowhere to be seen," he said.

"Like a ghost . . ." muttered Dray.

"So tell me . . . if he weren't Mr Reynolds . . . who the bloody hell was he anyway?"

Dray puffed out his cheeks, and made a point of exhaling loudly. "That man is trouble with a capital 'T', lad, and you'd do well to forget about him," he said, catching Jennings's eye. "But I'll tell you this much, laddie . . . if things were bad for Cornelius Quaint before . . . they've just got ten times worse."

CHAPTER
FORTY

The Betrayal

Cornelius Quaint stormed out of the fortune-teller's tent, with Destine trailing after him. "He's done *what?*" he raged. "After I explicitly told him *not* to? This is intolerable, Destine, it really is! I'll have to get there right away."

"No, Cornelius, I beg of you — wait," implored Destine. "He's been gone for hours, just after you left for the prison. You'll never catch up with him."

"Why on earth didn't you try to stop him?"

"What chance would I have of stopping a thundering titan like him? He is more involved in this than even you are, Cornelius. Do not forget that he stands accused of murdering the woman he loved. He just needs to *do* something."

"Madame, how could I forget?" Quaint paused, rubbing at the back of his head as he tried to think what to do next. "This is just typical. Just when we actually *get* somewhere, we end up taking two steps *back.*"

"I can see you're angry, Cornelius, but Prometheus is a big boy. He knows what he's doing, of that I am sure."

266

"He *thinks* he knows what he's doing, you mean! I told him that Crawditch was a dangerous place for him to be, and I warned him about Dray — but he's just ridden roughshod over it. I wanted him kept away from that place because I saw the look of desperation in Dray's eyes — they *need* him to be their killer, Madame, he's all Dray's got, and he's too perfect a fit to let slip through his fingers . . . the leopard has not changed his spots after all."

Destine placed her hand upon Quaint's shoulder, bringing the man towards her as she did so. "Cornelius . . . Prometheus feels his very soul is in torment, and unless he walks right into that police station — and at least *tries* to get them to listen to him — he will always feel the hunted quarry."

Quaint pulled away from her embrace, rubbing at his forehead furiously, as if trying to remove a dirty smudge. "Hell's teeth, Destine, now of all times — why did he have to go to Crawditch alone? With what I learned at Blackstaff, that district is the last place on earth that Prometheus can expect to see justice." Quaint rubbed his palms into his eyes, trying to clear the day's remnants from his head.

Destine moistened her lips, almost petrified to ask the question that formed itself in her mind, but she had to know what Quaint had discovered, perhaps giving her just enough breathing space to try and explain her actions to him. "And what did you learn, my sweetheart?" she asked.

"I learned much, Madame. Not only was someone named Bishop Courtney responsible for Tom Hawkspear's release, but also, more importantly than that . . . it seems I have been extremely foolish. I have misjudged someone very dearly . . . at the cost of others' lives. It seems there is betrayal on all sides in this caper, it surely knows no limits," said Quaint, striding away from the tent, the wind whipping at his clothes fiercely. "I just don't know who I can trust any more."

Destine gulped hard, remembering the haunting realisation of her deepest and greatest fear. The fire within Cornelius's eyes was something she had seen many times before.

"I have uncovered the person responsible for this whole damn mess, Madame," he countered, "and you'll not believe the trouble he's gone to, purely to get his revenge upon me, although I can't blame him — considering our history. I had thought never to set eyes upon him again, but it seems Fate had other ideas. Our foe is none other than —"

"My son," blurted out Destine. "Our foe is . . . Antoine Renard . . . yes I know," she said. The words tumbled from her mouth clumsily as if she were unburdening herself of a great weight.

Quaint spun on his heels, glaring at Destine. If the fire within his eyes was ablaze before, it was positively volcanic now.

"What . . . did you just say?" he asked.

"I know how you must feel, Cornelius, and I share your horror, believe me," protested Destine, pacing in circles around and around on the grassy verge. "I had a most terrifying vision of him myself just yesterday that shook me to the core. I . . . I'm so sorry that I could

268

not tell you sooner . . . please believe me, but I knew how it would affect you." The Frenchwoman buried her head in her hands and sobbed a distraught, weighty sob that came from the very depths of her soul.

Quaint approached her shattered form, mere inches from her face. His voice was calm and quiet, yet bubbling with rage. "Madame . . . what is this you're saying to me? Antoine Renard? Now, that's a name not spoken in my presence for a very long time . . . and you know damn well why."

"But . . . you said . . . you knew who was to blame," sniffed Destine.

"I do . . . or at least I *thought* I did. I was about to name Oliver Dray — for it was his man Jennings who countersigned Hawkspear's release papers. What has this to do with your son? The man's been dead fifteen years!"

"I had thought so myself . . . until recently. My premonitions were coming erratically, they made less and less sense, and after each one, I was left feeling exhausted. I had a vision such as this yesterday, a vision unlike any other, Cornelius. I felt an intense punch hit me right in my mind's eye . . . the last time I felt one as strong was in 1838 . . . the night you shot Antoine dead."

"Not dead enough, obviously," said Quaint.

He made several attempts to begin a sentence, to say something to Destine that would encapsulate just how he felt about her betrayal, but nothing seemed appropriate. He grabbed handfuls of his coat's material, squeezing them tight into his fists. He yanked, stretched

269

and tugged harshly at the coat, serving as a surrogate for the vocalisation of his anger. Tears flooded his dark eyes, and his lips trembled nervously. He couldn't even look at Destine, for he feared his heart would shatter into a million pieces.

"Cornelius, please say something," said Destine, approaching Quaint, but he turned away brusquely, leaving the fortune-teller's hand grasping nothing but air. "Please . . . let me explain. I knew that learning of this without confirmation would terrorise you. It would blind you; intoxicate your ability to think clearly."

Quaint's voice was shaky, his jaw clenched tight. "Madame," he began, turning away from her beseeching stare. "This is true, then? Is Renard still alive?"

Madame Destine lowered her head onto her chest, the word "Yes" barely audible.

"And . . . and why did you not sense him before? If he's been involved in this from the beginning, why did your foresight not give you — give *me* — warning?" blazed Quaint, the tears flowing freely now from his face, following the tracks of his ingrained wrinkles. "Fifteen years ago . . . when I pulled that trigger, I thought the man responsible for my wife's death — your blasted devil of a son, Antoine Renard — had finally faced justice, that I'd completed a circle of hate that'd been raging for so long. And now . . . you're standing there . . . after keeping this from me for God knows how long, telling me that I have been living naught but a *lie!*"

270

"No, Cornelius, I only suspected his return recently
. . . nothing definite. He appeared on the periphery of
my premonitions," protested Destine. "I had no way of
knowing for sure."

"Oh? And what clues do you have *now* that make
you so sure he's alive?"

"The vision I had last night . . . it was him, Cornelius
. . . and as much as I would like to deny it, he's my son.
Antoine shares my blood, and he and I do seem to have
an unnaturally clairvoyant link. Perhaps our kinship
shielded him from me before."

"What excellent timing," snapped Quaint.

"I do understand your anger, my sweet . . . as much
as I understand how much of a bloody monster he
was . . . and still is."

"Don't remind me," Quaint yelled. "For it was my
trust of you and your bloody monster of a son that
invited him into our house, remember? Where was your
damn foresight then? Notably absent — as it is *now* it
seems!"

Quaint stared blankly into Madame Destine's eyes,
unable to resist his memory recalling the first time that
he had met Antoine Renard, when the Frenchman was
nineteen and Quaint was twenty-four. As Destine had
been his governess from the age of seven, Quaint was
aware that she had a son. He had been educated and
raised by his father in Paris whilst Destine estranged
herself from her family to live in England — for what
reason, Quaint never asked. The subdued, inward-
looking boy had left his family home in Paris to seek
out his mother.

Antoine Renard's confidence was shattered by the break-up of his family, a condition made worse by years of indoctrination by his father. The young man had been raised to hate his mother, in fact only seeking her out to quell his curiosity rather than rectify any broken maternal bonds. But Antoine's own rage was not solely the by-product of his father, for the Frenchman was capable of breeding his own seeds of hate all by himself. He became convinced that Cornelius was the root of his evil, the reason why his mother had left Paris, the reason why she had never come to collect him, the reason why she had created a surrogate son in Cornelius — to replace him.

This bitter hatred festered, kept just under the surface of Renard's skin. He would search for anything with which to best Cornelius at, be it sports, intellect or duelling and, locked in a constant battle of one-upmanship, he and Cornelius were destined for disaster. The rivalry continued for nearly two years — until one fateful night when Antoine found himself alone with Cornelius's wife Margarite. Seeing Cornelius as his enemy, Antoine savagely assaulted Margarite, then fled the Quaint homestead, with the knowledge that it was one victory he would forever hold over Cornelius.

Cornelius returned home to find his bloodied wife barely alive, and she died in his arms that same night. It was only many years later that the Quaint family doctor informed the conjuror that Margarite had been pregnant at the time of her death. Pregnant with a child he would never see, never hold, never love. From that moment, a fuse was lit inside Quaint's heart that raged on unchecked as he spent the rest of his young years trekking across the globe on one fruitless quest after another. The search for Renard consumed him.

Horrified at what her son had become, Madame Destine turned away from Renard and promised to aid Quaint in his quest to bring Renard to justice. It took a further decade of uncovering many deceits and false trails before they found Renard, now working as a murderer for hire across Europe, selling his trade to the highest bidder. With Quaint's and Renard's paths seemingly irrevocably linked, a final confrontation between them was inevitable, and after many close calls and near-misses, in Paris in 1838 Quaint found himself face to face with Renard once again. The two opponents fought, and Quaint shot Renard in the chest. The Frenchman toppled over a wall into the River Seine — seemingly to his death — and Quaint had thought that was the last time he would ever hear the name "Antoine Renard". Hearing it again now, spoken by Renard's blood mother, Quaint felt a lancing jolt of pain hit him square in the gut.

"Please, Cornelius . . ." pleaded Madame Destine. "I am not your enemy. I did not commit his crimes! Until yesterday, I *too* thought Antoine dead." She reached out to him, resting her hand upon his wrist. "I could not have even *guessed* that he had returned. I did not set out to deliberately deceive you."

"Oh, but you *did* deceive me none the less, Madame."

"No! I merely did not mention all my feelings . . . my instincts."

"Renard is alive, and you *knew* it! How many more times have you misled me over the years, hmm? Or chosen not to *mention all your feelings*, as you put it?" Quaint tousled his curled locks severely. "I've known you since I was seven years old, and not once have I been forced to question your loyalty to me . . . until now."

"Cornelius, no!" wept Destine. "I have not betrayed you."

"I don't know how to *feel* about you any longer, Madame . . . knowing how I feel about *him*!"

"I have been torn! Since I began sensing these *feelings* about my son, they have dominated my thoughts. Should I tell you my fears and risk you running off to your death? What if I was wrong? What if it was all a mistake and I had reopened old wounds for nothing? I did not know what to do for the best, Cornelius."

"And so you did *nothing*?"

"Cornelius — please! I have been distracted."

"No, Madame . . . you have been distracting *me*."

"Only to keep your path from crossing Renard's!" Destine cleared her throat, the tears choking her, the guilt constricting her. "I only wished to guide you away from him . . . keep you safe."

Quaint grabbed her wrist, and forcefully removed her hand from his shoulder. "Your so-called *advice* has been leading me astray all week, hasn't it? Sending me to the fish warehouse in search of Prometheus? Sending me off to Blackstaff instead of Crawditch? I take it that was designed to delay me too?"

"I . . . I had to make sure your path did not cross Antoine's until I could fathom whether it was real. I have only been trying to protect you, my sweet. If I had told you of Antoine's return we both know what you would have done."

"I would have tracked the bastard down and squeezed the life out of him!" snapped Quaint.

"*Oui*, and what if he had done so to you instead? What then? How then would I have felt, knowing that I had led you to your demise? Think about it, Cornelius — this deceit may have *you* at the centre of the web, but the slightest touch to that web sends out shockwaves that cause disruption for all," Destine dabbed her eyes. "I . . . I had one such premonition that burned itself into my conscious mind."

"What? A vision of me discovering the truth?" asked Quaint.

"No. It was of you and my son. You were both locked in an eternal combat. Surrounded by corpses — victims of the battle that raged between you — and you were blind to them all, Cornelius. All you could see was your rage . . . pure and unrestrained. I was lying there too . . . as were Prometheus, Butter, Ruby . . . everyone we love was dead — because of your and Antoine's conflict — now, if I had to risk your loyalty in order to prevent that future from coming to pass, then *that* is my fate! That is my punishment."

Quaint wiped at his eyes with his sleeve. The afternoon light had faded completely now, and it was dusk. The cold wind bit at his tears, and his body felt weighed down by all that he had learned. He felt his age for the first time in many years. Quaint turned around and looked at the woman before him, a woman who had been an unfaltering constant in all his life. Now, it was like looking at a complete stranger. He wanted to run to her, to embrace her, and forgive her — but something inside his heart held him back. Something was tearing him away from her, and there was nothing he could do to regain his footing. Perhaps words were simply not enough.

"One question that I must know the answer to," Quaint said solemnly. "What can I do to mend this wound of ours?"

Destine walked towards him.

"One thing, my sweet boy," she said. "Hold me."

Quaint threw himself into Destine's arms, and squeezed her so tight, never wanting to release her. The tears fell from both their eyes, seemingly from the very pits of their hearts. From deep down within their souls, they wept in unified pain. Their faces were painted with agony, as they released their sadness, together as one. Quaint choked like a baby, his body quivering and jolting as he let the tears flow. It was such a relief, as if he had kept every tragic memory from his whole life bottled away inside him behind an impenetrable wall, and now . . . that wall was gone.

Destine gasped, grasping him by his cheeks. "*Mon cher, doux* Cornelius . . . I was a foolish old woman not to confide in you the very first moment. I had no idea that Antoine survived your previous encounter in Paris . . . please believe me."

Quaint pulled away from her. "Madame, I . . . I must go."

"Go? Go where?" Destine called after him. "Where are you going? What are you going to do?"

"Do you really have to ask?" said Quaint, his cold eyes scowling under his wind-beaten curls. "I'm going to Crawditch, of course."

"But, you can't go! Not there! I have foreseen your death, Cornelius."

"Oh, really?" asked Quaint. "Well, I have yet to *live* my death, so as far as I'm concerned, it can be averted. I wouldn't waste another tear on your son's resurrection, Madame, because after I've finished with him — he'll wish he'd *stayed* dead."

CHAPTER
FORTY-ONE

The Cold Embrace

"Commissioner?" called Sergeant Horace Berry, as he strode out into the exercise yard of the police station. "What on earth are you doing out here? Haven't you heard?"

"Haven't I heard *what?*" Dray asked, barely turning his head. A thin plume of cigarette smoke wisped from his mouth into the dark, early evening sky.

"Tucker just told me. There's been some kind of committee meeting or something. A group of locals have banded together and they're on their way here right now," said Berry. "Tucker says they want your head on a plate, sir."

"Tell 'em there's already a queue," said Dray.

Sergeant Berry walked around Dray, to stand directly in front of him, so he was unable to avert his eyes. "Sir . . . Oliver . . . what's going on? Are you going to speak to those people, or not?"

"Me? Why me?"

"Oliver, you're the Commissioner. This district falls under *your* charge. It's up to you to set these people right. Surely you can see it from their point of view? They're half-petrified!"

"Horace, I'm not in the mood. You deal with it."

Berry shook his head, pursing his lips as he selected his words carefully. "Commissioner . . . *sir* . . . those residents — the merchants, and business folk that haven't already absconded from Crawditch, of course — have a grievance with our handling of these murders, you *must* be aware of that."

Dray lifted his eyes to look at Berry. "Horace, what can I do about it? Our men are doing the best they can to find that giant, right? If that's not enough for this damned committee, then why the hell don't they *all* leave town?"

"Yes, but what about that Mr Quaint's thinking . . . about this Irish fellow? Surely it's worth checking out? So far we've been concentrating all our efforts on Miller."

"Horace, Cornelius Quaint is desperate to pin anything on anyone else other than his own people. You heard him, how he stuck up for his strongman, and all the while I'll bet he knew he was guilty as sin. Hell, he probably even helped the bastard escape!"

"How could he, sir? Quaint was with us *both* at the time. And that's the funny thing, isn't it? I mean, we checked the bars on that cell window . . . they looked like they'd eroded away, been eaten by rust or something, yet the rest of the cells were all fine." Horace Berry was trying to appeal to the man he used to know, a man who up until a week ago was level-headed and strong-minded. Since Cornelius Quaint's arrival and the recent murders, Dray had become anything but strong-minded, and he was

279

certainly not going to do anyone any favours by meeting with the soon-to-be arriving committee. "Look, I'll do my best to fend off this baying crowd. Please just do me a favour, will you?" Berry asked.

"What is it, Horace? What do you want from me, eh? D'you want me to fall honourably onto my sword like those Japanese wotsits?" said Dray hoarsely, hot breath billowing from behind his clenched teeth.

"What I *want* is for you to think about how it's going to look if you don't even bother to *pretend* to listen to what those people are asking for . . . all they want is to feel safe in their beds, Oliver, surely you can understand that?"

Berry didn't wait for a reply, and he turned away, glancing briefly over his shoulder at the stranger who stood in the station's yard. The man looked and sounded for the entire world just like his Commissioner, but this man was different. He was acting in a cold, emotionless manner that was very unlike the man he had known for many years. Berry only hoped that Dray would find his true self soon, for if any more of him were to flake away, how much of Berry's respect and admiration for him would erode with it? He prayed that his superior would make the right decision when the time came. Sergeant Berry opened the station door, and returned to his duties inside, leaving Dray alone in the chill November wind.

Dray's expression was fixated on the mist-shrouded moon above him, and he pondered Berry's words aloud. "The people want to feel safe in their beds?

280

Don't they know, man? Are they stupid? There aren't many places left in this world that you *can* feel safe in any more. Everywhere's gone to hell." Commissioner Dray watched distractedly, as his trail of warm breath curled up into the night sky. His eyes barely registered another misty plume swirling with his own, entwining into the night. Dray heard a long, breathy exhale at his back, and he froze.

"Sure, an' ye don't know how right ye are, Commissioner," said a strong Irish voice directly behind him. "Everywhere has indeed gone t'hell . . . and I've saved ye the best seat in the house."

A short time later, Sergeant Horace Berry was alerted to a cacophony of raised voices, screams and yells from outside. Berry rose from his desk, and stared across the station. He threw down his paperwork and scratched at his head.

"Marsh? What the blazes is all that noise?" he called over to the constable manning the front desk. "It's like a bloody zoo out there."

Marsh shrugged. "It's that crowd, Sarge, although, sounds more like a lynch mob to me. You want me to go out, try and calm 'em down a bit?"

There was suddenly a hammering on the station's door, as many fists pounded themselves on the hard wood. Berry scowled at the entrance, shooting a look to Marsh.

"No, let me," he said. "If I don't sort them out, they'll have the bloody doors off their hinges, and we'll be freezing our socks off all night."

281

Berry yanked the door open and was greeted by a horde of people. Some were being comforted by others, and some were pointing harshly at the police station. As he tried to get their attention, he stared across their faces. As well as being angered to the point of rage, there was another, more upsetting expression taking residence upon the townsfolk's faces. It was an expression of something that Horace Berry had seen before — fear. He held up his hands, imploring the residents for their silence, and gradually, one by one, he managed to calm them to the point where he could be heard.

"Now, listen to me, everyone," Berry said confidently, clapping his hands, trying to get eye contact with as many of the folk as possible. He knew most of their names, and all of their faces. Some were merchants and store traders, some were foremen, builders and dock workers, and others were elderly, or weak-looking residents. Berry blew on his whistle to halt the tumultuous baying.

"Please! I understand you're all very worried . . . but I want to reassure you that —" Berry was suddenly distracted as something pelted his shoulder, and he wiped away at it instinctively. As he touched the warm, wet substance he immediately recoiled, staring at his fingers — it was fresh blood. Berry spun around, nearly slipping from the steps in the spilt blood, and stared up towards the roof of the station, higher and higher to examine the source.

It didn't take him long to find it.

282

Commissioner Dray's corpse was stripped naked, wearing only his policeman's uniform jacket and nothing else, hanging from the roof of the police station by his neck. Bathed in the amber light from the station lamp, his internal organs and intestines hung like garlands from a vast open wound, dripping pools of crimson blood onto the front steps of the station. Of all the sights that clung to Sergeant Berry's memory, this was unlike any other, and its horror stained itself into his brain.

"Tucker! Marsh!" Berry yelled, as two constables tumbled out of the station looking decidedly flustered. Berry pointed up to the grotesque scene above their heads, and the two young policemen immediately lost their control over the power of speech. "Get up there, right now, and get him down, for crying out loud . . . I'll disperse these people . . . and get every available man assembled right here immediately. Get anyone and everyone. Whoever did this is still in the area — go!"

And, very quickly, all-out madness erupted on the streets of Crawditch.

Prometheus and Butter shrank back behind a blacksmith's workshop and watched pandemonium ensue, as hordes of policemen — hastily buttoning up uniforms and flattening down hair — rushed out onto the street at the front of the station. As Sergeant Berry held court and barked an assault of orders at his men, Prometheus glanced down at the small Inuit by his side.

"We were lucky we left when we did, mate," he said.

283

Butter nodded frantically, his jet black hair flopping into his eyes. He pulled the fringe apart in the middle like a pair of curtains, and looked up hopefully at his gargantuan companion. "What's we do now?" he asked.

"I'm open to any ideas," said Prometheus grimly. He squatted down, meeting Butter's gaze. "The main thing is we know who's behind all this, well, at least we sorta know . . . and we have to make sure that at least one of us gets through this to inform Cornelius, you understand?"

"Yes, I understand," Butter agreed. "What did Frenchman say about working for . . . 'heavenly connections'? What means this?"

"I would assume he means someone in high authority in the Church. And I heard him say something about a 'Hades Consortium', whoever he is." Prometheus grabbed Butter's shoulders. "Things've gone haywire here. This district wasn't exactly safe beforehand, lad, and now with Dray's murder, and his men runnin' around like headless chickens, they're still no nearer to catchin' Hawkspear."

"I do not think it good where we find ourselves," chirped Butter.

"Ye're a master of the understatement, Butter. Considerin' the mess things're in, I really don't know what t'do for the best."

"Return with me to the train, then. We must tell the boss about the Commissioner . . . and this Frenchman . . . he seemed to know the boss also."

"The problem is, we were possibly the last people to see the Commissioner alive, and if it gets out that we were hidin' in the bloody bushes at the time — we'll be right in the swill, good and proper," said Prometheus. "And I'll probably be hanged twice over."

"Prometheus, we have done well, yes? We have learned much whilst we dropped our eaves," said Butter emphatically. "Boss will be pleased, and we must not let it go wasted, I think."

Prometheus suddenly flattened himself against the wall, clamping his rough hands over Butter's mouth. A lone policeman walked briskly past their hiding place, a matter of feet from them, and Prometheus recognised the young man instantly as Constable Jennings.

"Where's he off to in such a hurry?" Prometheus asked his companion.

"The opposite direction to everyone else," noted Butter.

"I noticed. You don't need Madame Destine's powers to know that one's a bad seed," said Prometheus. "I think we should follow him . . . see where it takes us, hmm?"

"I wish Madame Destine were here right now," said Butter.

Prometheus looked down at his friend. "Oh, yeah? Why's that, then?"

"She would tell us to stay here," mumbled Butter. "I much better prefer *that* plan."

CHAPTER
FORTY-TWO

The Stab in the Dark

"Keep digging, men, I want as many of these graves dug up as you can manage, let's make use of the darkness. Double pay to the man that finds what I need," said the now exposed Frenchman Antoine Renard.

He could not care less whether Quaint knew of his existence now or not for his plan was nearly completed, but he needed to continue the charade for Bishop Courtney's sake, and so he had resumed his "Mr Reynolds" persona once more, and was striding across Crawditch cemetery towards the Bishop's waiting carriage. As usual, Melchin was perched like a pensive vulture waiting for meat at the front of the vehicle. Like slipping into a comfortable pair of slippers, Renard effortlessly shifted from his native French accent, and was now every inch the Cockney scoundrel that he had painted himself to be in front of the Bishop.

"All is set, Bishop. These blokes are hungry enough to dig until they drop for a pocket full of coins, and a hot meal," Renard said with a sniff, wiping the back of his hand across his nose. His transformation was nothing short of spectacular, and any detached observer would seek to question both their sanity and their eyesight upon witnessing the display. The Frenchman shared many characteristics with the snake, the least of which being the ability to shed one's skin.

Courtney darted his head out of the coach. "Jolly good, and should they fall, there are many men waiting to fill their positions." The Bishop gave Renard an unexpected pat on the shoulder. "You have done very well, Mr Reynolds. Very well, indeed. I shall have to retain you on my staff permanently."

Renard grinned. "Doubt that, Bishop — you couldn't afford me."

"Indeed! But if you manage to find the casket containing that elixir tonight, I shall ensure you are well rewarded. Perhaps even a share of the elixir yourself, eh?"

"Don't think so, Bishop. I would prefer to see an end to this husk of a life," Renard said with a cackle. "Death is the only thing I have left to look forward to."

The Bishop joined him in a throaty chuckle. "Yes, well . . . I shall take my leave for Westminster. Be sure to inform me immediately should you find the casket, no matter what the time."

"Yeah, will do," said Renard, motioning behind him. "They should be all right, this lot, but are you sure this place is safe? I thought the whole point was that you wanted to wait until Crawditch was cleared . . . last I saw, there were still folk about."

"Yes, well, the time for restraint has passed now that Hawkspear has worked his magic, my friend. By now Crawditch will be twinned with hell, and no one will

287

want to stick around long," said Courtney, gleefully rubbing his hands together. "Don't worry — all eyes will be on events unfolding down there in that borough, not up here in this graveyard. I will look forward to seeing you soon, Mr Reynolds!" said the Bishop, and he thumped on the side of the carriage door. "On, Melchin."

Renard watched silently as the Bishop's horse and carriage trundled off into the distance. "The time to dissolve our business partnership is almost upon us, Bishop Courtney," he said to himself. He knew that the next time he saw the man it would be their last meeting.

Renard approached a group of dark-clothed men huddled together, hastily digging at various gravesites. Even with the gang hard at work, the job would take the whole of the night — perhaps longer — and there was now no guarantee how much privacy they would have. Many of the graves had a nondescript, moss-covered headstone, with a name either defaced, or worn over time. It could even take weeks to find the right one containing the elixir — unless, of course, Antoine Renard was very, very lucky. With a sickening grin of pleasure, and his scar twisted into a malevolent sneer, Renard looked around himself. His piercing eyes scanned the graveyard in a sweep. Past the men, past the many stumps of moss-covered granite — something suddenly caught his attention at the far end of the cemetery, near the boundary wall, and he strode over to it. There it was — an unmarked grave; a beaten granite headstone. The years had eroded away all semblance of a monument to a loved one, and now the headstone was merely an emotionless lump of weather-worn rock. As nameless and lacking in identity as the person it represented.

Renard beamed proudly, as if he'd just found something he had cherished, but lost a long time ago. "Now . . . how to make this look convincing," he said under his breath. "Oi, you lot!" he called to the wraith-like men shovelling dirt from graves nearby. They froze at the sound of his voice, and rushed to his side. Renard squatted onto his haunches, and ran his hand gingerly through the layer of fine grass upon the top of the grave, as if it were capable of generating warmth. "I want you blokes to dig here," he said, pulling a stub of a cigar from his breast pocket. "Forget everywhere else, *just here!*"

He removed himself from the grave site over to a stout stone wall, and puffed happily on the cigar, his eyes sparkling as he watched the men attack the earth with their shovels and forks.

Within five minutes of digging, one of the men shouted in alarm. He lifted a dirty, grime-covered sack into the air. Renard rushed over, and snatched the sack roughly from the man's hands. He laid it onto the dirt, and unfurled the top. Inside was a small, dark-green wooden box with a strange, filigree figure-of-eight design on the top, etched in gold leaf. Renard's eyes blazed with interest. The man nearest to him leaned on his spade, and stared down at the nondescript box.

"Is that it, boss? Is that what you're after?" asked the dishevelled man. "That box?"

Renard spat the cigar onto the ground and smiled. "*Avec précision, monsieur* . . . this is what I'm after, all right," he said gleefully.

"But, hang on," said the curious man, "you said this job would take us all night, and yet you just plucked a grave right out've thin air . . . you must be the luckiest bleeder around!"

"Ah, *mais oui, monsieur,* I am very good at predicting the future, *voyez-vous?* You could say it runs in the family," said Renard with a grin, transfixed by the box. "Don't worry, men, I shall make sure you all receive a full night's pay . . . it's not like the Bishop will live long enough to spend his money."

CHAPTER
FORTY-THREE

The Bishop's Prize

In his Westminster Abbey annexe, the Bishop had just eaten a large supper, and the carcass of a chicken lay ripped and shredded next to an array of metal goblets, empty wine bottles and fresh fruit across the table, looking like the aftermath of a culinary battlefield. He was picking food from between his teeth when he heard a gentle knock upon his residence door.

"Enter," he boomed, dabbing at the corners of his mouth with a handkerchief.

A pensive-looking alumno with a floppy fringe and pinched features poked his head around the door. "Hello, Bishop Courtney, ah . . . Reverend Fox is here again to see you again."

The Bishop rose immediately from his chair, and shot a look to the clock on his mantel. "Fox? Well, show him in then, boy, and hurry up," Courtney snapped.

The alumno rushed to the door, and scuttled outside like a fleeing rat. Seconds later, dressed in his priestly disguise, the enigma that was Antoine Renard slid his wiry frame into the room.

"Mr Reynolds, you take me aback! I . . . had not expected to see you so soon," said the Bishop, approaching Renard, hurriedly closing the residence door behind him. "Surely you haven't found it already? It's been all of two hours. There aren't any . . . complications, are there? Some further delay?" he said breathlessly.

"Not at all, Bishop," said Renard. He pulled the hessian sack from behind his back, and offered it to Courtney. "Quite the opposite in fact."

"But . . . but, Mr Reynolds . . . surely you don't mean —"

"Look, if you don't want your bloody elixir, by all means — just let me know and I'll take it away," said Renard in a playful tone.

Courtney nearly choked with anticipation. "My Lord! You've done it, you've actually *done* it," he exclaimed, the paleness of his fat, greasy face accentuating his beady little eyes. "How? I mean . . . however did you find it so quickly?"

"Just a stab in the dark," said Renard, as he placed the sack-covered box upon the table in front of the Bishop. He untied the neck, and let the rough material fall open.

The Bishop's eyes lit up like Roman candles as he saw the dusty box before him. His lip quivered as he traced his fingers over the lid. "A very apt engraving," he said, examining the gold leaf, figure-of-eight design. "The symbol for Infinity — just like the gift that the consumer enjoys." The Bishop's breath was panting furiously, now, as if he'd just run up several flights of stairs. "How do you open it, Mr Reynolds?"

"Ah, if you don't mind, Bishop, I'd rather we concluded our business first," said Renard, placing his hand on top of the box's lid. "After all, you'll soon have eternal life . . . it's not like you're in any rush, is it?"

The Bishop couldn't tear his eyes away from the box, as if it were calling his name repeatedly. "Of course . . . of course," he said distractedly, and he shuffled over to a large oil painting on the wall of Saint Peter at the gates of Heaven. After a few anxious seconds of feeling his finger around the underneath of the frame, the painting swung slowly outwards, revealing a large metal safe behind it.

"My thanks to you, Mr Reynolds, for services rendered," Bishop Courtney said, handing Renard a small leather briefcase. "Without your savvy, I don't think I would have been able to achieve so much. Can I not convince you to stay awhile to watch me open my prize?"

Renard weighed the briefcase up in his hands. "Well, maybe I *will* for a little bit. Perhaps I can get your driver to drop me off in Whitehall?"

"Whitehall, eh? Yes, I'm sure Melchin would relish the fresh air. Won't you come closer and join me in toasting our victory?" said Bishop Courtney, hastily pouring Renard a goblet of wine. "To the future!" he said, lifting his goblet into the air.

"And your very good health, your Grace," said Renard.

"Indeed! A good health for all eternity," chuckled Courtney to himself. "This elixir does have properties other than longevity, you see. Once I consume the

293

liquid, I will be infused with God's light, healing any conditions that I may have, yet ensuring I can never again get sick. It stops time, you might say, to ensure that I shall always remain in the peak of health for all eternity."

"You know, once word gets out, everyone's going to be gunning for you, trying to get their hands on this stuff."

"Then I shall have to make sure that I keep it a secret, Mr Reynolds, won't I? Now, onto business," muttered the Bishop. "Lord, please be with me. I do this in your name," and with a broad grin spreading across his face, he delicately lifted the lid of the wooden box, and peered inside.

The box contained a lush, dark-purple velvet interior, with twelve inlaid pockets. Seated within one such pocket was a single glass vial. Topped with a cork stopper, and decorated with minute golden ivy leaves, the vial looked like something from a fairytale. The plump Bishop snatched it up with his stubby fingers, and held it towards the light.

"Only the one vial?" Bishop Courtney said, poking around inside the box. "I . . . I had expected to find more. The box has twelve indentations."

"Well, it ain't been opened since I left Crawditch — like I said, Bishop — I didn't want to open the thing and it blow up in my face." Renard rubbed a rough hand over his jaw. "I got me looks to think of you know, and anyway — what do you need with twelve vials of the stuff? You get eternal life no matter how many you have!"

"Hmm, well . . . I suppose you are quite correct, Mr Reynolds . . . one vial *is* all I need," the Bishop said, holding the small glass vial up to the light.

"Looks just like the other one, you know — the one you've got inside your cross," said Renard, admiring the sparkling clarity of the liquid inside the vial.

"Indeed it does, yes . . ." agreed Bishop Courtney, "the other sibling to the twin."

"You can name them Cain and Abel, eh?" laughed the Frenchman.

"I didn't have you down as a man of scripture," said Courtney, as he carefully uncorked the tiny stopper, and lifted the vial to his lips, pausing to savour the moment. "To your good health, Mr Reynolds," he said, eyes closed, feeling the warmth of the liquid trickling down his throat. He licked his lips deftly, and opened each eye slowly, looking around his surroundings as if expecting to be transported to another realm.

Renard stepped a little closer. "How do you feel, Bishop?"

"Wonderful!" The Bishop licked his lips, his eyes twinkling brightly. "Simply wonderful," he announced, lifting his arms into the air. "I can feel it, Mr Reynolds, like a gentle trickle of energy flowing through my veins. It's simply *wonderful*."

Eyeing the Bishop carefully, Renard teased at his lower lip with his teeth.

"Mr Reynolds, come join in my celebrations . . . I feel alive for the first time in years," cheered the Bishop.

"No thanks." Renard stood back and leant against the wall, watching the portly Bishop twirl and swirl

295

about the room like a ballerina, as the portly man's face beamed with elation, his eyes afire with a spark of something akin to sheer, unadulterated wonder. Almost stumbling over to Renard, he clasped at the gaunt man's fake priestly robes excitedly. His eyes were wide, and his pupils like pinpricks, and a fine, greasy coating of sweat decorated his corpulent face. It was as if the elixir that coursed through his veins had suddenly lit a fuse inside of him. The man stood in the centre of his apartment, his eyes now closed, just letting the feelings wash over him.

Suddenly, the Bishop was racked by a harsh cough, taking his breath away and bending him over double, and his eyes snapped open. He coughed again, a throaty, phlegm-hackle that made Renard wince. The Bishop stared down into his open hand. A thick, congealed puddle of blood sat there, and the Bishop's stare widened. He glared at the pool of dark blood, as if it couldn't possibly have come from his own body.

"Something's wrong," he gasped, wiping a trail of blood emanating from his mouth. He pulled his handkerchief from his sleeve and dabbed at the blood, but more was coming after each dab. This was no bitten tongue, or weeping ulcer; the Bishop could feel this dark blood seeping from the pit of his stomach. Each cough spewed it up through his throat, and it splattered onto the tiled floor. Staring in bewilderment at the pool below him, the man fell to his knees. "Reynolds . . . help me, something's wrong with the elixir. It feels . . . feels like . . . it's burning me up from the inside . . . eating away at me." The Bishop clutched madly at his

296

throat, pulling at his dog-collar, and clawing frantically at Renard. "Reynolds! Help me . . . I beg of you!"

"Get your hands off, *monsieur*," Renard said fiercely, swatting the Bishop's hands away from him. "You're bleeding all over me."

"What are you . . . doing? *Help* me, man," squealed the Bishop indignantly, grasping the crucifix that hung from a leather strap around his neck. "Antidote!" he wheezed, desperately trying to unscrew the cross. "Reynolds, listen to me!"

A wide, satisfied smile spread across Renard's face. "Hurts, does it, Bishop?"

"But I . . . I don't understand, man . . . the elixir . . . burns like acid." The Bishop's eyes now bulged horrifically, and tiny blood corpuscles burst like miniature red spiders across the iris, flooding the eyeball with a bright crimson wash of colour. "What's . . . wrong with me? You need to help me . . . take antidote."

"Take antidote? Don't mind if I do," said Renard, as he snatched the crucifix from Courtney's clammy hands, ripping at the leather strap around the fat man's neck. "You know, Bishop . . . I'm not so sure about this eternal life thing . . . it looks awfully painful to me."

Thick, dark-red blood-tears seeped from the corners of the Bishop's eyes as they beseeched Renard, imploring the man to help him.

"But why . . . Reynolds?" he said through blood-soaked teeth.

"I warned you once not to make a deal with the Devil, Bishop . . . because the odds are always stacked in his favour. You have been taken for a fool, and it is *I* that have done the taking."

"What? What are you saying? I . . . I don't understand. Have mercy! Why won't you help me?" asked the Bishop, spluttering on a mouthful of blood.

"Why?" Renard sneered, an inch from the Bishop's contorted face. "Because I want to watch you *die*, of course!" and in that instant, as the Bishop stared into the man's cold, blank eyes, it was as if his entire face changed before him. The Bishop witnessed the mask of Mr Reynolds fade away — and in his place stood Renard; a man twice as fearsome and a hundred times more cunning than a mere alleyway thug.

"Mr Reynolds, please!" begged Courtney.

"Sorry, *monsieur* . . . there's no 'Mr Reynolds' here," grinned Renard. Like a butterfly emerging from its cocoon, the Reynolds persona had shed itself completely now. As the dying Bishop mouthed empty, silent words, hysterically trying to figure out what was happening to him, Renard took great delight in telling him the entirety of his plan. "My true name is Antoine Renard, Bishop. I suppose that I should pass on my thanks to you, really. You see, I needed something from you — but I had no idea whether it was as deadly as I had been informed," Renard said, his French accent highlighting his machinations in a most roguish fashion. "But right now, Bishop, you are currently presenting quite startling proof of the elixir's power."

Renard grabbed hold of Courtney's jaw, squeezing his features into a squashed muddle in the centre of his fat face, as tendrils of blood-tainted spit dripped from the Bishop's teeth. "But not power as some holy gift of immortality . . . in fact quite the reverse. God's tools are the Devil's toys, after all."

Bishop Courtney snatched his face from Renard's grasp, and fell to the floor. With a wail of pain, he dragged himself along, finally resting against the door to his apartment. "You traitorous monster," he slurred. "You'll pay for this betrayal, Reynolds."

"That's *Renard*, my dear Bishop," the Frenchman said, smiling with faux warmth. His body language was now a lot more graceful, more feline, than the thuggish Reynolds, and he strode around the Bishop's room with renewed confidence, delighting in watching the deformities of agony pass across the priest's face. "It is strange to think that after years of research, my organisation should send me here, back to England where I spent some of my youth. When our scouts heard tales of you, Bishop Courtney — one of the Queen's most trusted advisors, taking an abnormal amount of interest in a little dockland cesspit called Crawditch — well, we just had to take a look for ourselves. Imagine my surprise when I learned what you were seeking." Renard pulled a long cheroot of a cigar from his pocket. He grabbed one of the Bishop's candelabras from the table and lit the cigar, squatting down to blow choking smoke into the Bishop's face. "An elixir of immortality, no less? Your Christian alchemists always did love committed devotees. A lifetime of servitude, and all that, *non?*"

"What . . . do you want . . . from me?" gasped Courtney.

"What do *I* want?" questioned Renard, yanking the white cloth from the Bishop's table, sending wine bottles, goblets and messy plates tumbling onto the tiled floor with a resounding crash. He sat himself upon the table, resting his muddy boots upon an upholstered chair. "My dear Bishop . . . I want *nothing*." Renard delved into his pockets and pulled out a handful of glass vials, each one identical to the Bishop's, splaying them out like a fan of playing cards. "I have in my possession everything that I need. Your Anglican friends spent decades perfecting this stuff — did you honestly think they only made the *one* vial?"

"What do you . . . plan to do?" seethed the Bishop, reaching for Renard, only to fall flat on his face on the floor. "After what you've seen . . . what it can do . . . it is poison! It . . . it's worthless!"

"Poison it may be, Bishop — but it's far from worthless. You're wondering how a godly elixir can become such a potent poison, are you not?" Renard cocked his head to one side, like a sparrow. "I'll take that as a yes, then! Now, I'm useless at all this chemistry stuff, believe me. I'm much more of a physics man, myself. You know, action . . ." Renard lashed out with his boot, striking the Bishop's ribs, ". . . and reaction, you see what I mean? Now, *that* I understand perfectly. But my organisation specialises in this kind of thing, so I don't *need* to know about it. Did you know that Crawditch cemetery, being positioned so close to the Thames as it is, contains a massive amount of sphagnum peat? I didn't, but then I didn't have a clue what 'sphagnum peat' is . . . I thought it sounded like

300

one of those dreadful American prospectors hunting for gold, until one of our scientific types told me that sphagnum is acidophilic moss, incredibly susceptible to the growth of bacteria." Renard slid off the table, standing at full height, towering over the Bishop.

"Over many hundreds of years, that gestation has transformed the elixir from a gift of eternal life into a harbinger of death, especially when the solution is combined with water." Renard grabbed the Bishop's scalp and Courtney spluttered again, spraying a shower of blood across the floor. "Are you taking all this in, Bishop?" he taunted, taking great pleasure in watching Courtney quiver. "Of course, I'm sure your lot had no idea that the solution inside that vial is extremely susceptible to contamination from bacteria, did they? Like most great scientific discoveries — we stumble upon them by accident." Reynolds paused to shuffle his footing away from a small pool of blood, spreading across the floor towards him.

Bishop Courtney's strength was ebbing away, as if his entire structure was being dissolved inside him. That was the poison doing its best to liquefy his internal organs. Like most intrusive chemical elements, it operated with an almost sentient awareness — picking off its victim slowly, stripping away one piece at a time. The poison savoured death as much as Renard did, and both were highly proficient at it. Beginning with the base organs such as the kidneys, the poison would force Bishop Courtney's bowels and bladder into overdrive to compensate for the signals being sent by the brain,

301

before moving onto the liver, lungs, heart and finally the brain.

Renard was enjoying his captive audience, watching the bulky Bishop drag himself along the floor. "Can you grasp just what damage someone with a creative mind could accomplish with a weapon such as this, *monsieur*? I doubt it. You're probably more interested in your own fate, *est-ce que je suis* correct? Well . . . you've just ingested pure, undiluted poison . . . it may take as long as three hours before you die, and the beauty of this poison is that you'll be conscious every step of the way."

Bishop Courtney was a broken man, in mind as well as body, as something pinched away handfuls of him at a time. He was flaking away, yet he knew that every word Renard spoke was the truth.

"There's nothing you can do, your Grace . . . for only the antidote can reverse the chemicals that are raging through your body right now."

"You're . . . insane," Bishop Courtney said weakly.

"On the contrary, my Lord, as you once told me yourself — I am a man of vision!" Renard said, preening his hair sarcastically.

"But, you said . . . you'd help me . . . you said . . ." pleaded the Bishop.

"I said a lot of things, Bishop. Surely you are not still blind as to how you have been deceived? Must you spend your last, few painful moments of life trying to work it all out? Do you really believe that the success of this little conspiracy of yours was due solely to your machinations? Come, *monsieur* . . . you are blind."

"Reynolds . . . how could you?"

"Surprisingly easily, Bishop. You see, there's one thing you need to know before you die," Renard said, a smile of mock sympathy on his thin, gaunt face. "I lie . . . I deceive . . . I trick, and I scheme — that's what I do best. That's Renard! Now hurry up and die."

CHAPTER
FORTY-FOUR

The Streets Aflame

Oblivious to both Commissioner Dray's fate and what was currently occurring in the annexe of Westminster Abbey, Cornelius Quaint stood underneath the lamplight of Crawditch police station and stared upwards. His eyes were drawn to dark-red stains of blood daubed across the upper floor of the station. He looked around him, trying to guess what had happened, but the tumultuous atmosphere of shock and desperation painted on the faces of the townsfolk around him suddenly stole his attention.

Quaint stepped inside the police station and witnessed a scene not dissimilar to what was occurring outside. As if he were invisible, no one paid him the slightest bit of notice as he walked around the partition near the enquiries desk, and strolled towards Commissioner Dray's office. Without knocking, he walked briskly inside.

"Ollie, what the hell is going on? It's like a bloody circus in this place, and I should know. What are you doing —" Quaint suddenly froze mid-sentence as he saw Sergeant Horace Berry, sitting at Dray's desk, his

304

head in his hands. "Sergeant? What's going on? It's like a madhouse — out there *and* in here."

Berry barely looked up, holding a glass of whisky to his lips. His face was pale, and he looked like he hadn't slept for a week. "Oh it's you, Mr Quaint . . . what brings you here?"

Quaint pulled up a chair, spun it around, and squatted astride it, resting his arms on its back. "Where's Oliver? I need to speak with him urgently about what's going on. I don't care *how* busy he is — I'm not taking no for an answer!"

"Well, you'll have to . . . because he's dead," said Berry, wiping his nose on his sleeve, leaving a slug's trail of mucus behind.

Quaint pounded his fist on the table, shaking Berry's glass. "I need to *see* him, Sergeant — it's *important*, and I don't have time for this nonsense. I know he's involved in whatever is going on in this district, and I will *not* be derailed!"

Berry held his hands out to Quaint, his palms coated bright red.

"You see this?" he asked shakily. "It's blood, that's what it is . . . Oliver's blood . . . so I hope you can understand that I . . . *really* cannot deal with you right now. If you don't mind, I've got things to be getting on with." He returned his vacant stare back to the tumbler of whisky.

"You're not serious," said Quaint. "Oliver's . . . *dead?*"

Berry glanced up, his eyes raw and bloodshot.

"It seems you are," said Quaint numbly. "My God, when *was* this?"

"Not long . . . perhaps an hour or so since we found the body . . . I'd only been speaking to him minutes beforehand. Someone . . . somehow got close enough to do it. Stabbed him in the back . . . then gutted him . . . his body hanging from the roof outside the station for the whole world to gawp at."

"So that's what that was," nodded Quaint. "I noticed that on my way in. And what can you tell me about the circumstances?"

"Circumstances? Mr Quaint, I know *nothing*. No one saw anyone arrive *or* leave the yard. The way things have got in this town of late, it could have been anyone," snapped Berry. "Last I knew, Jennings and the Commissioner were out back, having a chat about I don't know what. I went out to tell Oliver that there was this bunch of residents, formed themselves into some kind of committee or something. They were angry about how little progress we were making, and were on their way here to the station to force Oliver into contacting Scotland Yard — something he was dead set against."

"I'll bet," said Quaint. He took off his long overcoat and hung it over the back of the chair. "Horace, I need to tell you something. You seem like an honest and honourable fellow, and to last as long as you've done as a beat copper — then you're obviously trustworthy."

"How'd you work that out?"

"Otherwise, you'd have done what Ollie did, and get your father to pull some strings in Parliament. If you had an exit, there's no way you'd stick around as a street bobby, is there? In this day and age?"

"Maybe I've got a liking for cold nights and street scuffles, eh? So, what have you got to tell me, Mr Quaint?" said Berry, picking up his glass. He downed the half-full tumbler in one gulp, wiping his mouth with his sleeve, and pulled another glass from the desk drawer. "Have one yourself, why don't you? It's Oliver's Scotch . . . but he's hardly likely to complain now, is he?"

Quaint poured a small inch of whisky into the glass and swilled it around in his hands. "Berry — listen to me. There is a most dangerous and deadly conspiracy at play here in this district, and my circus has been drawn into it. What the scheme's exact purpose is, I don't rightly know at this point; but I do know who the antagonists are."

"The what?" asked Berry, struggling to replace the cap on the whisky bottle.

"Antagonists, Sergeant. Our adversaries, the main players in this game, our opponents . . . but not all of them are who I expected them to be."

"Considering that one of your employees is the prime suspect, you mean?"

"No, Sergeant, because I thought I'd killed him," said Quaint. "You might remember the name Hawkspear that I mentioned earlier this week — the Irishman who drugged my strongman? Well, it seems he was recently in residence at Blackstaff prison, so I popped along to investigate how he managed to escape, and what forces may have brought him here to Crawditch. I came upon this." Quaint unfolded a piece of paper and gently cast it onto the table in front of

307

Berry. "I'm sure you're familiar with a prison release form?"

Berry's eyes scanned the paper, his scowl increasing the more he read. "I don't understand," he said, looking up at Quaint. "This says our Jennings authorised Hawkspear's release . . . and . . . who's this Bishop Courtney character?"

"Unknown at this time, but I believe him to be an essential element of the plot, perhaps the man pulling everyone's strings. Tell me, Sergeant, where is Constable Jennings at this very moment?"

"I . . . I don't know, Mr Quaint. Out on his beat looking for Oliver's killer, I think. Here, you don't think *he's* involved in this nasty business, do you? I mean, the lad's a bit daft, but he's not capable of murder!"

"We don't always know people as well as they would have us believe, do we, Sergeant? Jennings countersigned Hawkspear's release papers with the authority of Commissioner Oliver Dray," Quaint tapped the letter on the table in front of Berry, startling the policeman. "There's more, and none of it is going to be easy to hear, I'm afraid. You see, many years ago, Oliver and his father were mixed up in some nasty business abroad."

"Sir George? You not saying that he's involved in all of this mess too, are you? Murder and the like?" quizzed Berry. "The man's on the board of every government business, has trading rights for God knows how many ports, practically owns the police, and has royal connections, to boot. He's a bloody knight of the realm, man. He's next to a bloody saint! I don't believe for one second that *he'd* be involved."

Quaint's stony expression didn't falter. "With all due respect, Sergeant, what you currently believe is irrelevant. I was there all those years ago, and I saw just what Sir George is capable of with my own eyes. During this nasty business, Drays junior and senior involved themselves with an old nemesis of mine, a French mercenary named Renard." Quaint paused, as he allowed Berry's naturally inquisitive mind to soak up the details. "Up until yesterday I was convinced that Renard was dead — by my own hand — but I have since discovered to my abhorrent surprise that he is very much alive, and it seems he has rekindled his past connections with Oliver. This has led me to conclude that this whole business with these murders has been the result of a triumvirate of evil — featuring the likes of Police Commissioner Oliver Dray, Antoine Renard and the man who is really responsible for those obscene murders, probably Oliver's included . . . Tom Hawkspear."

Berry rose from his seat, and squinted at Quaint. "You've been busy, Mr Quaint."

"Call me Cornelius, Sergeant. We're way past polite manners now."

"Right . . . you're saying Oliver is . . . *was* . . . in cahoots with a mercenary and a murderer? You know, I guessed there was bad blood between you two, but considering that he can't exactly stand up and defend himself, I find this in extremely bad taste, man!"

"Sergeant, know this: if Renard is in Crawditch, with a paid killer on his books, all hell could break loose to make Dante's Inferno look like a dinner party at Buckingham Palace," said Quaint. He ran his hands through his thick grey-brown curls, and placed his elbows on the desk in front of him. "I know Renard, Sergeant . . . I know exactly what he can do, and the havoc that can spiral out of his actions. You need to come on board with me quickly on this one, because doing nothing is not an option — you can believe me on that."

CHAPTER
FORTY-FIVE

The Killer and the Constable

Prometheus and Butter observed silently as Constable Jennings pulled away a wooden board from the disused bakery's door frame, and made his way through the rear entrance in Montague Street, about half-a-mile from the police station.

"It seems the constable did indeed lead us *somewhere*. The only question is where?" Prometheus toyed with his beard thoughtfully as he eyed the boarded-up windows of the bakery. "I wonder what awaits us once we go inside, lad."

Butter froze. "We are going inside?" he asked. "Are you sure that is wise?"

"Probably not," Prometheus smiled. "But if it makes ye feel any better, why don't I go in first?"

"If you are expecting me to argue, you will be disappointed," said Butter with a gulp. "Remember, if we die, no one can tell the boss about this plot."

"Well, I s'pose we'd best not die then, eh?" Prometheus said, with a smirk hidden under his beard.

The bakery had long since submitted to disrepair, and the windows were covered with wooden boards. A huge chimney left unused for over ten years rose from the centre of the premises, and its once proud silhouette breached the district's skyline like a memorial to what once was. In its heyday, the bakery was an essential part of the commercial life of Crawditch, with the Thames bringing barges of grain and the many mills over the water in Whitehall, but the present landowners had cancelled any attempts at restoration, and had stripped everything from the building. Whereas once hundreds of skilled workers busied from place to place inside, now only the rats inhabited the halls, workrooms and warehouses.

Prometheus pushed his bulk through the tight gap in the same wooden boards that the far more slender Jennings had entered. He and Butter found themselves at the foot of a steep stone staircase. Careful not to dislodge any of the debris that littered the steps, they made their way to the top. Prometheus looked around what appeared to be an office, and a massive bathroom area. Most of the sinks were missing from the walls, and exposed pipes were entwined like handfuls of worms everywhere they looked.

Butter tugged on Prometheus's sleeve and motioned towards a room not far away. They could hear a man's voice. Although he was unable to tell who it was, Prometheus stepped forward first. Butter stood glued to the spot, looking around him cautiously, and feeling petrified. He stooped down and picked up a crooked metal pipe from the dirt-littered ground. With a little bit more confidence, feeling his fingers gripping the pipe, he skipped lightly after Prometheus.

The voice was getting louder. A distinct London accent could be heard, and Butter identified it as their quarry — Constable Jennings. Prometheus and Butter waited outside the door from where the voice emanated, poised to enter. Butter shifted his grip on the metal pipe and looked up at Prometheus, who nodded down at him.

"After three," Prometheus whispered. "One . . . two . . ."

"Is this a private game or can anyone join in, Miller?" chirped a voice from behind them. Both Butter and Prometheus spun around to face a blade-wielding Tom Hawkspear, just as Constable Jennings wrenched the door open from the other side. "Well, well, well. Face to face, at last, eh?" taunted Hawkspear, stepping closer to Prometheus.

"Tom . . . what are you playing at?" the giant said slowly.

"This? I call it fun. Y'know, Miller . . . when they told me that I could play along wi'ye as much as I liked, but not kill ye, I nearly didn't take this job," Hawkspear said. "I wanted ye dead for what ye did to Lily and Sean. And then the Bishop explained . . . ye were just the bait. A target for the police t'pin their sights on, leavin' me free t'maim an' kill as much as I liked, so I guess I should thank ye for it."

Constable Jennings clapped his hands excitedly at the unfolding show in front of his very eyes. "I should've sorted you out the moment we brung you

313

in!" he said, aiming his pistol at Prometheus's head. "Could've saved meself a lot of bother."

Prometheus growled, his bearded face resembling a grizzly bear. Jennings gulped, and stepped back, deciding that perhaps he should leave the job of taunting the giant to Hawkspear.

"It's useless t'pull that face, Miller . . . your bullish posturin' ain't gonna help ye now. This is it for ye," said Tom Hawkspear. "Ye've got a knife and a pistol pointed at ye . . . and ye're such a big target, an'all. Hard t'miss, know what I mean?"

Prometheus grinned. "Ye know the problem with ye boys?" he said, his bristling beard twitching as he spoke. "Ye've got your weapons pointed at the wrong person."

Constable Jennings had just about enough time to glance down before Butter lunged at his groin forcefully with the metal pole. Jennings hit the deck like a sack of potatoes, and Butter spun on his heels, glaring at Hawkspear.

The Irishman seemed unshaken by the loss of his comrade, and he lifted his blade into the air menacingly. "Ye got lucky, ye little elf, but soon ye'll be just as dead as Miller will be!" he growled. "But it ain't even a fair fight . . . I've got a blade here, y'know."

Butter eyes narrowed into thin slits, flashed with a devilish spark. "I can see that. It is very nice," he said, as he pulled aside is jacket — displaying his tusk-handled knife nestled into his belt. "But I have one of my own . . . and it is bigger than yours."

Hawkspear's jaw dropped.

314

Prometheus took advantage of his confusion, and dived straight for him like a freight train, hitting the Irishman square in the chest at full force. Hawkspear's body slammed into the door frame, with Prometheus's sandwiching him. Forcing the circus strongman back with a swish of his knife, Hawkspear grabbed a handful of rubble and threw it with all his might. The cloud of thick dust and grit pelted Prometheus in the face, and he was temporarily blinded. Hawkspear grinned, and rose to his feet.

"I ain't as easy t'kill as that, Miller . . . I'm gonna carve one o'me crosses into yer heart, just like I did yer wee girlfriend," he said, and threw his weight towards Prometheus, this time slamming the blinded strongman into a wall on the opposite side of the landing. The wall crumbled like chalk as Prometheus's bulk and Hawkspear's force of will collided with it, and they both tumbled over the banisters of the staircase, landing in a crumpled heap of arms and legs at the bottom of the stairs.

Butter saw Jennings's focus was elsewhere, and he barged his weight into him, kicking the pistol out of his reach. He swung his elbow into the young constable's neck, and as the man went down, he reached into the constable's pockets, producing a pair of metal handcuffs. He swiftly snapped them on Jennings's wrists.

"Oi! What's your game?" whined Jennings.

"You are a policeman, you should be shamed," Butter scolded.

315

"Shamed? Bloody 'ellfire! What kind of nutter *are* you? You're *lecturin'* me?"

"Hush up, constable, or my friend will rip your arms off," Butter replied, hoisting the cuffed Jennings to his unsteady feet.

Prometheus and Hawkspear finally broke free of each other, but Hawkspear was up on his feet first, lashing out with his knife, slashing at the air to force Prometheus back. Again and again, Hawkspear sliced the air between them, but Prometheus never took his eyes from his opponent. As Prometheus stepped back, his heavy boots came into contact with a large stack of broken ceramic tiles, and he fell over backwards. Unable to hold onto anything, he tumbled head over heels down the small concrete steps that led to the outside. His weight shattered the dry, dead wood of the doors with ease, and Prometheus crashed down the steps into the bakery's yard. Hawkspear watched the giant's writhing frame as he lay stunned on the ground and leapt towards his prey, his greasy strands of black hair clinging to his forehead with grimy sweat. Hawkspear's knife was raised for the killing shot, and he lunged . . .

Prometheus flicked one eye open and smiled. In fights he rarely needed to employ tactics — his size and strength usually proved ample weapons — but with an enemy like Hawkspear, he had to use more than just his brawn. At the last possible moment, he side-stepped out of the way — as a large javelin of an iron pole pierced Hawkspear right through the stomach. The

Irishman's howl of agony echoed around the ruins of the yard. The pole went right through the man; it smashed through Hawkspear's spine, protruding from the other side of his back. Hawkspear spat blood, trying frantically to catch his breath. He gripped the metal spear and tried to pull himself off — wailing with pain the whole time, but it was useless. The metal pole was embedded straight through him, pierced like a butterfly in an entomologist's collection.

"Ye . . . lucky bastard, Miller," he said weakly.

"Ye know what they say about us Irish," Prometheus said, dusting down his clothes. He walked unsteadily over to Hawkspear, the loose stones slipping from underneath his feet. "Ye should have stayed in prison, Tommy . . . ye didn't deserve t'walk free for what ye did. Now . . . ye won't be walkin' anywhere."

"I ain't dead yet," Hawkspear said, his hair wringing with sweat. He spat a mouthful of dark-red blood in Prometheus's direction. "Ye talk about me walkin' free? And what . . . about . . . ye, Miller? How comes . . . ye're the one who's allowed t'walk free, eh? If not for ye . . . me brother and sister . . . would still be alive."

Prometheus grabbed Hawkspear's sodden hair, and wrenched it back furiously, the jar making the speared Irishman squeal anew in agony. "Listen t'me, ye slimy piece of filth, don't ye dare try an' justify what ye did t'Lily — t'Twinkle, t'them others! Ye're going t'burn in hell for what ye've done, Tommy — I swear that." He released Hawkspear's head roughly, causing the lank-haired Irishman's torso to slip further down the spear. His thick dark blood coated the pole like black treacle.

Just then, Butter and Jennings emerged from the bakery door and stepped out into the yard. Once Jennings saw Hawkspear's coughing and spluttering body speared through the guts, a dark, wet patch appeared on the front of his trousers.

"My God . . . is . . . is he dead?" Jennings gasped.

"Not yet," confirmed Prometheus. "But he soon will be . . . as will ye, lad."

Jennings mewed like a newborn kitten, and wept into his hands, as Butter prodded him forwards with his elbow. The constable fell awkwardly onto the gravel at Prometheus's feet.

"I see you were victorious," Butter said to Prometheus, eyeing Hawkspear's twitching form. "Now what shall we do?"

Prometheus stared intently at his Inuit friend as if he had just spoken a foreign language to him. "What do you mean 'do'? We watch 'em die, of course."

"Surely you cannot mean that?" asked Butter.

"Why can I not? It's nothin' less than they deserve, lad."

Jennings's jaw trembled. "I ain't like 'im over there! He's a bloody killer! Let me go . . . and I'll tell you what I know, eh? What d'you say?"

"Ye expect *mercy*, constable?" yelled Prometheus. "If ye aided Hawkspear, yer as guilty as he is, so ye are . . . and ye'll die by his side."

Butter's lithe form skipped across the loose shards of gravel, and clung to Prometheus's arm tightly. "No,

318

Prometheus, this is not right. These men should see justice . . . not revenge," he appealed. "We must see them delivered into law's grasp."

Prometheus considered his small companion's words. He looked over at Hawkspear, his body shivering and fidgeting on the pole. He would so dearly love to see the man dead. For what he had done, not just to him, but to Lily and to Twinkle too . . . death was far too good for him. Butter was right; it was justice that they deserved.

"Mebbe ye're right, Butter, lad . . ." Prometheus gripped the impaled Irishman by the thigh and shoulder, and tensed his muscles. He bent his knees, and sneered into Hawkspear's face. "Brace yerself, Tommy . . . this is going t'hurt," he said, as he hoisted Hawkspear into the air. The ripping and slurping of his body as it was pulled from the pole was inaudible over the sound of Hawkspear's scream.

Prometheus lifted the man clear of the pole and saw the gaping wound — as big as his fist — glistening in the moonlight. He knew that it meant only one thing — a slow, wretched death in agonising pain. Before long, Hawkspear would be begging for a quick release that would never come. That was perhaps the greatest act of justice.

"Come on, Butter," he said with a satisfied smile. "Let's get these two mongrels back to the station. And if Hawkspear dies on th'way, the rats'll get a feast t'night — if they can stomach his filth."

319

CHAPTER
FORTY-SIX

The Touch-paper
Is Lit

Sergeant Berry rubbed his palms roughly into his eye sockets, more to wake himself up than to disperse any tears. His sadness at losing not only his commissioner, but his friend too, was fading rapidly the more he learned from Cornelius Quaint, a man surprisingly yet convincingly in possession of a great many details. The more Berry heard, the more he knew it was all true.

"Curse that man," he said, slamming his fist onto the desk.

"Which one? Renard or Dray?" asked Quaint dryly, picking at his fingernails. "There's nothing you could have done, Horace . . . Renard is highly skilled at this sort of game . . . the man escaped getting shot in the bloody heart, for God's sake! That's one magic trick I've not quite managed to pull off yet."

"He sounds like the Devil himself, this Renard fellow," Horace Berry said.

Quaint toyed with a pencil on the desk. "Actually, he's more like the person the Devil aspires to *be*. He's

320

cunning, ferocious and fearless, just the kind of enemy you don't ever want after your blood, Horace."

"So, what's next then? I mean, if this Hawkspear is working for a man like Renard, and Dray and Jennings both got mixed up in it somehow, that still leaves us with a gaping hole in this whole mess. Murdering innocent folk — what's the point? What's the motive behind it all?" said Berry, scraping his chair against the rough wooden floor as he stood up. He approached a large black board affixed to the wall, and snatched up a mottled cloth next to it. As he took the cloth to the board and erased the remnants of handwriting, the brief recollection of Dray's fate sent a flare of nausea through Berry's veins. "Right, so if we look at the main players in this mystery like a pyramid, with your mate Renard at the apex, and Hawkspear and Oliver at the lower points, there must be a connection of some sort, unless they answered an advert for 'Mercenaries and Murderers' in the local rag! So what's their connection?" said Horace, tapping the chalk on the board in time with his words, as if he were thinking aloud. "You said that Renard knew Dray from way back, when Sir George was up to his tricks with his smuggling, right?" Berry drew a dotted line in chalk, linking the two names. "So that's *their* connection. But, either the Commissioner or Renard needs to have some kind of connection to Hawkspear — to be able to release him from Blackstaff prison is one thing, but out of all the murdering scum there — why pick him? Now, if Oliver was consorting with offenders — especially ones stuck in Blackstaff for a double manslaughter charge — that'd surely get noticed. If you're sent to Blackstaff, you're not likely to rehabilitate, know what I mean? I doubt he'd be that stupid."

"I like your thinking so far, Horace." Quaint joined Berry at the blackboard. "So, that means *Renard* had the connection with Hawkspear, which makes more sense. Renard was part of Sir George's pack once . . . so he may have come into contact with the Irishman . . . except that's not Renard's style. He's a solo operator, he likes to be in control, especially considering Hawkspear's mental state . . . I mean, gouging crosses into people's chests, and the like — it's unholy, and I doubt Renard would let him off his lead too frequently."

"What about that prison release paper?" Berry pointed to the note on the desk. "It's countersigned by someone called Bishop Courtney. Is Renard powerful enough to have contacts within the Church?"

"He's probably on first name terms with the Cardinal himself."

"And yet he seems to be a bit of a religious nut, if you ask me. I saw the crucifix he carved into your poor dwarf . . . I suppose that kind of eliminates the possibility that he and a bishop would dally in the same circles." Berry stubbed the chalk onto the board. "Hang on a mo, Mr Quaint, you said that Hawkspear was responsible for killing your strongman's love back in Ireland, didn't you? Isn't that why he got sent to Blackstaff in the first place?"

"Yes, that's true, as I have recently discovered . . . Why do you ask?"

THE TOUCH-PAPER IS LIT

"Well, think about it," asked Berry, his face alight with excitement as he fiercely stabbed his chalk onto the blackboard again, snapping it in two. "What if we're sat here looking at this all wrong, Cornelius? It's not what connection these men have to each *other* — it's the connection they have with someone *else*."

"Like who?" asked Quaint.

Berry stared at Quaint's blank face and raised his eyebrows. "You!"

"Me?" asked Quaint, jabbing his finger to his chest. "What do you mean 'me'?"

"You, Cornelius — it's you!" snapped Berry. "You're the link."

"Nonsense, Horace, I don't even *know* Hawkspear. I'd never even heard the man's name until yesterday."

"No, but if he's as connected as you say then I'll bet Renard had," said Horace Berry, clenching his fists tightly, as he always did when he was on the scent of the truth, and it was teasingly beyond his grasp. He was speaking in a stuttered, robotic fashion, as if his words were being directed by a higher authority. "You had a history with Oliver, and a running feud with Renard, right? You said so yourself. Renard also had dealings with Oliver and his father, you said . . . which leaves Hawkspear as the odd one out . . . with no connection to either man in the triangle. Come on, Cornelius, I know you're not trained to think like a detective but you're by no means an idiot."

"You noticed."

"Connect the dots — *you're* the link!"

Quaint suddenly went very quiet. "Can this be true? My god, Horace . . . Tom Hawkspear killed Twinkle . . . which set me and my circus upon this path in the first place. Prometheus was incarcerated for the crime, which led me to involve myself with Oliver once again, stoking up the past as we tried to prove Prom's innocence." Quaint stood up sharply, and downed his tumbler of whisky in one gulp. "Do you relly think that I am the trigger for all this insanity, Horace?"

Berry nodded. "So it would seem . . . yes. But there has to be more to it."

Quaint flopped his massive frame back down into his chair, as his legs almost gave way beneath him. "Renard used me. He involved my circus purposefully! Like a clockwork mouse . . . he wound up my key, and has watched me chase my tail in circles this whole week." He scratched frantically at his mop of curls. "So, now we know the connection . . . what's next?"

"You said this Renard character has a hatred of you, so how come it's taken him fifteen years to get his revenge? Why wait that long? And then, why sanction Hawkspear to kill Oliver, if he was on Renard's side?" Berry asked, loosening his collar and pouring another drink. "And we still don't know what this is all about . . . I don't believe Hawkspear killed all those women just to get revenge on *you*, someone he'd never had any personal disagreement with . . . He took too much pride in his kills for that."

There was a rap on the door, and Constable Marsh poked his head around it.

"Um, Sarge . . . Sorry to disturb you, but you're really going to want to see this," he said, and stepped back.

The door was pushed swiftly open and Prometheus walked in, with Hawkspear over his shoulder, writhing and groaning, closely followed by a guilty-looking Jennings and Butter behind him. Jennings fell to his knees, sobbing. Prometheus slowly lowered Hawkspear's bloodied body directly onto the desk, forcing Berry to hastily snatch up the half-full bottle of whisky from it.

"What's all this?" demanded Sergeant Berry. "Jennings, lad, you've got some explaining to do!"

Quaint looked to the newcomers. "Prometheus . . . Butter, would you care to enlighten us? I'm sure the sergeant is just as anxious as I am to hear what this is all about."

"Cornelius, man — thank God you're all right!" Prometheus said, clamping his huge hands on Quaint's shoulders, before turning to Berry. "Sergeant, ye may remember me . . . from earlier in the week? I was a prisoner here, do ye recall?"

Berry stared at the seven-foot bearded, bald giant with hands like tennis racquets and a body like a tractor engine. "How could I forget, eh?" he said with a polite nod.

"The sack of guts bleeding on yer desk is Tommy Hawkspear — the monster responsible for all the killings that've plagued yer wee district here this past week . . . includin' the murder of Madeline Argyle." Prometheus paused, gathering up his strength at the mention of Twinkle's name. "An' yer Commissioner,

325

n'all. I s'pose ye're already acquainted with that snivellin' worm on his knees over there mewin' like a wet cat?"

Jennings clambered to his feet clumsily. "Sarge . . . I've been stupid, I know that. But the boss told me to do it! He said I had to do what this Mr Reynolds fella wanted. He was blackmailin' the guv'nor . . . he had some dirt on 'im from some days in their past, we both 'ad no choice. Reynolds said this bishop character was wantin' somethin' from the cemetery and he was helpin' him get it . . . I don't know what, and I didn't ask. But I was only followin' orders, Sarge, you have to believe me!"

Quaint interrupted: "Constable, you saw this 'Mr Reynolds' character yourself?"

"Yeah, course I did. In the backyard of this very station, no less . . . shows you how cunnin' the man is! Looks like he ended up stabbin' the guv in the back after all."

"Describe him to me, this man," Quaint said.

"What? I . . . I dunno . . . tall, he was. Tall and thin, like a scarecrow . . . spoke French, although not when I knew him, he didn't. Seemed to be all an act with him. He was pretendin' to be a Londoner. I dunno why."

"Anything else?"

"Apart from the scar, y'mean?" sniffed Jennings.

"A scar? Where?" demanded Quaint.

"Down here," the Constable muttered, tracing his finger down the left-hand side of his face. "Right nasty one, an' all, it was."

326

"That's Renard, all right." Quaint said.

"It is?" asked Berry. "How can you be so sure?"

"Because I'm the one that gave him the scar," replied Quaint. "This Bishop you mentioned, Constable . . . it can only be the same one that countersigned Hawkspear's release papers. What does *he* look like, Jennings?"

Jennings shrugged. "Dunno, mate. Never seen 'im. Like I said, 'parently there was somethin' in the cemetery that he's after."

Quaint clenched his jaw, and pulled on his overcoat. "Sergeant . . . I think it'll be worth us taking a trip to this cemetery of yours, don't you?"

"What? Right now? What about this one?" asked Berry, pointing at Hawkspear's groaning body. "I can't just leave him to die on my desk, but if I lock him up — after what he's done to people round here, not to mention Commissioner Dray — my boys'll have his guts for garters."

"Then Butter and myself shall go and investigate this cemetery," nodded Quaint. "Prometheus, be a good chap and stay here, will you? Keep an eye on Hawkspear. See what else you can get out of him. We're a long way to discovering the entirety of what exactly is going on here, and I'm sick of being kept in the dark."

"Will do, Cornelius, don't ye worry," Prometheus agreed. "I'll do me best to keep him alive — so he can get what's comin' to him. But listen, there's something Butter and I overheard that you might make some sense of. The Frenchman seems to be working for someone else . . . someone called Hades something."

Quaint was striding towards the door, and froze mid-step. "What did you just say?"

"Hades. We overheard it . . . when Renard was talking to the Commissioner earlier tonight . . . it sounded like Dray knew who this bloke was too. He was petrified at the mention of his name."

"Mmmm," grumbled Quaint, "He should be."

"Cornelius, begging your pardon, but do you know who this Hades person is?" asked Sergeant Berry. "Do we need to focus on him as well as Renard?"

"It's not a person, Sergeant . . . it is *persons*. Plural. The Hades Consortium is a *group*," answered Quaint. "They are rumoured to have been in existence in one form or another for hundreds of years, perhaps as long as recorded history itself. Scattered across the world in positions of power, they slumber until their lords and masters require them . . . and then they arise . . . leaving devastation in their wake like a hurricane."

"What are you on about, man?" asked Berry. "I can't keep up with you."

"Sergeant, the Consortium is a secret organisation whose primary goal is to cause, and then profit from, the propagation of havoc and unrest across the globe. Politicians, businessmen, entertainers, royalty — the lot, nobody knows for sure who's in and who's not, not even their own members. They make the Freemasons look like a Sunday School group," said Quaint, pacing around the room. "The Hades Consortium thrives upon toppling governments, infiltrating vast conglomerates, influencing trading and generally causing massive unrest wherever they cast their shadow. Imagine all the

328

massive crises that have occurred in the past few hundred years, and it's a safe bet that the Consortium has had a hand in it somewhere along the line."

"Sounds preposterous!" Berry said. "I've never bloody heard of them!"

"That's why they're a 'secret' organisation, Sergeant," said Quaint.

"What? One single group, controlling all the world's wars and the like? It's all a million miles away from what's going on here in London, surely. If this group is as big as you say it is, Cornelius, they're hardly likely to be bothered with a place like Crawditch, are they?"

"Perhaps . . . perhaps *not*," said Quaint. "That all depends on whether there is anything they can take advantage of in this borough. In the sort of circles that I used to mix in, it has long been whispered in hushed tones that Sir George Dray himself maintains a prominent position within the Consortium's inner circle. No doubt he greased the wheels to appoint his son as Commissioner here, and the Consortium has been pulling Oliver's strings ever since, gaining a foothold in Crawditch."

Berry sucked air into his mouth through clenched teeth. "Then tell me this; if Oliver was working for this Consortium, then how come he's dead?"

"Something must have gone wrong. Either that or the Consortium has already concluded their business here. Perhaps Oliver outlived his usefulness."

Berry scratched at his head. "But — if they're involved in all that you say, surely someone would know

329

something about them? Can't be a real secret if *you* know of them, can they?"

"Sergeant, you'd be surprised what I have learned over the years. No law enforcement agency in the world knows for sure who they are, or where they are. They're like whispers! Phantoms that no one can ever find," Quaint slammed his fist against the door frame. "Let me just say this; if the Consortium has plans in Crawditch, then all of us are way out of our depths here. Renard is small fry compared to them."

Butter stepped forwards, and tugged on Quaint's arm. "Boss — there is another thing the Frenchman said," he offered. "It was another name. Perhaps this man also member of this Hades? He says someone named 'Oedipus' had 'nothing on him'."

The colour drained from Quaint's face. "Oedipus? Butter, are you absolutely certain he used those words?"

"Yes, boss, definitely. My English is poor, but my memory faultless."

"In that case; Butter, get up to that cemetery right now, and see what you can find. Prometheus, help the Sergeant restrain these men, and Horace — circulate Renard's description to all of your men — tell them to head to Hyde Park quick smart to the circus site. Time is most definitely of the essence here, gentlemen!" Quaint snapped, virtually running across the office.

"Wait, Cornelius," called Prometheus, "Where're ye off to in such a hurry?"

"If I understand Renard's meaning correctly, my friend," said a grim-masked Quaint, "I need to get to Destine before it's too late!"

CHAPTER
FORTY-SEVEN

The Kiss of Death

Cornelius Quaint was a man with a mission, and that mission was to find the fastest route back to Hyde Park. He sprinted down the road — his heavy-set frame pounding against the cobbles and sweat falling like salt rain from his hair — and he made a mental note to make sure the circus was somewhere more central next year. Next year? Ha! The thought of it made him smile. The way things were going, he'd be hard pushed to make it to the next sunrise, let alone next year.

Finding Antoine Renard was the task fuelling him now. His hatred went beyond anger, beyond rage. It was something long buried, but now fully exposed. Certain species of wild animals fear man even though they have never met one in the flesh, a genetic mistrust passed on from their predecessors. For Cornelius Quaint, hating Renard was as natural as breathing. Unlike most conflicts, where the origins may have faded over time, the murder of Quaint's wife was as raw to him that night as it was at the time; he just never allowed his memory the chance to access those thoughts. Now it was so many long years later, and Quaint could taste the same metallic burst of acid at the back of his throat as he pushed his body to the limit in pursuit of Renard.

Quaint knew that Renard had a loathing for his mother, something that Renard blamed the conjuror for entirely, and hearing of his words, "Oedipus had nothing on me", Quaint was in full understanding of the reference. It meant dire consequences for Destine. Renard was twisted and depraved, but, more than that, the devil was perfectly capable of carrying out his threat, and it was that which chilled Quaint's blood.

Quaint looked from side to side of the road as he pounded down the moonlit streets. He was barely at Vauxhall Bridge, and he'd been running for twenty minutes flat out. He needed to find a quicker way to get to the park, because the way he was heading, he would soon collapse from exhaustion — and not even his famed stubbornness would help him. His eyes scanned the streets and alleyways as he blazed through them, searching for a bicycle or anything remotely resembling a mode of transport, and then he saw a most refreshing sight: an old rag-and-bone shop, closed for the day many hours previously. Quaint hoped that the tall, wooden gates to the rear of the shop would hold salvation to him.

He wrenched back the slats of wood that served as a fence, and squeezed his not inconsiderable bulk through the gap. But as he reached a large pair of wooden doors, his progress was barred by an indomitable-looking padlock. Fumbling around inside his coat, Quaint removed his pocket-watch. He depressed a button on the top and, with a click, the face opened up like a locket. Curled within the watch was a long, hook-shaped piece of metal, the ideal hiding place for a tool that had come in handy during more than one stage act. Quaint removed the metal probe, and instantly began picking the lock. Fingers trained in the art of escapology deftly navigated the pins, shafts and cogs better than any locksmith ever could and, within thirty seconds, the heavy padlock fell freely onto the floor with a dull chink. Quaint pulled open the doors and stared into the darkness of a musty, straw-strewn warehouse.

He clicked his tongue against the roof of his mouth, and after what seemed an age, he finally heard a snort echo back at him. His luck was holding out — for the time being, at any rate. That's the problem with luck, it usually has a habit of running out just when you least expect it to. Like any half-decent rag-and-bone shop, this particular store hopefully contained something that Quaint could make good use of.

"Hello, you old nag," Quaint whispered into the darkness. "I do hope you're up for some exercise . . . I'm in an awful hurry."

As if in answer to his words, a huge shire horse sauntered out into the yard. Quaint tugged at the rope around his neck, and gently led it to the moonlight to get a better look. It was a magnificent, muscular beast, exhibiting its age with misted eyes and a beard of wayward white hairs protruding from its chin like an old man's whiskers. The animal was in its latter years, and it was in no particular hurry to go anywhere other than its warm and cosy stable. It would need some coaxing to do Quaint's bidding, and he spied the depressed look in the animal's eyes.

"You look just like I feel," Quaint muttered.

Meanwhile, at Quaint's destination in Hyde Park, the elusive Antoine Renard had arrived. He stood and stared at the huge yellow-and-red-striped circus tent, blowing into his dirty hands for warmth. He reached into the pocket of his jacket and caressed the small, velvet pouch beneath his fingertips. He looked around at the deserted circus tents covered with flags, banners and posters decorating the plot. Renard strolled silently into the area, his eyes flicking left and right searching for his quarry. He knew she'd be here, but he didn't know how prepared she would be for his arrival. As sensitive to feelings as his mother was, surely his hatred would announce his presence louder than a foghorn. After walking around the many tents, booths, stalls and cages he saw the tent that called to him: Madame Destine's tent. It stood out to him like a sore thumb amongst the others, his mother's scent all over it.

He was about three feet from the canvas door when it suddenly burst open, and standing there waiting for him was Destine — a grim, determined look upon her face. The rain clouds above suddenly broke, as a metaphor underlining the bitterness between these two people. Sheets of water fell straight down from the sky, pelting the grass and bouncing off the nearby canvas tents rat-a-tat-tat.

"We should have picked nicer weather for our reunion, Mother. Typical England, *ne convenez-vous pas?*" said Renard. A twisted grin seeped onto his face, drifting across its surface like oil upon water.

"I see that you did not meet Cornelius on your way here," Destine said.

"What makes you say that?" her son asked.

"Because you are still alive," Destine lifted her black lace veil, and stared at him with penetrating eyes. "What are you doing here, Antoine? Have you not done enough damage; you seek to cause yet more?"

"Oh, you know me, Mother," Renard said, placing his hand upon his chest in a mock heartfelt gesture. "I just couldn't leave without saying *au revoir*."

"Do not call me 'Mother' ... you are no son of mine. You are the spawn of a demon, Antoine; you have tainted my life with your poisonous mind. I told you once, all those years past, and I shall tell you now ... you are rotten to the core ... just like Phillipe."

Renard took a sudden step forward, causing Destine to flinch, but she bravely held her ground. "You aren't fit to even speak my father's name," he spat, his scarred face contorting into a violent sneer. "His dying wish was only to see you ... one last time, to make amends ... and you couldn't even do that for him, could you?"

"Did he seriously expect me to drop everything to go running *back* to the monster that I was running *from*?" Destine demanded.

"So ... not only did Cornelius Quaint take you from *me*, he took you from *Father* as well. Quaint has a lot to answer for. I have had such fun with him over the past week ... it's such a shame that it has to end."

"Cornelius knew nothing of Phillipe's death . . . I did not tell him," Destine said. "But why should I have? Phillipe was dead to me years ago."

"You lie! It was Quaint twisting your mind. Why do you always *protect* him?" Renard's eyes flared at the thought of Quaint. "You see him as a replacement for your abysmal failure of a son, *non*? A chance to rectify your past mistakes?"

"No, Antoine — it was not *I* who made the mistakes. You are so infected with hate that it taints every word that spills from your mouth — just like your damn father," Destine shouted through the curtains of pouring rain. "He was nothing but a coward and a monster, Antoine, who subjugated the fears of others to his own desires."

The tears flowed from her eyes, distorting her voice as she spoke, in fluent French now, in disjointed bursts — trying to ensure each word counted, for it might be her last. Even if she were to scream at the top of her voice no one else would hear her — for the rain spattered like rapid gunfire around them. She was praying silently in her head that Cornelius would turn up like a white knight and rescue her, but she knew he was miles away in Crawditch, far across the river — and heroes were few and far between in the real world. She was on her own, with her son walking a knife's edge between sanity and insanity, and her life hanging in the balance.

Renard's lips quivered in the rain as he tried to master his rage. He was like a steaming pot, boiling to the point where it reached critical overload. "No wonder Father hated you . . . why he was glad to see you go. He saw through you, you know . . . saw through you for what you truly are."

"Antoine . . . if you think your father was anything other than a lying, cheating bastard who put me — and you — through hell, then you are severely mistaken. Or do you not remember the nights you used to cry yourself to sleep after he beat you? Or when you walked in on him beating *me*? Do you know how many times I tried to get away, to get *you* away?" Each word was spoken through gritted teeth, the emotion barely held in check, but tangible in every syllable. "I used to just hold you and weep — hating myself for bringing you into a world of such despicable cruelty. If only my premonitions could have given me warning of what was to become your fate . . . of the pain that you would eventually cause others."

Renard glanced up from the ground with seething, vehement eyes. A grumble of distant thunder broke many miles away, symbolising the tumultuous emotions of hate bubbling over inside of his cold, dark heart. "Your gifts are dulled on your own flesh and blood, Mother, I know that. For you see, I am something of a seer myself, although not yet in your league, I admit. You have been blinded by your own hatred."

"Hate may be a powerful emotion, Antoine . . . more powerful even than love. They both have the power to blind a sensitive. But you are wrong, it is not hatred that I feel for you, it is sorrow. I was not as blind to you as you think."

"If you knew that I would come, then why are you alone?" Renard tested.

"For all your crimes . . . as much as I may deny it, you are still born of my flesh. You have to let me help you, Antoine," Destine pleaded. "You have to let me cleanse your father's anger from your heart once and for all."

"Cleanse me? Have you any idea how pathetic you sound? Cleanse me, like I am some filthy wound that cuts the surface of the skin? By now you must realise that I am who I am, what I am, through and through. Each sinew of every muscle and fibre of my being *loathes* you, Mother. I need no cleansing," mocked Renard. "I didn't come here to make happy families . . . I came here to watch you die." His hand came from nowhere, striking Destine across the cheekbone, and she fell to the ground.

"You even hit like your father," said Destine, as she wiped a thin crease of blood from the corner of her mouth. "You may speak these words to me . . . but it is with your father's voice. He has poisoned you."

"Poison?" yelled Renard, striding around the fallen Destine like a lion reviewing its prey for the best angle of attack. "What a simply wonderful idea, Mother." Renard reached into his jacket pocket, squatting down at Destine's side. She slowly rolled onto her back, her long wet dress clinging to her as if it were made of tar. "Unlike my father, *I* shall have the luxury of watching you die," Renard said, baring his teeth. He brandished a small glass vial in his wet hand.

Shards of rain-filtered moonlight bounced off its glass surface, and Destine squinted through the rain. "What . . . is that?" she whispered.

Renard glared proudly at the half-full vial of clear liquid. "Although a fool of a priest believed this to be an elixir of immortality, it is not any longer. Now it is the most potent poison ever concocted by man or nature, and it is the means of your death. I only wish I could spare more, but this stuff is in short supply. You're only getting dear old Bishop Courtney's leftovers, but it's enough to do you harm."

"You . . . you came all this way to poison me? Tell me, Antoine, do you loathe me that much?" wept Destine. Her son was now truly lost to her, lost to rationality, lost to reason.

"Don't flatter yourself, Mother. My business in England brings me just a few short miles from here in Whitehall . . . you are merely a bonus."

"Your business? What *business* do you speak of?"

"Do you really expect me to sit here and run off at the mouth until your prodigal son turns up? I'm afraid not, Mother . . . but I *will* let you in on a little secret . . . soon the River Thames will run with this poison, killing anything it comes into contact with. Mixing the stuff with salt water will augment its potency a hundredfold, and it will spread like wildfire, tainting not just the dockland districts, but it'll seep everywhere, right into London's heart. Not even the great Cornelius Quaint can stop what is in motion this time."

Destine shivered as the icy hand of dread stroked against her spine. If this poison Antoine gloated about could cause so much damage in a body of water the size of the Thames . . . what horrors would it inflict upon her?

Holding Destine by the throat, Renard uncorked the vial with his front teeth and waved it under her nose like smelling salts. Destine tried to twist her soaking wet face from his grip, but Renard easily overpowered her.

"You . . . you are still just a killer at heart," Destine spat, "no matter how grand you make yourself out to be."

"With respect, I am a lot more than *just* a killer," said Renard. "Killing is easy. On the other hand; *murdering* is a much more skilful business." The Frenchman held a finger to his ear as a loud crash of thunder exploded around them. "Do you hear that? That is your death knell sounding, Mother."

Destine tore her eyes away from him, staring through the drizzle into the distance. She was listening to an ominous rumbling sound, not just crashing in the skies above like thunder, but travelling against the wind. It echoed all around her from all sides, a droning, booming noise that grew ever louder. Destine began to grin to herself, as raindrops pelted her face.

"Accepting your fate at last, *non*?" Renard said.

"*Non*, Antoine," said Destine. "I am accepting *yours*."

"What are you talking about?"

"That sound you hear is not thunder," Destine said.

Galloping towards her at a furious pace through the liquid walls of rain was a horse. Sitting astride the horse — the moon-bathed light giving him a shining, silver aura — was Cornelius Quaint. As the rain pelted against his hard face, his black eyes narrowed, his brow furrowed, and he fixed his sights upon his target. Quaint dug his heels hard into the horse's flanks, feeling the creature lurch forwards, and he gripped the rope around its neck tighter. Renard, kneeling by his mother's inert form, was only a matter of yards away from him, and the sight re-energised his rage. The Frenchman was tantalisingly just out of his reach.

"*C'est impossible*! Quaint? You witch!" Renard snapped. He grabbed Destine by the scruff of the neck, and tipped the vial's contents forcibly into her mouth. "But you shall die long before I do, Mother. I have the only antidote, and unless you consume a cure within one hour — you are dead!" Renard gloated, discarding the empty vial onto the grass. "*Au revoir*, Madame Destine."

The Frenchman turned and sprinted towards the exit from the park where the Bishop's driver was sitting waiting for him — it was a sin to let that transportation go to waste, now that the Bishop could no longer make use of it.

Destine gagged, rolling over on the soaking wet grass, over and over again, fighting for breath. Her throat burned as the liquid made its way down. She tried to close it off, but it was useless. The poison would soon be in her system and there was not a damn thing she could do about it. Her vision was already

341

beginning to lose cohesion, and the curtains of rain didn't help. She reached out her arm towards the shadow thundering towards her, screaming Quaint's name into the rain-filled wind, before unconsciousness stole her words, and she slumped onto her back.

Within a fraction of a second, Cornelius Quaint arrived at Destine's side, and pulled the huge shire-horse to a halt. He leapt from the creature's back, skidding onto the grass next to Destine, and snatched up her wrist, wiping the soaking strands of hair from her face. He pressed his cheek to hers. She was so very cold.

"Destine," he shouted above the din of the downpour. "Destine, speak to me!"

He fell to his knees, cupping the Frenchwoman's head in his hands. Her breathing was shallow, and her eyes rolled. He looked around frantically for assistance. Lifting Destine up into his muscular arms, he cradled her close to his chest. Quaint's mind was flowing like quicksilver as he tried to think clearly, but he had no choice but to watch helplessly as Antoine Renard climbed into the rear of the carriage, less than two hundred yards away. Quaint fought every urge in his body. He wanted to give chase, but Destine shifted and moaned within his arms, snatching him back to reality. For once in his life, Cornelius Quaint had no idea what to do for the best.

"Help! Help me," Quaint yelled into the darkness. "Ruby! Jeremiah! Anyone, quick," his voice boomed once more. The rain fell relentlessly, and sparkles of liquid pelted Destine's pale, cold face. "I've got to get you out of this rain," Quaint said, holding his coat over her, offering a modicum of protection as he took her into her tent, laying her onto her camp bed.

In the distance, Quaint saw the faint glow of a lantern, and he yelled again for help, announcing himself. A few seconds later, a group of Quaint's workers joined him inside the tent.

"Harry! Bert!" Quaint snapped, not even looking the men in the eyes. "Get the tinder-burner in here, pronto. And we need some hot soup . . . and water," he said, noticing the specks of perspiration appearing on the surface of Destine's skin as a shiver ran through her body. "Christ, she's got a bastard of a fever . . . run and get Nurse Madoc, we need her skills here, right away! And can someone *please* go outside and check on my horse."

The group of men exchanged confused glances.

"What's up with her, boss?" asked one of them.

"God knows, Harry, I can't see any sign of a wound . . . so I'm thinking maybe it's her heart . . . but that fever . . . she's burning up good and proper," Quaint said, scratching at his sodden locks. "Plus, I know who was just here . . . I saw the bastard run off into the night. His appearance was probably enough to put her into shock."

Destine suddenly awoke and clutched at the air frantically, her arms and fingers outstretched as if electricity were animating her entire body. She screamed from the pit of her stomach, and arched her back. Her pale blue eyes rolled into the top of her head until only the whites remained, and her mouth trembled. Quaint shuffled himself forwards, taking her hands in his. Tenderly mopping at her brow with his handkerchief, he leaned closer.

"Destine . . . it's me. It's Cornelius," he said, the emotion stealing the usual confident edge to his voice. "Can you hear me, Madame?"

"Knew . . . you'd come," Destine said weakly, her eyelids fluttering erratically.

"Madame, where does it hurt? What did Renard *do* to you?"

Destine craned her neck to look at him. She slowly lifted her hand, and dropped the empty vial that Renard had discarded into his palm. "Forced me . . . to drink . . . some kind of poison," she said. "Too late for me . . . my love."

A middle-aged woman dressed in a thick dressing gown shuffled uncomfortably into the tent past the accumulated gathering, carrying a large medical bag.

"Mr Q? Where's the patient?" the sweet-voiced woman asked.

"Nurse, she's here. It's Madame — she's been poisoned," said Quaint. He snatched up the vial, and took a brief sniff. "This doesn't smell like any poison I've ever come across. It could be some kind of venom . . . perhaps snake? I don't know. I arrived a few moments ago, and found her collapsed on the ground. Is there anything you can do?"

The plump nurse squinted at the vial in Quaint's hand. "Poisoned?"

"Someone *did* this to her. Now there must be something you can do!" snapped Quaint.

344

"Gosh, Mr Q, I don't know . . . I'm not used t'stuff like poison, an' suchlike! Let me 'ave a good look at 'er," the nurse said in a thick West Country accent, "It all depends on what type o' poison it were, now don't it? And 'ow she took it, whether it be a bite, skin contact or orally."

Quaint was floored. "Orally, I think. She said he made her drink it."

"Right then," Nurse Madoc said, scouring Destine's face for clues, "we need to try our best t'flush it from her system quick-smart. I've got a nasty wee ointment 'ere that'll make 'er vomit like a first-time sailor. We need t'give 'er as much fluid as we can. If we're lucky, we'll dilute the poison's effects before it reaches the bloodstream, or it'll be all over 'er body in seconds. Now stand back, man."

The occupants of the tent froze as Destine suddenly screamed, and gripped onto the side of the camp bed until her knuckles turned bone-white. She lifted her arm, and motioned to Quaint. He stumbled onto his knees and pressed his cheek against hers.

"I'm here, Destine," he said.

"Renard plans . . . to poison the river," she gasped, her dry lips cracked like sun-hardened mud. "Stop . . . him."

"Madame, what are you saying? The river? Which river?"

"Thames. Oh, Cornelius, please . . . you must hurry."

"What? No, I can't go anywhere, Destine. I'm needed here . . . with you."

345

Destine gripped at his clothes, as if the effort took all of her strength. "No, Cornelius . . . no."

"But . . . the poison," he said, his hands shaking as he watched Destine's strength ebbing away before his eyes.

"Antoine . . . has cure," Destine said.

"I . . . I don't know about this, Destine. Where do I begin?"

Destine licked at her barren lips, trying to force the words to form themselves upon them. Her wild, tortured eyes implored Quaint's very soul. "Whitehall," she said exhaustedly, before crashing back down onto the bed. "Renard's gone . . . to Whitehall."

CHAPTER
FORTY-EIGHT

The Pursuit

Within seconds, Quaint had re-mounted his purloined horse and set off towards St James's Palace. From there the fastest route was heading down Pall Mall a little way before streaking right across St James's Park to his destination. Whitehall was a big place, nestled on the north-west side of the Thames in between the Westminster and Waterloo Bridges, and finding Renard would need some logical thinking and a fair amount of luck.

It was now just past a quarter-to-two in the morning, and the roads were silent and empty, thankfully bereft of horses and carriages. Quaint's cumbersome, though strong and muscular shire-horse was maintaining a steady speed — if not as swift as Quaint would have liked. His journey so far had been an arduous one, both physically and mentally. Never had he given chase at such a slow pace before, and he almost felt it'd be quicker to get off and walk, until something from his memory came from nowhere. A phrase that he had picked up from some cattle merchants in Morocco years before announced itself upon his mind. As the horse cantered amiably along the cobbles, its heavy footsteps echoing off the enclosed streets, Quaint held on tight to the rope around the beast's neck and leant towards its ear.

"*Az-Toray!*" he yelled.

The horse whinnied with a combination of shock and alarm as if woken from some deep slumber, and it instantly sprang to life, galloping forwards at double speed. Whatever that particular word meant to the animal, Quaint couldn't care less, and as he gripped the rope for dear life he patted himself on the back, mentally noting that gem for future use.

He was still none the wiser about what plot he was involved in, but Renard and the Hades Consortium's implication blinded him to the details. Right now, obtaining some kind of cure for Destine's condition was the driving force — of course, considering that he had already spent the best part of twenty minutes getting barely a few miles from Hyde Park, time was definitely going to be a factor.

Quaint was nearing St James's Park when he yanked hard on the rope to slow his horse down. A carriage was parked in the centre of the dark, deserted street, and a man lay on the ground beside it, writhing in pain. Renard was leaving a trail of bodies in his wake. Quaint was almost relieved. If the Frenchman kept *that* up, it'd be easier to follow than a trail of breadcrumbs.

In a flash, Quaint was off his horse and kneeling at the man's side.

"He . . . came from nowhere," wheezed the man, his face contorted in pain.

"Are you all right, sir?" Quaint said, reaching for the man's hand. "Did you see which way the felon went?"

The felled man slowly turned to look at him. "Yeah . . . he's right behind you mate," chirped Melchin — the Bishop's coach driver.

The sound of clapping filled the air, echoing off the confinement of the terraced buildings in the enclosed street. Quaint gradually rose to his feet, accepting the inevitable fact that he had just been taken for a fool.

"*Renard*," he said.

"Bravo, Mr Melchin," said Antoine Renard, as he stepped from the shadows of a nearby doorway into the streams of moonlight, continuing to clap his hands. "A cracking performance!" Renard walked up behind Quaint, and aimed a pistol at a distance of no more than eight feet. "You can relax, Cornelius. I am not about to shoot you in the back."

Quaint turned around slowly and his eyes met the physical embodiment of all his pain. It was almost a relief to look at him again, to prove to himself that the Devil did indeed walk the earth amongst men. Fifteen years of thinking that they would never meet again, fifteen years of a bubbling broth simmering on a stove, and fifteen years of searching for something that had no wish to be found.

"You've got to admire the irony," Renard said, "for was it not this same predicament that signalled our last meeting?"

"Except last time *I* was the one holding the pistol," said Quaint. "I should have dredged the Seine myself

349

and thrust a wooden stake through your damned heart, like the Devil you are."

"If only your intelligence was as smart as your wit, Cornelius," said Renard, stepping closer, the gun steady in his hand.

"Enough game-play, Renard, you know what I want."

"And what do you want, Cornelius? My head on a platter?"

"All I want is the antidote to the poison."

"The antidote, he says?" squawked Renard with a gesture of mock surprise. "So, you've seen Mother, then? Pitiful old wretch, isn't she? And that is all you want? You don't want me? You don't want revenge?" he taunted, intentionally stoking the embers of Quaint's hatred. "Not even after all these years? Cornelius, you really know how to wound me."

Quaint ground his teeth. "I wish that were so."

The two men patrolled around the street, circling each other slowly, neither one removing their eyes from the other. Both were now so focused upon the other that the world could have erupted into flames around them and it would have gone unnoticed. The street's merchant stores and guest houses were derelict and beyond repair. A ghost town, it provided the perfect setting for these two foes. The thunder echoed about them, the lightning throwing white cracks of radiance around the sky.

Renard waved his pistol through the air like a bandleader conducting an orchestra. "Let me hear you ask for it, Cornelius . . . let me hear you beg for it."

"The antidote, Renard," said Quaint.

"And the rest . . ."

"The antidote, Renard . . . *please*."

Renard clapped his hands with glee. "I propose a trade: if you give me what *I* want — I will give you what *you* want."

"What could *I* possibly have that you'd want, Renard?" asked Quaint, his calm exterior belying the maelstrom of emotions churning in his insides. He was watching his foe vividly, trying to guess what he would do next, but trying to outfox Renard was like trying to pinch quicksilver. Whereas Quaint's demeanour was reactive and defensive, Renard's was self-assuredly confident. He was effortlessly in control, and the Frenchman knew it. A crooked lightning vein sparked silver-white overhead, scarring the sky, and Renard was enjoying every second of his triumph.

"What do I want, *monsieur*? Hmm, well that's the fun part. All I want is to test your loyalty to my mother. You are more a son to her than I, and I am interested to see whether you could make the right choice if given a difficult dilemma," said Renard, the sudden flash of light accentuating the crooked scar down the left side of his face. "You can have the antidote for free; the only price I ask is this: I want to watch as *you* drink the poison too."

Quaint scowled at him intently. "You wish to *poison* me? Come on, Renard, where's the sport in that? Would it not be simpler to just put a bullet in my brain?" he asked, pointing to the gun in Renard's hand.

"Simpler, perhaps — but nowhere near as satisfying for me. You see, the problem is . . . there's only one vial of antidote . . . just enough for one dose. I thought I'd make this task a bit more of a challenge for you — I know how you have a flair for the dramatic. Such a choice . . ." gloated Renard, standing with his arms outstretched like a crucifix. "Your life on one side . . . Madame Destine's on the other. Who lives — it's up to you!"

"You're insane! How can you have so little regard for life?"

"I am a killer for hire, Cornelius . . . having a cold heart comes with the job." Renard flashed his eyes wider at Quaint, as if showing him the darkness inside his soul. "But this is your decision; I do not wish to sway your judgement."

"This is *your* decision, Renard, not mine! And it is you alone whom I will hold responsible should Destine die."

"Sounds fair to me," grinned Renard. "Of course . . . you need to live if you wish to make good on your threat . . . and that is highly unlikely, *monsieur*. If you choose to drink the antidote yourself in some vain attempt to try and stop me — my mother's death will be on *your* conscience. Her blood will be on your hands, and you must hold yourself responsible. Tell me, Cornelius; are you ready to make the ultimate sacrifice?"

CHAPTER
FORTY-NINE

The Burden of Choice

"You're twisted, Renard," said Cornelius Quaint ardently. "I always knew you were a cad, but to gamble your own mother's life . . . that's low even for you."

"I do like to surprise, now and again," Renard curled his tongue around his thin lips. "So . . . what do you say? Do we have a bargain?"

"You already know what I will choose."

"Indeed, for you truly have *no* choice," said Renard. He thrust his hand into his jacket pocket, pulling out the glass vial of the deadly liquid. "Don't worry about me. I've got enough poison to go around. I only need one single vial to do my job, and by now, the rest are well on their way to their destination."

"The rest?" asked Quaint. "How many of those damned things are there?"

"Enough."

"And where *is* their destination, Renard?"

"Cornelius, I'm surprised at you, I really am . . . and you call yourself a *conjuror*? Do you really expect me to give up *all* my secrets? Where is the drama? Where are the surprises? Where is the suspense of it all?"

Unmoved by Renard's sarcasm, Quaint pressed the Frenchman with the one thing that he had as ammunition. "What does the Hades Consortium plan on doing with the rest of the poison, Renard?"

Renard's expression fell. "What do you know of the Hades Consortium?" he snapped, resighting his target with the pistol.

"I thought you liked surprises," said Quaint deftly.

"It doesn't matter what you know, or think you know, Quaint. The Hades Consortium's plan for Egypt will proceed without interruption whether you know of it or not, unless you have a way of communicating from beyond the grave. In less than a month, the River Nile will run red with blood, and there is nothing anyone can do to stop it."

"The Nile? I thought you planned on poisoning the Thames?" asked Quaint, trying to tease as much out of Renard as possible in case he needed to make use of it later. If there was a later, of course — an optimistic mind is easily fooled.

"The Consortium has many irons in the fire, Cornelius, and in many locations. Egypt's fate is but one of these. But back to business . . . poor Madame Destine doesn't have all night, you know," Renard said. "I went easy on her . . . I only gave her a small dose, and the antidote is only effective within sixty minutes. This poison is very punctual."

"What exactly does it do?" asked Quaint.

"It kills," said Renard, holding the vial up to the moonlight. "With a hundred per cent success rate — that's all you need to know. Once this stuff mixes with the river, the current will do the rest for me. You should have seen what it did earlier. I have to give the stuff its due, although it's positively ghastly — it really is quite spectacular. Were Bishop Courtney still alive, I'm sure he would concur."

"Bishop Courtney? That name keeps cropping up all over the place. On Tom Hawkspear's release papers from Blackstaff prison, for example. By now that Irish fiend should be long dead."

"Well, that's *your* fault," said Renard. "Poor old Hawkspear is only a pawn in my game because of *you*."

"What are you talking about?" said Quaint.

"Bringing Hawkspear to Crawditch was all for *your* benefit, did you not know? This scheme has been well planned, Cornelius, that is the way the Consortium does things."

"How do you mean for 'my benefit'?" It was then Quaint's turn to falter. "Was Sergeant Berry correct, then? You involved me in your scheme intentionally?"

Reynolds laughed under his breath, squinting into the night sky. "Simple physics, Cornelius. Sometimes you need to apply force from obscure angles to cause the right amount of pressure elsewhere," a thin, crooked smile crept onto his face. "I have orchestrated everything, my dear Cornelius — what, who, when, where — even Hawkspear's release from Blackstaff prison was on my command."

"Twinkle's death, Prometheus taking the blame . . . Hawkspear was the one that did the killing . . . but you were pulling his strings all the time?" asked Quaint. "Why Hawkspear specifically?"

"That maniac's appearance on the scene was engineered for one reason and one reason only — to occupy *you*, the great Cornelius Quaint, to keep you out of my way. I needed someone with the right amount of passion to become our killer, and once I'd discovered that Hawkspear shared a history with your strongman, it was too deliciously perfect to believe. Your man was nothing more than a very visible target. With your mind focused upon *him*, I knew it would be *off* the Bishop's plan."

"So you were working for this Bishop character all along?" Quaint asked.

"When it suited me."

"And the rest of the time working for the Hades Consortium, eh? No wonder you dragged poor old Oliver into this scheme of yours. Tell me; is Sir George still in the inner circle of the Consortium?"

"My, it seems you *are* remarkably well informed after all, Cornelius. I almost wish I had time to find out exactly how much you *do* know . . . but I've got a schedule to keep. Hurry up and drink the poison will you, there's a good chap."

Quaint gritted his teeth, and measured up his situation. To save Destine, he would have to forsake his own life — that much seemed clear now. Renard was right; there was no choice, and no way out. The Frenchman was watching him like a hawk, his pistol trained at Quaint's head. There was only one way this would end, and both men knew it.

As Quaint raised the deadly vial to his lips, the stench of the acidic poison staggered him, scorching at

356

his nasal canal. With one last glance in Renard's direction, he tipped the contents of the vial into his mouth. He instantly tasted the harsh, metallic-tasting liquid flow upon his tongue, tingling against the roof of his mouth. With a sideways glance at Renard's smug face, Quaint threw the glass vial onto the ground.

"Satisfied?" he asked bitterly.

Renard nodded. "Very much so! I applaud your bravery, Cornelius."

"The antidote, Renard, give it to me," demanded Quaint.

"Take it . . . for all the good it'll do you. If Mother doesn't get that soon, she's dead, and you'll be following her not much later, so either way . . . I win," he said, tossing the glass vial high up into the air. "Catch!"

Suspended for an eternity, spinning in circles in the air, the antidote finally began to descend and Quaint threw himself onto the cobbles, and snatched up the vial before it hit the ground. He slowly unfurled one finger at a time to make sure the vial was intact.

"One day, it'll be just you and me, Antoine," he said, watching Renard walk casually away towards the waiting coach. "No tricks."

"Coming from a conjuror, that's quite rich," said Renard, skipping into the horse-drawn coach. "I'll await your resurrection with bated breath, *monsieur*. I think I shall almost miss sparring with you. Wherever will I find a nemesis as worthy as you? Melchin . . . let's get going."

Quaint winced as he felt an electric twinge wash over him from the pit of his stomach. The poison was already taking effect, as it had done so quickly with Destine. She was a woman in her seventies, more frail than she let on. She was in no position to put up a battle that was more about stubbornness and will-power than anything else. Fortunately for Quaint, he had those qualities in droves.

He rose unsteadily to his feet and stood in the centre of the street like a lost child, looking towards the area of Hyde Park, and then back down the street, as Renard's carriage melted into the shadows and faded from sight. Quaint watched his foe depart, with full knowledge that he was about to kill hundreds of people. Scratching furiously at his mop of curls, feeling the poison crawl slowly around his veins, Quaint looked up at the sky, feeling scattered raindrops pelt his face. He begged the grey clouds for guidance.

Quaint checked the time on his pocket-watch. "Oh, well — in for a penny, and all that."

CHAPTER
FIFTY

The Rooftop Highway

Cornelius Quaint ignored the acidic rush that flowed down his throat, and gripped the rope around the shire horse's neck tightly, literally as if his life depended on it. The word "*Az-Toray*" had an amazing effect on the horse's stamina once more, and the thunderous beast galloped down Spinnaker Street like a streak of lightning, much to Quaint's discomfort.

Renard's coach was in sight, and had been far ahead for a good five minutes, but Quaint was unable to shorten the distance, despite the horse's best efforts. The chill wind grew more bitter the closer he got to the Thames, which Quaint took as a good sign, for it meant Whitehall was only minutes away, as was the Frenchman's plot to poison the river. The sooner Quaint caught up with him and defeated him, the sooner he could get back to Hyde Park. It was a credit to Quaint that it all sounded fairly straightforward — but then again, it wasn't as if he had spent any time actually *thinking* about the magnitude of his task. His mind was busy elsewhere, trying to guess where Renard might do the most damage with that foul poison in his possession.

Whitehall was a large district, often regarded as the heart of London, the main location for most of Parliament's ministries and governmental offices. A teenaged Quaint had spent some time there as a young clerk, working for one of the many Thames trade ministries, and his familiarity with the area enabled him to make a sudden rash decision. He wrenched hard on the horse's rope, stopping the animal clumsily as its hooves skidded on the wet cobbles.

"Sorry, old chap, but I can make better progress on foot from here," Quaint said. He leapt from the horse's back and darted down an alleyway, his long coat trailing behind him like a pair of dirty wet wings.

The shops and merchant stores dissipated the further he moved into Whitehall itself, making way for row upon row of terraced housing buildings and waterfront storage facilities. If you knew where you were going and had a head for heights, by traversing across the rooftop highways, a man could easily shave valuable minutes off his journey and, if he were in pursuit, every second counted.

Taking advantage of the warren-like layout of the Thames-side buildings, Quaint sprinted through the narrow lanes, past delivery entrances and rear gardens strewn with rubbish. Using a stack of wooden planks, he vaulted up over a wall and his feet landed with a slap against the lane at the rear of a terraced tenement building. The sudden jarring of his uneasy landing sent a shock-wave of queasiness around him. Quaint wheezed, feeling every intake of breath bringing further waves of stinging pain. He leaned against the wall for support, desperately trying to catch his breath as a kaleidoscopic display of fireworks flashed before his eyes. The poison was spreading fast throughout his system now and he knew it. Was this to be his fate, then? To die a quivering mess in the garden of a squalid, urine-smelling building . . . and for Destine to die just as horribly in Hyde Park? Cornelius Quaint forced the pain to retreat behind his clenched teeth in stubborn defiance.

"I . . . won't give you the . . . satisfaction, Renard," he hissed, coughing a spit-ball of bloody phlegm into the gutter. He palmed the spots from his eyes and regained his composure. He needed to conquer this ravaging beast before it consumed him from the inside out.

The touch of the cold glass vial in his breast pocket was small consolation. He reached into it, and pulled out the antidote. With just one mouthful he could put an end to Renard's plan for good. The Thames, and the Nile also, would be safe. Finally, Quaint would be able to close a chapter that had remained stubbornly open. But the price he would have to pay was steep . . . for it was nothing less than Destine's life.

A thought suddenly struck him, and he allowed it to wallow around his addled mind undisturbed. Unsure exactly what he was doing, Quaint quickly uncorked the vial and raised it to his lips. Surely half an antidote was better than none, and the liquid might just give him the extra push he needed to keep up the chase. He paused. If he drank the antidote . . . did that not prove that his hatred of Renard eclipsed his love for Destine?

361

He hoped not. He could not allow the darkness to consume the light. But then the thought of Renard's plan drove into focus clearly in his mind. Many more could die — *would* die — if Renard had his way. Quaint was probably the only man alive who knew of it, and definitely the only man alive who would pursue Antoine Renard to the ends of the world to defeat him. He had no choice. He had to do something.

Quaint's decision to pursue his foe rather than race to his guardian's side would have bothered him more had he not been preoccupied with trying to keep from collapsing in a bloodied heap on the floor. He swallowed a metallic clot of blood back down his throat, raised the vial to his lips once again, and tipped half the antidote down his throat. Within seconds it was fluttering around inside him. Quaint felt partially revitalised in moments, and grabbed hold of the iron railings at the bottom of a weather-worn staircase that snaked up the side of the building.

As he reached the flat roof of the tenement, Quaint heard a strange yet recognisable noise, and he ran to the edge, scouring the dark lanes below that ran towards the River Thames. He could see the flaking whitewash on the embankment wall, and briefly, for a split second, a horse-drawn coach flashed into view beneath him. Quaint's ploy had worked; he had decreased the distance between himself and his quarry.

Renard's coach was slowing down. He must be nearing his destination, thought Quaint, but where the hell could the man be going? He used his hand as a visor and squinted into the distance, when the penny dropped. Quaint recognised the large, pale building that nestled upon the banks of the Thames in the distance.

Situated a mile or so along the road, the Whitehall Weir House was a sugar-white building on the north side of the Thames, housing a collection of weirs — the perfect place to administer Renard's poison. Quaint had been there before, and the memory of the roofed jetty that jutted out into the Thames was still fresh. A large watermill made use of the constant rush of water flow that the weirs provided to grind the flour at the neighbouring Grist Mill. The mill's location on the banks of the Thames enabled easy access for the huge grain cargo ships that trawled up and down the river from all points on the compass — but of more importance today was the knowledge that if someone wished to poison the river, a collection of weirs would do a most admirable job.

Fuelled by this recognition, a re-energised Quaint began to feel like a man half his age, and his full strength returned to form a barrier around the poison's effects, pushing it down into the recesses of his body. He needed to cut a swift dash to the Weir House, and the rooftop highway thankfully provided him with a shortcut. With slim gaps between each tenement, Quaint could traverse across each one in a straight line, unlike Renard's coach, following the slower, snaking road. The building opposite the one where he stood was a good ten feet away, an easy jump for Quaint at the best of times — but this was not the best of times — as his swaying vision reminded him. One miscalculation or

363

misstep, and he would plummet to the ground below. Well, he couldn't have that. If he died, who would stop Renard? There was no stand-in, there was no replacement, no Plan B. It began and ended with Quaint — the Alpha and the Omega.

"Oh, well," he muttered to himself. "Nothing ventured . . ."

He clenched his fists, and ran at the edge of the roof at full pelt, his heavy steps pounding away at the felted roof of the building. His feet touched the edge of the roof, and he propelled himself upwards with all his strength, soaring through the air towards the other building. Time seemed to slow to a crawl. Quaint could see his destination; he could almost imagine himself landing confidently. His feet slapped down hard on the tenement's roof with inches to spare, and Quaint rolled into a ball, skidding across the rooftop. He gathered himself together, and scrambled over the cluttered chimney stacks of the densely populated building towards the next edge. Placing himself parallel to Renard's position, Quaint ensured he never let the man from his sight.

"Feet, don't fail me now," he said.

Staring down at the road below him, Quaint caught another glimpse of Renard's coach. If he wanted to stop the Frenchman before he reached the Weir House, he probably had less than a mile in which to do it. Realising this steeled him to go forward, and he launched himself over the chasm again, across the rooftops from one building to the next. Cornelius

Quaint was panting and wheezing but his momentum was locked on course now, unable to deviate.

As he motored forward like a steam train from the edge of the building's rooftop, Quaint suddenly realised something quite horrifying — he had just run out of buildings . . .

This notion was extremely bad news primarily because he had already launched himself into the air. He had just leapt from the end of a terraced house, and it was a long, long way down.

Quaint's fingers groped the air around him, miraculously finding purchase on the edge of a massive brick chimney stack. His body lurched erratically in an arc through the air, but his grip held against the rough stone, and he was snapped back. His body slammed against the side of the building, but still his grip did not falter. Hanging by his fingertips, he managed to twist his body around, and swung himself towards the building's window frames. At least there he would find shelter from the searing wind that threatened to rip him from the building like tissue paper in a cyclone.

His heart pounding fit to burst, Quaint began to scale down the stone window-sill ledges at the tenement's front, ledges caked in pigeon excrement that assaulted his senses with the stench of ammonia. Pressing himself tight against the glass, he manoeuvred into the next window, and down, working his way towards street level via the grid-like windows.

Quaint looked down at the road below. His error had cost him dearly, and Renard's coach was now seemingly just out of reach. He had to reach street level fast, and straight down was the quickest route. He ripped off his scarf, and snagged the drainpipe at the end of the terraced house. He gripped both ends tight, and threaded his wrist around it. Stepping off the building's third storey, he cascaded down the drainpipe at a tremendous speed, with gravity as his transport. His knees and elbows were getting torn to shreds as he rocketed straight down, and the metal-tipped heels on his boots were throwing off sparks like a blacksmith's forge. Quaint suddenly hit the street with a touch more force than he had hoped for. He curled into a ball and clutched his stomach, his guts feeling like the squashed bellows of an accordion.

"Not now . . ." he snapped, as he felt a course of pain flooding his guts. It was not simply the fall that ailed him — it was the poison making itself known once more. Using the pain of the sudden itching beneath the surface of his skin as fuel, Quaint thrust himself forwards and thundered down the street in pursuit. He had to make up some valuable time. Then he saw a most invigorating sight. There was a coach . . . and it had just sped past his position. Quaint pulled himself to his feet.

The low moon animated his shadow across the tenement fronts, as the slap-slap-slap of his boots echoed around the lanes and alleyways. Renard's coach was now only six feet away and, with a final burst of speed, Quaint propelled himself forwards. He stepped up onto the metal rung at the rear of the horse-drawn carriage, and propelled himself up onto the roof. Instantly, the carriage lurched to the side, and a cacophony of voices shouted and screamed in alarm, most notably the driver, Melchin, who struggled hard to control the startled beast dragging the coach.

"Stop this damn coach, Renard!" yelled Quaint into the wind, clutching onto the coach's roof with all his ebbing strength as it swerved from one side of the road to the other. "With my dying breath, I'll see you dead!"

"You first, Cornelius," called Renard from inside the swaying carriage, responding with a volley of shots from his revolver, each one slicing up through the craft's roof mere inches from Quaint's sliding body.

It was only sheer dumb luck — thanks to the momentum of the careering vehicle — that all five of the bullets missed their mark, but Quaint knew he had only seconds. The exploding cracks of thunder sent the already manic horse into overdrive, and the carriage swayed even more violently across the breadth of the road. A quick glimpse through a seared bullet hole in the roof showed Quaint's assailant's position — brandishing the six-shot .32 calibre Adams and Deane pistol — and Quaint leaned into the veer of the carriage, landing a solid punch to Renard's head through the open window. Batting Quaint away with his elbow, Renard gripped the window frame and lunged up with the barrel of the pistol, catching Quaint a glancing blow to the cheek.

Ignoring the blazing pain, he stared through the mist, spying the Weir House just up ahead. He knew that Renard still had one bullet left — more than enough to send him on his way to his maker. He had to move quickly, for there was something else of concern to him.

Like a tremendous undulating acidic wave, something stirred within his guts, causing a nauseous cloud to blur his vision. That damn poison was nothing if not persistent. Just when his strength of will had forced one intense attack to dissipate, another was waiting in the wings, ready to pounce upon him. It was akin to being blindfolded in a boxing ring whilst your opponent was free to hit you at will. He knew the punches were inevitable, but had no idea from which direction they would come.

Quaint knew that Renard getting an accurate shot off whilst he was being thrown around the confines of the carriage was next to impossible. But his recognition of that fact was quickly dashed as the younger and fitter Renard hoisted himself up and out of the window, clawing his way up out onto the roof.

"Hold her steady, Melchin!" screamed Renard.

"What d'you think I'm *trying* to do, mate?" replied the driver over the din of the carriage's wheels. The short, stout man was wrenching on the reins as hard as he could, and the fight against the startled horse was lifting him clear out of his seat.

"You're as stubborn as ever!" Renard said, thrusting his palm hard towards Quaint's jaw, sending the conjuror skidding across the roof.

Quaint landed with a painfully unceremonious thump onto the large fender of the carriage's rear wheel. He was inches from the wheel, and the constant buffeting against the small of his back was sheer torture. Just as he reached for a handhold on the roof, the carriage hit a large bump in the road, and Quaint was cast aside, bouncing with the ricocheting vehicle. The vibrations of the wheel against the hard stone cobbles reverberated through his body, shaking the very teeth in his gums. His head was less than six inches from the whitewashed Thames wall and, with one last spurt of strength, Quaint reached out with all his body's remaining effort. His fingertips brushed against the luggage rack affixed to the roof, and the man clung on with all his might. Quaint threw his other arm up, gripping onto the rail, just as the Frenchman threw his weight towards him. Both men tumbled over the side of the transport onto the rear luggage rack in a jumble of awkward limbs. With a jab of his elbow towards Renard's throat, Quaint regained a handhold. The cobbled stone streets streaked past, inches from both Renard's and Quaint's heads. All it would take was one minor graze at that speed, and the flesh would burn off to the bone. With a well-placed punch to his foe's solar plexus, Quaint managed to gain the upper hand, and clambered back up onto the carriage's rooftop.

"Now it's your turn to beg, Renard," hollered Quaint, holding on desperately by his left hand. "Call a halt to this insane plan of yours now — before it's too late!"

"Cornelius, you self-righteous old fool . . . it's no good appealing to my conscience," Renard said. "I don't have one."

Renard swiftly produced his pistol from underneath his body. Quaint's eyes widened. As the Frenchman pulled the pistol's trigger, his face was briefly illuminated in a glare of amber light. The bullet struck his shoulder . . . The shoulder of the arm attached to the hand that held the fingers that gripped the roof rack of the carriage . . . and Cornelius Quaint fell. He fell clumsily, and he fell hard.

Seeing the lifeless figure of his fallen enemy lying in the middle of the street, Renard saluted. "A valiant effort, Cornelius . . . but in the end, was there ever any doubt as to which of us would be the victor?"

CHAPTER
FIFTY-ONE

The Endgame

The freezing wind chilled the cobbled stone ground, and as Cornelius Quaint tried to lift his battered and wounded body, its surface clung to his cheek. Wincing in agony as he put weight upon his shoulder, he slowly pulled himself up off the ground, like pulling a bandage from an open wound. Quaint lost his balance and crashed back down onto the wet stones. After what seemed like an immeasurable amount of time, he finally managed to force his body to obey his commands, and he rose to his feet.

It had been precious seconds since Renard had shot him, but the dull ache barely even registered. It was the endgame, and he only hoped that he could make it in time to prevent Renard from fulfilling his plan. Pushing the physical pain to the back of his mind, he continued the pursuit, making good use of his determined, single-minded ability to focus upon his quarry.

"You're going to pay for the pain you have wrought, Renard," Quaint said, as he picked at his tattered and ripped clothes with a limp hand. "Or, at the very least, you'll pay for my bloody suit."

★ ★ ★

After an arduous quarter-mile hobble, Quaint was less than fifty yards from the now battered and beaten carriage, when he saw Melchin tying up the coach's horse outside the huge Weir House. A bemused Quaint felt a small semblance of energy creep back into his body at the sight. The conjuror's unconquerable doggedness might just give him the edge he needed.

Sneaking as low as he could, Quaint scuttled through the long dark shadows and grabbed Melchin by his collar, dragging him to the ground. The man was flustered and cowardly, but Quaint was in no mood to play nice.

"Please don't hit me," Melchin yelped. "I don't want no bother, sir! I'm just a driver!"

"Run," Quaint sneered, his face up close to Melchin's. The poison was evident now on his face, the excited blood vessels creating red blotches on his cheeks, and he had rims around his eyes, accentuating his rage in a truly demonic fashion. "As fast, and far away as you can." Quaint thrust his face closer to the quivering driver. "Go!"

Melchin scrambled to his feet, and did as Quaint had ordered. He ran as if his life depended on it down the street, his footsteps echoing into the distance like castanets.

Quaint painfully removed his overcoat, and pulled his handkerchief from his pocket. He folded it into a square swab, and pressed it hard onto the bullet wound on his shoulder. Feeling the nub of the iron projectile just beneath his flesh, he winced. He was loathe to scream — he would not give Renard the pleasure. Quaint wiped a trickle of blood from his nose with his cuff, and stared towards the Weir House as if it were the Devil's residence itself.

"That's the *hors-d'oeuvres* done with . . . now for the main course," he said.

The outside of the Weir House building was a completely different affair than inside. It was essentially a large, warehouse-like containment building, with tall, vertical windows set high into the walls, and huge wooden struts that ran the length of the white building, leading down to the elongated jetty that ran parallel. Inside the building were housed over twenty mechanical weirs; small, metal plates with V-shaped notches cut into them, designed to measure and regulate water depth at certain times of the year. Each plate was fitted to spiralling metal domes housed in the water. The noise both within and without was tremendous; small wonder then that the only tenement buildings located nearby were one step shy of Cheapside, London's fleapit not too far up the river, a haven for users and abusers of opiates, absinthe, petty crime and prostitution.

Quaint made his way to the rear of the building and climbed the wall up to one of the church-like windows, peering cautiously inside. A giant, cog-powered metal construct could be seen clearly, and standing on an observation platform at the rear of the building was Renard. He was scouring the weirs as if he'd lost

373

something, searching for the optimum place to tip the poison. From the weirs, it would mix with the main flow of the water and be dragged down the length of the Thames. Feeling the acidic rush flow over him again, like a million tiny red ants scuttling under the surface of his skin, he was suddenly appreciative of the weapon's power.

With his back pressed hard against the rear wall of the Weir House, Quaint mouthed silently and counted upon his fingers. Renard had surely emptied that pistol of his by now . . . but had he reloaded it? He would be gambling with his life if he just strolled in through the front door. Quaint looked up at the roof of the building, but his pulsating left shoulder screamed against him doing anything even remotely strenuous, so an aerial entrance was out of the question. Quaint knew that a frontal assault was his best option . . . it was probably the last thing Renard would expect and, truth to tell, Cornelius Quaint did so love a good gamble.

Inside the Whitehall Weir House, Renard held the small glass vial in the palm of his hand. Not much bigger than a fountain pen, the deadly liquid looked harmless to the naked eye, and even Renard himself had questioned its potency, until he had watched the Bishop's veins implode as the acidic parasitic liquid devoured him from the inside out. That was just the latest image in a long line of nightmarish scenes that the man had seen — and caused — during his adult life. This current plot would certainly be his most ambitious, but the only drawback was him not being able to see for himself the deaths that it would surely cause. He usually enjoyed seeing the fruits of his hard labour blossom in front of his eyes, but it was an acceptable loss.

Renard was lost in this world of his. Above the din of the swirling weirs, he was oblivious to the sight of Cornelius Quaint stumbling into the Weir House through the two large wooden doors behind him.

The circus-owner — cum opportunist, cum sometime conjuror — took advantage of his foe's fascination with the swirling waters. His face knotted into a grim mask of fury, Quaint slammed his sizeable bulk into the wiry Frenchman. Both men crashed to the metal floor of the house's observation platform. Quaint's shoulder lanced a spark of acidic fire as he hit the ground. Every molecule of his body cursed him, but still he pressed onwards, his fists flailing wildly as he pummelled the French mercenary with rapid, powerful punches.

"Quaint? Alive?" Renard yelled. "You're signing your own death warrant."

"No, Renard," Quaint said, "I'm signing yours."

"And what about my mother, hmm? You just left her to rot?" Renard said, trying to twist his body from under Quaint. He punched Quaint's wounded shoulder, and the conjuror screamed with an uncommon wail of agony.

"There's more at stake here than just one life — even Destine's — what you propose is mass slaughter, Renard!" shouted Quaint, a spray of spittle forming between his clenched teeth. "You're planning on killing hundreds of people."

"Actually, our analysts predict *thousands*." Renard pulled at Quaint's coat, and kicked him aside. Getting to his feet, Renard towered over Quaint's hunched form. "Do you really think you have it in you to stop me, Cornelius? Look at you — lying there . . . half-dead. You're a washed-up, middle-aged, has-been conjuror . . . fit enough only to run a bloody circus!"

"Better what *I* am than what *you* are, Renard." Quaint lunged with his fist towards Renard's face, but the Frenchman easily avoided it.

Quaint gripped onto the metal railings of the platform and hoisted himself up to his feet. The worrying thing was that Renard was right. Quaint was practically running on fumes, his energy reserves depleted.

"You know, it's funny," laughed Renard. "You tell everyone that you're a magician . . . but in all the years I've known you, I've never actually seen you *do* any magic tricks." Renard lashed out with his fist, catching Quaint another blow square in his wounded shoulder. "You had a chance! You had a chance to *save* your precious Madame Destine . . . and you have squandered that chance. Now, both of you will die."

"You know me better than most, Renard," said Quaint, glaring menacingly at his foe as he nursed his bloodied shoulder. Red trickles of blood oozed between his fingers. "You know I'll stop you . . . even if it costs me my life."

"Well, you've got about five minutes, if you last that long; I've seen lepers who look more healthy." Renard stepped closer and looked Quaint up and down. "If you could only see yourself, Cornelius, you are nothing but a husk. A mere shadow of your former self, *monsieur*! It is almost unsporting of me; I think that maybe I should shoot you like the lame old nag you are, *non*?" Renard reached into his mud-stained jacket, and pulled out the revolver. "You may have got lucky before, but at this range, even *you* can't pull a vanishing trick."

"I won't *have* to if I've counted correctly," said Quaint dryly.

"Enough pithy conversation, Cornelius," Renard said. "*Au revoir.*"

Renard pulled the pistol's trigger.

An empty snap sounded out around the Weir House.

He squinted at Quaint, and then the gun. He pulled the trigger, again and again. The pistol's hammer struck nothing but an empty chamber. Quaint's gamble had paid off — luckily for him. Renard threw the gun furiously at Quaint, who side-stepped out of the way. His legs almost gave way beneath him, his muscles still unsteady. He gripped onto the railings for balance.

"You are a tired old man, and I hardly need a gun to finish you off," Renard said, edging slightly closer to Quaint. "It looks to me as if you are *already* dead." Renard crossed his arms, and a smug grin emerged on his gaunt face. "That poison's not eating away at your insides already, is it? I told you this was potent stuff." He removed a vial of the poison from his pocket, and waved it in the air. Quaint clutched at it drunkenly, miles off target, and Renard snatched it from his flailing grasp. "You're lucky that poison you consumed wasn't mixed with water, Cornelius, or it would be ten times as strong. You will soon have a front row seat to watch its effects!"

"You monster . . . I'll stop you!" said Quaint.

"How, *mon ami*? Look at you! Look at your hands. You are shaking like a leaf in autumn."

Quaint stared down at his quivering hands. Renard was right. They were gradually shifting from side to side, blurred into nightmarish mutations, replaced by mirror images of multiple hands, each one seeming to emanate from his wrists. This was the poison inside of him, transfixing his vision, betraying his eyes. His stubbornness alone had battled its effects so far, but now, in his weakened state, the poison was gaining the upper hand. It was reaching a crescendo inside of him, and his strength had finally given up the ghost. It was pointless to fight a battle you could not win . . .

He collapsed onto his knees, trying desperately to decipher what was reality and what was illusion. His mind was feeding his eyes falsehoods. His ears were hearing non-existent sounds all around him. Up was down and down was up, and the room was spinning like a feather in a hurricane. The more he tried to focus, the more blurred his sight became.

"If you think you are in trouble now, *mon ami*, just imagine what it would be like to drink a whole one of these vials," Renard gloated, tapping the vial with his fingertip, watching Quaint's face change from aggressor into something akin to a child experiencing pain for the very first time. "But you should be proud of yourself for getting this far, Cornelius."

Quaint looked up in confusion. "You'll hang for this."

"They will have to catch me first," said Renard with a vicious grin, strolling around behind Quaint. He snatched at the conjuror's scalp, wrenching his head back sharply, and he sneered close to his ear. "I may have been dead to you, these past fifteen years, but that doesn't mean you've been dead to me. I've kept an eye on you, Cornelius. Oh, yes! And were it not for you choosing now of all times to bring your circus here to London, our paths might never have crossed again." Renard let Quaint's head go, and it nodded limply. "And now . . . I really must conclude this little *tête-à-tête* of ours. I have more pressing things to do." Renard uncorked the glass vial, and held it teasingly over the side of the observation platform.

Quaint's beleaguered eyes scanned around for something to use as a weapon. He suddenly spotted a mechanical command console, which he guessed would be used for maintenance work and sifting flotsam from the water. An embryonic plan formed in his mind, which was quite a triumph considering how much of a mess it was inside there.

"Cornelius . . . this is the end," Renard said.

Quaint gripped the metal railings of the platform and rose unsteadily to his feet. His lip had been split by

Renard's flailing elbows, and he touched the wound gently, noting the blood. Instead of many blurred images of the blood spot, he could now see just one — and he knew instantly what that meant.

The antidote was working.

"You don't have to do this just to get revenge upon me, you know," he said, trying to steer Renard's attention in his direction.

Renard threw back his head and rocked with laughter. "*You?* You egotistical old man! Do you honestly think this has something to do with *you?*"

"Think about what you're doing — it's madness," said Quaint, edging forwards.

"I know, but it is *inspired* madness!" Renard said. "You put in a valiant try for a dead man, Cornelius . . . but do not forget . . . I inherited some of my mother's gift for foresight. I predicted my victory!"

Antoine Renard stared deeply into Quaint's wide eyes, his nostrils flared with delight . . . and he tipped the vial into the churning waters below. The Frenchman held up his arms and punched the air, a look of pure wonder on his face. He had done it. He had poured the vial into the Thames . . . and Cornelius Quaint had been unable to do a damn thing to avert it.

Quaint looked at the distracted Renard. He took his chance, and dived for the maintenance console. Before his enemy had a chance to work out what was happening, he wrenched the machine's lever with all his might into operation, and instantly, the machine obeyed with a grinding of metal gears. A mechanical arm sprang to life at the side of the observation platform, and swung out furiously over the water, striking Renard full in the chest — the Frenchman toppled over the railings into the thrashing waters below.

Quaint pushed the well-greased lever into its nook, setting the brake. The grating screech of metal against metal could be heard slowing down around the Weir House, as one by one, the mechanical weirs slowly ground to a halt and the brown-grey water calmed. Quaint peered over the side of the railings of the observation platform. Renard was splashing about in the water, trying desperately to climb on top of the dome-like weirs.

"This is pointless, Cornelius . . . the poison's already in the river. There's nothing you can do to stop it," Renard screamed through mouthfuls of frothy water. "In a few short days, a third of the population of London will either be dead or dying."

"Sadly for you, that's not true," said Quaint, reaching into his overcoat's pocket.

He pulled out a glass vial between his thumb and index finger.

"What the hell is that?" Renard spluttered.

"This is the poison. The *real* poison, I mean. You said earlier that you'd never seen me perform any magic tricks," said Quaint with a confident grin. "Any decent illusionist will tell you that the *real* magic is never letting your audience know they've *been* tricked until the last minute."

"I . . . I don't understand," said Renard, clinging to the side of a weir. "The poison!"

"Is safely in my possession," said Quaint, trying his best not to look *too* smug — even though it felt wonderful to see the look on Renard's face. "When you poisoned Destine, you left the empty vial behind. A scavenger like me never knows when something may come in handy, and so I took it . . . and filled it with rain water. All I had to do was wait for the opportune moment to switch it for the poisoned vial — and you kindly showed me earlier which pocket it was in." Quaint dropped the glass vial onto the platform, and stamped his heel down hard, shattering the vessel. "As a Frenchman, Renard — surely you must understand when you've had your Waterloo."

Renard's face contorted in the tumult of the water. "You . . . you're lying."

"Do you really believe that? Think about it . . . if that really *was* the poison you just tipped into that water, shouldn't you be dying right about now?"

"I know you, Quaint, remember? I *know* you," protested Renard, trying to clamber up on top of one of the weirs. "You're not just going to stand there and watch me drown."

"You're absolutely right," said Quaint determinedly. "I have to go and save your mother's life."

As he walked towards the exit to the Weir House, Quaint released the brake on the console, and wrenched the long-armed lever attached to the machine. Immediately, the weir mechanisms sprang into life. The huge cogs mounted at the rear of the Weir

House connected with well-oiled chains and instantly the array of mechanical weirs started up again, all of them spinning wildly. The scream of the weirs as they churned the water was deafening.

In the small, enclosed area, Renard had nothing to hold onto, and the swirling maelstrom of the current was impossible to swim against. Amidst the thrashing, spiralling water, he tried desperately to grab onto one of the weirs. The spinning metal dome was as sharp as a blade, and it cleanly sliced off four fingers of Renard's right hand. The Frenchman screamed in frenzied pain as rich, red blood seeped into the rust-coloured water. With nowhere to go and no escape, his face knotted into a frantic mask of panic, Renard's body was dragged under the water time and time again. Just seconds later, shreds of clothing floated grimly to the surface.

Quaint was already out by the horse-drawn coach that Melchin had helpfully left tethered to a nearby lamppost. It was easily a far more superior horse than his last one. Quaint looked at his pocket-watch. It had a long hairline crack across its surface, and he held it to his ear. It had stopped ticking some time ago, and he had no idea how many minutes Destine had left. He prayed that fate was smiling on him. After all, had he not just unravelled and foiled a complicated plot to poison the River Thames, saving thousands of Londoners' lives, and dispatched the architect of that plot to his death? Surely he deserved a *little* bit of luck as a token of good will.

His fracas with Renard had taken too long, and Hyde Park was agonisingly far away. Even with Bishop Courtney's purloined horse, it was unlikely that he'd make it in time . . . but he had to try.

CHAPTER
FIFTY-TWO

The White Knight

"Destine," Cornelius Quaint yelled, leaping from his horse. He ran straight for the fortune-teller's tent, ripped open the door and stepped inside — the antidote clutched in his hand at the ready. He stood in the open doorway, staring in disbelief at the sight laid before him. He shook his head, clamping his eyes shut to deny the image.

Destine's bed and tent were both completely empty. Quaint fell to his knees, exhausted beyond anything he had ever felt before. He noticed Destine's shawl, discarded on the ground, and he reached out to it. He scooped it up into his hands, and smothered his face into it as if he were trying to claw back a memory. The poison inside of him had abated now, the antidote miraculously conquering the effects just in time . . . for him anyway. As he looked forlornly around the empty tent it seemed that, despite his best efforts, he was now too late to save Destine. He cupped the shawl to his face, and smelt the familiar lavender perfume. She was gone. She was lost to him for ever and a part of him wished that he had died too. What was the point of all his struggle, all his sacrifice, if Destine were dead?

Just then Ruby Marstrand darted into the tent. "Oh! It's you, Mr Quaint. I . . . I didn't know you were back. I just came to collect a few things."

"Where is she?" demanded Quaint, rising to his feet swiftly.

"We thought Madame would be more comfortable inside the caravan," Ruby said tearfully. "She . . . she's so weak . . . I've never seen anyone in such agony."

"Lead the way, child! We don't have one single second to waste."

An elaborately decorated Romany caravan was parked up next to the Big Top tent, a single gas lamp flickering in the window, and Quaint sprinted quickly inside. Destine was laid out on the bed, her golden bracelet attached with its array of lucky charms twinkling in the stillness of the room. Her red-rimmed eyes went wide as she saw the imposing figure of Quaint enter.

"Madame," Quaint said breathlessly, kneeling by her bedside. "Drink this at once!"

With a great deal of effort, Destine's dry and cracked lips managed to take the liquid, and swallowed it down awkwardly. Quaint scanned her condition, praying that he'd reached her in time. He had remembered what Renard had said about the poison being augmented by water, and he'd topped up the remaining antidote with rainwater, wagering that perhaps that might work for the antidote too. If *he* had fought against the odds and survived, perhaps there was still hope for her.

Destine finished her painful swallowing, and Quaint lowered her back down onto the caravan's bed. Her eyelids flickered erratically, and her limp arm flopped onto the floor. Her energy was slipping away. Quaint picked up her hand and rested it upon her chest, kissing her cheek gently. Ruby shuffled closer to Quaint, her eyes raw with tears.

"Mr Q? Is . . . is she going to get better?"

"I don't know, Ruby . . . I really don't know," Quaint said, a lump rising in his throat. "We should let her get some rest and allow the antidote do its work."

"She's put up such a fight so far, Mr Q . . . I only pray she can win the final battle. Things just wouldn't be the same without her."

"Do not even contemplate it, Ruby. Madame has an effervescent spirit, and if anyone can survive such torment, it is she. I will pray for her," Quaint said, as he rose to his feet, and walked outside into the freezing cold. He was numb, unable to feel even the slightest chill. As he stood at the caravan's door, he turned to look at the still form of Destine. "Live, Madame. Fight!" he whispered. "Now, more than ever . . . I need you."

CHAPTER
FIFTY-THREE

The Slate Wiped Clean

Some time later, as the scent of sizzling bacon and freshly-cooked bread signalled to the circus encampment that breakfast was being prepared, Quaint was still lying awake and alone in Madame Destine's tent. He still wore his blood-stained white cotton vest, and he hadn't taken his eyes away from a dirty stain of mould on the roof above him for the past three hours. He lifted his hands and looked at them, clenching and unclenching his fists. To his surprise, his wounds from the battle with Renard had almost completely disappeared, leaving his skin itchy in the places where they had once been. His previously scraped knuckles had healed, his arms and legs felt stronger, tauter, and the recurring twinge in his lower back (compliments of the Hungarian Premier's wife) had vanished completely. Quaint felt like a new man, and even the lack of sleep over the past twenty-odd hours was causing him no fatigue. He was in immaculate condition considering the carnage his body had been through.

Whistling a happy ditty, Butter breezed into the tent, carrying a metal tray full of deliciously smelling fried eggs, black pudding, bread and bacon.

"Some food, Mr Quaint," the Inuit said proudly, placing the plate on a small stool in the tent. "I am overjoyed to see you well, boss. When Prometheus and I finally returned from Crawditch and there was a telling of what happened to Madame, well . . . I feared the worst things. For you both."

"And? How is Destine?" Quaint, asked hurriedly. "Is there any news?"

A broad smile illuminated Butter's face. "She is most well, boss. She is far from fully recovered, but she is awake now, and drinking and eating. She has asked for you."

"Thank the Lord she's recovering," Quaint mumbled. "When can I see her?"

"Once you finish your eat. You need it; you have not had so much as a scrap for nearly twenty-four hours, boss."

"Time flies when you're having fun, eh?"

Butter chuckled to himself. "It is good to see your smile once more, boss. I was beginning to think that perhaps I would never see it again."

"You're not the only one." Quaint fell back onto his camp bed, and rubbed at his eyes. "My thanks, Butter, for the good news, *and* the hot food. Both are greeted with welcoming arms."

"It is pleasure for me, boss," said Butter. He placed his arm around Quaint's shoulder and leaned him forwards, plumping up the pillow behind his employer's back. He rushed around the tent, and scooped up the metal tray, placing it upon Quaint's lap. "You sit up," he ordered.

As Quaint shifted his position to sit upright, something struck the china plate on his tray with a metallic "chink". He reached down to the ground and plucked up a dented metal object. "How bizarre," he said, holding it up to the light. "Where on earth did this thing come from?"

Butter shuffled to his side to get a closer look. "A bullet?"

Quaint looked around almost regretfully. "Can it be . . .?" His hand moved to his shoulder, and he began to rub it gently. "I'd almost forgotten all about it. Butter — I've been shot!"

Butter nearly fainted on the spot, and his eyes flared wildly. "Where, boss?"

"Right here!" Quaint pulled his vest to one side, and twisted his neck to get a good look at the bullet wound in his shoulder, courtesy of Antoine Renard. To his surprise, there wasn't much to see; just a purple-grey bruise where the bullet had impacted, and small, spiralling tendrils emanating outwards, like knots in a tree trunk. Rather than a wound less than five hours old, it looked as if the wound had been healing for years. Quaint lifted his arm and rubbed at his itching shoulder. The pain was almost non-existent. How could that be? There was a wound there, albeit only a remnant of one.

"Boss, are you feeling unwell?" asked a concerned Butter. "I can see no shot."

"Well, no matter, Butter. I'll worry about that another time." And, indeed, Quaint surely would. "I must say, my friend, it feels good to be back in settled climates, after recent events. How did things conclude in Crawditch after my departure?"

"Sergeant Berry acting as Commissioner until Scotland Yard finds Mr Dray's successor. He has everything well in order, and the local people are much relieved."

"I'll bet. I don't know what the Yard is playing at. Horace Berry would make an ideal Commissioner. I might just drop a little note to a few friends of mine; see if they can't stack the odds in Berry's favour. And what else have I missed?"

"Well ... seems body of a Bishop Courtney was discovered in residence at Westminster Abbey. The Church is in dark to what happened, and are investigating so I hear."

"And what of Tom Hawkspear?" asked Quaint. "What is his fate to be?"

"He died shortly after you left, boss. Prometheus said about him having 'hole in his gut the size you could ride a horse through'. It saddens me for people of Crawditch, justice was not truly done."

"Well, that all depends on your perception of justice, Butter. Some might say the manner of Hawkspear's death was a just reward. We'll let Hell decide his punishment."

"I suppose ... and the Constable Jennings is now in prison for aiding conspiracy and treason, to be sentenced in three days."

"Excellent!" said Quaint with a nod, tucking into his warm bread. "So, all loose ends are nicely wrapped up then. Just the way I like it. And how do you feel after all the excitement, Butter?"

"I have learned much from this adventure, boss."

"We both have, my friend. I have lain awake for hours trying to soak it all in," said Quaint with a wistful gaze.

"And how that make you feel, boss?" chirped Butter.

"Oddly enough, my friend," Quaint said, as he chomped on a rasher of smoked bacon, "for the first time in a very long while . . . I suddenly feel . . . revitalised!"

"That is good," said Butter, smiling warmly. "Even if you do not look so, I think."

"And what do you mean by that remark, you cheeky little scamp?"

Butter laughed. "I mean no offence, boss. I refer only to your hair."

"My hair?" asked Quaint. "What on earth are you talking about, Butter? What's wrong with my bloody hair?"

Butter picked up a small, hand-held mirror from Madame Destine's makeshift dresser next to the bed, and offered it to his employer.

"Take a peek," he said.

Quaint scowled and stared at his reflection as if he were looking at a stranger.

"Good Lord!" he gasped.

His formerly brown-grey curls were now silver-white curls.

"This is terrible!" Quaint said. "Butter, I look *ancient*."

"Actually, boss, I think it makes you look . . ."

"Distinguished?" offered Quaint, optimistically.

"No," replied Butter. "I was going to say . . . *wise.*"

"Wise, eh?" Quaint pulled at his spiralled silver-white curls in the mirror, stretching his jaw and inspecting his teeth as if this were the first time he had viewed his face. "Hmm, well . . . I suppose I can cope with '*wise*'. Heaven knows, I have been called far worse."

Quaint threw back his loose bed sheets and stood up straight, taking in a deep breath. "Well, hasn't this week just been *full* of surprises? I wonder what else we have left to discover, hmm? Now . . . I need to have a word with Prometheus before show time," he said, ominously. "There are a few things I need to say."

The conjuror left his tent, and meandered through the congregated pockets of his performers and crew, searching for Prometheus. As he did so, they clapped, cheered and patted him on the back like a soldier returning from war. Quaint was not expecting that, and by the time he had got halfway to the piece of open grass where Prometheus was doing press-ups, he almost felt like turning around — but he kept on going, for the conversation he needed to have with the Irish strongman was of the utmost importance.

Quaint's shadow drifted over Prometheus's sweating form, and he slowly registered that he had company. He rose to his feet, and greeted Quaint with a wide smile.

"Mornin' to ye, Cornelius," he said, cheerily. "Ye look well."

Quaint prodded his ivory locks. "Apart from the new look, you mean?"

Prometheus laughed. "Well, if ye want the truth, I think it makes ye look —"

"Distinguished?" suggested Quaint hopefully.

"Yeah . . . *distinguished* . . . that's it," replied Prometheus, none too convincingly.

"Prom . . . I wanted to have a quick word with you," began Quaint. "Things have happened so fast this past week. A lot of things have occurred . . . to us both. I suppose I just . . . I just wanted to make sure you were all right . . . with the upcoming show and all."

"Cornelius, I've known ye for a long time. I can see through ye just as well as Destine can, me old friend. Ye can say her name, ye know . . ."

"Madeline . . ." said Quaint, reverently.

"Twinkle, boss. Twinkle was her circus name . . . her true name," Prometheus said, drifting away from a group of engineers making last-minute adjustments to a nearby marquee. "She would want us to remember her as Twinkle."

Quaint nodded, and followed him. "Quite right too. Listen to me . . . if you don't feel like performing today, I do understand. To be honest . . . everything has happened so quickly that I've hardly had time to take stock. I swore to myself that I would grieve for Twinkle once my enemies were vanquished . . . but now I find my time taken up by other matters." He reached out with his hand, grasping the air. "I just . . . didn't want you to think we didn't care, Prom . . . that *I* didn't care."

Prometheus spun to face him. "Ah, don't be daft, man! Course I know ye care! I know what she meant t'ye . . . an' more importantly, so did she. Just 'cos of all that's gone on, doesn't make ye a heartless *monster*, does it? Look, I know what ye did." He grinned a broad smile. "Ye saved the whole of bleedin' London, man! Ye're a hero!"

Quaint rubbed the back of his neck shyly. "Well, I don't know about that."

"Well, *I* do!" Prometheus strode over to him, snatched up his hand and shook it hard, the action causing Quaint's teeth to rattle in his mouth. "Ye did a grand job, so ye did, an' I'm proud t'call ye my friend."

Quaint nodded in acquiescence. "Well . . . same here. Very proud . . . just keep it to yourself, all right? I have a reputation to uphold!"

Prometheus grinned, and folded his broad arms across his expansive chest. "So . . . we're goin' t'put on a damn fine show here today for the folk o' London, right? An' we're gonna make Twinkle proud of us too, right?"

Quaint smiled. "You took the words right out of my mouth."

"I may have been mute all them years, but I wasn't deaf! Just like I heard ye say so many times — we're a family! We stick together, an' we'll *pull* together . . . no matter what fate throws our way! We always do."

"Absolutely," agreed Quaint. "I have to prepare. I'll see you later, Prometheus."

The conjuror turned, and walked back through the throng of gaudily dressed performers, his eyes on his feet and his mind elsewhere. How could he tell Prometheus that he was about to leave the circus, that he was abandoning them all? However he said it, no matter how much he sugar-coated the words, it still amounted to a betrayal in his eyes. But as close as he was to his people — things had changed. The world had changed. True evil had arisen in the form of the Hades Consortium, and with its members . . . he had some unfinished business.

Fate, it seemed, was in the habit of throwing things in Cornelius Quaint's way.

CHAPTER
FIFTY-FOUR

The Missing Piece

By lunchtime the first matinée show of the circus had begun, and reams of people from all across London's many boroughs peeled themselves away from their chores and employment, and entered Dr Marvello's Travelling Circus. Hyde Park was alight with such uncommon electricity as seemingly everyone from miles around had put their lives on hold and come to the circus.

Flurries of children and adults alike moved from one tent to the next, marvelling at the spectacles they witnessed as the show in the Big Top started. Destine patrolled around inside the massive tent watching the faces of the audience as the spectacle unfolded. Ruby had the crowd's stomachs in their mouths with her knife-throwing skills. The clowns Jeremiah and Peregrine soaked the first three rows with buckets of cold water. The Chinese twins Yin and Yang scared everyone half to death with their gymnastic exploits, and Prometheus bent steel bars as if they were made of liquorice — with Butter scurrying around doing everything in between. A well-oiled machine, the circus was a self-propagating beast. Everyone knew their part and each played it exceptionally. Shocks and frights were tempered with thrills and laughter like any good circus, and the atmosphere both inside and outside the Big Top was next to paradise. Cheers, screams of excitement and laughter undulated everywhere.

Destine stood back from the crowds and smiled to herself. Something she had not done in a long while. The circus had an amazing power to invigorate and rejuvenate. Suddenly, all her recent troubles were pushed to the back of her mind, as the performer side of her brain kicked in, and Destine simply allowed herself to go with the flow. She was taking a welcome break from her role as circus fortune-teller and she was feeling agitated, without knowing why. Despite how much pleasure she gained from watching the embryo of the circus blossom into its present state of completion, something was niggling at her. Tiny warm butterflies floated around Destine's body, and her hands tingled. Although this was normality once more (and how she had missed its presence), there was still something missing.

Cornelius Quaint was nowhere to be seen.

The show's resident conjuror had made a decidedly swift exit from the stage after astounding the crowds with his illusions, and that was most unlike him. Destine left the canvas-covered cornucopia of delights and walked out into Hyde Park.

It was a surprisingly clear and dry day after the previous night's torrential rain, and she held her gloved hand to her brow, shielding her eyes from the low-lying sunshine that bathed the entire park in golden hues and amber washes. The leafless, skeletal trees held little shade, and the long shadows of their barren trunks created a crazy-paving effect across the lawns of the park. The French fortune-teller felt the warmth of the sun on her cheeks, and a smile crossed over her lips. She was safe now, thanks to Cornelius. She caressed her hands slowly. They had not looked so vibrant in years, her temperamental arthritis now seemingly evaporated into thin air. She wasn't certain why that was, but the more she tried to make sense of it, the more it seemed to slip from her grasp. She needed to find Cornelius; he would know the answers. He'd have to, because surely what Destine thought was occurring could not possibly be true.

Though Madame Destine felt younger than she had done in well over fifty years, there was one nagging concern resting at the forefront of her worries. Since she had regained consciousness she had not experienced even the vaguest hint of any sort of premonition. It was as if everything that had made her special had been suddenly switched off. This knowledge served only to prove to her what had happened — for what use does an immortal have for seeing the future? Believing in eternal life was like believing in fairy tales, and despite the fact that Destine was gifted with an amazing quota of all kinds of otherworldly gifts — there was something so ethereal about immortality that she could scarcely allow her imagination to entertain the thought.

She had shared her thoughts with her best friend Ruby after she recovered from the antidote's quelling of the deadly poison, receiving more than one quasi-sarcastic remark for her trouble. One of the first questions that the young knife-smith asked was: "How do you *know* you can live for ever?", and, in truth, she had no answer. It was just something she knew to be true, as much as she knew she hated spinach, she knew she liked lavender perfume and she knew she preferred the colour green to the colour blue.

She knew that something inside her had changed irrevocably. Something great and something miraculous . . . and yet every time she tried to put it into words, she was lost. She needed Cornelius to help her discover why that was, to make sense of it all, and there was another tingle of a wish inside her mind also. If she felt the way she did — if she had these suspicions as to her fate — how did he feel? Was he sharing her delight at this sudden sense of rebirth?

Something caught Destine's eye up on Stanhope Hill, and she knew it was him instantly, his dark cloak buffeted by the wind like a flag on a pole. He was standing alone, staring down at the festivities of the circus, detached from it like an outsider. For a man surrounded by the comfort and warmth of his friends and adopted family, Cornelius Quaint felt like the loneliest man on earth . . .

CHAPTER
FIFTY-FIVE

The Ending and Beginning

Destine made her way to him, watching the man's sullen expression gradually change to an altogether brighter one as she stepped into view up the small embankment. Despite the elixir healing his cuts and bruises while he had slept, Quaint's face was as worn and weather-beaten as usual, a mainstay of his mature years that he would have to live with. Not that it bothered him, and Destine was used to the craggy rock-face, and had rather warmed to it over the years. She smiled as she approached him and noticed his mop of ivory curls, peeking from underneath his top-hat.

"I love your hair," she said.

"Apparently it makes me look wise," replied Quaint.

"Well . . . that is certainly a much needed improvement then."

"*Et tu*, Destine?" asked Quaint.

She smiled, and wrapped her arms around him. "What on earth are you doing standing out here all alone, Cornelius?"

"Oh, nothing really, Madame, I'm just pondering the meaning of existence. Would you care for a tot of brandy?" he asked, offering Destine a small silver hip-flask.

"*Merci,*" Destine said, raising the flask to her lips. "So what have you learned?"

"About what?" asked Quaint.

"About the meaning of existence . . . are you any the wiser?"

"Not a jot."

"So what will you do? Continue as normal and hope to find the answers in time?"

Quaint looked at her and smiled, taking back his flask. "Madame, I doubt that I shall ever see 'normal' again." He quaffed a hearty mouthful of brandy, and wiped his sleeve across his mouth. "No, I have made a decision. I have signed over the circus to Butter as caretaker owner whilst I take a little sabbatical. I know it'll be in good hands whilst I'm gone."

"You're giving up the circus?" gasped Destine.

"Temporarily, Madame . . . I care for those people down there too much to desert them for ever. I just need to stretch my wings for a few months. I'll be back."

"My, you certainly *have* changed."

"I'm not so sure I have, Destine, and that's the point," Quaint said.

"How so?" asled Destine.

"I think that it is the world that has changed — and I have remained grounded. I have allowed the ghosts of my past to rule me for too long. It is high time that I concentrated on the here and now, and started to live again." A sudden wind whipped at Quaint's clothes, as if trying to drag him away with its breeze. "The world is a big place, full of wonders, Madame, and now I feel as though I have a renewed lease of life with which to see it all."

"So, you feel it too?" asked Destine.

"Like warm water trickling through your veins? Yes, I feel it too, Madame," Quaint said with a roguish smile. "Something happened to me ... to *us*, last night, something ... almost miraculous."

"So says the conjuror?"

"I am serious, Destine, think on it! I was shot only a few hours ago ... but that wound has all but disappeared. You yourself were on death's door ... and now you look more than ten years younger. I ask myself how that can be possible."

"When my ... when *Renard* gave me the poison, he said 'a fool of a priest believed this to be an elixir of immortality' ... apparently he assumed that it was not true." Madame Destine's concerned expression bloomed into understanding. "But now, I find myself thinking perhaps he was wrong. Perhaps there was a spark of the elixir's original purpose left dormant, and this was reignited somehow. It is obvious that the antidote reversed the poison's effects just in time — but more than that is bordering on the fantastical!"

"I agree," nodded Quaint. "Whatever befell us, I am just grateful we are still alive to ponder it, Madame."

"As am I. If you are to see the world, where will you go first, my sweet?" asked Destine.

"Egypt," answered Quaint without missing a beat.

"I rather thought you might say that," Destine smiled.

"Perhaps I need a holiday, Madame." Quaint turned to look at her, his jet-black eyes speaking more than his voice ever could. They held Destine's attention like a lamp attracts a moth, and pulled her into their dark, enveloping void. "I haven't set foot in Egypt for a long time, and you know how I have always wanted to return there."

"I seem to recall you mentioning it," Destine lied.

"Sampling the local delicacies; boat trips down the Nile; maybe a little digging around near the pyramids of Giza," said Quaint, a vague smile resting on his lips. "I hear that all sorts of things can be uncovered if you look in the right places."

Destine nodded in silent understanding. "And on this new adventure, my sweet . . . would you care for some company?"

"Madame Destine," said Cornelius Quaint, offering the Frenchwoman the crook of his arm, "I thought you'd never ask."

Also available in ISIS Large Print:

Snow Hill

Mark Sanderson

"Friday, 18 December, 1936. I went to my funeral this morning . . ."

So begins the diary of Johnny Steadman, an ambitious reporter on London's Fleet Street. When he gets a tip-off about a Snow Hill policeman's death he thinks he's found the scoop that will make his career. Trouble is, no-one at the station seems to know anything about it . . . or they're not telling.

Johnny's one lead takes him to the meat market at Smithfield where he encounters violent death up close and personal. Undaunted by this chilling message, his investigation drags him deep into a web of corruption reaching further than he imagined.

Johnny must risk everything to save his closest friend and expose a ruthless killer. But to bring them to justice he must first go undercover. Six feet undercover. After all, a dead man cannot be tried for murder . . .

ISBN 978-0-7531-8702-9 (hb)
ISBN 978-0-7531-8703-6 (pb)

The Devil's Paintbrush

Jake Arnott

Paris, 1903. Major-General Sir Hector Macdonald, one of the greatest heroes of the British Empire, is facing ruin in a shocking homosexual scandal when he meets the notorious occultist, Aleister Crowley. As they set out into the night on a wild journey through the sinful city, the story of Macdonald's tragedy begins to unfold — with startling revelations both for the general and the aspiring magician.

In a tale that ranges from the battlefields of Sudan to the backstreets of Edinburgh, Jake Arnott brings alive a fascinating, forgotten figure of history, and a world trembling on the brink of a brutal new era. Black magic, Baden-Powell and Islamic revolution are just some of the ingredients in this bold and exhilarating novel, which explores imperialism, sexuality and the very nature of belief with an immediacy that resonates into the present.

ISBN 978-0-7531-8618-3 (hb)
ISBN 978-0-7531-8619-0 (pb)

Sanctuary

Ken Bruen

Galway PI Jack Taylor is back on another dark, uncompromising road-trip through the underworld of Irish crime

Two guards, one nun, one judge . . .

When a letter containing a list of victims arrives in the post, PI Jack Taylor tells himself that it is nothing to do with him. He has enough to do just staying sane. His close friend Ridge is recovering from surgery, and alcohol's siren song is calling to him ever more insistently.

A guard and then a judge die in mysterious circumstances.

But it is not until a child is added to the list that Taylor determines to find the identity of the killer, and stop them at any cost.

What he doesn't know is that his relationship with the killer is far closer than he thinks. And that it's about to become deeply personal.

ISBN 978-0-7531-8654-1 (hb)
ISBN 978-0-7531-8655-8 (pb)

Nightfall

Stephen Leather

"You're going to hell, Jack Nightingale": They are words that ended his career as a police negotiator. Now Jack's a struggling private detective — and the chilling words come back to haunt him.

Nightingale's life is turned upside down the day that he inherits a mansion with a priceless library; it comes from a man who claims to be his father, and it comes with a warning. That Nightingale's soul was sold at birth and a devil will come to claim it on his 33rd birthday — just three weeks away.

Jack doesn't believe in Hell, probably doesn't believe in Heaven either. But when people close to him start to die horribly, he is led to the inescapable conclusion that real evil may be at work. And that if he doesn't find a way out he'll be damned in hell for eternity.

ISBN 978-0-7531-8624-4 (hb)
ISBN 978-0-7531-8625-1 (pb)